Jumping Jax

BLUE SPRINGS SERIES
BOOK ONE

JACKIE EGAN

For H.S.
This is my manifestation of your happy ending, because nobody deserves it as much as you.

Trigger Warnings

Brief mention and scenes displaying emotional and physical abuse

Jump Rope Moves:

Mummy Kicks
While jumping, alternate kicking one leg straight out in front, mimicking a mummy walk. Takes a "running in place" move and adds a leg extension.
Level—intermediate.

Side Swipes
Swinging the rope around the side of your body, not passing under feet, creating a sweeping motion across your torso. Moving the rope from one side to the other while maintaining a steady rhythm with your feet.
Level—intermediate to advanced.

Double Unders
Bringing the jump rope underneath your body 2x during a single Jump.
Level—advanced.

Crisscross
Movement of crossing your arms in front of your body while the rope is in the air, then uncrossing them before the rope passes under your feet.
Level—intermediate to advanced.

Boxer Skips
Shifting your weight from one foot to the other while jumping.
Level—advanced.

X-Motion
Incorporates side-straddle, alternating the front foot each time, while the rope swings underneath your feet.
Level—intermediate.

High Knee
Perform a high knee movement with each jump, mimicking a running motion in place, while simultaneously jumping over the rope.
Level—advanced.

Straddle
A movement where you expand your feet wide, into a "straddle" position, while jumping over the rope. Similar to a jumping-jack motion.
Level—intermediate.

Heel Touch
While jumping, intentionally tap the heel of one foot with each jump, alternating each time, creating a heel-to-toe pattern.
Level—beginner to intermediate.

Toe Touch
While jumping, intentionally tap the toes behind yourself with one foot, alternating with each jump.
Level—intermediate.

CHAPTER 1

Melody

I've never wanted to spit in a customer's food before but today might be the day.

Brenda has sent her food back three times already, and if she does it one more time, I'm seriously considering adding some extra *seasoning* to her dish. If I didn't need this job so badly, I would have done so weeks ago.

Moving to Blue Springs, Colorado a month ago was supposed to make my life easier. Unfortunately, this dedicated regular has been placed in my section every single shift without fail, bringing me to the brink of tears.

"Here's your club sandwich, and your *fresh* order of fries," I emphasize, because even though I watched them being pulled from the fryer, Brenda insists we gave her old fries. Never mind that Blue Bistro is a local favorite, known for their made-to-order dishes. I've decided that Brenda takes pleasure in others' suffering.

The woman glares at me while I set her plate down in front of her. "Mm-hmm, we'll see if you got it right this time."

Deep breaths, you need this job.

I hold my composure, giving her my best customer-service smile. "Enjoy."

Walking back through the kitchen doors, I attempt to keep my head up, when all I want to do is kick my feet up and cry. This shift has been nonstop, and being down one server has made today especially hectic.

I place both of my hands on the metal counter and hang my head. I need a moment to collect myself before going back out and plastering that painful fake smile on again.

"Oh honey, you look beat." Mary, one of Blue Bistro's longest-standing employees, comes up beside me, giving my shoulder a comforting squeeze.

I glance up at her. "It's Brenda. She's sent back her plate three times. THREE. I'm about to snap."

Mary is in her fifties, has dark hair that's always teased and voluminous, and caramel-colored eyes. Her kids have grown and gone off to college in other states, and as an empty nester, was looking for something to fill her days. She claims to love working here, but with customers like Brenda, I can't fathom why.

She rolls her eyes. "Lord, that woman sure has it out for you, doesn't she?"

I nod.

"Want me to go have a chat with her, honey?" she offers, her brown eyes sympathetically boring into mine.

I shake my head. "No, I can handle it. Thanks, though. I just needed a minute to breathe."

Mary, although closer to my mother's age, has become one of my closest friends since moving here. Actually, my *only* friend. Being a single, working mother doesn't leave time for much else. But my daughter is my entire world, and she makes it all worth it.

Running around for the last six hours has my hair in a

sweaty mess at the nape of my neck, so I take a minute to secure my golden-brown hair in a messy bun at the top of my head. I wash my hands and head back out to check on my tables.

Luckily, the third time's the charm, and evil Brenda doesn't make another complaint, although, predictably, she asks for a discount, for the "inconvenience." I caught on pretty quick that it's the sole reason she runs my ass off every time. She's lucky this is a small town, this shit would never fly in a big city.

The owners are a sweet older couple who don't have the heart to kick anybody out. Seeing the good in everyone, Brenda always gets the benefit of the doubt. They hired me on the spot when I came to town, having abruptly left my old life. It was obvious I was desperate for a job when Gracie and I arrived that first day.

We shared one entrée, and when I asked if they were hiring, Bud, the owner, came out and handed me an apron, telling me to arrive at 10 a.m. the next day. No questions asked. After I tearfully thanked him, he proceeded to bring out an extra entrée and a piece of their famous Blue Springs blueberry pie for Gracie and me to share.

He and his wife, Kat, have been my personal angels since we got here. We were down to our last few dollars and hadn't yet found a place to stay. Like a Hail Mary in the fourth quarter of the Super Bowl, they swooped in and offered us a vacant property they owned a few blocks away. I was ecstatic and jumped at the offer.

It's a cozy one-bedroom, one-bathroom, cabin-style home, and it's perfect for Gracie and me. A bed and a roof over our head is everything we need. There's a modest kitchen where we love to bake and make lemonade with lemons from the tree outside, adorned with a wraparound porch and an adorable flat porch swing out back. We may have come from a very different lifestyle, but Gracie doesn't seem to mind the drastic change. At four years old, she sees everything as an adventure, which is lucky for me since I chose this location at random when we left in a panic.

I packed the car and hightailed it out of LA, hoping this small town would be far enough away to hide us from all of our problems. Even if just for a short time.

After the night shift arrived, I finished my duties, turned in my paperwork, and practically sprinted out the door, eager to get home to my daughter. Having been able to stay at home her entire life, up until recently, has me missing her like crazy by the time my shifts end. Going from sharing every moment with her to having our time cut to a few hours a day hasn't been easy, but it was necessary.

The Blue Bistro is only a few blocks away from the cabin, so when the weather's nice, I like walking to work. Colorado's weather is notoriously unpredictable, especially in a mountain town, but so far, it's been favorable. May has given us warm, sunny days, with only a few afternoon summer showers.

On the walk home, I count the meager tips I made for the day, wondering how I'm ever going to keep us afloat on this.

$64.50.

Guess who the fifty cents came from. After complaining three times, and getting her food at a heavy discount, Brenda left me a whopping $1.50. I don't like to complain, because every dollar counts, and it's one I didn't have before I went into work today. I try to remember this is temporary, and I'll figure something out. My sweet Gracie deserves it.

"Gracie, baby. Mom's home," I announce into the cabin as I walk through the front door.

Our current sitter, Vicki, is sort of a grouch, and I wouldn't call her "hands-on," but she's always willing to babysit and lives right down the road.

"Mama!" Gracie comes bouncing out of the bedroom, with Vicki trailing behind.

Gracie jumps into my arms and I pick her up, squeezing her in a tight hug. The apple scent from her shampoo fills my nostrils and I inhale deeply. She smells like my baby girl. Her light brown hair is in braided pigtails that hang just above her shoulders. Her bright blue eyes that are a match for mine are misty when she pulls back.

"Hi baby, how was your day? What's wrong?" I say, noticing her wet eyes.

I glance over at Vicki, standing in the doorway with her arms crossed, who shrugs. "She was fine the whole day. We were looking for some of her dolls in the bedroom when you walked in."

"I missed you, Mama. I no see you." She means she *didn't* see me. Since she's still learning how to structure her sentences, her words are often jumbled. Even though it's wrong, I find it too adorable to correct.

"Aw baby, Mama was at work. But I'll always come home to you. Okay?" I tell her, caressing her cheek with my thumb.

She nods, and I set her down to walk Vicki out. I pull some cash out of my apron and hand it to her. "Thank you again, you're a lifesaver."

"No problem. Send over some of those cupcakes next time y'all make them," she requests without a hint of a smile.

A babysitter who doesn't mind that half of her pay is in the form of baked goods is why I overlook her not being especially great with kids. A desperate mother doesn't get to be picky. I'm grateful for how little she charges me. Having left Los Angeles with nothing, money is very tight.

"You got it. Thanks again." I close the door as she walks down the steps.

Finally off work, I can do my two favorite things: after

hugging my baby girl, stripping out of my bra, and kicking off my work shoes. There's nothing like ditching an underwire bra that's been digging into the sides of your breasts and shoulders for eight hours straight.

Whoever invented bras hates women.

"Did you have fun with Vicki?" I ask like I always do.

Gracie shrugs.

I know Vicki wouldn't be her first choice, and I hate leaving her with somebody I know she doesn't particularly enjoy being around. Yet, I'd choose this over enduring the life we had back home.

Home.

One day I'll stop calling that place home, but like a knee-jerk reaction, the word sits on the tip of my tongue whenever I think about our life back in Los Angeles.

"Sweetie, I'm sorry," I tell her, pulling her into a hug as I sit on the small brown couch. "I'll see if I can find somebody else to come and hang out with you when I'm at work. This is temporary."

She won't look at me, instead she twists her fingers into the frayed fabric on the knee of my jeans.

I give her a squeeze and she lets out a high-pitched giggle. "Hey, Mama loves you. Do you love me?"

This time she glances up at me, giving me one of her big smiles that melts me. "Yes. I love you, Mama."

"Good. What do you say we go pick some lemons and you can make me some of your delicious lemonade."

Her eyes light up, and just like that, she's in a good mood again. I envy the way my daughter lets things roll off her back, never letting one thing ruin her entire day. I find myself questioning every day whether packing up our lives and making the hasty move to Blue Springs was the right choice or not, but when I remember that last night in Los Angeles, with *him*, I know that as hard as this is, it was the right decision.

"Mama, more sugar!" Gracie shrieks at me, trying to dump in another spoonful of sugar to the lemonade. Although, at this point, let's be honest, it's sugar water with a hint of lemon.

I laugh, attempting to snatch the spoon from her before it goes into the glass pitcher. "Sweetie, that's enough! It won't taste good if it's too sweet."

Gracie is quicker than I am and tips the spoon into the liquid, giving me a sheepish grin. "Oopsie."

"Mm-hmm, oopsie." She knows if she feigns innocence, she'll avoid repercussions. She's usually right.

"Mommy, can we do a lemonade stand one day?"

I give her a quizzical expression. "How do you know what a lemonade stand is?"

"On the TV. The girl had one," she tells me excitedly.

I laugh. "Sure baby, we can have a lemonade stand."

Although, thinking about serving others on a day off doesn't sound all that appealing.

"Okay, you can have half of a glass and then let's get to the bathroom and hop in that bath. You are very sticky."

She sighs heavily. "Okay, Mommy."

After we've had dinner, and Gracie has had her bath, it was time for me to finally wash off the grueling day I had.

The small bathroom has a tub/shower combo that can't compare with the bathroom I've been used to, but even a gas station bathroom with peace is more appealing than all the luxury in the world with a toxic man.

Stepping out of the shower, standing before the oval sink mirror, I use my towel and clear the fog. I used to be such a confident woman. A woman who took pride in her looks and was a frequent gym goer. But now, all I see are the flaws. Flaws that were frequently pointed out.

The stretch marks on my stomach and hips from pregnancy. The widening of my hips. The "love handles" that I loathe. The lower belly pooch that I tried forever to lose but hangs on for dear life.

I'm not the size two woman I was before I had Gracie, and I made peace with that. It's a reality I could accept. This body created the life of my favorite person.

But that was before. Before I was made to believe that I was a disgusting failure. Prior to knowing what it was like to hear every one of my insecurities thrown in my face like stored ammo whenever he was displeased with me.

It's been two years since I've been brave enough to show my face in any gym, but much longer since I've been able to look at myself in the mirror without picking myself apart.

Your stomach is too big.

Your stretch marks are ugly.

Your hips are too big.

You're being lazy.

Every day this goes on for several minutes without fail, until I remember that I'm raising a daughter. The only thing more heartbreaking than hating yourself is thinking that one day your daughter might look at herself the same way.

Like working a new muscle, I have to keep training myself to stop the negative talk. But it's hard when all I hear is his voice in my head telling me I'm not enough.

This is why we left, and this is why we are here now. Because, no matter what it takes, I refuse to let my daughter grow up hating herself. Moving us here was the hardest thing I've ever had to do, but not as hard as waking up each day in that house to him.

CHAPTER 2

Jackson

Sweat drips down the sides of my face, making a few of the curls on my head stick to me. I brush them off with the side of my arm as I take a breather between jumps.

"What's wrong, Jax, losing your steam?" Summer heckles me.

I send a playful glare in her direction as her blonde ponytail whips back and forth while she seamlessly continues to send her white jump rope around her body. "Well, I have been here since 6 a.m., Sum, so I think a small break is warranted."

Summer works for me at the local gym I own, Jumping Jax. It's a typical gym stocked with all the cardio and weight lifting equipment you could dream of, but with one detail that sets us apart from other gyms.

I have been a professional jump rope athlete most of my life and have thus thrown my love for it into this gym with a designated jump rope area. Most gyms don't accommodate an area to do this, so I decided, why don't I do it?

A lot of planning, a couple of loans, and a lot of work later, Jumping Jax was born. The building sits in the heart of Blue Springs, Colorado, which I adore, having grown up here. It's the perfect small mountain town. Never too crowded, and everything is practically within walking distance.

My mother was worried at first that opening a niche business in a small town wouldn't garner enough business to keep me afloat. But thanks to my large social media following, people travel from all over to visit my gym, and I've been able to open two more locations in Denver. And thanks to social media, the number of sponsorships I've accrued has created a living income on its own. I'm also looking at a possible location in LA, so suffice it to say, I'm doing okay for myself.

"Come on, let's take a break. I need to refuel," I tell Summer, hanging up my blue jump rope.

Summer does the same with her white rope, and then reaches into her bag, pulling out two insulated bottles with post-workout smoothies.

"What are my options today?" I ask her as she holds them both out in front of her.

"Blueberry with banana, spinach, almond milk, cinnamon, and of course, protein," she says with a knowing grin.

"Of course. What about the other one?"

"Lemon, honey, Greek yogurt, ginger, turmeric, and a lemon meringue protein," she tells me excitedly, shaking the container.

"Uh, I don't know how I feel about turmeric, so I'll take the blueberry one."

She hands it over, taking the lid off hers and taking a large gulp of it. "You're missing out, this is one of my new favorites."

Summer and I go way back, meeting at a jump rope competition when we were kids. She was one of the best jumpers that year, and I had barely beaten her. I panicked when I saw her storming toward me after the competition, thinking she was going to give me an ear full. But instead, she stuck her hand out and congratulated me. We've been friends ever since. That's what's great about Summer, she may be beautiful, have toned muscles (with impressive, chiseled abs), yet she's one of the most genuinely humble, kind people you'll ever meet.

Every day, Summer brings us new smoothie concoctions for us to try. She's an avid fitness lover, but nutrition is her real passion. One day she'll do amazing things with all her knowledge, but for now, she works for me at Jumping Jax and we train together daily for fun, but also for my social media videos.

Summer is my best friend, and even though people still think we're hiding a secret relationship, it's never been that way between us. Hell, she's more like a sister at this point, so I could never look at her that way.

Not that I'm looking at *anyone* that way, not after the last failure I called a relationship. Sure, I could make time for a relationship, but I don't want to. I've always been happy to pour myself into work and training. Last time I heard, Summer was happy living the single life as well.

Taking a heavy swig of the smoothie, I unintentionally smack my lips. "Damn, this one is amazing, Sum. You're really good at this."

She dramatically gives herself a pat on the back. "I know, right?"

"And so modest, too," I tease.

She rolls her light blue eyes. "Oh please, I am modest. But there's nothing wrong with acknowledging that you're great at something. And *this* I'm great at."

I laugh. "Fair enough. Listen, I'm starving and this smoothie isn't going to do the trick today, want to head over to Blue's with me and grab a burger?"

She caps her bottle and stuffs it back in her gym bag. "Can't. I have a date."

"A date? I thought you were, quote, 'done dating men until I'm thirty-five.'" I repeat the words she told me after coming back from her last disastrous date.

She shrugs. "Well, ten years turned out to be too long to wait for Prince Charming."

"It's been, like, two months."

"What can I say, I'm weak. But if this guy sucks, I'm officially done with men in this town."

"Fair." I chuckle.

I take the last sip of the smoothie she offered me, and hand her back the bottle. She packs it with the other one. "Wish me luck."

"Good luck, Sum. Call me if you need an out," I joke, although I'd absolutely be there if she needed me.

She waves a hand in front of her face. "Please, I have no problem telling a man I'm not interested."

I can't help but laugh. Summer has a heart of gold, but she's direct. If a man disrespects her, she has zero issue sending him back where he came from with his tail tucked between his legs. She's a firecracker.

"See you tomorrow!" I shout and she tosses me a wave over her shoulder, walking out the front doors.

I grab my belongings from my office in the back, and head out to Blue's. It is time to eat.

"JAX! OVER HERE, HONEY," Mary, one of Blue Bistro's sweetest employees, waves me over to a booth as I wait at the hostess stand.

That's what I love about small towns, everywhere you go, you're family. Blue Springs has definitely become my family, especially after my father left us all those years ago.

"Thanks Mary," I say, sliding into the booth, and glancing up to give her a warm smile.

"The usual?" she asks.

I nod. "Yep, you know it."

"One Blue Bistro burger, extra bleu cheese. Would you like a beer?"

"No, I just got done training. I'll take a large iced water, please."

"You got it."

I thank her and then pull out my phone to check my emails. You'd think that spending all day at the gym, I'd have time to get more than enough done, but it never seems to stop.

Be your own boss, they said.

You'll have more time, they said.

Don't get me wrong, I love being my own boss, but it's a lot of work. Even with a rock star employee like Summer, there's still always something to be done. And let's face it, she's more part-owner at this point.

About ten minutes later, Mary returns with a burger piled high with bacon and bleu cheese, and a side of the best fries you'll ever have. Traveling to my other gym locations puts me in the city a lot, and I can say with full confidence that small towns absolutely have better food.

"Enjoy, and let me know if you need anything else."

"Thanks Mar."

The warm bacon and melting cheese aromas waft into my senses, and I'm about to take that first bite when I hear a commotion behind me.

"Excuse me?!" Brenda, a Bistro regular, is shouting at a woman I haven't seen before.

The waitress, with golden-brown hair, stops in her tracks, and slowly turns back toward the customer. Once she reaches Brenda's table, I see her plaster on a smile that's faker than the vegan burger they added to the menu last year for tourists.

"Is there something wrong with your meal?" she asks kindly, albeit a little timid.

"Yes. First of all, I asked for *extra* ice in my diet soda. Second, these fries are cold, just like last time," Brenda snaps at her.

I feel for the woman; Brenda is older and generally bitter about life. She lives at home with a small yappy dog who shares the same aversion to people. Rumor has it that her husband left her for a younger woman years ago, so now, whenever a mildly attractive woman enters her orbit, she catches the wrath of Brenda.

It's easy to see why this woman would have triggered Brenda, she is stunning. She's shorter than my six-one, with curves that any man would love to explore. Her golden-brown hair glistens when the sunlight catches it through the windows, and her big deep blue eyes are like pools of water that I'd love to dive into.

"Ma'am, I'm sorry. I watched the cook pull them directly from the fryer. I immediately brought them out to you, so I'm not sure how they could have gotten cold that quickly," the waitress responds, trying to defend herself.

Brenda scoffs, dramatically clutching her chest. "Don't call me ma'am, I'm not that much older than you. And are you calling me a liar?"

I'm usually a man who minds his own business, but I'm having a hard time taking my eyes off this woman for some reason.

The waitress must feel me staring. Her eyes leave the bitter woman at the table and meet mine. It's quick, but that's all it takes for me to see a thousand emotions in her eyes.

Hurt, frustration, desperation, exhaustion.

I can see she's hanging by a thread.

"Hello?!" Brenda shouts, snapping her fingers in her face.

The woman's attention snaps back to the table. "I'm sorry, I'll have them remade for you."

She removes Brenda's plate, and scurries back through the kitchen door.

"Good, let's see if there's any brains in that pretty little head of yours," Brenda spits out, even though the waitress is no longer in earshot.

I don't know what compels me to do it, except for the fact that insulting someone personally over *food* is so juvenile I can't possibly sit and listen to this poor waitress get berated for another second.

Standing, I turn around and head for Brenda's table. She's chugging her diet soda and doesn't see me approach.

I clear my throat, and she startles. "Oh, Jackson. I didn't see you there, handsome. What can I do for you?"

Her attempt at flattery only infuriates me more. "I couldn't help but overhear the conversation with your waitress."

"Oh, she's new. Doesn't know what she's doing. Every time I'm in here she screws *something* up," she says, flipping her hand around.

"Well, if she's new, one would think you'd be a little more patient with her."

"I, well, I..." Brenda stumbles over her words, not expecting to be confronted for her behavior.

"I see you're at a loss for words, and that's great, actually. You've said enough. Bud and Kat are close friends with my mother, which you're aware of. I know they're too nice to kick you out of here themselves, so I'm not above having my mother talk with them and ensure you're never allowed to set foot inside this bistro, or any others in all of Blue Springs if you ever talk to another waitress that way."

"But, I—"

I don't let her finish. "I don't care if she dropped your entire plate on the floor and tried to serve it to you. If you have anything else to say to her for the remainder of this visit or any future visits, it better be an apology or a thank you for waiting on your miserable ass. Got it?"

Brenda gives me a tense nod, and I don't miss the way her now-folded hands are shaking.

"Good. Have a great day, ma'am."

Once I've made my point, I head back to my table.

Mary walks up with a mischievous grin. "Jax, if I weren't old enough to be your mother, or already married myself, I'd whisk you away right now after that."

I chuckle to myself. "She do that often?"

She gives me a pained expression. "Yep, every time."

I rub my forehead. "How long has…"

"Melody. Her name is Melody," Mary fills in for me.

"Right. How long has Melody worked here?"

"About a month."

"Good lord. She's been dealing with *that* for a month?"

"I've offered to take over for her every time Brenda comes in, but she always refuses. She's such a sweet woman, but very independent. Wants to handle things on her own, ya know?"

I do know.

Melody. She's got a beautiful face, a beautiful name, and she's been dealing with bitchy Brenda for a month, which tells me she's tough as nails.

"Well, if she ever talks to Melody like that again, please come next door and let me know. Also,"—I pull a hundred dollar bill from my wallet and hand it to Mary—"will you make sure she gets this? You don't have to tell her who it's from, but something tells me bad behavior isn't the only thing Brenda has been dishing out to her."

Mary folds the bill and sticks it in her back pocket. "Absolutely. You're a wonderful man, Jax. Your mother should be proud."

When I glance behind Mary, I see Melody standing in front

of the kitchen with Brenda's new plate of food. Her eyes are locked on mine, and I find it hard to look away. I give her an encouraging smile.

Like I said, I'm a man that usually minds his own business, but in a split second, something about Melody has drawn me in, prompting me to jump to her rescue. Suddenly I don't want to mind my own business at all.

CHAPTER 3

Melody

"Who was that?" I ask Mary, once the man at her table left.

"Who?" she asks, standing at one of the kiosks, counting out change for a customer.

"The guy at table twelve. The one who told off Brenda."

In my entire life, nobody has ever stood up for me the way that man did. A perfect stranger. He did what the people who claimed to love me never could. It was insanely sexy, and I don't even know his name.

After tossing some cash in a check presenter, she looks up with a smirk, and pulls something from her back pocket, handing it to me.

Money?

"What's this?" I ask, taking the cash from her hand.

"It's from him. That was Jackson Pierce. He wanted to make sure I gave this to you."

"What? Why? That was your table, not mine. I didn't even talk to the guy!"

She laughs at me, placing a calming hand on top of mine.

"Because it's Jax. He's just a good man. I may or may not have told him that you've been Blue Springs's unlucky recipient of our bitchiest customer for the last month. He figured she hasn't been leaving you much in the way of tips, so..." she says, nodding to the cash in my hand.

I unfold it. "A hundred dollars?!"

"Shh!" Mary laughs.

I can't help but giggle back. "Sorry. Wow, that's so generous."

She shrugs.

I shake my head. "I can't accept this. He was in your section, I didn't work for it. This belongs to you."

When I try to hand it back to her, she closes a fist over my hand and shoves it back toward me with a wink. "Oh honey, he took care of me too, don't worry. Take it."

Why would this random stranger leave me a hundred dollars before we've even spoken?

The eye contact we shared was intense, I can't deny that. He is one of the most handsome men I've ever seen. With medium-length wavy brown hair that stuck out from underneath a base-ball cap, gray sweatpants, and a simple white tee, he managed to make me feel things that I never thought I would for anybody else. Who am I kidding, he was sexy as hell.

The expensive Rolex on his wrist screams money, so of course this is the first man I find myself attracted to. As if the universe is testing my restraint against wealthy men, it places this sexy individual crashing directly onto my path.

But he would never be interested in someone like me. He looks like he spends hours in the gym where I'm sure there's dozens of chiseled gym babes at his beck and call. I'm a mom with a soft belly and stretch marks.

Pity, that's what this is. But it's too much and I can't accept it. When he comes back in, I'll tell him exactly that. Right after I thank him for his words to Brenda. He managed to bring to life every waitress's wet dream of a perfect stranger telling off a shitty customer when we can't.

After I dropped off her new plate, I braced myself for another onslaught of insults but was instead met with a forced smile as she nodded and hung her head low. She never said another word to me. She also didn't leave a tip, but that's fine by me. Not having to endure another round with her in the ring was more than sufficient.

For the first time, I'm leaving work with a smile, eager to spend the next two days off with my baby girl. Things may be hard right now, but that man's small act of kindness was enough to make me believe that maybe, just maybe, things are going to be okay.

"I'M GOING to get a sprinkle one. Ooh, ooh, and a chocolate one! Oh, and those yummy pink frosting ones are soooo good." Gracie is practically drooling as we walk into town for donuts at the local bakery.

"How about we start with one, and see how things go? That's a lot of sugar, baby girl."

She attempts a pouty face, but she's too excited to make it believable.

It's a beautiful sunny day, so we decide to head into town for an early morning snack before we build the lemonade stand. I have the next two days off before I have to work through the weekend, so I plan on soaking up every minute with my sweet girl.

We are headed to Main Street, where the majority of the town's businesses are located. Being such a small town, there's not much else outside of Main. The restaurant I work at, Blue Bistro, is up ahead, next to it is the local gym, Jumping Jax, and next door is the building we're looking for.

Bread Pitt is the local bakery, known for their fresh loaves of bread and incredible donuts. We've only been here once in my attempt at limiting Gracie's sugar, but I struggle to not give her everything her heart desires.

Main Street sits at the base of the mountains here in Blue Springs and is surrounded by lush pine trees that border the street on both sides. Down the center is an idyllic brick road with sidewalks on each side and old-school oil lamps that run the length of the road. A few streets over, there's a crystal clear river running through town, where the locals can be seen splashing around on a hot day.

About ten minutes from here, hidden among the trees, you can find hot springs the residents swear by. Apparently they're the best way to unwind.

Although I'm used to big cities, and have always felt quite comfortable there, I'm starting to understand the appeal of small-town life. Life moves slower here. There's less chaos. Less rushing, and more people walking leisurely to enjoy the day. And there's not a single view in the city that can compare to this.

"Look Mommy, there it is!" Gracie shrieks and bounces up and down, jerking my arm as we hold hands, making our way through Main Street.

I giggle. "I see it, baby girl."

We push through the front door with black lettering that reads *Bread Pitt* depicting a French loaf image beneath it. The name is hard to forget and always makes me smile.

I'm immediately hit with the sweet smell of fresh baked donuts, coffee beans, and warm bread. Two of my favorite things, carbs and coffee.

"Hi Gracie! Hi Melody! How are you?" Trish, the owner, greets from behind the counter.

She's in her forties with curly brown hair pulled back into a large jaw clip. She's wearing short jean overalls over a white T-shirt donning the bakery name on the left breast. She has small frame glasses on her face, and she looks like what I picture every kindergarten teacher to look like.

One of the perks of a small town I didn't expect to appreciate was the fact that everyone knows you. We have been here exactly *one* time, but because Blue Springs doesn't often get new residents, we've become the shiny new toy.

"Hi, Trish. We're doing great. How are you?" I beam at her.

She gives us a bright smile. "Wonderful! You two enjoying the day?"

Gracie has her face pressed to the glass, already scoping out the donut selection, and I walk up to the register where Trish stands. "Yes, it's beautiful out. We thought we'd grab a delicious treat before we work on a project today."

She puts her hands on her hips, intrigued. "Oh, that sounds delightful. What sort of project are we doing today, Gracie?"

I love the way these people always include my daughter in the conversation. She's a child, but her input still matters.

Gracie glances up from the glass to answer. "A lelomade stand! Want to come and buy some?"

I laugh at her mispronunciation of lemonade. "Yes, we will be making fresh *lemonade*. But we won't be set up today, baby girl. We should be ready tomorrow. We were going to set up in front of our house if you'd like to come by."

Trish claps her hands together joyfully. "That sounds wonderful!" She taps a finger to her chin pensively. "Actually, what do you think about setting up shop right here? You'll definitely catch more foot traffic."

"That's so generous. But isn't that sort of competing with

you? That can't be good for business." Now this is definitely something you'd never get in the big city.

She turns slightly and waves a hand around her shop. "I don't see any lemonade here, do you?"

I laugh. "No, I guess not."

"Great, then it's settled. Come back tomorrow and I can help you set up! A new attraction will be great for business. It'll draw people inside for some treats to go with your delicious lemonade, Gracie."

My heart squeezes. I'm not used to such benevolence from people I hardly know. It's foreign, and I can't help but wonder what are the ulterior motives. Much like with the way Jackson left me a hundred dollars. It's not that I have reason to distrust either one, but in my experience, people are rarely giving for no reason.

"Thank you so much. Okay Gracie, did you decide which one you'd like?" I ask, bending down so we're both eye level with the rows of baked goods.

"That one!" she squeals, pointing to a pink frosted donut with sprinkles.

Of course. The usual.

"Okay, baby girl, one pink frosted with sprinkles, and a raspberry jelly filled one for me."

I pay and Trish hands us the donuts. We take a seat at one of the small round tables inside, and Gracie finishes hers in record time. I am halfway through with mine, when we say goodbye to Trish and walk back outside, ready to make our way home.

Next to the bakery is the local gym, and it's surprisingly busy for the early hour. I glance inside as we pass by, and there he is.

Jackson Pierce.

The generous mystery man.

He's shirtless, wearing gray sweatpants, and black Converse. With a jump rope in hand, he's doing some of the most intricate tricks I've ever seen a person do. I always thought there were two ways, forward and backward. Wrong.

Jackson is whipping that rope around like a pro, crossing it in front of him, switching the handles from one hand to another. It's impressive and surprisingly sexy. The way his skin glistens as his body jerks up and down elicits desires I thought had gone dormant. But with the way I'm staring at him through this glass window, I'd say those urges are beginning to stir awake.

Next to him, I see a bubbly blonde with a perfect face and perky boobs a few feet in front of him, performing similar stunts with her own jump rope.

Does everyone in this town jump rope like they're in the Olympics?

They're facing each other, with huge grins on their faces. The way they're giggling and talking back and forth, there's a sense of familiarity and comfort there. Probably his girlfriend. She's stunning in her matching light blue sports bra and leggings with tall white socks and matching sneakers. She has a white jump rope and looks equally impressive whipping it around her body.

I glance down at the dirty jeans pulled over my stomach, and flowy white tank top with a fresh donut stain on it, feeling painfully inadequate. This woman is a stranger to me so I shouldn't be comparing myself to her, or anyone, but I can't help it. Once someone points out your flaws on a daily basis, it's hard to silence the voices that demand to agree with them.

Internally, I scold myself for allowing a fantasy about this man to evolve for even a moment when he's got a woman like that within reach. She looks like she's sporting six pack abs, and her smile is blinding me from here. I can only imagine what a woman such as her is like in bed.

I'm sure Jackson knows.

"Mommy, what are we doing?" Gracie asks, pulling me from the chaos of my thoughts.

"Nothing, sweetie," I tell her, then to myself, I mutter, "Just what could have been."

What could have been if I wasn't afraid to step into a gym. If I was the person I used to be, and if I was the kind of woman a man like Jackson would ever go for.

I tug her hand forward, and back to reality.

CHAPTER 4
Jackson

"What's on the menu today?" I ask Summer as we finish training for the day.

"Raspberry oatmeal or strawberry blueberry."

"Oatmeal?" I grimace.

She rolls her eyes. "I swear it's good. Just try it, you big baby."

I reach for the strawberry smoothie. "I'll play it safe today."

"Still scared to try anything outside your comfort zone, I see," she teases.

"Beats the alternative and ending up with diarrhea at a jump rope competition."

She nearly chokes on the sip of smoothie that was in her mouth, before coughing it up. "That was one time! And I've never made that one since. Nobody ever told me too much apple juice does that."

A laugh bursts out of me, and she throws her gym towel at my face.

"You're an ass," she says, grinning, knowing it's all in fun.

"Speaking of ass, how was your date?"

We're resting on the gym mats, and she leans back on her hands with her legs outstretched. "Ugh. Awful."

"What was wrong with this one?" I ask with an exasperated look.

"Hey, don't make it sound like a *me* problem. Men out there are seriously disturbed!"

I twist my baseball cap so it sits backward on my head, giving her a cocky expression. "Welp, hate to break it to you, Sum, but they can't all be like me."

Summer sticks a finger in her mouth and pretends to throw up. "Gross. Don't even joke about that. It would be like dating my brother, and I'm firmly against that sort of thing."

Another laugh bubbles out of my chest. "I have to agree with you there, Sum. So tell me what his issue was."

Her mouth pulls to the side while she thinks. "It's nothing *too* big. But he was really close with his mother. Like, *really, really* close."

I mock gasp. "Hey! I'm really close with my mom."

She shakes her head and her eyes bulge out. "No, not like this, Jax. He talked about her the entire time and showed me a whole slideshow of pictures of her like she was his child. It was giving serious Norman Bates vibes."

My nose wrinkles in disgust. "Yikes. I'm definitely not Norman Bates close with my mom."

"Exactly," she states, taking another swig of her smoothie.

"Better luck next time."

"Nope," she says, shaking her head. "I'm officially done with men. There's nothing but freaks out there. I will just be the old lady with cats and jump ropes."

"Cheers to that, Sum." I hold up my bottle to hers and we toast to the single life.

She leans forward and taps hers to mine. "I don't know why

you're still choosing to stay single. There's plenty of incredible eligible women here that would give their left tit for a date with you."

I shrug, not wanting to get into this with her again.

Summer gives me an exasperated look. "That was so long ago. You can't still be holding onto that. Not all women are like that. You have to let somebody in someday."

"I disagree. I have a booming business, a wonderful family, and the best friend anybody could ask for."

She gives me a warm smile. "Okay, okay. I won't push it. But you know I'm right."

While Summer might be right about the reason I'm refusing to date, I'm not sure there's anyone I'd be willing to trust enough to let in again. I did that once. Gave my entire heart to a woman I thought I'd spend forever with. But it doesn't matter. What's done is done, and it's okay because I'm happy now. Or at least, happy enough.

Before I can think of a comeback, my phone rings on the ground next to us.

"Ah, saved by the bell," Summer singsongs.

I glance at the name that pops up. "Nope, saved by Mom."

She chuckles. "You men and your moms. Tell Jane I said hi. I'm gonna go shower and get back to work."

I push the green icon on the phone. "Hey Mom."

"Hi, my sweet boy, how's your day going?"

"Pretty good, I just finished training with Summer. She says hi."

"I miss her. Tell her I said hello."

"Sure thing, Mom. What's going on?" I ask, though it's not abnormal for her to call just to check in.

It's been my mother and me since I was a young boy, so I've never known anything else. We've always been each other's best friend and biggest cheerleader. She worked her ass off to support us after my father ditched us, taking all of our savings. I can't remember a single day that my mother complained or led me to believe there were hard times. But I knew.

As I got older, I became aware that we didn't live the way other families did, never had the same things. While other kids went on beach vacations during the summer, I helped around the house or tagged along with my mom to odd jobs. It would have been easy to complain, but I wanted to prove that I could be strong for her. The way she worked endlessly, I knew she was exhausted. She had enough to worry about, I didn't want to be another cause of her stress.

"I was getting hungry. I thought I'd see if you wanted to grab a bite to eat."

"I'm still at work for a while. Can I bring some food over later for you? And I'd be happy to accompany you anywhere you like tomorrow when I have the day off," I offer.

"No, no. You don't need to bring me anything tonight, let's get together tomorrow."

There's disappointment in her voice. I feel bad saying no. My mother gets lonely. She never remarried or had any boyfriends, as far as I knew. As much as I wish she would put herself out there, I know firsthand how scary it can be.

"Okay, Mom. Call me if you change your mind. I'd be happy to come by with something."

"I don't want you fussing over me. You're a young man, you should be going out and meeting a woman or something."

A young man?

I'd hardly say twenty-nine warrants a "young man," but I suppose age is relative.

"Well, don't count on that. But I should get back to work, Mom. I love you."

"Love you, too!"

I rinse off in the locker room showers and change into a

black T-shirt and a clean pair of dark gray sweats and my black Chucks. The afternoon slump hits, and I'm tempted to go next door and grab a cup of coffee but decide to tough it out. I force myself to go through the dozens of new emails I've received since this morning.

Updates from both Denver locations, spending reports, new memberships, etc. Summer takes care of these in the mornings before we train, but I take over in the afternoons when she's out on the floor assisting with customers and trying to create new memberships through existing clientele.

Summer is easy to love. Clients like that she's spunky, funny, and sweet. She's charismatic and able to draw in new customers, not just because she's beautiful, but because she's honest and hardworking as well. That's what I love about her. She never lets her looks create her success or be all she has to offer. Summer has always been determined to be the hardest working person in any room, and I've always found that to be true.

But with Summer out front, it leaves me back in my office, trudging through emails. Easily the most boring part of this job. But a vital one.

I'm about halfway through the emails when my mind starts to wander back to what both Summer and my mother said today. That I should be opening myself to dating, to women again. I haven't considered dating in a long time, so I don't know why their comments are sticking with me today.

Maybe I just need to get laid. It's been a long time since I've done that, too. The last time I slept with a woman was six months ago on a weekend trip to one of the Denver locations. We met at a bar, and sure, she was beautiful, but it was never anything more than that.

Since my last serious relationship, I've been able to completely separate sex from any feelings. While that might sound harsh, I refuse to open myself to that sort of heartbreak again. I still crave sex as much as the next guy, but I don't ever let it go beyond that. All of my hookups are well aware and fully understand it can never lead anywhere. Just because I don't let women in doesn't mean I take advantage of them or lead them on. I'm not an asshole.

Maybe the upcoming Denver trip in a few weeks can take care of the foreign thoughts in my head. The ones that keep inviting unwelcome feelings of needing someone to call my own again. And the ones circling back to the new waitress at Blue's.

Melody.

Her name rings through my mind like a song. I picture the way her wide hips sway back and forth when walking, all those alluring curves. The way her pouty lips parted when my eyes locked with her deep blue ones. She was an unexpected sight in such an ordinary place.

I've never felt compelled to interfere with someone else's affairs the way I was with her. But when I saw the look on her face, the way she was trying so hard not to fall apart, I jumped in. I didn't think. It wasn't an option not to help.

Even here, alone in my office, my thoughts are consumed with a woman I've never met. A voice that keeps poking and prodding at me from the inside to find out more than just her name.

I pull up my phone and shoot a text to my mom.

Jackson: Let's have lunch at Blue's tomorrow.

Mom: Sounds great honey! I'll meet you there around 1.

Jackson: See you then ma.

I was excited to see my mother, of course, but I found myself jittery with anticipation of seeing a particular curvy brunette again. I only hope she'll be working when we go in, because I'm dying to find out more about this mystery woman who did what no other woman has been able to: make me want more.

CHAPTER 5

Melody

Why is it that when you're in a hurry, you suddenly can't find anything you need? Car keys, shoes, bra? Okay, so maybe I didn't technically lose my bra. But I only have one comfortable one that holds these bad boys up, and it's currently hiding from me.

"Gracie, baby, come on, we gotta go!" I shout, as I'm yanking my too-tight jeans up my thighs, only to be met with annoying resistance.

"Mama, don't go to work today." She plops on the bed and gives me her best pouty face as I'm performing my jump-and-pull motion to get the pants up over my hips.

"I have to, baby, they need me today." *And we need the money.*

"What about the lemonade stand today at the donut store?" she reminds me. Though, I haven't forgotten, I've simply had to make a choice. Time with my child, or money to keep a roof over our heads and food on the table.

When those are the options, is it really a choice?

Kat and Bud have been our life boat since we met. When Kat came over today with a casserole dish for dinner and asked if I could cover tonight, I couldn't say no. Not only have they given me a job and a place to stay, but they regularly keep us fed, bringing over homemade meals a few times a week. They don't do it so I'll be at their beck and call, but I don't want to leave them hanging when they do so much for us.

We gathered the supplies we needed yesterday after our donut stop, but today's setup has officially been put on pause.

Once my pants are up and buttoned, I lean down to her level and put my hands on her shoulders. "Baby, I'm so sorry. I have Monday off, and we can do it then. Promise."

She considers my offer and shrugs. "Okay."

It's not what she wants, but she knows it's what she's got, so she agrees.

Usually I walk over to work, but since our neighbor can't sit for Gracie last minute today, I am taking her with me and hoping she can sit through my shift until I'm off. Since it'll be dark when I get off work, I don't want to walk with Gracie back to the cabin.

I find the keys inside one of her pretend plastic purses—one of the perks of having kids—and we race out the door and into my older model Honda Civic. A vehicle I bought with cash when I sold the obnoxiously overpriced luxury car I had back in LA. It provided us with a vehicle and a few extra bucks to spend.

Luckily, there's no traffic in this town, *ever*, so we arrive at Blue Bistro in under five minutes.

"Okay, baby, see that booth back there? Take your tablet and your coloring books and go sit while Mommy works, okay?"

Mother of the year award goes to...

"Sure Mommy," she replies sweetly, and hops into the booth with zero fuss.

Thank God.

Tying my apron around my waist and securing a shift towel to the back of the apron, I glance around the restaurant, noticing that it's, in fact, dead.

"Mary," I call, shuffling over to her as she pushes through the kitchen doors into the dining room.

"Hey honey, what are you doing here? I thought you had the day off."

Giving her a forced smile, I wave a hand over to the booth where Gracie's sitting quietly, playing a game on her tablet. "Yep, I was supposed to. Someone called out. Again. But it's dead in here, so I'm not sure why I'm here."

"Hold on, let me drop these off to table twelve real quick," she says, and my eyes follow to where she drops food off to none other than Jackson.

I quickly sift through my apron for the hundred dollar bill he gave me, since I have no intention of keeping it. Just because he has money and likes to flaunt it doesn't mean I have to accept it. I'm sure he's used to women fawning over him the second he starts throwing his wealth around, but I'm one woman that won't work on.

The cash isn't there. I grimace, remembering that I took it out to wash the apron, and in my hasty exit, forgot to put it back.

Mary returns to where I'm standing in front of the kitchen doors. "Sorry honey. I heard something about a large seventieth birthday party coming in later. I guess they didn't want to be a man down when they came in."

I nod. That makes more sense than the ghost town it currently is.

"You don't have a sitter for Gracie?" she asks softly.

"No. The one person I know that can sit for her has plans today. It was pretty last minute, so I can't even be angry. I hate having her sit here for my entire shift." I rub my forehead, feeling the beginning of a headache coming on.

"Oh my gosh, I have the best idea!" Mary suddenly shrieks, grabbing my hand and dragging me over to, yep, you guessed it: Jackson's table.

He's sitting across from a woman who appears older than him. She has kind brown eyes and short curly brown hair. They share a passing resemblance so I can only assume they're related.

Once we approach the table, they both glance up with confused expressions, though they're both smiling.

Fuck, he's got a great smile.

"Mary, we've hardly had time to take a bite, I don't know how it tastes yet," the woman jokes.

Mary laughs. "Sorry, Jane, I actually have a favor to ask."

Jane looks back and forth between us and sets her hands in her lap. "What is it, dear?"

"Well, Melody here," she says, using both hands in a very Vanna White manner to direct all attention to me, "is without a sitter for her sweet little girl over there. And I was wondering, if you don't have plans after this, if you wouldn't mind watching her for a few hours."

Alarm bells start screaming at me, and I interrupt. "Whoa, Mary, uh…I appreciate this, but I don't even know this woman." I look back at Jane. "No offense."

Jane laughs. "None taken, sweetheart. Well, to answer your question, I'd be delighted to watch her little one, permitting approval, of course."

Jackson grins in his seat with his stupid, sexy baseball cap and gray sweats. What man wears those out in public, looking like sex on a stick, unless he's a man whore?

Nervously, I'm glancing between the three of them, unsure what to say when Jane breaks the silence.

"If you'd like my references, I grew up in Blue Springs. This is my son Jackson who can vouch for my mothering skills. I'm CPR certified. I'm also a longtime friend of Bud and Kat, whom I think you're familiar with," she says, giving me a wink.

I bite my lip, feeling put on the spot. She's clearly excited about it, which is already a step above my current sitter.

"She's really great with kids. Actually, she sits for a lot of the local families from time to time," Jackson adds.

I consider Jackson's words, turning back to Jane, my voice low. "Why would you want to help a complete stranger?"

She offers me a kind smile. "You're not a stranger. You're in Blue Springs now, darlin'. You're one of us, and we take care of our own."

Her words come easily, and without hesitation. As if offering to help me is the most obvious thing in the world. I've never known such kindness, not without strings, anyway. Between my family and Gracie's father, I've never had anyone who was willingly in my corner simply because they wanted to be. Hearing those words come from a stranger makes my heart pinch. The fact of the matter is, I had been settling for far less than I even thought possible.

It's not only that I don't know this woman, but I also don't want to announce that I can't give her a fair wage. I am barely paying our current sitter.

"I, uh, I don't have much to offer in the way of pay right now," I sheepishly tell the woman.

Her hand flies to her chest like I've offended her. "Oh my gosh, honey, I wouldn't take your money. I'd be happy to help. I know it's scary to trust your little one with someone new. It's the scariest thing in the world. But I am wonderful with children, and I truly enjoy spending time with them. They keep me young."

The three of them chuckle lightheartedly.

I give her a warm smile. It's easy to like Jane.

Recognizing that I don't have many other options, and that spending time with this sweet woman is better than Gracie having to sit quietly in a restaurant for eight hours, I agree.

"Okay, when you're finished eating, I'd be happy to introduce you, and then give you directions to our home."

"You're staying in Bud and Kat's cabin. I know exactly where that is."

Oh yeah, "long time Blue Springs resident" and best friends with everyone in town. Small towns are smaller than I thought.

About twenty minutes later, I hear my name being called by Jackson. I glance over to his table, and he's waving me over as Mary is clearing their plates. I guess it's time.

I make my way to where Gracie is now coloring a picture of a unicorn.

"Hey sweetie, I want you to come meet someone."

"Who?" she asks, still intensely concentrating on her picture.

"A nice lady who wants to hang out with you today while Mommy works."

"Not Vicki," she groans.

"No, not her," I quickly tell her, feeling even worse that I've left them together so many times.

"Oh, okay," she says, satisfied, finally looking up at me.

"And listen, you can say no. Whatever you decide, I'll support. Come on, sweetheart," I tell her as I take her hand and lead her over to their table.

Once we approach them, Jane's hands grip her chest as she greets a shy Gracie who's hiding halfway behind my legs. "Oh my gosh, this beautiful girl must be Gracie."

"Want to say hi, Gracie?" I ask, trying to pull her out from behind my legs.

She shakes her head, refusing to move.

"That's okay, sweetie, I get nervous meeting new people, too. I was talking with your mommy here, and I was wondering if you'd want to spend the day with me because I have a bunch of cookies to bake, and this new craft project I wanted to do. But I need some help," Jane says, trying to cajole her out from behind me, and like a switch, Gracie's ears perk up.

"Cookies? What kind?" she asks quietly.

I stifle a giggle, and when I glance up, I see Jackson's doing the same, his intense green eyes locking onto mine.

Does he look at all women with the same intensity he gives me?

"What kind do you like?" she asks Gracie sweetly.

"Sugar cookies. With frosting."

Jane excitedly slaps her knee. "Oh my gosh, what luck! That's exactly the kind I was going to make. What do you say, should we go make cookies at your place, while your mama finishes her work? Would that be okay, Gracie?"

Gracie comes forward, no longer hiding behind me and smiles at Jane. "Sure," she answers slowly. "What's your name?"

"Jane. I'm Jackson's mama," she says, reaching across and grabbing Jackson's forearm, giving it a squeeze.

I expect him to pull away or get embarrassed, something a typical guy would do. But he gives his mother a wide grin and then turns to Gracie. "She's the best mom. You're going to have a lot of fun with her today."

"Will you come bake cookies with us, too?" Gracie asks him, catching everyone off guard.

"Uh..." Jackson's gaze quickly jerks back to me, pausing for my reaction.

"Maybe, sweetheart, but I'm sure he has plans with his girl-friend," I tell her.

His eyes narrow slightly at me, and an expression I can't read flits across his face. "I'd love to bake cookies with you two. I love cookies."

His resolve takes me by surprise.

"You do?" I blurt out before I can stop it.

Now it's his turn to look offended when his head jerks back. "Of course I do, who doesn't love cookies?"

Maybe it's because of his rock-hard body that's covered in well-defined muscles, but I can't picture a man that looks like him sitting around a kitchen, baking cookies all day.

I bite my bottom lip, unsure how to respond. Jackson's full of surprises.

Before averting my eyes, I don't miss the flicker of heat that flows through his gaze. The look startles me.

"Yeah, Mommy, everyone loves cookies," Gracie chimes in.

The four of us laugh in unison.

"Then I guess you guys will be making cookies. I'll give you my number so you can reach me if you have any questions or concerns. She doesn't have any allergies, and she's usually very well-behaved," I tell Jane, and she reaches out for my hand.

I place my hand in hers and she gives me a reassuring smile. "We'll be fine. We're going to have the best time. Aren't we, Gracie?"

Without hesitation, Gracie pushes through our hands and hops up into the booth, sitting right next to Jane, and proceeds to fire off questions. In five minutes, she's created better rapport with this woman than in all the weeks she's spent with Vicki.

I release a calming breath knowing I made the right choice.

"You can put your number in here," Jackson offers, holding out his cell phone for me. He continues when I stare down at it in confusion. "So we can reach you, and you can check on Gracie."

I shake my head, as if it'll untangle my thoughts, embarrassed I thought for a second it was for any other reason. "Oh, right."

Taking the phone, I punch in my name and number and then send myself a text so I have the number, too. "Thank you again for doing this. You don't know what a lifesaver this is," I say, passing the phone back.

Our hands graze in the exchange, and the heat radiating not

only from his skin, but from the way his green eyes bore into mine, momentarily makes me forget that I'm at work, standing in front of my daughter and his mother. Instead, in my mind, I'm pinned beneath him, his strong arms framing me. His hand reaches down, pushing my legs apart, and...

"Mommy, we are going to make signs for the lelomade stand!" Gracie's words pull me from my trance-like state, and I quickly yank my hand away.

I don't know who this man is, but one thing is for sure, I need to be very careful around Jackson Pierce.

CHAPTER 6

Jackson

We'd barely made it the short drive back to Melody's place after stopping at the market for cookie ingredients before I'd gotten the first text from Melody.

> Melody: Aprons are in the second drawer next to the fridge. Gracie knows to wash her hands before baking, but sometimes she forgets.

> Jackson: We will be fine. She's sweet and my mom is the best sitter. There's not a kid in town that wouldn't jump at the chance to spend the day baking and crafting with her.

> Melody: Thank you. Our current sitter isn't quite so hands-on, and Gracie doesn't particularly enjoy their time together. So I worry about her when I'm gone.

I snap a picture of Gracie and my mother in matching aprons standing in their quaint kitchen smiling at each other. Sending it to Melody, I follow it with a message.

Jackson: I think it's safe to say she's enjoying herself.

If I've learned anything from my own mother, it's that mothers are going to worry. It's a skill they've mastered, and they can't unlearn it. So, if there's anything I can do to lessen the anxiety Melody feels for sending her daughter with us, I will.

Melody: 😍

Jackson: We will see you at 8.

Before we left the restaurant, we offered to get Gracie down for bed since Melody wouldn't be off until eight, but she wanted to be there to put her down. So, we're going to keep her busy and fed until her mother comes home.

With this being my only day off this week, I had planned on hiking up to the hot springs to take a dip. Between workouts and training with Summer every day, the strain pretty much keeps me in a constant state of soreness. A dip in the hot springs would have been exactly what my aching muscles needed. Although, seeing the desperation in Melody's face today, and knowing that we could help, I can't say I'm upset with the turn of events.

Aside from my mother and Summer, I don't spend much time with women, nor do I find myself eager to insert myself into their life like some sort of knight in shining armor. I never wanted to.

But every time I see this woman, I have the overpowering urge to jump in. To protect her. Even if my mom had declined, I would have offered. Something in the way she carries herself, and the genuine shock when we offered to help watch Gracie, tells me that life hasn't been easy for her.

I don't know what my draw to her means, but I tell myself it's because she's new in town, and like my mother said, this is how we treat our own.

"I'M HOME," Melody whispers as she walks through the front door.

The day flew by, filled with paint and glitter, and the smell of sugar cookies. I figured with the guarded way Melody carries herself that Gracie would behave similarly, but boy, was I wrong. This little girl is a ball of energy and sunshine. She's outgoing, hilarious, and exudes sweetness and confidence.

After I helped my mother and Gracie make cookies—and by help, I mean "taste tester"—I assisted with making signs for a lemonade stand that Gracie can't stop talking about. I took a few urgent calls from one of the Denver locations that's reporting low numbers the last few months, but other than that, the day was a lot of fun.

"Hi," my mother greets at the same time Gracie shouts, "Mama!"

Melody closes the front door behind her and joins us in the living room on the couch. Her hair is in a messy bun on the top of her head, and her mascara is creating a slight raccoon effect under her eyes. She looks exhausted and relieved to be home. I can't help but smile at her. Even after an eight-hour shift of slingin' plates for Blue Springs's finest, she still looks absolutely beautiful.

"We ate five cookies and made sparkly signs for the lelomade stand. Do you want to see?" Gracie starts talking a mile a minute, excited to tell her mother about her day.

Melody laughs, and it might be the sweetest sound I've ever heard.

"Oh wow! That sounds like a great day, baby. Let me walk them out and I'll come look at your beautiful signs. It's late and I'm sure they want to get going," she says and then looks at my mother who begins to stand from the couch where we've been relaxing.

"Gracie, you were a delight, sweetheart. Anytime you need a friend for the day, have your mommy call me," my mother says, bending down to hug Gracie, who hopped up with her.

"Thanks for making those amazing cookies, Gracie. They were delicious," I tell her, and then join my mother who's now walking to the door.

Melody follows us outside and closes it behind the three of us. She pulls a few bills from the apron she's still wearing. "Thank you again. I didn't make as much as I hoped tonight, but this is for you."

I make no move to take the money from her hand as I gaze down at it, and then to my mother who's slightly shaking her head and smiling.

"I already told you. You're one of us. You're family. We don't take advantage of our family."

Placing my hand over hers, I push her hand back. "Keep it, Mel."

Mel? I hadn't even been properly introduced to her yet, and here I am giving her a nickname.

I feel the same warmth from earlier in the day when our hands touched and can't help but wonder if she felt it, too. The way she ripped her hand away, I would presume not. Maybe it's all in my head, the attraction simply one-sided.

But this time she's not moving, not pulling away.

Her eyes are wet when they meet mine, and I don't know where the sudden emotion is coming from.

"I'm going to meet you in the car, Jax. Melody, she was an angel. Please call me if you need someone to watch her again, I'd love to spend more time with her." My mother retreats down the few stone steps and hops into her white SUV.

"Thank you. Your mom is really great. I'm sorry you had to spend your day babysitting," she tells me.

"What do you mean?" I ask, noting that our hands are still intertwined between us.

"I'm sure there's a hundred other things a guy like you would rather be doing than spending his day baking cookies with a four-year-old and his mother."

I raise an eyebrow at her. "I happen to love my mother. We spend lots of time together, actually," I say, releasing our hands, and then gently gripping her forearm, drawing us together and leaning into her ear. "And for the record, I loved spending time with your daughter."

Pulling away, I see the stunned look on her face, but she doesn't respond. The corners of her lips begin to pull upward, and I turn and walk down the stairs to the SUV. "Good night, Mel."

As I climb into the vehicle, I can't divert my gaze away from the gorgeous brunette who stands on the front porch. A woman who's currently giving me the same undivided attention while we back out of her driveway.

"How was your day off?" Summer asks, sitting in a chair across from me while I reply to a slew of emails that have come in this morning.

"It was good," I tell her, not planning to elaborate more, because knowing her, she'll read more into it than necessary.

"Did you make it to the springs? It sounded so good, I thought about going, too. But I decided to take an afternoon nap after my run. I regret nothing," she tells me with a dramatic hand gesture.

"No, I didn't. I was helping my mom with something."

Her eyes narrow. "With what?"

"She was babysitting a little girl, and I decided to tag along and help out."

One side of her lips curls into a smirk. "Ooook. Whose little girl?"

"You don't know her," I quickly respond.

"Uh, it's Blue Springs. I know everybody you know."

"Her name is Gracie. She and her mom are new in town."

She leans back in her chair, placing one ankle over the other knee and crossing her arms in front of her in full detective mode. "Okay. Who's her mom?"

This is why I didn't want to tell her. She's about to make this a bigger deal than it is.

I sigh, shooting her an annoyed glare. "Her name is Melody. Like I said, she's new in town, and I was just being helpful."

"Okay," she replies, her eyes filled with mischief.

I lean back in my own chair and cross my arms, mirroring her posture. "What?"

"Oh nothing." She stifles a laugh.

"What is it, Sum? Something funny?"

"I'm just wondering why you didn't help Mrs. Winthrop when she moved to town last year."

I roll my eyes, tugging on the brim of my backward cap, annoyed. "That was different."

She barks out a laugh. "How so?"

My eyebrows pinch together, but I don't respond, so Summer continues.

"I remember your mom sat for her twin boys a handful of times, and I don't recall you volunteering to help her then."

My eyes meet Summer's and she gives me a look as if to say *Well?*

"I was at lunch with my mom, and the whole thing was sort of set up in front of me. So I offered to tag along. It wasn't a big deal, and anyway, her daughter is the sweetest kid."

"Coming from 'Mr. I Will Never Settle Down or Have Kids'?" she says, using finger quotes.

I lean forward, feeling annoyed at the way she's pushing this, when I don't understand it myself. "You're reading into this for no reason. I'm not settling down with anybody. So let's chill with the third degree."

She holds both hands up in front of her in surrender. "Okay, okay. I'm not judging. It's kind of great, actually. Like a whole new side of you. Jump rope enthusiast by day, hot stepdad by night."

I roll my eyes and she laughs at me, slapping her knee, clearly amused with herself.

"How about a little more 'best friend' and a little less 'detective.' And please don't say 'hot stepdad' to me again. It's weird to hear you say that."

We both laugh. "Well, what do you say, 'daddy,' are you ready to go train or what?"

I grimace at her and have a full-body shudder. "Gross. Get out of here, I'll be out in a minute. And for all this sass today, your smoothies better be your best ones yet."

She rises from her chair and stands in the doorway. "Oh Jaxy, they're all my best ones."

I shake my head and laugh when she turns dramatically with her blonde ponytail flipping over her shoulder as she bounces out of my office and down the hall. Whatever is going on with my attraction to Melody is going to have to be better hidden than this, otherwise I'm never going to escape the scrutiny of my best friend, the ballbuster.

After sending two more emails to management at the Denver locations, I grab my blue rope, and head out front where I see Summer racing toward me with a mischievous grin on her face.

"What?" I ask when she reaches me on the jump rope mats.

"You have a visitor," she singsongs.

"Okay, who is it?"

"She said her name is Melody."

Shit.

CHAPTER 7

Melody

There is no greater joy than knowing you have a happy child.

After my shift, Gracie could not stop talking about Jane and Jackson. She had the absolute best time baking cookies with them. My hesitation to leave her with them vanished once I saw how attentive and respectful they were to my caution, as well as Gracie's feelings.

I had already planned on giving back the one hundred dollar bill that Jackson left me that first day I saw him at Blue's, and now there's no way I can keep it. He and his mother saved me yesterday, and I owe them everything. The last thing I wanted when I left LA was to be indebted to another rich man.

The great day with Jane only made today that much harder when Vicki came over to babysit as scheduled.

Gracie fought me this morning, which she's never done, and I had to promise her I'd talk to Jane about becoming her regular sitter before she unlatched from my leg and let me leave for work. Now I'm standing at the front of Jackson's work where I was greeted by a gorgeous blonde, who, let's face it, is a real-life Barbie doll.

Her long blonde hair is pulled back into a sleek ponytail, and her white sports bra and pastel low-rise pink leggings look like a second skin on her perfectly sculpted body, forcing an uncomfortable glance downward, judging my own unkempt appearance.

Faded blue jeans with a fray at the knee, black nonslip work shoes, and my white Blue Bistro T-shirt with the logo name on the left breast pocket. A far cry from how this woman looks. If she's Barbie, then I'm, well, the opposite of that.

She bounced away to find Jackson for me, and I can't help but curse my damn luck that it was her at the front when I walked in. I can only imagine the things she's thinking about another woman coming to look for her man.

Not that she would ever be jealous of someone like me.

The gym is full of people in their own element, in all corners of the building. Some on cardio equipment, others using free weights, and a few on mats utilizing jump ropes. There's loud, upbeat music playing, and the energy is inviting and fun. But with my sordid past with fitness, I feel out of my comfort zone. As if there's a spotlight on me and everyone's eyes are directed at me.

Tugging on my shirt, I wait awkwardly in my work uniform and an apron that smells like ketchup and ranch dressing. I should have run it through the wash last night, but with the excitement of the day, Gracie's nonstop chatter kept me side-tracked.

"Mel."

My head jerks up at the sound of my name being called by Jackson, who's striding toward me with a blue jump rope in his hand and a wide grin plastered on his face.

Why does he look so happy to see me?

And why is he calling me Mel, like we're close friends?

More importantly, why do I like it?

"Hey," I say blandly, because I'm lost for words, and suddenly can't remember why I'm here.

His smile stretches even wider. He's wearing black Converse, gray sweatpants, and a black T-shirt that has a Jumping Jax and jump rope logo on the front. I can't help but picture his glistening body underneath. The same one I saw a few days ago while passing by the gym.

"Are you here to join the gym?" he asks, startling me from the unwelcome dirty thoughts.

"Excuse me? Are you saying I need to join a gym?" The words bolt out harshly before I can stop them. They're a reflex of old habits, old conversations. The constant need to defend myself, and why I'm not what others need me to be.

His eyes widen and he scratches the back of his head. "No, not at all. It's just...why are you here, then?"

I avoid eye contact, realizing that I am, in fact, standing in a gym, so his question had to do with my presence here, and not at all with my appearance.

I reach into my apron and pull out the hundred dollar bill, and extend my arm to him. "Here. I can't keep this."

He doesn't take it or respond.

I glance up to see what he's doing.

Smirking. He's smirking at me.

"Here." I shake my arm. "I appreciate the sentiment, but I don't take handouts. I can take care of myself."

He crosses his arms and widens his stance, his rope dangling at his side. "I never said you couldn't."

I've been holding my arm up for so long, it's starting to get sore. "Please take it. You don't even know me."

He sticks his hand out but doesn't take the money. "That's a great point. We haven't officially met. Hi, I'm Jackson Pierce."

I cock my head and lower my hand. "You already know who I am."

He scratches the back of his head, pretending to be confused. "Wait, but you just said I didn't know you. I'm starting to get lost here, Mel."

"And that. Stop calling me Mel. You don't know me," I snap at him.

The anger in my words doesn't deter him, and his smile doesn't falter. "Yeah, but I could if you let me."

Jackson seems like a nice enough guy, but I came here to get away from men. One man in particular, and all men. For mine and my daughter's sake, I made a promise to myself that I'd never get mixed up with another man after what happened with her father. I can't do that to us again. The risk is too high.

Before I have time to respond, his phone chimes in his pocket and he pulls it out and reads a text message. He glances behind him toward the blonde that greeted me. The one who's currently staring in our direction.

Oh hell.

I'm sure she's wondering what the hell he's still doing talking to a random woman for this long.

"Look," I say, and his gaze is drawn back on me. "It seems like you've got all the female attention you need, and I'm not really interested in getting to know you."

He clutches his chest. "Ouch."

"It's not personal. I'm not interested in getting to know anyone. And that's beside the point. I think the longer you stand here, the angrier your girlfriend is going to get."

He gives me a dazed look. "My girlfriend?"

"Yeah, blondie over there can't take her eyes off you," I say, jerking my head in her direction.

When he looks back, she bursts into laughter. I don't know what to make of it. She doesn't actually look angry, so maybe this is a game for them.

"Is that what you think of me? That I have a girlfriend while I'm over here trying to get to know you?"

I shrug and try to hand him the cash again.

He shakes his head at me, and this time his smile fades. "You're right, Melody, you don't know me at all."

He turns and walks away, and my heart sinks. I had intended to thank him for his help and return his cash. But somehow, I wound up offending him.

Since we've arrived in town, I've had my guard up to protect myself and Gracie, but I never wanted my armor to harm someone else.

NOW THAT MEGAN, the waitress who called out, was back at work, I was able to get home to Gracie at a reasonable hour tonight and have dinner with her without rushing her to bed.

I'd be lying if I said I didn't have the urge all day to text Jackson to apologize. But I'm not even sure what I'd say. I know why I reacted the way I did, but he doesn't, and I'm not ready to share that with anybody yet. Maybe ever. I don't want to be a bitch to him since he's never been anything but kind. Him and his mother. But I can't let myself get involved with another man, or any man, for that matter. And it seems like opening the door to any kind of friendship with this one could get messy.

Who am I kidding, he's not interested in me like that anyway. I'm reading too much into it, when he's likely trying to be nice because of his mother. He is self-admittedly a mama's boy, so that would make sense.

Why does that make him even sexier?

It's why I decide not to text him. It's better this way. If he thinks I'm a bitch, he won't want to get to know me. Problem solved. I can admire him in silence and nobody has to know. Nobody gets hurt.

Gracie and I are spread out on the couch watching *Ferdinand* after downing some bison burgers that Kat brought over. Being on my feet for more than six to eight hours a day makes it hard to find time to make a decent meal for us, so nights when Kat brings us dinner makes all the difference. And I love that Gracie will eat pretty much anything that's put in front of her.

It's also gratifying to enjoy a meal without agonizing over every single calorie that goes into it. While I'm not a petite girl by any means, I'm not overweight. But I spent too many years beneath someone else's thumb, demanding that I look a certain way. Now, every time I consume something that isn't a chicken salad, or chicken and rice, it feels like retribution. Payback for every time I had to choke down that boiled chicken to make someone else happy.

Gracie is cracking up at something the goat Lupe is doing onscreen when my phone vibrates next to me. Since I left Los Angeles, and cut everyone off, or they cut me off—it's hard to tell which sometimes—I don't get many messages. Not from family or friends. Mary will text me from time to time, but I know she's out on a date with her husband tonight so it's unlikely that it's her.

I flip it over to see a text from Kat. She will reach out and check in occasionally to see how we're doing at the house, make sure everything is in working order, and ask how we're fitting in. It may not be much for some people, but to me, it's everything.

> Kat: Thank you for your hard work today. Let us know if you or Gracie need anything at all! Hope you enjoyed the burgers.

> Melody: We have everything we need, thank you so much. Please tell Bud thank you as well.

JUST AS I'M about to set my phone down, another message pops through, but from someone new.

> Jackson: I'm sorry that the tip offended you. I never meant to insinuate you were incapable of anything.

AN APOLOGY. I went to his workplace, insulted *him,* and he's apologizing to me. I really am a bitch.

> Melody: Don't be sorry. I just don't feel comfortable taking money from a stranger. I didn't work for that.

WHAT I DON'T TELL him is that I refuse to be indebted to him in any way. In my experience, men only do nice things for you to hold it over your head to get their way.

Three bubbles pop up as he types a new message.

> Jackson: I disagree. A month of serving bitchy Brenda. You absolutely earned that, and then some.

I giggle, smiling at the screen.

> Melody: "Bitchy Brenda," so that's her official town name then? And here I was thinking I was so original calling her that.

Jackson: Oh you're original all right. I've never had someone get furious with me over a tip.

Melody: About that… I'm sorry. I said things I shouldn't have. I went there to thank you for what you and your mother did for me.

Jackson: I missed the gratitude memo you came to deliver.

Melody: Hey, I said I'm sorry.

Jackson: You're forgiven. So have you decided?

I REPLAY our last conversation through my head, trying to place if he asked me anything.

Melody: About what?

Jackson: If you're willing to let me get to know you.

Melody: I don't think that's a great idea.

WHY IS he on this again? I thought we established that it wasn't a good idea. Really, I'm shocked that he messaged me to begin with. If he were any other guy, he would have deleted my number and moved on to the next girl in town.

Three bubbles appear and disappear for the next few minutes. I don't expect a reply so I put my phone down and get up to start Gracie's bedtime routine. We brush our teeth, use the restroom, wash our hands, and I sing her two favorite songs before turning out the lights.

It's only 8 p.m., so once I feel her heavy breathing, indicating deep sleep, I sneak out to the living room and look for a movie to watch before I go to bed. I work the late shift tomorrow so I don't need to be out of the house early, though that won't stop sweet Gracie from rising with the sun.

When I return to my phone, I see I have a new message waiting for me.

Jackson: Why not?

Melody: It's complicated.

Jackson: That sounds like an excuse.

Melody: It most certainly is.

Jackson: For the record, I don't have a girlfriend. I would like to get to know you. As friends.

Melody: Why do you want to be my friend?

Jackson: Who couldn't use more friends? Hang out with me one time, if I'm an absolute bore, I'll never bother you again.

I DON'T KNOW why he's so persistent with this. What do I have to offer him? Maybe he doesn't have a girlfriend, but he and blondie sure seem awfully close.

Nothing good can come from us hanging out. I need to tell him no. It's not happening.

So tell me why that's not what I sent back.

CHAPTER 8

Jackson

Who is this person I've suddenly become? I'm not the man who chases women. Hell, I'm not the man who cares whether or not a woman chases me. But I can't ignore the way my stomach does a flip-flop when Melody's text comes through.

> Melody: Let me think about it.

I WOULD HAVE BET my entire fortune that Melody was going to say no, maybe tell me to fuck off.

I'm never this forward or persistent. Sure, there's women pursuing me, both here in town and one woman in Denver in particular who can't take no for an answer, but I never open the door to them. For me, it's simpler to keep women at arm's length. They're either after my money, or they only want me for how I look. Nobody's ever interested in getting to know me.

Last year I had one date with a woman—if you can call coffee at her apartment and her proceeding to strip down and give me a lap dance a date. The entire evening was bizarre, and even though she was what anyone would consider a perfect ten,

I wasn't interested in seeing her again. She messaged me for weeks saying she knew I was the one, and knew we were soulmates. Summer calls her a stage five clinger. I blocked her number after she didn't get the hint, and I haven't wanted to hang out with anyone new since.

So why can't I leave Melody alone? Why do I have this innate desire to be there for her? Clearly, she's an independent woman who can take care of herself, so why do I care?

At the risk of scaring her off tonight, I send back a simple text.

> Jackson: I'll take it. Good night, Mel.

I'M LYING in my oversized bed, legs outstretched, while the flat-screen on the wall displays one of my favorite comfort shows: *Friends*. I don't have a lot of time for starting new shows. Even as I lie here, I have my laptop open next to me, going through emails, and working on finalizing vendors for the upcoming end-of-summer jump rope festival. The work never stops, which makes having *Friends* on as background noise comforting for me. I don't have to pay much attention to it and can still recite every line to every episode.

My home, while some might say it's too big for a bachelor, is something I'm proud of. My mother raised me on her own, so we never had a fancy large house. It never bothered me, but I did always dream what it might be like to be someone who could afford a home like this.

The Colonial Revival style home has two floors, plus an oversized, fully furnished basement/man cave, six bedrooms, three bathrooms, and a lush large backyard with a waterfall spa that pours directly into my pool. Once my business took off and I was able to acquire two more gyms, I celebrated by buying both my mother and I homes. Hers is a few minutes from here, and isn't quite as large, per her request, but it's more extravagant than anything we could afford growing up. It was the least I could do for all the years she worked multiple jobs to keep us afloat. I know it wasn't easy, so now that I can give her a relatively worry-free lifestyle, it makes me feel like I'm doing something right. She gave me a wonderful life, and now I want to do the same for her.

I'm scrolling through pages of jump ropes, trying to narrow down the ones I want to order for the festival in August, when my phone buzzes.

Hopeful that it's Melody, I quickly snatch it off the bed and flip it over.

> Summer: I'm bored. What are you doing? Hot stepdad things?

> Jackson: No, smart ass. Looking at what jump ropes I want to order for the festival.

> Summer: Ooh! Fun! You're saving a spot for my booth again right?

> Jackson: Duh. It's not a jump rope festival without Summer's smoothies.

> Summer: Haha. That's what I like to hear. I think Ember is coming to town to help me run it again this year.

EMBER IS Summer's younger sister who lives in Denver. She's basically Summer's doppelgänger, only a few years younger, and way more reserved. Where Summer is loud and outgoing, able to walk up to anyone and start a conversation, Ember is more shy and keeps to herself. I'm not as close with Ember as I am to Summer but growing up with them both makes her feel like a sister as much as Summer.

Summer sends another text.

> Summer: But seriously, when are you going to dish on the situation with that hot mama?

> Jackson: Well, you know her name is Melody, and there's nothing going on.

> Summer: So, you admit you think she's hot? Interesting

> Jackson:

As I suspected, once Melody left the gym this morning, Summer could hardly contain her excitement. She was frothing at the mouth for intel and was disappointed when I didn't have any juicy details. There was a vomiting gesture when I told her Melody thought she was my girlfriend, but other than that, I shut down the conversation and I assumed that would be the end of it.

Apparently, I was wrong.

> Summer: I don't know why you're being so weird about it. She's gorgeous, and there's nothing wrong with liking her.

> Jackson: I hardly know her. We're just friends. Or, we're trying to be.

Summer: Listen, you know I'm bustin' your balls. I don't want to see you get hurt. You're my best friend. But I will say, I don't think I've seen you look at a woman this way since Shaina.

LEAVE it to Summer to bring up the sole reason I no longer date. The woman who betrayed me, ripped my fucking heart out, and had the nerve to ask if we could still be friends. That was a hard no for me.

Jackson: Can we not talk about her?

Summer: 10-4. Can I come over and help you pick jump ropes? I'm so bored, and if I sit here any longer I might actually consider hopping back on these dating apps and giving another local a date.

As HARD OF a time as she gives me, she means well and hasn't had an easy go of dating, either. Although, I do have to say that hearing about her failed dates sure does keep me entertained, so a small part of me hopes she gives some poor schmuck a chance.

Jackson: You've got a key, let yourself in.

SUMMER ENDED up staying the night in one of my guest rooms, which she does from time to time. She brought over a six pack of Colorado Native, an amber lager we both enjoy, while we chose jump ropes for the kids.

Every year, my gym, along with a handful of other businesses in town, host the annual jump rope festival, giving away jump ropes to every kid that attends. It's a great cause that encourages kids to get active in an era when they spend most of their time sitting in front of screens. This is my way of giving back to the town I love in the hope that kids will get back outside. Not only for their health, but because it's fun. The festival is great for the entire community. Parents love it, and it's extra revenue for the businesses that have booths.

We usually go with all black ropes, but I'm feeling adventurous and wanted to choose something more outgoing this year. So after bickering back and forth for two hours, we decided on pink, blue, green, and purple ropes. We decided to order five hundred for now and will likely need more once we start selling tickets in the next few weeks.

Summer left before me this morning to head into the gym, and since my arrival, it's been nonstop chaos. The warm weather always brings with it a slew of new memberships, which is great, but that means more paperwork and more wear and tear on the equipment. Work seems to double in the summertime.

It's nearly 3 p.m. before I'm able to sit down and eat, but I left in a hurry and didn't pack anything. Though I'm not too upset because it gives me the perfect alibi to go see my new friend Melody.

I push open the front door to Blue's and I'm greeted with the curvy sway of Melody's figure exiting the dining room, carrying dishes back to the kitchen.

Get your head right, friends don't stare at each other's asses.

"Hey Jax, just one today?" the hostess asks.

"Hey Maybelle, yep, just me. Is there room in Melody's section?"

Maybelle, who's all of seventeen, gives me a playful grin. "Melody? Oh sure, she has a few tables open right now, actually."

I nod and hold my arm out for her to lead the way.

Once I'm seated in the booth, I glance up to see Melody making her way over to me with a quizzical expression on her face.

"Jackson," she greets as she stands in front of me.

"Melody. What an honor it is to see you here."

Her eyebrows furrow. "Well, I work here, so. What are you doing here again? This town isn't that small. Isn't there some other watering hole you enjoy?"

"You wound me," I joke, clutching my chest dramatically.

"All I know is, I didn't see you the entire first month I worked here, and now you're here every day. What gives? A guy that looks like you can't possibly be eating the blue burger this often."

I purse my lips and turn my baseball cap backward. "Have you been shamelessly checking me out, Mel?"

I'm teasing, tossing my line in the water, and she's biting.

She places a hand on one of her cocked hips. "Don't flatter yourself. Your ego doesn't need any more compliments."

"Well, as a matter of fact, I love the blue burger. And believe me, my body can handle it just fine with how much I put it through. You don't have to worry about me, Mel."

"So, you're really just here to eat?" she asks warily.

My lips twitch up into a sly smile.

She throws her hands up. "I knew it."

"I figure if I keep showing up, you'll have no choice but to see what a great friend I am to have around. I'm not so bad." I smirk.

"Yeah, yeah, that's what they all say. I'll be right back with your order," she says tersely, walking away. Not at all fazed by any charm I'm attempting to exude.

I think, in part, that's what draws me to her.

"I'll take a Pepsi, too!" I shout as she walks to the computer to punch my order in.

Once I've finished eating, Melody returns to clear my plate and drop off my check. She doesn't seem any more charmed by my presence.

"Should I expect to see you again tomorrow?" she asks with my empty plate in hand.

"Do you work tomorrow?" I grin innocently.

She raises an eyebrow and hesitates. "Yes."

I pull out some cash and toss it in the check presenter, handing it to her and standing up from the booth. "Well, then, I guess I'll see you tomorrow."

Exiting the front doors, I begin walking back toward Jumping Jax when I hear my name being called.

Turning around, I see Melody storming toward me holding the check presenter in the air, but when she approaches me, she simply stares at me.

"Yes?" I ask.

Maybe it's in my head, but I know there's interest on her end as well. I can see it in those fiery blue eyes. I can't quite read her, but there's more than frustration there. Whatever she's feeling, she's working really hard to hide from it.

"What the hell is this?" she asks abruptly, shaking the black presenter at me.

"Uh, the bill?"

"You left me a hundred dollar tip again. Why do you keep leaving me this much? Nobody tips like this. Your bill was twenty-five dollars. It's absurd."

"Maybe I'm just a nice guy."

"Those don't exist," she replies without hesitation.

I've never been a man who wished for special powers, but right now, I'm wishing I was a mind reader. To be able to see what's going through her mind, and why she seems so scared of me. Why she's convinced that all men are bad. And damn me for wanting to be the man to prove her wrong.

I take slow steps toward her, but she backs away until she meets the side of the Blue Bistro. I inch into her space, slowly raising my right arm over her head, pressing my palm against the brick building.

I look down at her beautiful eyes and lean in as I whisper, "Maybe not where you're from, sweetheart. But I'd be happy to show you how a nice guy should treat a woman like you."

Her chest begins to rapidly rise and fall as her breathing quickens. She's not responding, not making a move to push me away or get away from me. When I glance down, I see her pouty full lips part slightly.

Fuck me, I want to kiss her, and I can't help but wonder, what would she do if I leaned down right now and pressed my lips to hers?

CHAPTER 9

Melody

Why do I want to reach up and close the distance between us?

Oh right, because I've been daydreaming about his mouth on mine every chance I get. The way it would feel. The way it would taste.

This doesn't feel like real life. Men like him don't go for women like me. I'm a mom with a soft belly and stretch marks, and he has muscles I didn't even know could *be* sexy. He can have any woman he wants, so why is he pursuing me?

Any and all words are caught in my throat as I stare into his intense emerald gaze. The proximity of his body to mine, and the way his arm is caging me in against this building is making the butterflies in my stomach flutter wildly.

I need to go back inside, but I don't want to move and pop this bubble we're in. So I stare right back into his gaze, getting lost in him. Momentarily allowing myself to feel something for Jackson and find myself unintentionally biting my lower lip.

Did he just growl at me?

Jackson places his other hand firmly on my hip. "Say yes.

Tell me you'll give me one day. One chance to show you I'm not like the men you know. What a great friend I can be."

Friends.

This doesn't feel like friends but fuck it if I don't want to find out what perks this friendship might have.

My voice is low and breathy. "Friends?"

His thumb gently moves back and forth over my jeans. "If that's what you want."

I manage a tight nod.

"What do you say?" he asks, his eyes pleading, begging me to say yes.

"Okay."

Fuck me. What did I just agree to?

The lust in his eyes intensifies and a wide smile spreads across his face. "Yes?"

I nod again, not trusting myself to open my mouth again. Not trusting what else I might say to him. What he might get me to agree to.

I take a deep breath in an attempt to center and pull myself out of this lust bubble I'm trapped in, but all I smell is Jackson.

Fuck, that was a mistake.

A man who spends his days inside of a gym, with a jump rope in hand, should never smell this good. It's outdoorsy, like blue skies meet lush landscape and citrus. It's clean and intoxicating. As I inhale, I close my eyes, letting his aroma surround me.

When I open them again, he's smirking at me, like he knows what I'm thinking. I place my hand on his chest, pushing him backward, and turn to walk back toward Blue's.

"Have a great day, Mel," he shouts after me.

But I don't turn around, because if I do, he'll see what I've been trying to hide. What I've been trying to run from, and there's no rational way to explain how I have feelings for a man I hardly know in such a short amount of time. It's reckless and it's crazy.

Walking back through the bistro dining room, I check on my tables and then head to the restroom to gather myself.

I look in the mirror and tell myself that I will absolutely not catch feelings for a man. Moving here was intentional. This is a tiny-ass town, and I wasn't supposed to find any men here. The plan was to escape our life in Los Angeles and focus on my daughter. So we could both heal and move on from the past.

Jackson Pierce is fucking up my plans.

Taking a deep breath, I repeat my new mantra over and over until I believe it.

We are only going to be friends.

We are only going to be friends.

We are only going to be friends.

As I walk back out to the dining room, I swear my reflection in the mirror is laughing at me.

GRACIE and I are placing the finishing touches on the lemonade stand before bathtime. I found some wood in the shed behind the cabin, and Bud and Kat told me I could use as much as we needed. While I'm not a carpenter by any means, I'm proud of the little creation I made for Gracie.

She's painting in the last few lemons I outlined in Sharpie, when my phone vibrates with an incoming phone call. I flip it over and see none other than Jackson's name on my screen.

"Gracie, I'm going to take this phone call real quick. Keep painting and I'll be right back."

"Okay, Mommy," she replies without looking up.

I hit the green button. "Hello?"

"Hey Mel, I was wondering if my mom could talk to Gracie."

"What, why?" I ask, laughing.

"Well, earlier today you told me you didn't feel comfortable leaving Gracie with the sitter so we could hang out. But if memory serves me, I recall her having a blast with my mom. If you're okay with it, of course."

He texted me not long after he had me nearly pinned against the side of Blue Bistro, already having the perfect "friendly get-together" planned. His persistence has me curious, and as much as I want to fight it, I want to give in more.

I consider his offer. Did I love leaving Gracie with Vicki? No. Do I love the idea of leaving Gracie on a day I didn't work? Also no. But do I want to spend the day with Jackson after he told me he had the perfect day planned? Fuck yeah, I do.

Mom guilt is a bitch. You spend all of your time with your kids, and then burn yourself out, needing a break. But the minute you're not with them, you feel like the worst mom in the world. Being a mother is definitely not for the faint of heart. Though, thinking back on everything we've been through, maybe I owe it to myself to see what this attraction is about. The last few years have been really tough, and it's time I start doing things for myself. Even if I use the term *friends* as a front to hide behind.

"Okay, I'll put her on," I concede.

"Great! I'll pass the phone to my mom."

Padding out to the living room to Gracie, I click the speaker button. "Gracie, do you remember Jackson's mom, Jane? The one who watched you the other day and made cookies with you?"

"Jax's mommy? She was so fun!" Gracie answers enthusiastically.

"She wants to talk to you," I say, kneeling down and pushing the phone toward her.

Her small hand curls around the phone when Jane's comforting voice comes through the speaker. "Gracie, sweetie, I wanted to ask you something."

"What?" she asks and covers her mouth with her other hand, stifling a giggle.

"Would you want to come hang out with me tomorrow? I was going to do some more baking and crafts. I thought you might like to help while your mommy runs some errands," Jane offers.

Gracie lets out a loud shriek of excitement that no doubt pierces Jane and Jackson's ears the same way it does mine.

"I'll take that as a yes," Jane says through her laughter.

"Can I Mommy, please?" Gracie asks me with her best pouty face.

I smile at her. "You know that means we won't be doing our lemonade stand until the next day, then. Are you okay with that?"

She nods passionately.

"Okay, you can go, baby girl."

"Mommy, thank you, thank you!" she squeals, throwing herself into my arms, almost knocking me over.

Jackson's voice breaks through the squeals and laughter. "It sounds like a yes to me, Mel."

I laugh and roll my eyes. "It's a yes."

"My mother and I will meet you at your place at ten," Jackson says before hanging up.

There are a million other things I should be focusing on: finding a better job, looking for a bigger place for Gracie and me, and keeping a low profile in case anyone comes looking for us. Going on a "non-date" date is the last thing I should be doing.

So why am I this excited?

"MOMMY, WHERE ARE YOU GOING?" Gracie asks as I'm getting dressed.

Jackson told me to bring a bathing suit. He refused to tell me exactly what we're doing, so I can only imagine. Blue Springs is a very outdoorsy town, so that's what I'm going to assume it will be.

I dress in my favorite jean shorts (also the only ones that still fit), white sneakers, and a loose-fitting white tank top with pink flowers over my one-piece bathing suit.

"I'm actually going to hang out with Jane's son today."

"Jax?" she asks, her eyes going wide.

"Yes." I laugh. "Why do you call him that, sweetie?" As far as I know, his name is Jackson.

She shrugs. "That's what his mommy calls him."

Mary introduced him as Jackson, so now, as I'm toying around with the name *Jax* in my head, my body breaks out in chills and my stomach begins to roil when I realize why he works at the gym.

He doesn't just *work* there, he owns the damn gym.

Jumping Jax.

He's Jax.

The obnoxiously large tips, the expensive Rolex, it all makes sense now.

I'm sure he gets all sorts of attention for being a rich business owner, but when I moved here, not only did I promise myself no more men, but I specifically promised myself no more *rich* ones.

Apparently, I only attract rich assholes, and I refuse to go down this road again. Not after everything we've been through.

It was hard enough for me to consider being friends with this man after I thought he worked at a gym, but to find out he owns it is completely different. Our lifestyles will never mesh and I refuse to change myself for a man ever again. I can't make myself live under a microscope of what he'll want me to be.

Maybe right now I'm intriguing because I'm the new girl, but eventually the excitement will fade and he'll want someone who's more his speed. That will never be me. Where I was filled with excitement a few minutes ago, I'm now filled with dread. And I can't help but wonder why he didn't tell me.

Jackson

When Melody opened her front door, I couldn't believe how beautiful she looked. Her light brown hair, with blonde pieces peeking through in the sunlight, hung in loose waves at her shoulders. Her curvy legs in tight jean shorts and full breasts threatening to spill out over her white tank top had me staring for longer than appropriate. I consider myself a respectful man, but one look at her, and I can't tame the dirty thoughts playing in my head. Particularly her splayed out underneath me, naked.

"You're quiet today," I tell her after we've been walking for a few minutes.

Today, I wanted to give her an official Blue Springs tour. I've planned to walk through town and then hike up to the hot springs nearby. It's quiet and private, but not too far of a walk. Melody is typically wound tight, so I'm hoping this will be a relaxing day for her.

She shrugs. "I'm always quiet."

We're walking side by side as the sun shines down on us. It's not too warm yet, but it will be later this afternoon. She's carrying a small purse on her shoulder, and I'm carrying two towels under my arm.

I cock an eyebrow and turn my head to look at her. "Are you saying I'm going to have to carry all the weight of conversation in this friendship?"

I'm joking, but she either doesn't pick up on it, or doesn't care to. *If she didn't want to come today, she would have said so, right?*

The longer she's silent, the more anxious I become. I can't help but wonder if I pushed too hard and pressured her to be here when she really didn't want to be.

I gently grab her forearm, bringing us both to a stop and turn to her. "Hey, if you don't want to do this, I can take you back home. No hard feelings, honest."

Her eyes drop to where I'm holding on to her, and then she takes a deep breath. I can see her sorting through her thoughts, some internal battle she's wrestling with. Without explaining, she looks back up at me with a forced smile. "No, I want to be here. I just have a lot on my mind."

I nod. "Let's make a deal."

An apprehensive smile spreads across her face as she responds. "What kind of deal?"

"We're going to be friends, right?"

She gives me a playful "we'll see" look as her head bobs from side to side. "Pending friends."

I laugh at her lightened mood. "Yes, pending friends. So, let's promise to always be honest with each other. If you're not ready for a...*friendship,* and I'm pushing too hard, tell me. I want to break you out of your shell, but I don't want to ever pressure you into doing something you don't want to do."

She scoffs.

"What?" My eyebrows pull together.

She shakes her head. "Nothing." Rubbing her forehead with

her index and middle finger, she seems to consider my offer. "Okay, honesty. I'll agree to be honest, if you will."

I stick my hand out to her. "Deal."

Looking at my extended hand, she slowly takes it in hers and we shake. She gives me an expression that I can't read. Whatever is going on in her head, she's clearly not ready to share with me, so we press on.

We are walking through a neighborhood that runs parallel to Main Street instead of going through it, that way I can take her through the history of Main on our way back into town.

"See that house over there?" I ask, pointing to a light blue house on the other side of the street.

"The blue one? Yeah."

"That's where I got this scar," I tell her, lifting up my cloth short slightly to show her a long vertical scar running up the length of my right knee.

"Ouch. What happened?" she asks, eyeing the wound.

"When I was eight years old, me and my friend Mark were skateboarding. We thought we were so cool, right? We wanted to learn all these amazing tricks and impress everyone else on the block. We built this make-shift ramp out of this warped old wood we found. It was completely unsafe, but we were so proud of it. Of course, I had to be the one to try it first. As soon as my board got to the top, the wood bottomed out and it sent me flying through the air. I slammed knees first on the sidewalk where one of the nails sat that we hadn't put back in the box. I slid across it and it left this little beauty behind."

A sweet laugh slips through her pouty lips and I mentally start searching for stories just to hear her laugh again.

"You sound like every reason a mother has anxiety," she jokes.

"Yeah, I guess I could have been a little less reckless. I'd like to say it got better once I picked up jumping rope, but I've acquired quite a few injuries from that too, believe it or not."

"Oh, I believe it. Those tricks are so impressive. I've never seen anyone do anything like that," she confesses.

I smirk. "Have you been spying on me, Melody Miller?"

Her cheeks flush pink, and her response is flustered. "No. I mean, only when I pass by, but..."

I place my hand on her arm. "Hey, I'm just teasing you."

A nervous giggle slips through her lips and she tries to blow past it. "How did you get into jumping rope, anyhow? Were you in the jump rope Olympics or something?"

She's joking, but she's not far off. "Not exactly, but I did win my fair share of competitions growing up and in college. That's actually how Summer and I met when we were younger. She's really talented and keeps me on my toes."

"Yeah, she's really something. Beautiful, too."

Is that jealousy I detect?

"Not as beautiful as you," I say, allowing myself to be bold. I don't like the insecurity I hear in her voice. She's the most beautiful woman I've ever seen. How could she not see that?

Her cheeks flush again. "Yeah, right."

I see her eyes roll.

"Melody Miller, are you calling me a liar?" I tease.

"Why do you keep calling me by my full name? How do you know my last name, anyway?"

"You wear a name tag."

She cocks an eyebrow at me. "That only has my first name on it."

"Okay, so I asked Mary for it. Sue me," I reply jokingly.

"You asked her about me? Why?"

We're almost to the dirt path beyond the houses that will lead us to the hot springs when I stop her in her tracks.

"Hey, listen to me. You've made it clear that you don't want to be anything more than friends, and that's fine. For now," I say with a wink. "But you're going to have to accept that I like you. So, maybe I asked about you because I was curious. I'm not sure what sort of men you've been with in the past, but I'm not them. So, when I'm around, just know that I won't tolerate you thinking or talking negatively about yourself. Got it?"

She pulls her bottom lip between her teeth as her eyes begin to water.

Melody nods, and we both carry on. This was meant to be a lighthearted, relaxing day, so why can't I help going deeper with her?

There's still so much to learn about her, but one thing is for certain: someone out there sure did a number on her.

About ten minutes later, the path takes us to a slight hill, where we can look down and see a small body of water hidden perfectly between the trees.

"It doesn't smell very good," Melody says, scrunching her nose, as we make our way down the path toward the hot springs.

I laugh. "The hot springs are natural so they don't have the best aroma, but the water feels amazing. You've never been to one?"

She shakes her head.

I like getting to claim one of her firsts.

"You're gonna love it, come on."

We make our way down to the springs. Steam rises from the water, and a log nearby has been carved into a make-shift bench, so we drop our belongings and sit to remove our shoes. It's a warmer day, so we've lucked out and have the whole place to ourselves. But come wintertime, it's unlikely we'll find it vacant.

I begin to pull off my shorts and T-shirt when I notice Melody hesitating next to me.

"Everything okay?" I ask her.

She gives me a shy smile. "Um, can you turn around?"

"Ooh, did you forget your bathing suit?" I razz, waggling my eyebrows at her.

Giving me a coy smile, she shakes her head. "It's underneath my clothes, but can you, please?"

"I'll even cover my eyes. A perfect gentleman," I announce, holding one hand up, and the other to my chest.

I turn to face the woods, and after a moment, I hear the gentle sloshing of water.

"Okay, you can look."

"Sheesh, thanks for waiting for me," I joke when I turn around and see that she's nearly waist-deep in the water.

She's wearing a spaghetti strap, one-piece white bathing suit that has a deep V cut, and the straps are ruffled. Her large, perky breasts are peeking out of the water, and I'm trying my hardest not to stare. But damn, she looks good.

"I didn't want to get cold," she says, but it feels like a lie.

I dip a toe, testing the water. "Whoa! Yep, that's hot. How did you get all the way in so fast?"

She shrugs. "It's not much hotter than my showers are."

"Good lord, woman," I say, shaking my head in disbelief.

"I'm from Los Angeles, I don't like to be cold."

"Well, you might not like Blue Springs come wintertime. It's nice now, but we get hit pretty hard with snow."

She bites her bottom lip again, and I swear my dick twitches every time she does it.

"Yeah, I guess I didn't think that far ahead," she confesses. I can see the anxiety in her eyes.

"Don't worry, there are plenty of ways to keep warm." I wink at her.

Her eyes roll playfully. "You're incorrigible, Jackson."

"What? I'm talking about the hot springs, get your head out of the gutter."

"Mm-hmm, sure." Her words drip with sarcasm.

"Whatever you were thinking probably works, too."

She splashes me with water, and I can't help but smile at her. *Is she flirting with me?*

We spend a few moments moving around in the water on opposite sides, facing each other. The water is warm, almost too warm for a day like today, and I can't help but picture sneaking up here with her on a cold winter day, with the snow blanketing everything around us.

"So, what's the big deal about floating around in this stinky water?" She's being sassy, but I can see the way she's slowly relaxing.

"Right, let me show you the best part." I reach under the water, scooping up a handful of mud and make my way over to her. "You might want to put your hair up."

"What, why?"

"You'll see." I smirk at her.

Her eyebrows pull together into a skeptical glare, but she dries her hands off on the nearby towels and tosses her hair into a messy bun on the top of her head.

"Now what?" she asks once her hair is secured.

I move into her personal space, with my hand outstretched. "May I?"

She nods.

This woman doesn't seem to trust very easily, so I can't suppress the exhilaration of this small victory.

Slowly, I lift my hand and begin to rub the mud into her skin. I spread it across her chest, and slightly up her neck. Our faces are so close, I can feel every warm exhale. My eyes are downcast as I gently massage the mud into her soft skin. Neither one of us speaks, and the only sound is the rustling of leaves and birds chirping nearby. She lifts her arms out of the water, holding them out to her sides, so I reach for more mud and begin rubbing it on her shoulders and down her arms.

"That feels good," she murmurs.

Her voice has the same breathy inflection it did the other day when I had her up against that brick wall. She can tell me she doesn't want this, but her body can't hide it. Her heavy breathing and gooseflesh say otherwise.

Once I'm finished with her chest and arms, she reaches under the water and grabs a fistful of mud and moves closer to me. "Can I do you?"

Goddamn, woman, that's a loaded question.

CHAPTER 11

Melody

I'm covered in mud that smells like sulfur, yet somehow, this is one of the most intimate moments I've ever had. The air between Jackson and me feels charged, like it could zap either one of us at any moment if we're not careful.

The water at its deepest is about waist-deep, at least to my five-foot-six build, but hits below Jackson's hips. Depending on where we are in the water, we can sit and relax comfortably in the warm well, but in the middle where Jackson is rubbing mud on me, we stand facing each other.

He nods when I ask if I can rub the mud on him, so I wade over, back into his space, and our faces are close. Too close. But also not close enough.

His chest begins rapidly rising when he breathes and I find myself peering up into his gaze against my better judgment. Jackson has made it clear he wants to be more than friends. We both know this friendship thing is only a ruse. Although, I'm still confused as to why he's pursuing me. I can't give him what he wants. Whether it's sex or a relationship, I'm incapable of giving either. I'm not a girl who does casual hookups, and a relationship is absolutely out of the question. There's no reason I should be here, but I can't seem to fight my curiosity about him.

When our gazes meet, his emerald eyes are intense and unwavering. My hands continue to rub circles in his chest as we stare into each other's eyes, though it's likely been covered for several minutes now. But he makes no attempt to stop me, nor can I stop myself from touching him. I'm surprised when he makes no attempt to put his hands on me.

He really is a gentleman.

He keeps his hands still under the water, and I find myself slightly disappointed that he doesn't make a move. But this is what I said I wanted. What I need.

I don't know how many minutes have passed with me rubbing his chest and shoulders, both of us locked into a gaze that neither one seems able to break. Or maybe we just don't want to.

"Melody." Jackson's husky voice is barely a whisper.

My eyes drop to his lips.

His tongue swipes across his lips and then he grins. "I think we've surpassed the appropriate time limit for friends to be rubbing one another."

I yank my hands back like I've touched hot coals. "Right. Sorry."

I retreat to my side of the hot springs. His gaze never leaves mine, though the amusement on his face grows the farther away I get.

"You didn't have to stop. I don't bite. Unless you want me to."

He's an insufferable flirt, but it doesn't stop my body from reacting to his words or his presence. My nipples immediately harden, and chills break out over my skin as I picture his teeth sinking into my neck, my nipples, my lips.

Down, girl.

Attempting to ignore the throbbing between my legs, I shift

the conversation. "You never answered my question from earlier."

He makes his way backward until he can recline in the water, his arms resting on the outside of the pit. "What question was that?"

"How you got into jumping rope in the first place."

We're both settling into the water, leaning backward against the earth, its calming properties clearly taking effect.

"Ah, that one. Well, I guess it started when I was around five or so. My dad left when I was a baby, so my mom worked a lot. I don't remember a time when she didn't have at least two jobs. She worked so hard for us. I bounced from sitter to sitter, and even when I was at home with her, she was usually so tired that I played by myself most of the time. She tried, but even then I knew she was spread too thin." He pauses for a moment, treading his hands in the water, lost in memories. "Anyway, one of my sitter's children had this cheap plastic jump rope I picked up one day and couldn't put down. She let me take it home, and it became a way to pass the time. The next Christmas, my mom got me a more expensive one, and I was hooked. I started challenging myself and learning new tricks. The rest is history."

I can't help but focus on the fact that he grew up without a father. It's going to be my daughter's story, too. One day she'll be telling the person she's dating the story of her life without a father, and I'd be lying if I said that those thoughts didn't keep me up at night. Being a mom is terrifying enough without having the added strain of worrying about how the absence of your child's father is going to affect her.

Before responding, I take in his words, not wanting to take his candor lightly, but also unable to suppress my own curiosity. "What was it like growing up without a father?"

He purses his lips like he's trying to retrieve a memory, a feeling he hasn't paid attention to in years and sits dusty in the corners of his soul. "If I'm honest, I didn't really notice. I mean, I knew he wasn't there. Other kids had dads and I was aware I didn't have one. But for me, I never knew the feeling of having one in the first place, so it didn't feel like I was missing anything. My mother worked her ass off and made sure we had a roof over our heads and food on the table. We never went without anything. Sure, we didn't have the nicest things, but you know what I have that most people I know don't?"

I shake my head.

"A great relationship with my mom. I tell her everything, and she truly is my best friend. Well, aside from Summer, of course. They've been all the family I've needed. As burned-out as my mother was for all those years, she still found time to read me stories at bedtime and always listened to me when I had something to say. She never made me feel unimportant or like I was a burden. Not for one moment of my life. We were equals."

My nose stings, and I feel a lump at the back of my throat. While I grew up never having to worry about money, I've also never had a real relationship with my parents.

Popular belief is that money equates to happiness, and sure, it helps. But looking at the joy on Jackson's face as he talks about his mother and his childhood, I know without hesitation I would have swapped with him any day.

Swallowing the lump in my throat, I sniffle and try to hold the tears at bay, but I know the cracking in my voice betrays me. "That sounds pretty great."

Jackson gives me a sympathetic look. "You're worried about Gracie."

A half-hearted laugh slips through my lips. "Always."

He gives me a sad smile. "What happened with Gracie's dad?"

My body immediately stiffens, and though we're in near-boiling water, it feels like I've had ice water poured down my back. Whatever relaxation I felt is long gone.

I shake my head.

Not only do I not want to talk about him, I'm also not sure I could get through a conversation about him without completely falling apart. I'm not ready to face whatever it is I'm starting to feel for the man in front of me, so I'm sure as hell not ready to discuss the man that forced me to pick up the pieces of my life and flee to another state.

"That's okay, you don't have to tell me. But whenever you're ready, I'll be here," he says to me with a comforting smile.

"Thank you."

We move around in the water, allowing the mud to soak into our skin for a few more minutes and letting nature be the soundtrack to our day. In the chaos of the last few weeks, the weight of my decisions have been clouding the good in my life. I've been telling myself I'm being positive, but maybe all I've been doing is masking how I feel.

I wade through the shallow water to where Jackson is leaning his head back, his eyes shut. My hand finds one of his and I give it a squeeze.

His head jerks up, his gaze locking with mine.

"Thank you. I needed this," I confess.

His eyes, that somehow look even greener among the trees, brighten at my words. "I'm glad. I was worried I ruined the day with my intrusive questions."

I shake my head. "No. It's hard for me to talk about. Things are still fresh."

He squeezes my hand back, giving me a reassuring smile. "What do you say we get out of here and get some lunch?"

"That sounds amazing. Let's go."

AN HOUR LATER, after scrubbing the mud off ourselves the best we could, we are dry and dressed as we sit in a local brewery called Blue for Brews. Jackson ordered a local IPA, while I decided on a much tamer blonde ale. We ordered a large soft pretzel, rosemary truffle fries, and green chili pork tacos to share. It's not the healthiest lunch, but Jackson insisted they were their best dishes. Truth be told, I can't remember the last time I was out with a man who didn't automatically order me a salad.

"Melody, you've hardly eaten anything. You're going to have to help me. I can't eat all of this by myself. Do you not like it?" Jackson asks me. I was hoping he didn't realize I had hardly taken any bites of the savory dishes.

I feel my cheeks heat, embarrassed that he's noted my behavior. "No, it's all delicious."

He gives me a playful glare. "Whatever is going on in that beautiful head of yours, stop it. I ordered these because I wanted to enjoy them *with* you."

Somehow, in the short amount of time I've known him, he can see right through me. He knows when my mind is working overtime, and when I'm starting to shut down. It's something Gracie's father couldn't accomplish in all the years we were together. Or maybe he didn't care to.

"You're right," I say, lifting my beer glass between us. "Thank you for a wonderful day."

He lifts his glass, clinking it to mine as we mutter "Cheers" in unison.

After we finish the plates and one more beer each, I decide it's probably time to be getting home to Gracie, so he pays the bill, even though I offered to pay, and thanks me for my company.

The walk home is nice, now that there's a breeze. Though, the slight buzz from the beers doesn't hurt. Somewhere along the way, Jackson reaches for my hand and I let him. Even though I still stand by what I told him, I don't have it in me to fight it right now. The longer I'm around him, the harder it is for me to find reasons to stay away.

We finally reach the cabin and walk up the stone steps to the front porch.

"Tomorrow you and Gracie have your lemonade stand?" he asks.

"Yeah, she's been so excited about it. Trish said we could set up in front of Bread Pitt."

We both chuckle at the bakery name.

"Good ol' Bread Pitt. Did she tell you how the bakery got its name?" he asks, turning toward me, so we're standing face-to-face outside my front door.

I shake my head.

"Back in the early 2000s, Brad Pitt and Jennifer Aniston came here for a weekend to escape the big city, I guess, and they came into her shop every day they were here. Said Trish had the best pastries and bread they ever tasted. After they left, she immediately changed the name. If you look, you can see the picture she took with Brad behind the register on the wall."

A burst of hearty laughter shoots out of me. An honest-to-God, genuine laugh, and it feels so good, it almost brings tears to my eyes. I don't know the last time I laughed this hard or felt this relaxed. But I have one person to thank for that now.

The man in front of me. Jackson Pierce. The jump rope god of Blue Springs, who, for whatever reason, has taken an interest in me and is slowly reminding me that there are still good men out there.

Once my laughter dies down, I take a step toward him, invading his personal space. I reach my right hand forward and slip it into his left one. He responds by copying the movement with his other hand. Rising slightly on my toes, I start to close the distance between us. I can feel the heat between us, the way he wants to kiss me. But I know he won't make the move. I've told him that I'm only interested in being friends, so he will respect that.

His eyes widen, and when he realizes what I'm doing, he bends slightly. My lips part, anticipating his mouth on mine. My body is starting to quiver with anticipation, and my heart is beating wildly in my chest. I want this so fucking bad, so I ignore the terrified voices in my head telling me this is a bad idea. Our lips are about to meet when the front door swings open.

"Mommy, I knew I heard you!"

Fuck. Me.

CHAPTER 12

Jackson

As I lie in bed the next morning, my cock is rock-hard underneath my boxers, and all I can picture is the look Melody gave me yesterday. The way her pouty lips parted as she leaned into me.

All day, I fought the urge to pull her into my arms and press my lips to hers, and then she surprised me when we got to her door. Neither one of us had seen my mother's SUV parked on the side of the cabin, so it's a good thing we didn't get further than we did.

Fuck, I want her bad.

Sure, sex is great, but I've never been a man who craved it like this. When the thought of being with a woman consumed my consciousness. I've always enjoyed it while it was happening, but I never needed it like others seem to. There's been moments I've thought maybe there was something wrong with me when I never wanted to see the same woman more than a few times. I haven't been able to feel anything for another woman since Shaina.

The woman who broke my heart and sent me on a trajectory of meaningless sex with women who all thought they'd be the one to "change" me or lock me down. I don't blame her for my behavior, I'm responsible for my own actions, but she humiliated me in such spectacular fashion that I haven't felt true desire to be with another woman since.

Until Melody.

My attraction to her was immediate and obvious. Aside from that, I can see the way she strives to be an incredible mother for her daughter. Her independence is admirable, but I can see the pressure she puts on herself to be and do everything at once. It weighs heavily on her. She has the same look in her eyes at work that I saw in my mother's when I was younger. Having seen first-hand how difficult life can be for single moms, the many responsibilities and decisions they have to tackle on their own, I can't stand by and watch Melody believing she needs to do this alone.

My attraction to her aside, this is still the way of Blue Springs. We take care of our own the way the town came together for my mother when I was growing up. I don't know where I'd be if there weren't so many willing families to watch over me while my mother worked those endless hours.

As long as Melody lives in Blue Springs, she will never have to do this alone.

Last night left me confused about our...er, friendship. She made it clear she wants nothing more than to be friends, but the way she lingered while rubbing mud on me, and then almost kissing me, left me disoriented. I want more, but I don't want to scare her away.

Was last night a lapse in judgment, or a sign that she wants more?

I'm debating sending her a text when my phone goes off on the black nightstand next to my bed. I flip it over and see a text from Summer.

The time on my phone reads ten thirty. I'm usually in the gym by eight.

Luckily, the gym is only a few minutes away, so I get there in under ten minutes to find Summer in our shared office, looking frazzled.

Her eyebrows are pulled together and her forehead is creased with worry.

I make my way into the office and set my gym bag down. "If you keep making that face, it's gonna get stuck that way."

She lifts her head and gives me a look that sends chills down my spine.

"What is it?" I ask when I realize the seriousness of the situation.

"Denver West location is blowing up on Instagram right now. Not in a good way."

"What do you mean, why?"

She pulls up the profile for that gym location and navigates to the comment section on the most recent post.

Don't go to this gym, management are fat-phobic pigs.

Whoever is running this place needs to do a better job.

I will never support any of these gym locations after hearing what happened.

You all should be ashamed.

This gym and the managers are disgusting.

I scroll down and there are over four hundred comments that reflect similar emotions. "What the hell happened there?"

Handing her phone back, she takes it and drops it onto the

desk. "Randy was in the gym this last weekend, I guess, and he was going around the gym with Rick, the sales manager."

"Okay, and?" I ask impatiently.

"They were approaching all of the, uh, larger clientele, telling them they needed to sign up for personal training if they ever wanted to look good."

My face heats with rage. "What?"

Her lips form a thin line.

I pull the baseball cap off my head. Running my hands anxiously through my hair, I clasp my fingers at the back of my skull. "What the fuck. This isn't that kind of gym. My training specifically advises against this sort of thing."

Summer lets out a heavy breath. "I know."

"I would never allow this kind of behavior in my gym," I continue as if Summer isn't aware.

"I know, Jackson."

"Fuck."

Randy is the current general manager at Denver West—until I have a chat with him, of course—and he should know better than anybody that this type of approach will never be permitted in my gyms. Not only does it go against my anti hard-sales training, it's also downright degrading.

"What do you want to do? It's bad," Summer says.

"I know it's bad. I see that, Sum."

"Hey, don't shoot the messenger."

I take a deep breath and let it out slowly, trying to expel some of the rage boiling inside my chest right now. "You're right, sorry. I didn't mean to snap. I need to get over there."

"I'll hold down the fort here. Go. Get rid of those assholes."

The gym empire I've built has been carefully curated to make everyone feel safe and welcome. Some beginning their fitness journey will likely feel insecure and intimidated walking into a gym for the first time. My goal was to create an environment that was inviting, friendly, and fun. It's part of the appeal of Jumping Jax.

We have the typical weight and cardio sections but having an entire area specifically for jumping rope is a fun way for people to let loose and find their inner child again. Jumping rope isn't about who has the biggest muscles, it's about having fun.

Summer has been here since the beginning, and I can see she's seething as much as I am. She has always been a "girl's girl," which is why I always have her up front, on the floor. She's wonderful with new customers and has this incredible ability to make everyone feel right at home, even if they're a little shy or unsure if they want to be here. Somehow, she always makes a connection with them, turning strangers into customers and customers into friends.

"I'm going to step outside for some air. I'll be back in five," I tell her, slipping my hat back on my head and standing.

"No problem, I'm going to turn the comments off on the profile for now."

"No." I stop her.

"What, why?"

"Because it will look like we're trying to hide what happened, not taking accountability. I don't want to lie to anyone. I will make a statement soon, but don't silence them."

She gives me a sympathetic smile. "I'm proud to call you my best friend."

"You think Randy and Rick will feel that way when I'm done with them?" I ask jokingly.

A boisterous laugh escapes Summer. "Yeah, I doubt that."

Typically, I'm a pretty easygoing guy, but when you mess with my business or the people I care about, you'll find a version you wish you hadn't awoken. They crossed the line when they went after people who were simply trying to better themselves, only to be embarrassed by two meatheads who I mistakenly put in charge.

I won't be making that mistake again.

Making my way outside, I notice a small group gathering in front of Bread Pitt bakery. Melody and Gracie are standing behind a homemade wooden stand with brightly colored lemons on it. They both look blissfully happy as they hand out small cups of lemonade. I make my way over and stand in line, waiting my turn.

Melody glances up at me, a sweet smile dancing on her lips.

When I reach the front of the line, Gracie squeals. "Jax! Are you here to buy lemonade?"

"I sure am, pretty girl. How much for a cup?" I ask Gracie directly.

"It's fifty cents for one cup. Would you like regular or blueberry?"

I glance up at Melody in surprise. "Blueberry? That sounds delicious. I'll have a cup of that, please."

I reach into my sweatpants pocket and pull out a ten dollar bill.

"Mommy, will you help me count how much change to give him?" Gracie asks.

"Keep it, Gracie, but can I take a cup to Summer?"

"Sure!" Gracie answers with excitement, but I don't miss the flicker in Melody's eyes at the mention of Summer.

She may not be ready to admit she likes me, but the look on her face tells me she's jealous.

"Jax!"

Speak of the devil.

When I look up, I see Summer sauntering toward us with a confused grin on her face.

"I'm coming back, I promise. I was just getting some of Blue

Springs's finest lemonade. Here, I got you a cup," I say, handing over the second cup Gracie poured for me.

Summer takes a sip. "Holy shit, that's amazing!"

When I glare at her and tilt my head toward Gracie, she slaps a hand over her mouth. "Sorry! I'm not around a lot of kids these days. Unless you count my sister Ember, although she's twenty."

Melody laughs uncomfortably. "Don't worry about it. I have my fair share of slips, too."

"I don't think we've been properly introduced. I'm Summer Hart," she announces, sticking her hand out to Melody.

I can see both the surprise and hesitation in Melody's eyes, but she places her hand in Summer's. "Hi, I'm Melody Miller. This is my daughter Gracie."

"Hi Gracie. This lemonade is amazing. I love the frozen blueberries," Summer compliments with her typical megawatt grin.

"Thank you!" Gracie beams, clearly no longer shy.

Summer turns toward me and smacks me in the chest with the back of her hand. "Jax! This would be perfect for the jump rope festival, wouldn't it?"

"What's that?" Melody asks me.

"It's a festival we host every year at the end of August. It's a way to get kids outside and promote exercise, primarily for children, but for all ages. I wanted to find a way to get kids back outdoors, so we host this event and give out jump ropes to every child that attends. Everyone in town comes, and a lot of the local businesses have booths set up. It's beneficial for everyone, really," I proudly tell her.

Her eyes light up. "Wow, that's amazing. I would love to help support it any way I can."

"Mommy, that sounds like so much fun, I want to go! I want a jump rope!" Gracie begs.

Summer chimes in. "Yes! You have to be there. Let's trade numbers and we can coordinate."

"Sure," Melody says, turning around and bending down to her purse, reaching for her phone.

"Oh my God. Melody, I would kill for an ass like yours," Summer blurts out unapologetically.

Gracie gasps at the curse word and giggles.

Melody's cheeks flush as her body snaps upright. "Oh, uh, thank you?"

"I'm serious, you're really stunning. No wonder Jax here won't shut up about you," Summer blurts out as they trade phones.

"Summer!" I chide.

Her blonde ponytail whips from side to side as her gaze dances between Melody and me, both of us sharing horrified expressions.

Summer giggles. "Sorry. I'm going, I'm going." She hands Melody her phone back. "Melody, you have my number. I'm going to text you and we should definitely get coffee or drinks sometime so I can officially welcome you to Blue Springs."

Melody's eyes soften. I think I even hear quiet laughter. "Sure, that would be great, Summer."

Luckily, there has been nobody else in line behind us during this entire exchange, because if anybody overheard Summer, it would spread like wildfire and definitely spook Melody.

Summer waves and bounces back toward the gym, leaving the three of us standing together. Melody is giving me a weird look, and I hope Summer didn't just say too much and scare her off.

"I'm really sorry about her. She means well, but sometimes she talks too much," I tell her jokingly.

"Jax?" she asks.

"What?"

Melody's attention drifts from me to my gym sign.

"Jumping Jax. It's your gym, as in, you own it?"

"Yes," I reply slowly.

Telling women I'm a business owner, especially of a very successful chain of gyms, isn't something I typically broadcast, because people are shady and full of greed. My reservations are due to the fear of being taken advantage of. I liked that Melody was unaware. It wasn't exactly a secret. I knew she'd find out eventually, but I didn't expect this reaction when she did.

Why does she look so angry with me?

CHAPTER 13

Melody

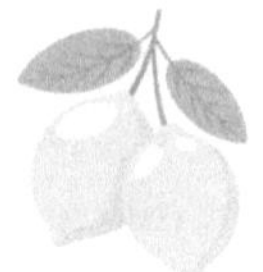

Cat's out of the bag now, and it's squirming.

He told me to be honest with him, yet he hasn't been honest with me about the simplest aspect of a person, their job.

During our date, the issue drifted to the back of my mind like every other concern I have about becoming close to this man. Jackson has this incredibly obnoxious way of making me forget every reason I had to stay away from him. He doesn't owe me an explanation, but I can't help but feel like it was purposely hidden.

Most women probably throw themselves at him because he's successful and has money. That's great for him, but it's not something I'm interested in. Wealthy, successful men are full of secrets and lies. I told myself no more rich assholes, and I meant it. This morning, no longer under his spell, I woke up with renewed frustration at the situation.

With him admitting he's the owner of Jumping Jax, I'm suddenly grateful that last night didn't go further. The voices in my head were right, that would have been a huge mistake.

"You didn't think that was worth mentioning to your friend?" I ask as he gives me a quizzical expression.

"I don't know what the big deal is. You know I work there."

The mood swing from last night to today is giving him whiplash, I can see it.

"It just does. Look, this isn't the time. I need to help Gracie with these customers," I snap, hoping he'll go back to his gym, and let me process my frustration in peace.

He turns around at the line beginning to form behind him, so he steps to the side, and lowers his voice next to me. "Can I come over to your place and talk about this?"

Why does he always have to smell so damn good?

"Like the other night when you were kissing?" Gracie interjects, giggling.

"What?" I panic, my head snapping in her direction so fast I nearly smack right into her.

"You and Jax were kissing. Your faces were like this," she says, pressing her two hands together, making a kissy noise.

"Sweetie, we were *not* kissing," I say as firmly as possible.

"What were you doing?" she asks innocently. She was so sure of what she saw and is now looking at me as she questions herself.

"Yeah, Melody, what were we doing?" Jackson challenges.

Could I feel more like an asshole right now?

This is why I shouldn't be getting mixed up with men.

"Your mommy was just wiping something off my face," Jackson tells her, sensing my panic.

"Oh. Okay." Gracie shrugs, her attention already back on the lemonade.

When I look back at Jackson, he looks wounded, though I'm not sure why. I'm the one that's been lied to.

"Thanks for the business," I tell him dismissively.

He gives me a forced smile and says bye to Gracie before going back to his gym. I watch him walk away, and I can't help the small twinge in my chest. I'm sure I did the right thing. Clearly we would be a disaster, so it's best if we stop before someone gets hurt. Because in the end, someone always does.

"TABLE SIXTEEN, ORDER UP!" one of the cooks shouts from the kitchen.

"Got it!" Mary shouts back, rushing through the kitchen doors. She drops a few empty cups in the dish pit and reaches over to grab the tray of food for her table. "I didn't expect it to be so busy today."

"Me either," I reply as I fill three glasses with soda for a new table.

"I'm going to drop this off, and then I want to hear how the lemonade stand went with your little one!" she exclaims on her way out.

The conflict yesterday with Jackson aside, the day was a complete success. Gracie had the best time, and I absolutely loved watching her interact with the townspeople and the way she lit up when they loved her lemonade. We made three large pitchers and somehow ended up going through them all and making close to fifty dollars. People were extremely generous, dropping five dollar bills into our jar when they ordered one or two glasses. There's something to be said about the kindness and hospitality of a small town.

Mary bursts through the kitchen doors and strides toward me. "Okay, I have about two minutes before Mr. Newstrom needs another soda. Did Gracie have the best time?"

"Oh my gosh. She was so cute. You should have seen how

outgoing and professional she was. She greeted people, poured lemonade, and helped count cash back. It was so much fun. I had a great day with her. Afterward, Trish gifted us a box of donuts for directing so much business in her direction."

"Aw honey, that's amazing. Seems like you two are really settling in nice here." She pauses. "Maybe too nice."

She gives me a wink and I squint my eyes at her. "What do you mean?"

Mary lowers her voice. "I heard that you and Mr. Pierce are getting quite cozy together."

My eyes go wide. "Why would you say that?"

"Honey, you're not in Los Angeles anymore. In small towns, people don't have much else to do other than talk. I overheard some folks saying you and Jackson had drinks at Blue for Brews. And a little birdie may have told me he bought some lemonade from your daughter's lemonade stand."

I chew on my cheek, because it's all true. Though, it doesn't mean what she thinks it means.

"Lots of people bought lemonade from us. We're just friends."

Lies.

She gives me an incredulous scowl.

"We are!" I defend.

More lies.

"Well, not according to my sources."

"Who are these sources?" I ask, because the only one who has seen any interaction between us, other than friendship, is Gracie.

Mary shoots me a sly grin before turning to exit the kitchen. "Table three."

Who the hell is at table three?

I take my three glasses of soda and push through the kitchen door, my eyes going directly to table three.

"Melody!"

Summer Hart.

Plastering a smile on my face, I drop the drinks off at a nearby table and then walk over to Summer at table three.

"Hi, how are you?" I ask, noticing that even as she sits here in workout clothes, without makeup and sporting a messy ponytail, she's still an absolute goddess. I wish I didn't feel so envious of her, but it's hard not to when she looks like that, while I'm always in my uniform, covered in condiment smears.

"Pretty good! I'm glad you're here. I was going to see if you wanted to go for drinks tonight or tomorrow."

"Oh! Um, I'm not sure. I'd have to get a sitter, and Gracie doesn't particularly love the one we currently have." It's mostly true. I haven't had a chance to secure Jane as our main sitter, but it's not the only reason I'm hesitant.

Summer seems really amazing, and as much as I could use a friend my age, I'm not sure getting close to Jackson's best friend is a good idea.

"Oh. I thought Jane was watching her now?"

"She's watched her a few times for me. They actually had a wonderful time together."

"Have you asked her if she could watch her again? Because she totally would. Jane is amazing."

"Oh, it's okay. I'm sure she's got plenty else she'd rather do," I lie, knowing damn well that Jane would watch Gracie anytime I asked.

"Are you kidding me? Jane lives for this sort of thing. She's great with kids."

I shrug.

"You really don't like letting others help you, do you?" Summer asks, and although she said it kindly, it feels like she just kicked down a locked door in my soul.

I give her a sad smile. "Not particularly."

It's not easy for me to let people help me, even when they offer. The last person I trusted with that power threw every single thing he ever did in my face to lord over me. It's the same person that was supposed to love and protect me, so I have a hard time processing why strangers are so eager to help. Accepting help puts me in their debt, and it's not a position I plan on being in ever again.

"You don't know me, but I would like to get to know you. Jackson thinks very highly of you, so therefore, so do I. From what I hear, so does his mother."

"I don't want to bother her," I hedge.

"Oh please. Hold on," she says, grabbing her phone and her fingers fly across the screen.

"What are you doing?"

Please don't call Jackson.

"I'm texting Jane to see if she'll watch your little girl tonight," she says matter-of-factly.

"You text Jackson's mom?"

Summer looks back up at me, flicking her wrist. "She's basically my second mother. My mom and I were never super close, but Jane has always treated me as one of her own since I've known her."

Some people have all the luck. I can't count on one hand the people I have in my corner, and Summer has parental figures to spare. Now I'm jealous for a whole new reason.

Summer's phone chimes in her hand and she glances down at the incoming text and squeals. "She said she'd be happy to!"

Her eyes meet mine, waiting for me to agree to a night out with her. The way she can see right through my facade reminds me of Jackson. And Jane. And Mary. These people see me in a way nobody in my old life ever did. People in Blue Springs aren't worried about money, fame, or status. They might indulge in the latest town drama, but they don't use it to tear others down.

Maybe I've been cold to her for no reason. Summer has been nothing but kind to me, and now she's here, offering me friendship.

I give her a warm smile. "That sounds fun. Let's do it."

Summer claps her hands together and lets out another victorious squeal. "Great! I'll text you later. I can pick you up at your place and go from there. Does that sound good?"

I nod. "I'll be off in a few hours."

"Perf! I gave Jane your number and she's going to text you so you can set up a time for her later this evening. I'm so excited!"

Her bright smile is infectious, and despite my best efforts, I find myself excited to go out with another adult after the sun goes down. Being a mom doesn't typically include a lot of after-sundown adventures. My evenings typically include Gracie's bath time and bedtime routine, showering myself, and snacks and TV show binging in bed.

Even before I left Gracie's father, this is how every night looked for me. He wasn't what you'd call an "active father." He loved the idea of having the perfect family but never wanted to actually put in the work or time to participate in said family.

I spent most nights alone until he'd roll in well past midnight, smelling of alcohol, among other things. Sure, he worked late *sometimes*, but that was rare. And never that late. His job didn't require those sorts of hours, and considering he made his own schedule, his absence at home was hard not to take personally. After shit hit the fan, I had to face the harsh reality that he wasn't interested in me or our daughter.

It's not easy to face the fact that the person you saw forever with doesn't care that his decisions hurt you and your child. I spent a lot of tiring years attempting to hold the pieces of our life together despite his constant absence and disrespect. It felt like I was trying to hold onto a stray dog that didn't want to be captured or domesticated, and the harder I held on, the more I got attacked

But these people are proving to be the exact opposite of him and his family. Blue Springs has been nothing but good to me, and yet I've held them at arm's length, shut them all out. Maybe it's time I start letting a few of them in.

CHAPTER 14

Jackson

The towering skyscrapers come into view as I make my way into Denver. While I much prefer the small-town atmosphere over city life, when the sun goes down and the entire city lights up, I can't ignore the appeal. The congested and bustling vibes of daytime gives way to the bright lights of the night life granting the city a completely different feel. Instead of stuffy, it's fun and exciting.

Having such a blissful high the other night with Melody, I never expected waking up and walking into the shitstorm the last twenty-four hours has been. The disaster with the Denver gym was infuriating enough, but Melody's cold demeanor toward me was the punch-gut-cherry-on-top of a shitty day.

I would have left yesterday but had to take care of a few things at work and return home to pack before I could make the drive to Denver. With the heavy traffic, I just made it here and won't actually be able to take care of the work situation until tomorrow morning, so it looks like I have the night to myself.

Dropping my large duffle bag on the couch in my room at the Four Seasons, I resolve to unpack the few things I've brought with me in the walk-in closet later. I make my way to the large floor-to-ceiling windows and take in the lively city that'll be my home for the next few days. Once I let both managers go, I'll need to stick around while I look for a temporary replacement.

I feel my phone vibrate in the pocket of my blue jeans, and I pull it out to check the notification. With the influx of bad news, and hateful social media messages, I'm almost afraid to check it.

Summer: Did you make it there?

Jackson: Yes, traffic sucked. Just got to my room. I'm going to take care of things in the morning.

Summer: Good call. How are you going to spend the rest of your night?

Jackson: I'm exhausted. All I want to do is climb into bed. What about you?

Summer: I'm getting drinks with Melody tonight!

Jackson: You're hanging out with Melody? How did that happen?

Summer: I invited her out and she said yes.

Jackson: I'm surprised. Getting to hang out with that woman is like hiking uphill. In flip flops. Over small gravel.

Summer: 😬 Yeah, she's definitely a little closed off. There's a reason for it though. There's always a reason. I'm going to work my magic and get that woman to crack like a pistachio tonight.

> Jackson: A pistachio huh? Listen, just don't push her too far. She's been through some things. I'm not sure what, but it's still fresh for her.

Summer: Look at you being all protective over her.

> Jackson: 😳

Summer: Don't sass me. I like it. "Protective Jackson" is a good look for you.

I WANT TO ARGUE, but she's right. I do feel protective over Melody for some reason. The pull I have toward her doesn't seem to be going away, only strengthening each day. A part of me hopes Summer can get her to open up, but the selfish part of me wishes Melody would open up to me instead.

> Jackson: Have fun. Thank you for getting her to go out. She could use a good friend like you.

Summer: I am pretty great, aren't I?

> Jackson: And sooo humble.

Summer: 😏

> Jackson: Have fun, I'm going to turn in and watch some mind numbing tv before bed.

Summer: Friends again?

> Jackson: Always.

SUMMER and I both know she's only half kidding, but fuck me if I don't reread that text a few more times.

It's barely 10 p.m., and a *Friends* episode is serving as my emotional support background noise while I go through emails and work on my apology statement. I've worked my ass off building my gym empire and have always been very hands-on in picking each person hired into the company, especially at the managerial level. It doesn't matter if you have great, dedicated hourly employees, if management sucks, your business will suffer. This entire situation has been a slap in the face for me. It's damage control time, and it will need to be handled delicately.

Once something this negative comes out about a company, or how it's run, it's hard to overcome the sour taste that's been put in people's mouths. These days, people are very mindful of the companies they support. It's a mindset I can relate to. Hell, it's why I created Jumping Jax to begin with.

My anger begins to boil again, thinking about the damage these two idiots have caused, when my phone vibrates on the bed next to me.

Assuming it's a text from Summer making some sort of crack about me and Melody during her night out, I flip it over with a smile. A smile that quickly fades when I see who the sender is.

I groan and toss the phone back on the bed. Scrubbing my

hands down my face, I debate whether or not I should reply. I'm not sure how she knows I'm in town, but knowing Natasha, she's probably paid someone at the front desk to call her anytime I check in. I wouldn't put it past her.

Natasha and I met at an athletic convention a few years ago and get together every once in a while when I'm in town. She's an aspiring model, or influencer, I'm not sure which, and resides in Denver. The convenience factor is the only reason I've kept in contact with her.

At first it was a fun, no-strings-attached situation. But after she started following me on Instagram and learned that I own the Jumping Jax gyms and noticed all of the partnerships I've acquired via my social media following, she quickly turned into a leech. I have nothing against her, and overall she's a decent girl, but she got her wires crossed.

I always made it clear that I was not open to anything more than a casual fling, but once she found out what I was worth, it was clear her intentions were to sink her claws in, not only into me, but into my bank account.

I pick up my phone and send a text to Summer instead.

> Jackson: Guess who just texted me.

ABOUT TEN MINUTES go by without a reply, which I take to mean that her night with Melody is going well, keeping her off her phone. At least I hope it is. I begin to think I won't be hearing back from her when my phone buzzes.

Summer: Umm, a tall, dark and handsome man, who's honest and is just waiting to sweep me off my feet by going through my best friend first?

Jackson: Not quite. Sorry.

Summer: Okay, I give up. Who?

Jackson: Natasha.

Summer: Oh god, your Denver booty call? The tall blonde Instagram model with the fake ass?

Jackson: Well, when you put it like that, you make it sound really awful. She's not all bad.

Summer: So why are you complaining to me about her then?

Jackson: You make a good point. 

Summer: I usually do.

Jackson:

Jackson: Natasha asked to come up to my room.

Jackson: I just pulled up her Instagram. I forgot how hot she is.

Jackson: Is it a terrible idea to invite her up one last time?

Jackson: Hello? Earth to Summer, where did you go?

ANOTHER TEN MINUTES GO BY, and I'm guessing she's too caught up with Melody, which is fine. Except now all I'm thinking about is Melody. Though, when am I not?

Feeling like an idiot for even sending those last few texts, deeply regretting even thinking for a moment of meeting with Natasha, I send Summer another text.

> Jackson: I'm not going to invite her up. Honestly, there's only one girl I want in my room, and she's currently in Blue Springs having drinks with you.

SOMETIMES LONELINESS IS A BITCH. It can land you in situations you shouldn't be in, with people you shouldn't be with. Natasha is one of those people. She'll probably make some rich guy happy one day, but not me. I need something more than a wild cat in bed with good looks. If I'm being completely honest with myself, she could never hold a candle to Melody.

I need to end this situationship once and for all.

I don't know why I considered seeing her for a second. I decide to send her a text, because if I don't, she'll show up here anyway, and I really don't need her making a scene at the Four Seasons while I'm in town to put out a fire.

> Jackson: Hey Tash, I'm on a quick work trip. But, I've started to see someone. I hope you can respect that.

Her response comes immediately.

> Natasha: That's not a problem, I have a boyfriend, too. They don't have to know. It can be our not-so-little secret.

Her flirty little innuendos used to make my dick hard, but this makes me nauseous. The blatant disrespect she has for other people's feelings. She sounds just like my ex. I guess I have a type.

> Jackson: Whatever you do with or without your boyfriend is your business. But I'm not that kind of man, and I never will be. Take care.

I DON'T EXPECT her to respond, and when she does, I wish I never responded at all.

> Natasha: I'll see you soon Jax.

FUCK. Something tells me this isn't over.

Melody

I can't be the only one that feels like I'm going on a blind date when I meet up with a new friend for the first time. There's something nerve-racking about not knowing if you'll get along, finding things in common, or if the conversation will flow. I've spent the last twenty minutes dreading that awkward silence as my mind blanks for a way to fill it, should the crisis arise.

Summer is the nicest person I've met in a long time, but as I stand in front of my bathroom mirror in one of my little black dresses and black heeled sandals, I can't help but feel like I'm going to be rejected.

My relationship with Gracie's dad has left me with residual false notions of myself. Where I was once the most confident woman in the room, I now find that I'm constantly comparing myself to every other woman. Wondering if I'm underdressed or too overdressed. The paranoia of thinking they're all staring at my back rolls, or the belly pooch that's been near impossible to lose since I had my sweet Gracie. The self-inflicted insults are endless, and it's a hard habit to kick. Some people bite their nails, or even pick their nose, but my worst habit is picking *myself* apart.

I hear a knock on the door and take a calming breath. Jane is in the living room with Gracie, coloring farm animal pictures and giggling at Gracie's unwillingness to stay in the lines. She can, but she won't. It's what I love most about her. Her refusal to conform to what's expected. She's my strong-willed little girl, and she's going to need that in this harsh world.

Jane answers the door and Summer's cheery voice floods the home. "Jane! You're the best for agreeing to watch this gorgeous little girl while I take her mommy out."

I listen from the bathroom, taking one last look at myself and smoothing a few strands of hair.

"Not a problem, Gracie and I are already having such a great time! Aren't we, sweetheart?" Jane asks.

"The best! Can we make cookies again?" Gracie asks sweetly.

"Hey, don't use your pouty face on them to get your way, they're not immune to it yet," I warn Gracie, emerging from the bathroom.

"Melody! Oh my God, look at you!" Summer gasps, her eyes scanning me from head to toe.

My hair is in loose waves that hang at my shoulders. The tight black thin-strap dress I have on hits just above the knee with a sweetheart neckline, and my black heeled sandals make it dressy, yet casual.

"It's not too much, is it? I wasn't sure where we were going," I tell her, feeling self-conscious under her scrutiny.

Looking at Summer's body-hugging high-waisted skinny jeans, closed-toe ankle booties, and fitted black cropped T-shirt with a Blue Springs logo on the front, I'm starting to feel overdressed.

"Girl, no. You look fucking phenomenal! That'll be perfect for Rocky's," Summer reassures me as she takes my hand, forcing me to do a dramatic spin. "Oh yeah, the men in this town are going to lose their minds tonight."

I can't help but wonder, is there a chance Jackson could show up?

"Mommy, you look beautiful!" Gracie tells me, her eyes lit up with astonishment.

Say what you want about kids, but when I'm feeling bad about myself, Gracie will be the first one to make me feel better about myself. Whether I'm in bed with crazy hair, or I'm all dolled up, she will kiss me on the cheek and call me beautiful just when I need it the most.

"Thank you, baby," I tell her, bending down so we're eye to eye. "Mommy will be back later, okay? Be a good listener for Jane. I love you so much."

I lean in to hug her and she gives me a quick squeeze. "Okay, Mommy. I will be on my best behavior!"

The three of us giggle in unison at her response. "That's what I like to hear," I say, giving her a gentle tap on the end of her nose with my pointer finger.

I stand and face Jane. "If you need anything at all, please call. I'll have my phone on all night and can come back for any reason."

Jane plants a hand on my arm. "Sweetie, I've got this. She's an angel, and we're going to have a great time together. Go, enjoy your night. You deserve some time to yourself."

"Are you ready?" Summer asks me with a wide grin.

I take a deep breath, feeling guilty for leaving Gracie for anything other than work. But as I watch her attention already back on Jane and their drawings, I know it'll be good for us both to interact with new people.

"WHY THE HECK is this place so busy on a Wednesday night?" Summer announces as we walk into Rocky's Tavern.

Summer told me it's a local dive bar, but with its exposed brick, large black leather cushioned booths, and cozy patio firepits, this place is anything but a dive.

I follow her swaying blonde ponytail as she leads us through the bar, waving and saying hello to a handful of people as we pass by. She leads us through a side door leading to the patio where she takes a seat at a small outdoor couch in front of the firepit. "Is this okay?"

Taking a seat next to her, I smile. "Yeah, this is great. It's nice out here."

"I love this place. It's not usually so crowded, but they've got great drinks and they're not

overpriced, which is always nice."

Especially when you've barely got the money for drinks in the first place.

Worrying about money isn't something I had to do in my life back in Los Angeles, so

having to account for where every dollar goes is new for me. I wasn't an out of control spender, but I also didn't have to think about how much a cocktail was.

We turn toward each other on the couch, our phones lying in between us, while we peruse the drink menu a server handed us on the way in.

"Blue Springs tonic? What the heck is in that?" I ask, browsing the long list of small-town themed drink names.

Summer laughs at my question. "It's basically a vodka tonic with a splash of blue curaçao."

"Oh my gosh, that sounds awful." I grimace, laughing.

"Yeah, it's not great, but it's colorful. Makes people feel fancy."

"What do you usually get here?" I ask, scanning the rest of the menu for something that sounds good.

"I really like the boujee bootlegger. It's an old-fashioned but has edible gold flakes in it."

My eyes go wide. "Gold flakes?"

"It sounds funky, but it's really good. Makes me feel fancy," she says with a sly smile and a shoulder shimmy.

I laugh. "I'll try that one, too."

She claps her hands together excitedly. "Oh my gosh! You're gonna love it!"

We set the menus down on the edge of the concrete ledge in front of the firepit and give our order to the waiter who hurries off to retrieve them. While we wait for our drinks, Summer turns her full attention to me with a glimmer in her eye and I just know she's about to bring up Jackson.

"So, what is going on with you and Jax?"

I knew it.

Twisting a lock of hair around my finger, I shrug. "Nothing, really."

Her gaze narrows at me slightly. "Hmm."

I can't help but laugh. "What?"

"I definitely sensed some *tension* yesterday at the lemonade stand. And when you two were chatting in the gym, it looked like a couple quarreling."

I shake my head vehemently. "No. Oh no. Not at all. We're friends."

"Girl, you know he's my best friend, right?" she says, raising an eyebrow at me.

My lips form a thin line, and luckily, the drinks arrive and I don't need to answer right away. We thank the waiter and then Summer lifts her glass in the air.

"Here's to new friends," Summer announces brightly.

"To new friends," I repeat and raise my own drink. We clink our glasses and then take a long sip of the beverage.

I have to admit, it's a gorgeous drink, with the red cherries and gold flakes floating on top. It tastes even better.

"Good, right?" she asks me.

"*So* good." I take another greedy pull, feeling myself already relaxing.

She flips her ponytail back behind her shoulder dramatically. "See, I have great taste." She pauses, and a disgusted look spreads across her face. "Well, not in men. But with drinks, anyway."

Boy, is that relatable.

"I have to ask. Have you and Jackson ever..." I trail off, not knowing quite how to ask my question.

"Been more than friends?" she finishes.

Yeah, that'll work.

I nod.

She grimaces. "Never. Don't get me wrong, he's a great guy. But he's basically my brother. So, even talking about that just grosses me out."

I laugh. "Sorry. It's not often you see men and women having honest-to-God platonic friendships."

She waves me off as she takes another sip of her drink. "I get it. We've heard it our whole lives. Even my sister Ember has asked me before."

"How many siblings do you have?"

"Just Ember. She lives in the city right now for work. She just graduated from college there, but I'm hoping we can get her back here someday. It's hard being without her."

"Are you the oldest?"

"Yes, and I'm very protective over her. But it's hard to be protective from so far away."

I feel a sad smile spread across my face.

"What's that look for?" The concern in her honeyed voice is genuine and refreshing.

"It's nice that you look out for her. Not everybody has that."

I'm staring into my drink, stirring it mindlessly with the straw when I feel her hand latch onto my arm, giving it a squeeze.

"Hey, you're in Blue Springs now. We're a big family, and we have your back."

A phrase I keep hearing in this town.

I muster up another smile, but I fear it reveals the same uncertainty and sorrow.

"From what I hear, Jackson is pretty protective of you already," Summer says slowly.

I blush. "What do you mean?"

"Bitchy Brenda has been torturing waitresses for years, and he's never gone off on her the way I hear he did for you."

"I have to admit, that was probably the nicest thing anyone has ever done for me. The look on her face was priceless. And she's been quiet as a mouse ever since. She still tips like shit, but at least she's not verbally harassing me anymore."

"God, that woman is miserable. We have all tried getting to know her and understand her motives. But she's just a nasty human. I don't get it."

I shrug. "Some people are just that way."

I should know. Gracie's dad was a prime example of that.

One of our phones vibrates, and thinking it might be Jane texting about Gracie, I lift mine but don't see a notification. Summer does the same and grins.

"Speak of the devil," she says.

"Bitchy Brenda?" I ask, horrified.

Summer lets out a boisterous laugh that echoes through the patio. "No. Jackson."

Oh.

I pretend to be very interested in the contents of my drink as I stare into the glass. I spin the straw around and try to sound as casual as I can. "What's he saying?"

When I glance up at Summer, she's smirking at me as if to say *Mm-hmm, sure, there's nothing going on.* But when she begins to read the text, her expression changes to something akin to disgust.

"He, uh. He had to go to Denver to take care of a situation at one of the gym locations. So he's just telling me he's getting settled into his hotel room."

I can't help but feel disappointed that we won't be bumping into him tonight. There's a chance that I may or may not have scanned the bar when we walked in, hoping to see his curly brown hair sticking out from underneath his backward baseball cap.

Sure, I put a stop to anything going further between us, but I can still look, can't I?

"I hope everything is okay. How long will he be in Denver?"

She looks to be typing back a few responses and then puts her phone down before responding. "Sorry. Uh, he's usually gone for a day or two. But with this situation, I'm not really sure. Could be longer."

Why do I feel disappointed that I won't see his face around town for the rest of the week?

I take the last sip of my drink at the same time Summer does, and we set our glasses down on the edge of the firepit.

"Another round?" Summer asks.

"Let's do it. Those are dangerously good."

"I know, right? Okay, I'm going to open the floodgate, you order us more drinks when he comes by. I'll be right back."

Summer stands up, and as she makes her way inside, I see everyone's eyes zero in on her. Not only is she beautiful, but her energy draws people in. She's the kind of person you want to be near because their presence makes you happier, lighter. It's the same way Jackson makes me feel, come to think of it.

I tell the waiter we want another round, and when he walks away, I see Summer's phone light up. Our phones are right next to each other, so it's a knee-jerk reaction to look. But when I see the text that pops up from Jackson, my stomach sinks. But I can't tear my eyes away when a few more pop up back-to-back.

> Jackson: Natasha asked to come up to my room.

AND ANOTHER.

> Jackson: I just pulled up her Instagram. I forgot how hot she is.

And another.

> Jackson: Is it a terrible idea to invite her up one last time?

And another.

> Jackson: Hello? Earth to Summer, where did you go?

After the last text, I flip her phone over, feeling like an intruder. I didn't mean to look. Didn't mean to read them. But I did, and I can't unread them.

We're just friends. What or who he does is none of my business. So why do I suddenly feel crushed, knowing he's with someone else in Denver tonight?

CHAPTER 16

Jackson

The entrance to Jumping Jax Denver is an absolute zoo. We haven't even opened the doors yet, and already there's an angry mob gathered out front.

From my car I can see signs with angry red lettering on them: *Fat Shaming Is Wrong, Shame on YOU, Body Shaming Anybody Is Wrong, All Bodies Deserve Respect!!*

Fuck, this is bad.

The worst part is, I completely agree with all of it. What those two idiot managers did is not something I'd ever condone, and doesn't represent my company, yet it's my mess to clean up.

I take a calming breath and make my way out of the car and to the front entrance where the crowd turns their attention to me. They must recognize me, because they immediately begin chanting loudly and shaking their signs at me. I even see a few phones held up with the flash on, so I know they're recording me, just hoping I make their case. Waiting for any ammunition to send my company crumbling into ashes.

Not wanting to further upset them, or cause a scene, I let them say what they need to. Sometimes you're better off letting people say their peace before you act. Several minutes later, I hold my hands up and plead with them to quiet down to let me speak.

When they quiet down, I give them an appreciative smile. "Thank you. Seems like we're all aware of the unfortunate events that took place here. Just know that I do not, nor will I ever, tolerate that sort of behavior. Both Randy and Rick will be terminated, effective immediately, and I will be holding a full investigation. I don't take these accusations lightly. My sincerest apologies go out to everyone who was affected by their behavior. Those men do not represent Jumping Jax. I have spent years pouring my soul into these gyms to ensure you all would have a safe place to work on your health, to escape the rigors of everyday life. I am deeply sorry for what has transpired, and I promise I will make things right."

After I've finished speaking, I expect the crowd to explode into another uproar, but they don't. They stand there staring at me. Some with small smiles, others with shocked expressions. I guess in a world where so few take responsibility, it's easy to catch people off guard when you're a person who does.

Forcing a small smile, I give the crowd an unassuming wave and unlock the front door, making my way inside. It's dark. Nobody has arrived yet, so I begin performing the opening duties. When the staff shows up I want to take care of the situation before anything else.

About thirty minutes later, I'm sipping my coffee in one of the offices when I hear the crowd getting riled up again.

Those two assholes must be here.

"Get out of here or we'll call the cops! You can't be here! This is for members only!"

I hear Randy shouting at the crowd, and just when I thought he couldn't make things worse, he does.

"If you ran with your legs as much as you do your mouth, you wouldn't be this angry!"

OH FUCK.

I jump out of my seat so fast, I knock over the cup of coffee, and the liquid spills across the desk. Racing to the front door where Randy and Rick are trying to squeeze through the crowd, I open the doors and wave my arms at them to get inside as quickly as I can.

Once the doors are closed, I turn to see the two men smirking at each other.

"What the hell is funny about this?" I thunder at them.

Their smiles fade, and Randy raises an eyebrow. "Didn't expect to see you today, boss."

My eyes narrow at him. "Really? You thought you could verbally attack our clientele and what, it would fall on deaf ears?"

Silence.

"Ah, so you know what I'm referring to then."

"Jax—" Randy starts.

I cut him off. "Save it. I was willing to hear your side. Give you the benefit of the doubt. But after what I just witnessed, I don't need to. You are absolutely disgusting. How you treat people is shameful. Those people have every right to be angry. What were you thinking?"

"They were shouting in our faces," Rick whines defensively.

"So? They did the same thing to me. I managed to get through the crowd and have a civil conversation with them." I shake my head at them, rubbing my forehead with my fingertips. "I hope it was worth your job. Get your things and get out. You're fired. Both of you."

"This is bullshit!" Randy shouts at me.

"You're right. But it would be in your best interest not to say anything further, or you'll be hearing from my lawyer. You have tarnished my company name, and you better hope I can salvage it after you two scumbags are gone." I point to the offices, letting them know the conversation is over.

They only take about three minutes to grab a few belongings and slink out through the back exit. Shortly after, the rest of the staff starts filing in with confused expressions.

The crowd out front let out a boisterous cheer when they saw the two men darting out front to their cars, and since then have been quiet, though they're still present.

After the morning crowd is all checked in and are working out, seemingly unaffected, I call a meeting.

We pile into a large room typically used for one of our group jump rope classes. The crew quietly waits for me to begin.

"Hey guys, thank you for being here. I wanted to fill everyone in on what's going on. I'm sure you've heard rumors, so I want to clear up any confusion. Without going into too much detail, as of today, Rick and Randy are no longer with us. I will be doing an investigation into what happened here, and any other staff found to be involved will also be let go.

"Since it's apparently not common knowledge, let's go over a few things. We never comment on a client's body. We never body-shame, nor do we approach any person and tell them what they need to do or should be doing. If there's a risk for danger, and you're assisting to prevent an injury, of course, do your best to assist. But we never, under any circumstance, create a hostile environment for our clientele. They're our paychecks, and aside from that, they're human beings. Be nice. Treat them with respect." I pause, looking around the room and seeing a lot of head nods. "If any of you see anything disrespectful from anyone, including management, I'm going to leave Summer Hart's information with the store. I know some of you have met her. She's my right hand in Blue Springs. Please do not hesitate to email or give her a call if you ever need anything, and she will relay the information to me. Anonymously, if need be."

I'd give them my information, but with the way my daily inbox looks, I wouldn't want something this important to get lost in the sea of emails. Summer has a special talent of always keeping her inbox clean and organized. She's on top of paper-work, making sure our books are consistently up to date, and ensuring everything is tidy.

The staff nods and I hear murmurs of agreement. After they all scatter off in different directions to begin work, I make my way outside to give the crowd another update.

"Did you fire them?" one of the women in the crowd asks.

I nod. "Yes. They won't be coming back, and I will be sure to do a more thorough job when putting the next managers in charge here. This is still a safe space for you all, should you choose to give me another chance."

Slowly, each person in the crowd begins to clap, and a few of them drop their signs and embrace me. Though plenty of them are still glaring at me. I know there are more angry people out there, ones who didn't show up today. But this gives me hope that Jumping Jax still has a chance at survival.

"Jax!" a woman's voice calls from behind the crowd.

I peer around the group of people, only to see the one person I wanted to see less than an angry mob in the front of my gym.

Natasha slips through the crowd in her nude stilettos. It doesn't matter that it's 11 a.m., this woman is always dressed like she's headed to a black-tie event.

"Jax, baby, I was hoping I'd catch you before you left!" She leans in to embrace me like we're old friends, and I immedi-ately catch a whiff of her overpowering perfume. It's some expensive crap she's always loved, but to me it's musky and makes me a little bit nauseous, if I'm being honest. Sometimes less is more.

When I pull away, I see a few phones held up, pointed

directly at us, though I'm unsure why. I plaster a fake smile on my face, attempting to look unbothered in front of the crowd.

"Natasha, what are you doing here?" I ask, eyes narrowed at her. Our conversation did not continue last night, nor did I have any intention of starting it up again.

A smile spreads across her face, and her pearly white veneers stare back at me. Natasha is a gorgeous girl, but our relationship was only ever surface level. I was clear from the beginning that we could never be more, and she was happy with the arrangement. There was one night I thought maybe I should give our relationship a chance but learned quickly where her priorities lie. She only wants two things in life, fame and money.

"Aren't you happy to see me, baby? It's not like you to come to Denver and not see your favorite blonde," she says, dragging a long red acrylic nail down the side of my arm. She thinks it's sexy, but it's making my skin crawl.

Gazing back up at the crowd, I realize there's a lot of listening ears, and this gym already has one scandal to deal with, so we don't need anyone catching wind of any situation with this city's biggest drama queen.

"Let's talk inside," I say through a toothy, fake smile, holding the door open for her, and I follow her inside.

I lead her to an office, close the door, and sit behind the desk. She decides to forego the chair on the opposite side and sits on the corner of the desk directly in front of me instead.

"How have you been? I've missed you," she says in her whiny baby voice that I can't stand.

"Cut the crap. Why are you here? I told you I was seeing somebody," I remind her.

She scoffs and throws her head back, much like a toddler would. "It can't be serious. Jackson Pierce doesn't do relationships."

My lips form a thin line.

"Are you fucking kidding me?" she shouts.

"Natasha, keep it down. Please."

"No, fuck that," she shouts again, baby voice long gone, standing up so she towers over me. "I have spent years giving myself to you, and now you're dating someone else? Just like that? What the fuck?"

"I was always honest with you. I never led you on or lied."

Her lips make a *pfft* sound, and she crosses her arms over her large fake breasts. "I can't believe this. Who is she?"

"Natasha, don't," I warn.

"Is she some granola from that small-ass town you're living in? You know she can never give you what I can."

I stand and make my way to the office door. I open it and hold out an arm for her to leave. "I hope you're right about that."

She storms out, her heels clicking angrily against the flooring on her way out. I watch as she throws the front door open and pushes through the crowd. Now more than ever, I am eager to get home to Blue Springs. Because in a way, Natasha is right. We spent years together, in a lot of intimate ways, and not once did I ever feel for her the way I've felt about Melody in such a short time.

This whole time, I thought relationships weren't for me, but maybe I wasn't looking in the right place.

THE REST of the day goes smoothly, the remaining employees going about their day as usual and seem generally happy to have me here.

I've been in contact with my other Denver location, hoping they have a manager they can send my way, since this branch is down not one but two managers, with no luck. They just lost one to maternity leave, so they can't spare anyone. It's not until I'm back in my hotel room, vegging out on the bed with a cheeseburger, fries, and a cocktail I ordered from room service, that I remember one person who might be able to help.

Jackson: Hey, weren't you telling me that your sister was looking for a new job?

Summer: Yeah, why?

Jackson: I can't pull from another branch. I remembered that Ember worked for me briefly before she left for school. With her experience, she would be perfect. And frankly, she's the only other person aside from you that I'd trust in this place after this debacle.

Summer: Yeah, she finally quit after her asshole boss made a pass at her and tried to force her to keep it quiet when she turned him down.

Jackson: Yikes. I'm glad she left. Smart girl.

Summer: If she hadn't begged me not to come beat his ass, I would have.

Jackson: I believe you. Hell hath no fury like a Summer scorned.

Summer: Damn right. But I think she'd be a great fit at the gym. I'll call her!

Jackson: Thanks Sum.

I TAKE a large sip of my cocktail and try to put this shitty day behind me. The sooner I can get Ember in and squared away, the sooner I can get home.

Melody

"Mommy, is daddy going to come see us?" Gracie asks out of nowhere, completely catching me off guard.

Most of her questions come at random, and with almost zero explanation, but this one hits me square between the eyes because it's one I wasn't prepared to answer.

"Um, I'm not sure, baby."

Smooth.

It's not the truth, but it's not a lie, either.

When we left Los Angeles, we left Alexander behind, but he wasn't really there for us to abandon. We've been gone over a month and he hasn't tried calling me or sent as much as a text, so I think it's safe to say we aren't missed. But that's not something I'm going to tell my four-year-old.

They say a harmful truth is better than a useful lie, but I don't think that applies when a four-year-old's heart is on the line. I'm happy to shield her from this for as long as I can.

"Is he going to come live here with us?" The way she asks it leaves me uncertain whether she wants him to, or she's scared that he will.

The innocence in her voice causes a lump to form in my throat.

I swallow, choking back the sob that threatens to erupt. "I don't think so, sweetie."

She shrugs and goes back to playing the matching game on her iPad, and I've never been more grateful for the distraction. I'm not sure where the question came from, but she's old enough to realize we no longer live with her daddy.

Though, to be honest, he was away from home so much there was a part of me that wondered if she would notice at all.

Who am I to talk? Jackson has been gone two days, and I've definitely noticed. After I saw his texts to Summer last night, I told myself I wasn't going to think about him anymore. I promised myself I would extinguish everything I felt for him, but here I am, ignoring my own advice.

I never found the courage to tell Summer I saw the texts from Jackson. With it being a new friendship, I didn't want her to think I was snooping. I'm not that kind of person.

We finished our second drinks and chatted for a few more hours. She used that time to somehow convince me to take jump rope lessons with her at Jumping Jax. I don't know why I agreed, but I'm going to blame those two Boujee Bootleggers. I figured I could make an excuse to get out of going, but she brought over my 7-day free pass at work this morning and texted me to meet her at the gym tomorrow at 8 a.m. It's safe to say she's going to hold me to the commitment.

Even though I was nervous to meet up with her, Summer was really great to talk with. She opened up about her dating woes, and while I haven't been comfortable enough to talk about what happened with Alexander yet, I feel like she can sense what we've been through. Sometimes it feels like everybody can.

Today I worked the early shift while Jane watched Gracie. Apparently, the two made a deal last night that she would be

Gracie's permanent sitter, and neither of them would allow me to argue otherwise. I could have protested that it would be too much for Jane, or too inconvenient, but when I see how happy Gracie is with her, I lose the will to do so.

I have been hell-bent on doing everything on my own out here, making sure I don't wind up in the same situation I did back in Los Angeles, but right now, I'm looking at the bigger picture. Gracie has always and will always be the bigger picture. If she's happy, I'm happy.

Gracie is playing her matching game quietly, and there's a movie on the TV that I'm half paying attention to. I'm tired after my shift this morning, so I am resting my feet until I have to get up and make us dinner.

I'm scrolling through Pinterest, looking for dinner recipe ideas, when I get an incoming text.

Summer: Hey girl! Don't forget, 8am tomorrow! I have a rope for you!

I CAN'T HELP the smile that crosses my face. She sure is persistent.

Melody: How could I forget, you've reminded me twice since last night. Haha.

Summer: Jackson may have warned me that you're a flight risk, so I'm doing my due diligence.

FLIGHT RISK? What the hell does that mean?

. . .

Melody: I'm not sure he knows me well enough to be saying things like that.

I DON'T KNOW WHY, but the comment stings. It makes me sound like a coward.

Summer: It's a joke! He meant nothing by it.

Melody: Will he be there tomorrow?

IF THIS WAS YESTERDAY, I'd be asking in the hopes of seeing him, but now I hope he stays in Denver. The last thing I need is another man trying to tell me who or what I am.

Summer: I don't think so, he's still in Denver.

Melody: Ok, see you at 8.

I SET my phone down and try to concentrate on the movie that's playing, but my mind is elsewhere. It's focused on one particular subject. One man.

Once again, I'm feeling like an emotional liability when it comes to Jackson. One minute I'm craving him with undeniable need, and the next all I can see are reasons why we won't work.

Last night, Summer filled me in on the situation with the Denver store, and I recall her saying their social media was getting bombarded with nasty messages. That must mean Jackson has a social media profile because who doesn't these days.

Picking my phone back up, I open Instagram. I haven't used this since, well, before we left Los Angeles. I had a meltdown one night after an awful argument with Alexander and deleted every picture but one. The first picture I have of Gracie and me. I'm cradling her, wrapped up in a pink blanket and a little crochet beanie on her head. It's one of my favorites, because we're both looking into each other's eyes. It was the moment I vowed to always protect her.

I type *Jackson Pierce* into the search bar, and his profile comes up first with the blue official check mark. He has 1.2 million followers.

How the hell does anyone have that many followers?

I suppose it helps that his profile picture shows him shirtless with his jump rope. As I scroll through his page, I realize that most of his posts are shirtless jump rope videos. Not only that, but he coordinates them with songs that create a lethal combo for any woman's panties.

Why does he have to be so irresistible? The man oozes sex.

His most recent video is a few weeks old, and shows him in the gray sweatpants that, let's face it, might as well say *I know how to fuck*, and his black Converse. He's using a white jump rope and wearing a dark-colored baseball cap. His muscles are glistening like he's worked on the video a long time. Beads of sweat drip between his muscular pecs, down to his chiseled abs. My tongue slips out and glides across my lower lip before I pull it between my teeth.

Why am I picturing running my tongue all over his sweaty body?

I don't know how many times I watch the video, but enough to notice how graceful his footwork is. The way it seems like his body is moving through the rope, instead of the rope moving around his body. The moves are quick and seamless.

Carefully, I swipe out of each video I click on, making sure I don't accidentally tap one of them. The last thing I need is to alert him of the stalking I'm doing. Technology has given us a brand-new, inventive way to embarrass ourselves. Oh, the joys.

I swipe too quickly and somehow end up on a tagged picture that's been recently uploaded. But not by him.

A picture of him and a blonde female. At first glance, it could be Summer, but no. It's definitely not Summer.

There's a few pictures, so I swipe through them to get a better look at the woman. I click the tag link in the bottom corner, and two names pop up: Jackson Pierce and Natasha Redding.

My heart begins to race, and my ears ring hot. It's one thing to think he's going to sleep with someone else, but to see her face makes it too real. If I can't picture her, she doesn't exist. Once you put a face to a name, the betrayal becomes real. Though, it's not betrayal, is it? He's not mine, nor do I plan on being his. We're friends, so why does it sting so bad?

Like the dairy-intolerant glutton who refuses to stop eating ice cream, I keep the pictures up, swiping through them over and over. I tell myself, just a little more, I can handle it.

The first picture shows them hugging outside of his gym. They have their arms around each other, and it looks like he's pulling away to kiss her. They're talking in the second one, inches apart, smiling at each other. The last picture shows Jackson holding the door for her as they both enter the gym.

The pictures were taken today by a girl named Sarah who lives in Denver. The caption reads *Jackson Pierce makes an appear-*

ance at Denver West gym to address body shaming rumors with his girlfriend Natasha Redding. The two head inside for a private moment.

It was bad enough to see the texts where he gushed over how hot she was, but to see him with her is way worse. He wasn't wrong, though, she's a knockout. The glossy long blonde hair, giant fake tits, legs that go for miles, and the way she dresses tells me she knows how beautiful she is. The confidence is seeping through my phone screen. Much like the jealousy that is seeping from every pore in my body.

The woman could stop traffic.

For a brief moment today, I considered sending Jackson a text. Replying to the one he sent me last night, shortly after I saw the texts on Summer's phone.

He sent me a simple *Hey, hope you have fun with Summer.*

I was too mad to reply at the time, and now I'm glad I never did. Jackson might be sexy and know how to reel in any woman he wants. But I don't want to be just any woman, and it's not just me. I'm a full-grown woman, a mom with far too much to lose by playing around with playboys. Being friends with Jackson Pierce is no longer an option.

"SUMMER, I've done this for thirty minutes straight. I don't think my body can move like that."

I met Summer bright and early at Jumping Jax, while Jane took Gracie to the park to run off some energy before they make some lemonade and bake whatever pastry they've decided on today. Gracie and Jane have a great time together and manage to act more like grandmother and granddaughter than the preschooler-babysitter relationship I've been accustomed to.

They immediately clicked, and I don't know how I've lived in Blue Springs all this time without her.

"You will get it, I promise. It takes time," Summer tells me optimistically.

"How long did it take you?"

"Oh gosh. Years! You're just getting started," she says with a smile.

"Years?"

She laughs.

"Sooner for you, since you've got one hell of a coach." She winks at me.

I nod, still catching my breath from my last attempt at two tricks called mummy kicks and side swipes.

Noticing the defeated look on my face, Summer grabs her backpack and hands me one of her insulated bottles. "Let's take a break. Here, take one. It will replenish you."

"What is it?"

"One of my Blue Springs famous smoothies." She laughs. "Okay, well, maybe not famous, but they might be one day. These are strawberry-orange and banana."

Opening the bottle, I can already smell the fruity goodness, and I eagerly take a sip of it. "Oh my gosh! This is really good. Why is this so good?"

Summer takes a sip of her own and then laughs at my reaction. "My secret ingredients. I add lemon juice and honey to it."

"This is incredible. If you keep bringing these, I definitely won't have trouble showing up to our workout sessions."

"Deal!" Summer replies, clinking her bottle to mine.

Bringing myself here wasn't easy. For starters, I haven't seen or talked to Jackson since I saw those text messages or the pictures online. But more than that, my history with gyms is an emotional one.

Before I had Gracie, this was my happy place, my zen.

Nobody tells you that once you have a baby, your priorities completely change. Sure, I knew my baby would take up most of my time, and I would always put her first. What I didn't expect was that I would no longer care about being a gym rat and getting ripped.

Do I still love the idea of it? Of course. But whenever I found the time to get into the gym, I realized I wanted to spend time with Gracie instead. I'd rather bake cookies, snuggle, or watch a movie with her. Everything I wanted to do was anything with her.

But her father quickly voiced his disapproval of the person I'd become. Overnight, we became strangers to each other. He quickly went from being a man that I thought loved me to a man that kept track of how many steps I took a day, how many calories I consumed, and how often I missed a workout. The workouts that used to be therapy turned into punishment, and Gracie's father turned into a drill sergeant that couldn't stand the sight of me.

Glancing around the gym, I can't help but wonder who's here for their therapy session, enjoying themselves, and who's here by force, silently hating themselves.

"Are you okay?" Summer asks, noticing my drift into the past.

I give her a sad smile and nod. "Yeah."

Her eyes narrow at me skeptically. "Why don't I believe you?"

A small laugh escapes me. "Because you're a good friend, Summer Hart."

This morning it was cold when I first came in, so I wore a sweater over my sports bra and high-waisted leggings. Turns out, jumping rope is a lot harder than it looks. I pull the gray Colorado sweatshirt over my head and set it off to the side so we can start again. I'm already dripping sweat, and at this point, my usual self-consciousness loses to the desire of not getting sweat in my eyes.

I take a few more sips of Summer's hydrating smoothie and grab my pink rope. "Okay, show me one more time. I really want to get the side swipe thing down."

Summer laughs, standing to show me again, step-by-step, how to create the motion. After a few more attempts, my rope starts to emulate what hers is doing, and Summer lets out an excited shriek. "You're getting it! I knew you would!"

She's looking at me as though I've just climbed Mount Everest. I can see the pride and excitement she has for me. I'd be lying if I didn't have the same emotion coursing through me. Not only for completing a jump rope trick, but for being in a gym in the first place.

This is the first time I've voluntarily set foot in one without being pressured or bullied into it. Summer was a little pushy, but the difference is, she came from a good place. A place of wanting to spend time with me doing something she enjoys.

We are cheesing at each other like goofballs when a low voice cuts in. "Very impressive, Mel."

I whip around so fast, the rope smacks me in the shins.

"Oh my gosh, you're back!" Summer shouts and throws herself into her friend's arms.

Jackson glances at me over her shoulder, bestowing a kind smile. I don't have the heart to return one. My mind is all over the place. I'm mad, though I know I shouldn't be. But mostly, I feel stupid. Stupid for thinking a man like him could ever be into someone like me. The pictures of him and that woman made far more sense than him and me ever could.

Summer pulls away, throwing a friendly arm around him, and gesturing to me with the other. "Did you see how amazing our girl is? She just completed her first side swipe! She's a natural."

His eyes darken as his gaze stays locked onto mine. "Yes, she is."

Like the rattled mess I am, I begin fumbling for words, looking for a way out of this conversation. "I, uh, Gracie. I should go."

"What? Already? Stay a little longer, we're just getting it," Summer begs.

I shake my head, grab my keys and towel off the ground next to us, and bolt for the door. "I really should go. I'll see you next time."

I reach the entrance, throw the front door open, and practically sprint home. I'm halfway to the cabin before I realize I didn't grab my sweatshirt.

There is no fucking way I'm going back wearing only a sports bra with Jackson looking at me like that.

CHAPTER 18

Jackson

The last time I saw Melody, it wasn't exactly on the best of terms, but this was different. She could barely even look at me. My presence completely spooked her. She was smiling and giggling with Summer one minute, and the second she saw me, her face paled and she looked angry.

Clearly, my owning the gym and not being upfront with her is still bothering her, though I'm not entirely sure why.

"So, tell me everything? What did those assholes say? How good did it feel to fire them?" Summer asks me, sitting across from me in my office.

After Melody bolted, we retreated to my office so I could fill Summer in on the trip.

"Well, first of all, Ember is a life saver. She called me right after talking to you, dropped everything, and showed up, like, an hour later."

"Ember is the best," Summer says with the flick of her wrist. Her and her sister are very close, but Ember currently lives in the city. Summer does her best to be supportive, but I know it's hard having her sister so far away.

"Yeah, the timing was sort of perfect. I got her all squared away, and the staff was really receptive and embraced her right away. She's the only reason I felt confident coming back here. It would have taken me forever to find a trusted replacement."

"I saw the speech you made. Someone uploaded it. You did a great job. This won't go away overnight, but Jumping Jax will be okay. People know you. Your apology was authentic, and you acted immediately. Didn't make excuses. People resonate with that."

I sigh, feeling the toll of the last few days weighing heavily on me. "I guess."

"It's true. You'll see. On the plus side, things are going great here. We got ten new sign-ups over the weekend, and everything went smoothly here."

"Thank God something's going right. I appreciate you holding down the fort so I could go take care of things."

"What are best friends for?" she says with a smirk.

"No, really. I couldn't do any of this without you. Thank you," I tell her, slumping into the chair.

"Are you okay?" she asks, seeing the look of utter exhaustion plastered on my face.

I rub my forehead with my fingers, feeling irritated with having to talk about the other situation. "Fucking Natasha."

Her lips form a thin line. "Yeah. I saw the pictures."

All color drains from my face, and my fists clench in my lap. *"What pictures?"*

Summer looks hesitant to speak. "One of the protesters uploaded quite a few pictures of you and Natahsa looking pretty cozy together."

I raise an eyebrow, feeling my irritation rising. "Cozy? Fuck no. She showed up uninvited to the gym, and I took her inside and told her to fuck off. For a second time."

Summer shrugs. "I know you sent me the text about Melody, but did you meet up with Natasha after all?"

"Absolutely not. She is five kinds of crazy," I say firmly. I wasn't aware of any pictures, since I haven't been on social media to avoid the onslaught of hatred that's been flung my way. But if Summer saw the pictures, I'm wondering if maybe Melody has, too. "Fuck, has Melody seen them?"

Her lips pull to the side as she thinks. "I'm not sure. She hasn't said. Though, that could explain the way she ran out of here once you showed up."

I pull my baseball cap off and run both hands through my hair in frustration. "Fuck."

"Are we finally being honest about your feelings for her?"

"Yeah, I'm really into her. But now this shit with Natasha. Fuck." I groan, scrubbing my hands down my face.

It may not seem like much to others, but for me to even openly admit I have real feelings for the woman is a huge deal for me. I thought that factory setting had been shut off for good. But in a short amount of time, I've grown very strong, very real feelings for Melody, and a crazy influencer might fuck it all up for me.

"Talk to her. I'm sure she'll hear you out. If there's really nothing going on with Natasha."

"There's not!" I shout defensively, then rear my head back with a grimace. "Sorry."

A laugh bursts out of Summer. "Wow, you do get defensive about Melody. I like this protective side of you."

I roll my eyes. "What are you talking about? I've always been protective over you the same way."

We both know it's a lie.

Summer narrows her eyes at me. "Definitely not the same, Jaxy boy."

One side of my lips pull up into a half smile. "You do know that I'm older than you, right?"

"Then be a grown-up and call her," Summer scolds, and

then abruptly exits, leaving me alone in the office with my thoughts.

Even though nothing happened with Natasha, I can't help but feel like I've wronged Mel. The pit in my stomach churns. Any excitement I had at coming home has completely soured. Somehow, things are more fucked-up than before I left.

I pull my phone from my pocket and type out a quick text to Melody.

> Jackson: It was good to see you. I was hoping we could get together and chat.

AFTER HITTING SEND, I toss the phone down and drop my head into my hands. For several minutes I wait to hear the vibration of my phone, but it never does. I finally found a woman that makes me want to try, and Natasha has single-handedly fucked it up before we even had the chance to see what could be. Rather than sit here awaiting a reply that might never come, I head back out to the gym floor and put in some face time with a few clients.

Summer is training a woman in the rope room where she spent the morning with Melody. She catches my eye and waves me over.

"Hey, Melody left this here," she says, handing me a gray sweatshirt. I fight the urge to bring it to my nose.

I stand there holding it, giving her a confused look. "Okay?"

"Could be a cold night, she might need it," Summer responds facetiously with a wink.

Not only is Summer a fantastic friend, but she's brilliant.

Having a woman for a best friend might be the smartest thing I've ever done.

I HAD two jump rope classes to teach and follow-up with our new clients. Reaching out with a welcome call is something I like doing with each person who signs up at Jumping Jax. Where most gyms begin spam calling clients with extras they want to charge you for, ours is more of a *Welcome to the family* call. In my experience, it's those little things that separate us from everybody else.

After both classes, I scarf down a protein bar in my office and pull up my Instagram account to see what pictures Summer was referring to.

I try, and fail, to ignore the sinking feeling that Melody never replied to my message.

Sure enough, there are about three hundred new comments on my recent video. Some negative, but mostly positive in reaction to my speech to the protesters. Summer was right, the majority of people are standing by us, so the damage should be minimal. Though, I still feel sick about it.

There are also notifications for tagged pictures, and I groan as I reluctantly click on them. A handful of photos show Natasha and me talking out front of the Denver West gym. Unfortunately, if I were an onlooker, I'd think these do look rather cozy and friendly. Trying to hide the panic and frustration I had at seeing Natasha show up the way she did has only come to bite me in the ass. I never should have taken her inside.

We are smiling, albeit fake, embracing each other, and I even hold the door open for her, looking like a loving, doting boyfriend.

Fucking hell.

I close out of the app, pocket my phone, and head for the front door. It's near closing, and there are still a handful of customers getting their workouts in, but Summer offered to stay and close up. Not wanting to get to Melody's place too late, I didn't argue.

Summer stands at the receptionist desk at the front, greeting and saying good night to each client, when she spots me. "Good luck."

With Melody's sweatshirt in hand, I give Summer a hesitant smile. "Thanks. I'm gonna need it."

The walk to Melody's cabin isn't very far, so I try to come up with what I'm going to say other than *Here's your sweatshirt. I only smelled it four or five times like a creep. Also, you smell fucking delicious.*

I make a mental note to figure out what perfume she wears. It's the perfect mix of citrus and delicate florals, and it's seductively warm.

Attracting women has never been an issue for me. In fact, I've turned down enough women to likely raise suspicion to the state of my sexuality. After the way Shaina fucked me over, I haven't let myself get close to another woman. Natasha was as close as it ever got, and she's also currently trying to fuck me over.

But with Melody, it's different. She doesn't want anything from me. The way she resists the large tips I leave her tells me she would never pursue me for my money. Something I've found to be incredibly rare since acquiring my wealth.

Her cabin comes into view, and immediately my heart rate quickens.

Get it together, you fucking coward.

I climb the few small steps to her porch and stand in front of her door. Pulling my cell from my pocket, I check one last time to see if she ever responded. Nope. Which means my being here likely won't be welcome.

Here goes nothing.

I raise my fist and knock three times and wait. Inside I can hear Gracie's small voice calling for her mom and asking who's at the door, and her mom telling her to stay put and to always let the adult answer the door.

The door swings open a minute later, and I see Melody standing in tight black spandex shorts that stop high on her thigh and a loose-fitting gray tank top. The hard nipples protruding through the fabric tells me she's not wearing a bra.

Fuck me. Focus.

She tucks a strand of her loose hair behind her ear and crosses her arms. "Can I help you?"

Ouch.

I outstretch my arm, handing her the sweater she left at Jumping Jax. "You, uh, left this at the gym today. I thought you might need it."

She tilts her head slightly, narrowing her eyes. We both know it's a warm evening, and there was absolutely zero urgency to bring her this sweater. I'm grateful she's not calling me out on it, but she's definitely sizing me up.

She takes the sweater. "I was going to grab it tomorrow at my next session with Summer. But thanks, I guess."

I give her a weak smile. "No problem."

She clears her throat. "Was there something else?"

I sigh, accepting defeat. "No, that's all."

"Alright. See you later." Her words carry a sharp bite.

Melody has always been guarded, and overall pretty reserved, but I've never seen her this way. Ice-cold. She's looking at me like I'm a stranger, and as much as I don't want to admit it, it hurts.

The door begins to close, but I decide that I can't leave things like this.

"Melody, wait."

Slowly, the door reopens, but she stands wedged between the frame and the door, waiting for me to continue.

"Can we talk for a minute?" I ask, gesturing to the porch.

She licks her lips indecisively, pulling the bottom one between her teeth. Holding up one finger, she leaves the door cracked and takes a few steps back inside to say something to Gracie. A moment later, she walks outside, shutting the door behind her with a soft click.

Her arms are folded across her chest, and she leans against the house with one foot propped up behind her. "Well?"

"Nothing happened with Natasha. I don't know if that's why you're avoiding me, but I just wanted you to know." The words fly out of me before I lose the nerve.

Her face is stern, even as she scoffs. "Alrighty. Thanks for the update."

She's angry, and she won't look at me. Her gaze is pinned to something off in the distance. Nothing, maybe.

"I don't know if you saw the pictures of us, and I know they make us look like a couple, but there's nothing going on between her and me."

She doesn't look at me when she replies, "You don't owe me an explanation, Jackson."

"I wanted to. You seem angry with me, and I wanted to make sure I didn't do anything to upset you."

I can see her chewing on the inside of her lip and the fire in her eyes. I've hardly said anything, yet she seems to be getting angrier.

"Melody. Talk to me."

"No," she says firmly.

"Why not?"

She pushes off the wall and finally faces me. "It's not about the pictures, Jackson. How was your time with her in your hotel room?"

I give her a blank stare that she misinterprets as guilt. A person caught in the act.

"Yeah, I saw your texts to Summer about Natasha asking to come to your room and how sexy you think she is. So please get off my porch."

I flex my hands at my side in frustration. "For fuck's sake. Did you see what I said *after that*?"

"What, did you tell Summer how great of a lay she is? Sorry, not interested," she says, and then begins trying to make her exit, but I place my right hand on her hip, pressing her against the wall.

Our faces are inches apart, and I can see her chest rapidly rising and falling. With a lowered voice, we lock eyes and I tighten my fingers on her hip. "If you had continued reading, you would have seen me tell Summer that I didn't invite her up. I told her there's only one girl I wanted in my room, and she was in Blue Springs having drinks with her."

"What?" Her voice cracks, and her eyes mist.

"Melody, you were all I could think about. I couldn't wait to get home and see your beautiful face. Hear your sweet voice. I don't know why I said any of those other things. She is *nothing* compared to you."

Her watering eyes never leave mine, but she doesn't respond. My eyes drop to her lips, and she parts them slightly.

"Melody," I whisper.

"Jackson." Her voice is breathy, and my name comes out as more of a moan.

When I glance back up to her eyes, I see the sparkle before we collide. Our lips join, and her tongue sweeps into my mouth, causing a full-body tingle outbreak.

Taking both of her hands in mine, I place them firmly above her head and hold them in place. Her lips are even softer than I imagined. She tastes like peppermint and honey, and I decide right then and there that it's my favorite combination of flavors.

The kiss is intense and passionate, like two people who have been deprived of their favorite treat for too long and are now binging on it. Like going from eating nothing but bland chicken for months to my favorite cheat meal. Melody is mouthwatering and delicious.

When she moans into my mouth, I find myself involuntarily pressing myself up against her. My hard cock strains against my pants, begging for attention. I start to pull back, worried that I've taken it too far, when I feel her press her hips into mine.

I let her hands go, eager to touch more of her. As soon as she's released, her hands fly into my hair, pulling me closer. My tongue swirls around her mouth, trying to savor the way she tastes, when she takes my tongue between her lips and begins to suck.

I'm not sure what noise escapes me, but it's akin to a growl or a roar. This woman is awakening every primal instinct I have inside of me. My hands move to her perfect, plump ass, and I squeeze both cheeks before sliding my hands down to the back of her thighs and lifting her up to my waist. Her legs immediately wrap tightly around me.

If I thought my mind was consumed with her before, it's about to get so much worse. Because now I know how she tastes. I know how she smells, I know how she *feels*.

Kissing Melody is more effective than all the pre-workout in the world. Right now, I'm invincible. We're in a trance, unable to separate. I'm consumed with her delicious tongue in my mouth, her juicy ass in my hands, and the perfect way she fits in my arms.

"Mommy! The TV turned off!" Gracie yells from the other side of the door.

Our mouths halt, and we both freeze. Two deer in the headlights of reality. It's not until the doorknob starts to turn that I let her legs go and we part.

Melody opens the door, and Gracie emerges. "Jax! Did you come to play?"

I look at Melody, wondering, *hoping* she'll invite me inside.

"No, honey, he's just returning my sweatshirt. He has to go," Melody tells Gracie, and my ego deflates.

"Aw, okay," Gracie pouts.

"Good night, Jackson," Melody says before quickly retreating inside and shutting the door, once again leaving me alone on the porch, wondering what the fuck she's thinking.

CHAPTER 19

Melody

I'm like a sex-crazed teenager.

I consider myself a levelheaded woman. Rational and realistic. Until Jackson comes around with his gray man-whore sweats and backward baseball cap, turning my brain into pudding. All logic gets twisted up in those perfect brown curls on the top of his head.

A moment of weakness had me giving in to the sweet temptation that is Blue Springs's jump rope king.

What is it about seeing that man on my porch that makes me weak in the knees every damn time?

The sun is just starting to rise up over the mountains, but I'm wide-awake, replaying everything with Jackson from last night. His words, like an earworm, run on a never-ending track in my mind. The way his hands ran over my skin, grabbing me like I was his, has me clenching my thighs together.

A large part of me wants to believe what he told me. But I never did see the text he claims to have sent, and I sure as hell can't ask Summer about it. She doesn't know I saw the other texts to begin with. Having made such a fuss about only being friends with Jackson, I'd look like an absolute lunatic if she knew.

Maybe he invited Natasha up to his room, and maybe he didn't, but the bottom line is, there's something going on there and I can't be getting caught up in drama like that. I have a daughter to think about, and she will always come first.

I have got to stop getting caught up in his intoxicating haze.

"Mama." Gracie's tiny voice startles me when she stirs awake.

I turn over and drape an arm over her. "Good morning, sweetie pie. How did you sleep?"

She yawns and stretches her limbs. "Good, Mama. I'm hungry."

I giggle. "Already? You just opened your eyes."

Instead of replying, she boops me on the nose with her finger and makes a weird noise.

Gotta love the preschooler stage.

With only a few hours of sleep, I'm praying to the server gods that none of my tables are difficult today. I'm particularly hoping not to see bitchy Brenda today. Even though she doesn't verbally scold me anymore, just seeing her face puts me in a perpetually bad mood for the rest of the day. Miserable people like that are like a plague, infecting everyone around them.

Gracie and I get up to use the restroom, and then we head to the kitchen where I make us a quick French toast breakfast. Let me tell you, French toast is a lot better when you're not using carb smart, low-cal bread, only egg whites, and sugar-free syrup. Gracie seemed to like it okay back home, but since I've started making French toast this way, it's her most-requested meal. The whipped cream on top doesn't hurt, either.

When I wasn't dropping the baby weight and "bouncing back" as quickly as Alexander thought I should—the way society thinks women should—he started doing all of the grocery shopping, so our version of most meals looked vastly different from what people are typically accustomed to.

After we've had our fill of the syrupy goodness, I shower and dress for work while Gracie plays an alphabet game on her iPad. I'm slipping into my work shoes when I hear a knock at the door. Having heard a cheery humming coming up the stairs, I know it's Jane.

"Come in, it's open!" I shout, hunched over on the couch next to Gracie, tying my shoes.

"Hello, hello!" she singsongs, stepping inside, making her way to Gracie. "Good morning, sweetheart! Oh, look how wonderful you're getting at those letters!"

Gracie smiles at the praise and gives Jane a big hug. "I missed you!"

Jane and I share a look, and stifle a laugh, because it's been less than twenty-four hours since she was here last.

"I missed you too, sweetheart." Jane humors Gracie and goes along with it. Though, she probably means it, too.

"I should be off around five, and then I have a class set up with Summer for more jump rope lessons, if you don't mind staying. If not, I can absolutely reschedule and go another time."

Jane takes a seat on the couch next to Gracie and shakes her head at me. "No, no. You deserve more than to work and come home. Go, please. Jackson and Summer have done a wonderful job with those classes. I'm happy you're able to enjoy them."

Gracie, Jane, and I have formed such a comfortable connection that sometimes it's lost on me that she's Jackson's mother. I know they have a very close relationship, but she's never alluded to knowing about Jackson and me. Maybe she's waiting for me to bring it up to her first.

"Thank you so much. It's nice getting back into the gym. I have fun training with Summer."

"Were you an avid gym attendee back in Los Angeles?" Jane asks innocently, not knowing how loaded that question is.

The corners of my lips involuntarily pull downward, and I shrug. "Sort of. It was important to Gracie's dad that I go."

I wonder if she can see the pain behind my eyes. The years I spent silently suffering, so as not to rupture the already strained relationship between Gracie and her father. Even though he was a rat bastard, I never wanted to expose Gracie to what he was doing to me. Up until our last night there, I told myself that I could be strong for Gracie, that I could take all of the pain necessary to protect her and still give her the relationship I wanted most for her: father and daughter. Not having a relationship with my own, I am cognizant of the ways a little girl can be hurt without that bond.

Jane gives me a pained look, so I force a smile and lean over to hug Gracie goodbye. "Please be good for Jane. I'll be home tonight. Maybe I'll bring home a treat from Bread Pitt. How does that sound?"

"Yes, Mommy! Thank you! Thank you! I'll be good!" Gracie shrieks and latches onto my torso, squeezing a little too tight.

"Gracie, sweetie, I don't think Mommy can breathe," Jane tells her playfully.

Gracie unlatches and pulls her hands to her mouth, giggling. "Sorry, Mommy."

Standing, I grab my apron off the small table by the entrance and swing the door open, but Jane stops me. "Melody, sweetheart?"

I turn around, unable to refrain from smiling at the term of endearment she so easily gives. One I never had before. For a brief while, Alexander called me babe, but even that quickly dissipated once he realized I couldn't uphold the perfect Stepford wife standards he had for me.

"I don't know what you've endured, but I'm proud of you for

getting back in the gym. It takes a lot of courage to revisit the place that broke you."

My eyes sting, and my cheeks flush hot. I don't trust myself to speak, so I pull my lips inward in an attempt to hold myself together and give her a nod before leaving and closing the door behind me. For the next few minutes, I stand there with my back against the door, and silently weep.

I weep for the little girl that never heard those words, and I weep for the woman that needed to hear them now.

Not only has Jane acted as a stand-in grandmother for Gracie, but she's become the mother figure I never had.

Most people think of their parents and the memories evoke feelings of nostalgia and longing. Whenever thoughts of my parents arise, it's a reminder to do things differently than they did. To create a different relationship with my daughter. A safe place for her to evolve into whoever she wants to be. So that one day, when she's grown and I'm old and gray, Gracie's memories of me will be that of longing and love.

Before walking into work, I stop by Bread Pitt and pick out two of Gracie's favorite donuts. Trish even threw in an extra lemon curd pastry for me in honor of the successful lemonade stand we had. It's like her generosity is a bad habit she can't seem to kick.

When I passed by Jumping Jax, there's a chance my gaze may have wandered over to see if I could spot Jackson training shirtless. I'm running on about two hours of sleep, and just had an emotional meltdown, but somehow, thoughts of Jackson Pierce shirtless are still at the forefront of my mind.

That, ladies and gentlemen, is the power of a backward baseball cap and a man that can fill out a pair of gray sweatpants in all the right places.

He's performing mummy kicks and side swipes—much better than I can—and doesn't notice me walking by. Which allows me to stare at all his sweaty glory without getting caught and sucked into his orbit.

Though, I wouldn't mind doing some sucking of my own.

I slip through the back door of Blue's and clock in at the computer in the kitchen where I see Mary walking to the dish pit with dirty plates.

"Thank God you're here," she tells me, her shoulders drooping.

"What's going on? Is it slammed?" I ask, peering through the little window in the kitchen door.

"No, but it's just me and *you know who.*"

"You know who" is Elana. She's another server who's been here for years, yet I've found myself correcting her on just about everything. She's also the server who has left us high and dry a few times by calling out last minute. Basically, she makes our jobs harder and is a giant pain in the ass.

"Lord, help me. I am not rested enough to deal with her today," I whine with an exaggerated eye roll.

Mary gives me a smirk and sidles up next to me, giving my forearm a squeeze. "Late night?"

A boisterous laugh slips out. "No. I wish. I mean, I don't wish. I just couldn't sleep."

She cocks an eyebrow at me. "Why's that?"

I try to avoid her gaze while I tie my apron around my waist. "I may or may not have had a small, inconsequential make out session last night that left me feeling like I chugged a pot of coffee."

Mary gives me a full belly laugh. "Oh, I remember those days. Young love is so much fun."

I purse my lips when I look up at her. "No, no. Nobody said anything about love. Let's jump off that track right now."

She holds both of her hands up in surrender. "Take it easy, I come in peace. So, who's the stud?"

Pulling my lips inward and shaking my head, I fight a smile.

"Melody Miller, you better spill the beans right now!" she playfully scolds me, and then she gasps. "I know who it is."

"You do not."

"Of course I do, it's so obvious," she says, flipping her wrist.

"What's obvious?"

"How much you and Jackson are into each other. I've heard that you guys have been seen all around town. This is no secret."

"You're right, there's no secret. But there's nothing going on between us."

"So you're telling me you weren't locking lips with Jax last night?" she asks with her hand on one protruded hip.

I try and fail to stifle the growing smile on my face when I remember the way his tongue felt in my mouth, and the way his hands felt on my body.

"Ha! I knew it," she shouts.

"Maybe it was. But there's nothing going on. There can't be. I didn't come to Blue Springs just to wind up in the arms of another rich man."

She rolls her eyes. "I know you've got a sordid past with Gracie's father, but Jackson, he's a good one. Ask anyone around here. Whatever you're holding onto that's keeping you from letting him in isn't something you need to worry about with Jax."

The more I hear this, the more I want to believe it. Jane, Summer, and now Mary have sung his praises, yet I still find myself getting cold feet whenever I think about anything beyond the attraction we have. I manage to continually talk myself both in and out of it.

The hostess pokes her head in the kitchen. "Hey Melody, are you clocked in? I just sat a two-top in your section."

"Yeah, I'll be right over, thanks!"

"Saved by the customer," Mary says jokingly, walking out of the kitchen.

It's not that I don't want to have this conversation, but more that I don't know what to say about it. Mary is the only person who knows what I've been through with Alexander. Even she doesn't know the full story about the night that broke me and sent me running to a new town with my daughter. So this conversation will end the way it always does, with me telling her I'm not interested in a relationship and likely never will be.

The shift ends up being busier than we expected, which is always nice. But when I glance at the clock, it's almost six, roughly when I was supposed to meet Summer at the gym. I sneak into the walk-in freezer to cool off and pull out my phone to let Summer know I'm going to be late.

Melody: Hey, work is slammed. I probably won't get out of here until closer to 8. Will you still be around?

I CAN'T HIDE in here too long, because I have food to run out, orders to take, and a drink order to fill, but luckily, Summer texts back right away.

Summer: Usually I wouldn't mind staying late, but I have to take care of something tonight. I'm sorry.

Melody: That's okay, we can reschedule.

Summer: Actually, if you're up for it, Jax said he'd train with you.

WARNING bells are going off in my head, telling me what a terrible idea this is. Last night went too far, and what I need now is space, not more time together. But when I start to text back, I don't think the rest of my body got the memo.

Melody: Okay. I'll be off around 8.

CHAPTER 20

Jackson

Treadmill minutes, insomnia minutes, and waiting-for-Melody-to-show-up minutes are the longest I've ever experienced.

I'm taking over Summer's training session with Melody tonight, and after what transpired between us last night, *feeling anxious* is an understatement. I can't be sure if she's spooked because Gracie might know there's something going on between us, or because she's going to pull away again. But tonight, I plan to get to the bottom of it.

The gym is starting to empty out now that it's almost 8 p.m. We stay open until nine, but there's usually only a few people in here at that time. Melody and I will basically have the entire place to ourselves.

And fuck, does that excite me.

I took a quick rinse in the showers. The training will only get me sweaty again, but at least I'll smell halfway decent when she arrives. Not that anything is going to happen, but a man can be hopeful, right? I don't need to give this woman any more reasons to run from me. Although, the only clothing I have is what I arrived in this morning, which leaves me in jeans for tonight's coaching session. Not my first choice of workout attire, but there's no way I'm slipping back into what I sweat through today.

Summer took off over an hour ago; she's spending the night with her sister in the city and checking on her at the Denver location. I was a lucky son of a bitch that she was able to step right in the way she did. Ember has always been the kind of person you can count on.

I'm working my way through the gym, wiping down cardio equipment, putting plates back on the racks, and making things tidy. The music is quieter now that it's later, so I hear the minute Melody steps through the front doors.

Like a magnet, my head snaps to her. She's still in her work uniform of tight jeans, a white T-shirt with the Blue Bistro logo, black nonslip sneakers, and her apron.

Is it normal to find a waitress uniform this fucking sexy? Or is this a Melody thing?

When our eyes meet, she gives me a wave and a half smile. I jog over and smile back.

"Hey, sorry I'm so late tonight. If you have plans, I don't mind rescheduling," she offers with a sympathetic scan of the room, likely noticing the way it's emptied out.

Oh no, she's not getting out of this that easily.

"Nope. No plans," I tell her with a coy smile.

She bites her lip, thinking. "Okay." She glances down at her appearance. "Let me change, then, and I'll be right back."

I nod, and she makes her way to the women's locker room. A few minutes later, she emerges, looking like a whole-ass snack.

She's wearing high-waisted pastel-purple leggings and an oversized white T-shirt that says *Los Angeles* across the front. Her tall white chunky socks and white and black Adidas complete her ensemble. I assume she's wearing a matching sports bra underneath her tee. Not that I'm picturing it or anything.

"You look great," I tell her, earning a shy smile.

She self-consciously glances down at herself. "Oh. Uh, thanks."

For some reason, she looks confused by the compliment, like she thinks I'm lying, and I can't help but wonder when was the last time someone gave her one. She's a strong-willed woman, yet she lacks self-confidence. I can see it in the way she hides herself from not only me, but everyone around. It makes me wonder who took the time to chisel away at her, leaving behind the unsure woman who stands before me.

I hand her the pink rope that Summer set aside for her. "What did you want to work on today? It looked like you were practicing side swipes with Summer last time?"

She nods, adjusting the rope in both hands. "Yeah, I was starting to get it. I think. I see you two do that one all the time, and it looked fun. It's harder than it looks."

I laugh. "Yeah, that's usually how things go."

"But you're the pro, so I'll leave it up to you."

"How about I show you a few different jumps? You can try each one and we'll start with whichever is easiest for you and go from there?"

"Sure," she replies timidly.

We spend the next forty minutes trying out a variation of jumps, including double unders, crisscross, boxer skips, and mummy kicks. The one she really wanted to nail down is the side swipe. Her footwork is really good, but I can see the minute she starts to doubt herself and then gets tripped up in the rope. I can see she knows how to do the moves, but her mind needs the extra encouragement.

Once we're both dripping sweat, and the last guest has left, Mel and I decide to rest on a nearby bench to hydrate.

"You're a quick learner. You take direction really well," I tell her and then immediately regret my choice of words when my cock twitches in response, considering what other situations she'd be great at taking direction in.

The smirk on her face tells me her mind is traveling a similar track. "Thanks, Jax."

I raise an eyebrow at her. "Oh, it's Jax now, is it?"

She takes another drink out of her water bottle, shrugging. "That's your name, isn't it?"

It's playful, but I know it's a dig.

"I'm sorry I didn't tell you."

"Why didn't you? I was bound to find out. Aside from this being a small-ass town that loves to gossip, your name is right in the logo. I feel dumb I didn't figure it out sooner, honestly."

"I wasn't hiding it. I knew you'd figure it out. But ever since I acquired my wealth, there's only been one reason women seem to be attracted to me. I wanted to get to know you before you looked at me differently. It's not often I meet women who don't already know of me or follow me on social media."

She's looking down at her feet, bouncing her head up and down. "That's fair." She lifts her head and turns toward me. "For the record, your wealth is what I like least about you."

I sigh. "Well, I don't want it to be a reason you dislike me, either."

"I don't dislike you. I'm just being cautious. Having known plenty of men with money, it's become more of a deterrent."

"Wow," I say softly.

"Sorry. I'm not trying to be rude."

I shake my head. "No, it's not that. I'm sorry for whatever some rich asshole did to you."

Melody doesn't open up much, or easily, but this small crack explains why she's been so hot and cold with me. Whatever happened in her past has to do with some rich prick, and I can't blame her for thinking we all might be the same. Money can make people do really ugly things. I've seen some of the best people turn into monsters because of the "power" money brought them.

Shrugging, she caps her bottle and changes the subject. "Ok, I want to see your best move."

"You sure you can handle it? It's pretty intense." I bump shoulders with her, a wide grin spread across my face.

She playfully rolls her eyes. "I think I'll be fine."

I stand with my rope, making my way over to the host stand, and plug my phone in. The song I click on is a remix of Ginuwine's "Pony."

I make my way back over to where Melody sits and keep a safe distance in front of her. Her eyes are glued to me, and I can't wait to give this girl a show.

"I don't show this routine to just anybody, so buckle up, baby," I tell her, lifting my shirt over my head, and tossing it to the side.

The music plays, and I begin with an intense side swipe/mic drop to my left, stopping the rope underneath my right foot with a snap. I perform an x-motion/high knee/straddle combo, then switch to heel touch/toe touches, straight into crisscross jumps. I repeat the rotation a few more times, and then, once my body is slick and glistening, I end with a swipe/mic drop, back to center, and toss the handles in front of me, setting me up for my signature move. The one I haven't used in a long time, for obvious reasons.

With one hand, I pull the end of my belt, and jerk it out of the buckle, yanking it back through all the loops, and fling it to the side in two quick motions. I keep my eyes locked to Melody's gorgeous blue's the entire time, so I see the minute her jaw drops before she catches herself and quickly closes it.

Her lips are spread, and I can see her squeezing her legs together tightly while she's watching me.

The song continues while I stand in front of her, sweating and panting. Both of us are staring the other down, daring each other to make the first move.

"What did you think?" I ask in between breaths.

She licks her lips and leans back, giving me the perfect view of her hard nipples poking through her shirt.

That's right, baby. There's my girl.

She nods but doesn't speak.

"Cat got your tongue?" I quip, slowly walking toward her.

I can see that she wants this. She's scared and won't let me in long enough to let me show her I'm not someone to be scared of. To show her that, fuck, I'm scared, too. This routine was the ace up my sleeve, and from the moment I found out I would be training her tonight, I knew I wanted to show it to her. If this is how I get her to stop running from me, then so be it.

She clears her throat, but her voice cracks anyway. "That was…"

Her words drift off as she searches for the right word. "Impressive?" I supply.

I take one last step and now stand over her so she has to lift her chin upward to see me. "No. Sexy."

Using my thumb, I caress her jaw and chin. She leans into it, and fuck if this isn't the most beautiful view with her under me. She closes her eyes briefly and then opens them to speak. "Jackson."

"What is it, baby?" I ask, getting lost in her perfect features. The plump lips that are made for kissing, and now that I know how they taste, I crave even more. Her beautiful deep blue eyes, and her creamy tan skin that feels like velvet under my touch.

"Are you going to kiss me?"

I smirk. "Do you want me to?"

She nods.

I pull my hand away and wag my finger at her. "Uh-uh, tell me."

"Jackson, kiss me. Now." She whimpers and reaches up to pull my face down to hers.

Melody might still be fighting her feelings for me most days, but I'm done pretending.

Melody

I'm a liar. A big, giant, astronomical liar.

From the moment I knew Jackson Pierce existed, I told myself I'd be careful around him, that I'd steer clear of him, yet, here I am with my tongue in his mouth. The worst part is, I'm not even sure who made the first move.

His hands move from the back of my head, down to my waist as he pulls me up so we're both standing. I feel his fingers continue their way downward until they're planted firmly on my ass, causing me to automatically arch into him. My hands are tangled in his hair, and I give it a gentle tug. A moan escapes me before I can stop it, and he pulls back and begins kissing down my jaw, neck, and chest.

I don't know where the boldness comes from, but I spin us around and push him down onto the bench and straddle him, hovering over him slightly.

"What are you doing?" he asks.

Thinking I've taken things too far, I begin to lift my leg back over to stand, when he grips my leg tightly and yanks me back down flush against him. "Sit. I want you right here. Let me feel you."

Doing my best to stifle the self-consciousness of feeling like I'm going to crush him, I try to stay in the moment.

We continue kissing and running our hands over each other, familiarizing ourselves with this newfound paradise. A destination we've wanted to visit for so long and now see for the first time. Soaking up every touch and every kiss, I ignore each warning inside my mind telling me to run. Telling me that if I continue down this road, it'll only end in heartache. I ignore it all, because right now, with the way he makes me feel, I think heartbreak might just be worth it.

"You feel so fucking good, Mel." His deep, raspy voice is turning me into a wet mess.

I wonder if he can feel it through my leggings.

Since I've met Jackson, I feel like there's two versions of me. One that's levelheaded and determined to steer clear of men. And then there's the other version. The one that wants to finish what he started during his routine and unzip his pants and pull them off. This version wants to slip out of my leggings and see the way he fits inside of me.

His hard cock is pulsing underneath me, provoking my body to grind back and forth, creating delicious, torturous friction. My pussy is drenched and aching for him. I can feel the heartbeat pulsation that I didn't even know was still possible.

Reaching between us, I grab hold of his cock over his pants, fighting with the angels on my shoulders.

Should this be happening? Or should I be stopping this?

He groans with pleasure when I grip his cock, and it only makes me want more.

His fingers release their hold on my hips and begin moving under the hem of my shirt as he begins to lift it.

My hands quickly cover his, pulling my shirt back down, and like I've been burned by fire, I hop off his lap so fast, I stumble backward.

"What's wrong? Was that not okay?" he asks, worried lines creasing between his eyebrows.

I cover my mouth with my hand for a second, the adrenaline wearing off, and the shock of what we were doing settling in. "No. I mean, it's okay. I just need to go slow."

"Of course. We can slow down."

I bite my lip, nodding.

"Are you okay?" he asks, standing.

An embarrassed giggle slips through my lips. "I'm fine. I should probably get going, though."

He strides toward me, taking both of my hands in his. "Please, Mel. Don't run again."

His gorgeous emerald eyes bore into mine with sadness. It's impossible to be around him when neither of us can control ourselves. The inimitable attraction between us is too strong. Being around Jackson *literally* takes my breath away. It's hard to breathe, and I feel like I've chugged five espressos in five minutes.

To be near him means betraying the promises I made to myself. Continuing this "friendship" will only escalate our attraction, and I don't know if I'm ready for that. But I know I can't keep doing this to him. Also, I don't want to.

"I won't run." I reach up and softly press my lips to his.

His thumbs rub back and forth on my hands. "I like you, Melody."

I look away, feeling self-conscious when the doubt creeps in.

"Hey. Don't do that," he says tenderly.

I lift my gaze back to his and shrug. "I don't know why you like me."

"Are you kidding me? Look at you."

I lift an eyebrow, as if to say *And?*

"You are the most beautiful woman I've ever seen. I don't

think I've been able to look away from you since the minute I saw you in Blue's."

If the fluttering in my chest were actual butterflies, they would have exploded out of my chest by now.

I take in everything he's saying as he continues. "Aside from that, you are an incredible mother, you're independent, and strong-willed, maybe to a fault." We both laugh. "But more than that, you're an amazing human."

"A man like you could have any woman he wants," I say, unable to stifle the self-deprecating thoughts that tell me this all might still be a scam.

"If that were true, you'd be mine already."

My breath catches.

When my eyes meet his, a playful smirk dances on his lips. He's confident, but there's a sensitivity that lies underneath. Maybe there's more to Jackson Pierce than I thought.

"Jackson," I whisper, exasperated, planting my face into his muscular chest.

He wraps his arms around me. "Have dinner with me."

Lifting my head, I give him a knowing look. "Like our last friendship outing?"

I laugh softly, but his face is serious. "No."

"Well then?"

"A date. A real one."

"Oh."

"You want to take things slow, and I think that's great. I want to get to know you, Melody. You and Gracie."

"I don't know," I say with hesitation at the mention of Gracie. She's the one thing I hadn't fully considered when letting my guard down with Jackson. This will very much affect her as much as it will me. My decisions aren't just mine to make anymore. I have a four-year-old to think about.

His shoulders drop. "You said you were done running."

"I'm not running. I'm thinking. It's complicated with Gracie."

"What's complicated about getting to know me?" he asks with genuine curiosity.

What's complicated? Oh, just the fact that I could easily fall in love with you, and you could break not only my heart, but that of my four-year-old, too.

"Do you have any kids, Jackson?" I ask, and then internally face-palm. This is a question that should be asked *before* straddling a man.

His eyebrows pull together. "No."

"Well, I do. I have to think about how this could affect her if we get...close."

I can see as he considers what I've said. He's not being judgmental or pushy, he's curious. He's trying to understand.

"One date. Let's get to know each other a little better. We can talk about a game plan at dinner."

"Game plan?" I ask, the corners of my mouth lifting.

"Yes. A game plan for how to deal with everything else when you fall in love with me."

"Oh, I'm falling in love with you, am I?" I ask, grinning.

He shrugs, lifting his hand to caress my cheek. "Maybe. Can't count it out. Not with the way I plan on pursuing you, Melody Miller."

His hands on me are like kryptonite, and I'm melting into his hand, ready to agree with anything he's asking. I've never been very good at hiding my emotions, which is why Jackson uses this moment to ask me again.

"Let's go on a date. Have dinner with me."

With my head slanted sideways, resting in his hand, I glance upward into his deep green eyes. "Okay."

He pulls me into him and kisses me again. "Yes?"

I nod in between his hands. "I still don't know why you want to go out with me."

He releases me, and his lips pull to the side. "We're going to have to work on that."

"What?" I ask, walking over to gather my belongings next to the bench.

The way you talk down to yourself."

I swallow hard, not knowing how often I've probably done it in front of him. It's become an ingrained habit I hardly recognize as a negative one. To me, it's just a standard conversation between me, myself, and I.

I bend over to grab my bag, and when I right myself, he wraps his arms around me from behind. "One day, I'll get you to see what I see."

"What is it that you see?" I ask hesitantly, bracing for the answer while simultaneously thumbing through my memory catalog of the insults Alexander used to hurl at me.

"Everything I ever wanted."

A lump forms in my throat. Doing my best not to get emotional, I turn in his arms and give him a quick peck. "Good night, Jackson."

He offers to take me home, but with his mom and Gracie there, I don't want anyone getting the wrong idea. Already, people are taking notice. But more than that, I need the time to reflect on what the hell I just got myself into.

I moved here certain I'd never be in another relationship as long as I lived, yet, I have agreed to go out on a date with Blue Springs's most eligible bachelor.

So much for being smart around Jackson fucking Pierce.

CHAPTER 22
Jackson

If you told me a year ago I'd be pursuing a woman, I'd have laughed. After what I went through with Shaina, I convinced myself there wasn't a woman alive who could make me want to go down that road again. But there's something about Melody that keeps pulling me in. I have this innate desire to protect her. To take care of her.

"A real date? I never thought I'd see the day," Summer expresses with the same shock that I feel.

"Let's not make a big thing of it," I plead, knowing that's *exactly* what Summer's going to do. The girl can't help herself.

"Maybe you'd like to finish updating all this paperwork by yourself," I half-heartedly threaten.

She sits across from me in our shared office, sifting through applications, and sorting through new memberships. My mind is all Melody, but there's still work to do. Our date isn't for a few days, and yet it's at the forefront of all of my thoughts.

Summer dramatically places one palm over her heart. "On my best behavior."

I roll my eyes. "Sure."

She laughs, creating a bounce in her blonde curls. "I swear!

Look, one of us should be dating. And since I've decided against it again, it's only right that you get back out there."

"It's one date. Neither of us is looking to get serious."

She cocks an eyebrow at me. "Why are you two going on a date then?"

Her question catches me off guard, because it's the question I've been asking myself. It seems counterproductive to be actively pursuing someone that doesn't want to date, and by someone who isn't looking for a relationship. The truth is that for so long, I haven't wanted a relationship, but since Melody arrived, it seems to be all I can think about.

I'm internally battling the two extremes, not wanting to open myself up to possible heartache again, but unable to stay away from this woman.

I avoid her gaze, thumbing through a stack of papers. "I don't know what this is, aside from our attraction. This *date* is so we can get to know each other better. That's all."

With a flick of her wrist, she shoves a pile of blonde curls behind her shoulder and shrugs.

I huff. "I've been meaning to tell you, Wes confirmed he'll be at the festival this year, and he's interested in talking to you."

"Your big shot investor friend? Why? For my smoothies?" she asks, surprised with the subject change.

I nod.

Summer has been dreaming of opening her own smoothie shop for years. I've offered to front her the money to get her going, but she's refused every time, saying she never wants to feel like she's taking advantage of our friendship. Though I've assured her that would never be the case, she's determined to find another way.

"Why would he be interested in *my* idea?" she asks warily.

"He's an investor, it's what he does. He's always looking for something new to pour his money into. He's incredibly smart. A little rough around the edges, but he's a great guy."

Summer rolls her eyes and sighs.

"What?" I ask.

"Whenever someone says 'rough around the edges' or 'you have to get to know them first,' it always means they're an asshole."

My eyes go wide. "I've never heard that."

"Well, it's true."

I try to keep my features neutral, but Summer knows me too well, and detects even the slightest upturn of my lips.

"Ha! I knew it!" she shouts, pointing at me with her index finger.

A laugh bursts from my chest. "Okay, he's definitely not Mr. Sunshine, but this is a great opportunity, and he's excited to meet with you."

"Should I be worried about meeting this guy?"

I shake my head. "No, he's going to love you."

Sure, he might be a notorious playboy, but Summer shouldn't be worried about that. This is strictly business.

Her lips widen into a gracious smile. "Thank you for setting this up. I can't believe I could actually have my own shop."

"You deserve it, Sum."

She lifts an eyebrow, and suddenly her face takes on a conspiratorial edge. "Now, where are you going to take Melody on your date?"

I stand and proceed to exit the office. "I'm never telling you anything again."

Truth is, I don't care where we go, as long as she's there. But I don't have the slightest fucking clue where I plan on taking her.

I'M LOOKING through my closet when I hear my phone ping on my bed. When I flip it over, a text from Melody flashes across my screen and it instantly brings a smile to my face.

> Melody: You haven't said where you're taking me. I'm not sure how to dress.

I'VE BEEN WORKING out the details of our date, and tonight is finally the night. I'm racked with nerves, and after not seeing her for the last few days, I'm eager to see that beautiful face of hers. A few text messages a day isn't enough to feed my craving.

> Me: You'll be beautiful in anything you wear.

> Melody: 🙄 That wasn't very helpful.

MY INSTINCTS ARE to spoil her. Take her on an extravagant date and blow her mind. But the way she's resistant to my wealth—the way it was practically a turnoff—tells me she's had that treatment before and it doesn't impress her. So instead, I've opted for a much simpler evening for us.

Me: Wear something you feel confident in.

Melody: Okay, so my gym clothes then? LOL.

Me: If that's what you feel best in, absolutely.

Melody: Is our date at the gym? You're taking me to hump rope, aren't you?

I BURST out laughing at the typo, and before I can respond, I see her typing again before more panicked messages pour in.

Melody: *Jump* rope. Stupid autocorrect.

Melody: Ignore that please.

Melody:

Me: Don't tempt me with a good time.

Melody: You know what I meant, Mr. Jump Rope.

Me: It's okay Mel, you can tell me what you really want ;)

Melody: You're incorrigible.

Me: Naw, just hopeful. 

Melody: Jackson...

Me: I'm kidding. I'll see you at 7, beautiful.

Melody: See you at 7.

I TOSS my phone on the bed and walk back to my closet where I'm agonizing over my own outfit. I don't want to look like I'm trying too hard, but I don't want to appear like I haven't made any effort, either. Melody is a tough woman to crack. Like a wild animal, I'm scared any wrong move will scare her off.

Tonight will be about us getting to know each other better, without any onlookers, and without any pressure of getting physical. I want her to be comfortable in her own skin, because something tells me it's been a long time since she has been.

Summer's question lingers in my head, making me second-guess this entire evening. I don't want to lead Melody on. I've always been up front with women, never wanting to earn the title of playboy or asshole that other men seem comfortable with. What scares me most is falling for a woman I can't commit to. I've tried before, and every uncomfortable and embarrassing emotion that Shaina brought out of me came roaring back with a vengeance, sending me back behind my wall.

I'm not an asshole, I'm trying to protect myself.

After deciding on a pair of nice jeans and an ironed black button up, rolled halfway up my forearms, I make my way to the kitchen where I've stocked up on some fresh groceries and wine.

Tonight, instead of taking her to some fancy dinner with a bunch of nosey, wandering eyes, I've decided to make us a three-course dinner with dessert and wine. I could have had my chef prepare us dinner, freeing up more time for us to connect, but I wanted her to see I'm more than just a man with money. I want her to get to know me beyond the physical.

To know my money doesn't define who I am, and that I won't wield it as a weapon. When I do something nice for her, I want her to know it's because I want to, and not to portray some false persona to win her over. Phony isn't in my DNA.

This morning, I had the entire place deep cleaned and organized, because even though I'm a fairly tidy guy, I wanted to make sure everything was perfect for Mel.

I've always loved the spaciousness of this place. It's six bedrooms on three acres, complete with infinity pool and spa. I've never been self-conscious about it until tonight. Tonight it feels too big. Too unnecessary.

Will Melody see me as just another rich asshole who overindulges?

I don't know what sort of life Melody had before coming to Blue Springs, and it's one of the many things I'm hoping to learn about her tonight. If she can give me a chance, I hope she'll see that my worth isn't what my bank statement reads.

I make sure the bouquet of flowers I'm bringing her tonight are sitting in fresh water. The last woman I bought flowers for never appreciated the gesture, and although tonight is sure to open old wounds, I want to make the effort for Mel. It's cheesy, and if I had another way to describe it, I would, but all I can say for sure is that I have a feeling about this woman.

Melody

The small oval mirror in my bathroom isn't doing me any favors. My flowy black button-up dress, while cinched at the waist with a gold belt and paired with my black cowboy boots accentuates my curves, makes me feel frumpy.

Jackson told me to wear something comfortable, but something tells me he didn't mean showing up in my favorite cow print pajama set that I'd rather be in.

This is dressy, but casual enough to appear like it's effortless. Though, this look has been anything but. The curls in my hair that took me forty minutes are now losing their hold and sit limply on my shoulders. The makeup I took my time with, attempting to look "natural," feels cakey.

Or maybe it's my inner demons playing tricks on me.

"Mama, why are you all dressed up?" Gracie asks, spying on me from the hallway.

I spin around in a panic. "I look dressed up?"

Gracie smiles and nods excitedly as she reaches for the fabric. "I like your beautiful dress."

"You look wonderful. Don't worry, honey," Jane assures me, peeking around the corner.

I don't know why I'm so worried. This is just a date. With a regular person. One date. Harmless, right?

I sigh, smoothing my hands down the front of the dress. "Thank you again for watching Gracie."

She waves me off. "You have to stop thanking me, you know I love my time with this sweetheart."

Janeand I make our way over to the couch, where there's a movie playing for Gracie while I get ready. The girls have puzzles and some sort of craft planned for the evening that includes glue, colored paper, pipe cleaners, and a bunch of fuzzy balls that are littered across the small coffee table in front of the couch.

I sit in between the two, turning toward Jane. I lower my voice. "Is this weird?"

She gives me a puzzled look.

I glance at Gracie, making sure she's preoccupied with the movie, and then turn back to Jane. "Me going on a date with your son?"

She stifles a laugh. "Believe it or not, I'm aware that my son has an interest in women."

I smile at her. "I know. I mean...I don't know what I'm trying to say."

"It's okay, dear, just say it."

"Well, since I don't know what this means for either of us. I don't know if I'll ever be ready for a relationship, but he's a persistent man."

She laughs again, this time earning an echoing laugh from Gracie who has no idea why she's laughing but wants to be included.

"You're worried about hurting him," she states. It's not a question, and she's not wrong.

I nod. "Yes. And no. I'm worried I'll hurt him in the process of protecting myself."

She gives me an understanding look. "Don't overthink things. Go out tonight, have fun. Follow your instincts. You're allowed to explore things even if you're not sure. Especially when you're not sure. That's the beauty of dating. It's not a commitment, it's an exploration to see if two people are a good fit."

Her response surprises me. As a mother, I'm not sure I'd be as gracious toward someone telling me they weren't sure of their interest in my child. But all I can do is be honest with her and myself.

Before I have a chance to respond, there's a knock at the door.

I stand, smoothing out my dress, and make my way to the door before Gracie can beat me to it. We're still working on her letting the adults answer the door.

I swing the door open and I see Jackson standing in front of me looking like sex on a stick.

I thought his gray sweats were deadly. Dear lord.

I take in his black dress shoes, intentionally faded blue jeans, and black dress shirt rolled up to his elbows. His muscular fore-arms are doing things to me that I should be ashamed of with my daughter and his mother standing right behind us.

"H-hi," I sputter.

A sweet grin stretches across his face. "You look beautiful, Melody."

My cheeks heat from the compliment.

"These are for you." He extends his arm out, holding a bouquet of red roses.

Oh. This is a *date* date.

I smile and take the flowers. "Thank you. Please, come in."

We both step inside, and he closes the door behind him.

"Jax!" Gracie shouts, running toward him.

I watch as he instinctively bends down and lifts her up into a hug. Her little feet dangle in the air, and the grin on his face tells me that he's equally happy to see her.

My heart squeezes against my better judgment. My stomach does somersaults at the scene playing out in front of me and what could be. But my mind sends flashes of warning lights through my mind, snapping me out of my trance.

"Jax, you look so handsome," his mother tells him as he sets Gracie back on the ground.

He walks over to his mother, greeting her with a kiss on the cheek. "Thanks, Mom."

"I'll set these in some water and we can go."

We say our goodbyes to Gracie and Jane and make our way to his car in the driveway. He follows me to the passenger side, gallantly opening my door for me. Once I'm settled, he quickly circles the front and hops into the driver's seat. His black Rolls-Royce sedan screams luxury with its matte black-and-blue leather interior. It's the kind of car most of my inner circle back in LA would have driven.

A subtle shudder flickers down my body as I try to suppress the familiarity of the lifestyle, the painful memories of the life I used to know.

"I hope you like the roses. I wasn't sure what your favorite flower was, so I played it safe."

I turn my head and smile as we back out of the driveway. "They're beautiful. If I had to pick a favorite flower, it would be peonies."

I see him mouth the word *peonies*, but he doesn't reply.

I clear my throat. "So, where are we headed tonight?"

He places his hand on my knee, inducing a full-body tingle. I'm a strong woman, but when I'm around him, my body seems to forget what restraint means.

"If it's okay, I planned a quiet evening for us at my place."

"Oh." Is this his clever way to get me to sleep with him?

He turns toward me, likely seeing the panic on my face. "Don't worry. I have no expectations for this evening. If you're uncomfortable at any point, I'll take you home right away."

Reassurance. Without having to ask for it. Without having to beg for it. This is a new one for me. It's never been freely given to me without a fight.

The simple gesture comforts me in a way that Alexander never managed to do in our entire relationship, and I find myself placing my hand over the one he's resting on my knee.

I still have my guard up, but if Jackson Pierce is truly the man he appears to be, I'm in big fucking trouble.

"Wow, this is your place?" I ask as the car makes its way up the long semicircle driveway.

"It's a little big," he responds, sounding almost self-conscious, and for some reason, it makes me like him even more.

Men with money typically come with an ego the size of their McMansions. But sitting next to me is a man who seems to have everything he could ever need, and yet, I can sense the insecurities that still linger.

"No. I mean, yes, but it's amazing. Beautiful."

Jackson turns off the ignition and quickly makes his way around to open my car door, offering me his hand. Placing my hand in his, I step out of the vehicle and glance up at his home. It's grand and stands out in a place like Blue Springs. There aren't many homes in town with this sort of status and grandiose nature.

It's the kind of home I've lived in all my life. The kind of house anyone would love to live in, but right now, all it does is give me flashbacks to the cold, unhappy home I once lived in.

Walking through the front door, the place smells inviting and lived-in. While the lack of decoration and clutter screams "bachelor pad," it's still more inviting than my home with Alexander ever was.

I see lots of warm gray color throughout his house as he leads me hand in hand through the main entrance to his living space, down a long, wide hallway. What surprises me is that he's incorporated pops of color throughout each area. While not fully decorated the way a woman might, I see colorful art on the walls and vases of orange and yellow flowers throughout the abode. I swallow hard, taking with it the jealousy and insecurities attempting to creep up.

"It smells amazing in here," I say as we pass by the opening to his very large kitchen, where I see a large granite island filled with an array of fresh vegetables and bottles of wine.

"Thank you. I wanted to make you dinner tonight. I hope you don't mind that we aren't going out."

My heart does an embarrassing flip-flop. A man who so easily could have flaunted his wealth by taking me to any high-end restaurant has decided to make me a meal himself. It's sadly one of the nicest things anyone has ever done for me.

I choke back my simmering emotions. "That sounds wonderful."

He leads me to a couch that's dark gray, oversized, soft, and so deep, I could comfortably take a nap on it. The white accent pillows are large and fluffy, making it very inviting.

"Sit, get comfortable. I'll make us a drink. What would you like?" he offers.

"Wine would be great."

He nods, giving me a bright smile. "You got it."

Across from the oversized couch, against the wall, is a large wooden stand with bottles of wine, decanters of alcohol, and glasses set up, along with a bucket of what I assume is ice. He uncorks a bottle of red and fills two glasses. He brings them over and sits next to me, handing me one.

He holds his glass out to me. "Thank you for coming tonight."

I clink his glass. "Thank you for inviting me."

I take a sip of the wine, and at the same time, he asks, "How was your day?"

I set down the glass on the large square glass coffee table in front of us. "It was good. Gracie and I ran some errands, and she helped me clean the cabin." I pause, hearing the mundaneness of it. "It sounds boring, but it's nice to spend time with her. She's a really great helper."

I can feel my heartbeat racing with my lame response. This man is a millionaire who owns his own company, and I'm sure running errands with a four-year-old is not his idea of a "good day."

He smiles at me. "I really admire what you're doing."

My eyebrows pull together. "What do you mean?"

"Being a single mother is an incredibly difficult thing to do."

My breath catches. It's not the response I expected, nor is the emotion it generates. I lift my glass and take another sip, stalling until I find the words to respond.

He continues when I don't speak. "I was raised by one, and I know firsthand how hard they work. How demanding it is. How lonely it can be."

We are about five minutes into this date, I cannot get choked up already.

I sigh. "It is the hardest thing I've ever done. Though, I don't really know any other way."

Jackson puts his glass down and scoots closer. "Was Gracie's father never in the picture?"

"Yes and no. Physically, he was there, I suppose. Occasionally. He wasn't what you'd call a 'hands-on' father."

Jackson shakes his head. "That's a shame."

I nod.

"Gracie is such a sweet girl. I can't imagine anything more important than her."

I scoff. "Oh, he found things."

The *things* he found were not only work, friends, and extracurricular activities, but other women as well. In Alexander's eyes, all of those came before me and Gracie.

"He's an idiot."

"What happened between him and me, I don't care. But I hate the way he broke her heart. She asks for him, and I don't know what to say. I feel like I'm failing her every single day."

Well, I sure didn't mean to unload all of that on a first date.

"You're wrong."

"About which part?" I ask.

"All of it. I've seen that little girl. The way she is with you, with other people. She's loving, sweet, thoughtful, smart, and beautiful. Whatever choices you made, I know it was for the benefit of that girl. She's perfect. You're absolutely not failing her."

I have to look away, because I'm not very comfortable being emotional in front of others, and when it comes to my daughter, I become incredibly emotional. The tears in my eyes threaten to fall, but I hold them at bay. I don't want to show Jackson all the pain I have inside. All the wounds that are just starting to scab over and heal. They're still tender, and the slightest nick would pry them right open again.

When I turn my head back toward him, he's moved closer. Our faces are mere inches apart. He's looking at me, not only with heat, but a tenderness I can't place. A look I'm not sure I've ever seen.

He lifts his hand to cradle my cheek, and as I lean into it, he does the same. The self-conscious part of me panics and pulls away. I want to kiss him so badly, but not like this. Not with my insecurities sitting out in the open, between us like an exhibit of trauma.

He gives me a warm smile. "What do you say, should we start with the first course?"

I nod.

He stands and takes my hand in his as we make our way to the dining room across the hall. The large dark wood table has eight chairs but is set for two. Dim lighting is created by candles arranged on the table. It's a little over the top, but it's beautiful and romantic.

Jackson pulls out my seat and sets off for the kitchen to retrieve the first course. He returns and sets a plate in front of each of us filled with crisp greens and a citrusy-smelling vinaigrette.

I take a bite, savoring the fresh flavors, when I realize he's not eating, he's watching me. I clear my throat and try not to let it make me awkward.

"So tell me. If you weren't Blue Springs's jump rope god, what would you be doing?" I ask before forking another bite of the pear salad into my mouth.

He laughs. "Oh, is that what I am?"

I shrug. "That's basically the sentiment I get from anyone who knows you."

He playfully rolls his eyes like he's not comfortable with the outlandish compliment. "I'm not sure. I've always been drawn to it, so it's hard to picture anything else. I love what I do."

A derisive laugh huffs out of me.

"That was corny, wasn't it?" he asks self-consciously.

I shake my head. "No, sorry. I was just thinking how nice that must be. To love what you do."

"What would you love to do?" he asks.

I ponder it for a moment. My family has always had money, and then I married into another family that has always been well-off. I never had to think about what I wanted to do, because everything was already set up for me. But now that I'm on my own with Gracie, doing a job I'm grateful for but loathe, there's one thing that keeps popping into the forefront of my thoughts.

"I think I'd like to help people."

"How so?" he asks, leaning forward on one elbow, his hand pressed under his chin, gazing at me attentively.

I smile. "I've never really told anyone this, but I think it would be really great to set up a group home or safe house. For women who leave or are trying to escape abusive relationships and don't have anywhere to go. I think I would like that."

"Wow," Jackson says softly.

The puppy dog look Jackson's giving me right now is exactly what I don't want. The pity and sorrow. The weepy *what has she been through* look. There's a stigma around women who have been through what I have, and the last thing I need is for another man to look at me like I'm weak.

And just like that, we have tacked on another reason I have no business getting mixed up with a new man.

Fuck, Melody, you should have kept your mouth shut.

CHAPTER 24

Jackson

I don't know if it was the look on my face, or the fact that she verbalized her dream out loud, but something shifted. I don't want to upset her, and I know she's not fragile, but I can't help but feel like she just admitted to going through something horrific.

"Did I say something wrong?" I ask, feeling the sharp turn in mood.

She pulls her lips inward, taking her time to respond. "It's been hard to start over, to stand on my own two feet," she starts. "But I'm really proud of myself. So what I don't want is anybody feeling sorry for me."

My face scrunches into confusion. "Melody, I don't feel sorry for you."

"The look of pity said it for you."

"I apologize for whatever look my face gave off. Whatever you've gone through, I can see how strong it's made you. I don't pity you. If anything, it makes me angry that some asshole felt comfortable enough to wrong you and Gracie in any way."

She seems to mull over my words, then gives me an accepting nod.

"For the record, I think that's a wonderful idea. It might be the most selfless thing I've ever heard," I tell her in between bites of salad.

She shrugs.

"I mean it, Mel, you've got a great heart. Gracie's lucky to have a mom like you."

If there's anyone who would be perfect for this job, it's Melody, and I can't help but remember my friend Wes is coming to town soon. This could be a fantastic project for him to jump into.

She swallows her bite and responds. "Thank you for saying that. I do my best. If I have a happy child, that's all that matters."

"You remind me of my mom sometimes."

Her eyebrow raises, and she laughs uncomfortably, sitting back with her hands in her lap. "I remind you of your mom? That's..."

"No, I mean in the way you're so strong and independent."

Her gaze softens.

"I can recall my mother saying very similar things to me as a child. I never had a strong male father figure to look up to, or take care of us, and so my mom took everything on herself. I've always admired her work ethic, her strength, her resilience. I see those things in you. You should know they're very admirable."

She smiles. "Your mother is great. Gracie and her have the best time together. It's so nice to have someone I fully trust with her."

I nod. "My mom is crazy about her."

She's pushing the food around her plate, deep in thought. I can see the wheels turning.

"What is it?" I ask.

Her gaze stays glued on her plate. "I don't know what this is between us. But I think it's important to not flaunt it around in front of Gracie. Things are confusing enough for her, and I don't want anyone to get hurt."

I can't help but think she's not only referring to Gracie.

I reach over and place my hand on top of hers. "Hey, it's okay. We can take things as slow as you want. I'm happy just to get to know you."

Her gaze meets mine, and she gives me a soft smile.

"Turtle's pace. Snail's pace. Whatever you need, Mel."

She nods, and it seems to be exactly what she needed to hear as I watch her release a tense breath. Just like that, the tension has subsided and we continue through the evening.

I lead her into the kitchen and she sits on a bar stool while I make quick work of cooking our steaks and lobster to perfection. Melody watches as we chat back and forth about nothing in particular.

We drink our wine and finish our plates. Afterward, I bring out a blueberry cheesecake I prepared this morning and coffee for dessert. As we nibble on small bites, the conversation progresses to less serious topics. Melody tells me what she's liked most since moving here, how Gracie is adjusting, and about her time at Blue Bistro. We laugh and swap stories about Blue Springs's notorious grump, Brenda.

When we finish up, I clear our plates and offer to show Melody the rest of my home.

I give her the full tour of the downstairs, and then we make our way up the staircase, and I show her the guest bedrooms, and arrive at my bedroom door last.

"Is this your room?" she asks.

I nod. "Do you want to see it?"

She smirks. "Do I want to see how a jump rope god unwinds? Absolutely."

I laugh at her teasing and push the door open. I extend my

arm outward, inviting her in and stand back as she takes in the space.

She walks over to my king-size bed and runs her hand across the gray and black striped bedding. My laptop sits on one of the bedside tables, next to my cell. The other side table has a small vase of yellow flowers in it.

"You have a lot of flowers," she says, turning toward me with a smirk.

I walk toward her. "Summer made me sign up for a weekly delivery because she said it looked too much like a bachelor pad without them."

She laughs. "I knew it."

"What?"

"That it was the work of a woman. Men typically don't care about decorating their homes with floral arrangements."

"Is that bad?" I ask self-consciously.

It hadn't occurred to me with Melody and Summer's growing friendship, but maybe my close relationship with Summer bothers her.

She shakes her head. "No. I can just pick up on other women's influence when it comes to men."

My lips pull down at her comment. I want to dive into her brain and find out what she's been through so I can do everything in my power to be the opposite of everything that's hurt her.

I try to keep the mood light. "I don't bring women here. Summer is the only one that's been here, and she forces me to get flowers because she's a control freak."

Melody laughs. "I could see that. I love the way she knows what she wants. She's so sure of herself. So confident."

"She's a spitfire, alright."

Melody lowers to the bed, and I take a seat next to her.

"You've never brought a woman here?" she asks.

I shake my head.

"But you brought me here."

My lips turn upward and I nod. I place my hand over hers. "I don't know if you've noticed, but I like you, Mel."

She sighs heavily. "I like you, too. Things are just... complicated."

"Complicated how?" I ask, automatically dreading the worst.

Another man she's been seeing. Her ex.

She pulls her bottom lip between her teeth, thinking. "With Gracie and everything."

She has already made it clear she doesn't want to flaunt whatever this is in front of her daughter, so I can't help but wonder what else she's alluding to.

I nod. "You're not ready to let another man into her life."

She confirms with a nod.

"Like you said, we're going slow. There's no pressure. And whatever else you're worried about, we'll figure it out as it comes."

Her blue eyes bore deep into mine. "Are you real?"

The question surprises me, causing a laugh to burst from my chest. "I think so."

"You're a very patient and understanding man. It's refreshing."

"Look, I know I can be a little pushy, but I want you to be with me because you want to. Not because you feel like I've forced you to."

My last serious relationship is a prime example of that. I held onto her so tight, scared to lose her, and in the end, all I did was chase her away. I've always wondered if things would have turned out differently had I given her the space she needed. Would I still have wound up heartbroken and humiliated?

"I do want to be here. But I don't want to lead you on. I don't want to hurt you. I've been on the receiving end of pain in a relationship, and I don't want to be the person delivering it."

Her and me both.

"I'm a big boy. You've been very transparent with me. If this becomes too much, we can pull back and just be friends."

Am I scared to have such strong feelings for a woman I have known for such a short time? Fuck yeah. But I'm also smart enough to know that women like her don't come around very often, so whether we progress or fizzle out, I need to see what this is.

She leans forward and plants a soft kiss on my cheek and pulls back slowly, lingering close. "I don't think I can be your friend, Jackson."

Her voice is quiet, almost a whisper. It draws me in, like a moth to a flame.

"Why not?" I ask.

"Because I've never wanted to do to my friends what I picture doing with you."

My heart rate accelerates as I envision all the things Melody could possibly be thinking.

"Maybe we shouldn't be friends, then," I whisper back.

I caress her cheek with the back of my fingers and then wrap my hand around the side of her neck and slowly pull her closer to me. Our mouths are so close I can feel her warm breath on my face. I think she might pull away again, but she closes the distance and presses her lips to mine.

Her lips are soft and supple, and as we deepen the kiss, her tongue slips into my mouth, giving me full-body chills. I feel her hands slide around my back, pressing me into her, and I respond by moving my hand into her hair, holding her even closer.

A small, quiet moan slips from Mel, and damn if it doesn't turn me on instantly.

This woman has had a hold on me from the moment I saw

her, and now that she's here in my bedroom making these noises, I don't know how I'll ever get her out of my system.

The kiss takes on a life of its own, becoming more fervid and needy. We're both breathing heavily, our hands roaming each other's bodies, becoming familiar with the shape and slope of each other's curves. Melody suddenly pulls away, gasping for air.

I take my hands off her, leaning back slightly. "Everything okay?"

"Yeah." She pauses with a hand to her mouth. "Sorry. That was...intense."

I smirk. *Fuck yeah, it was. The raging hard-on in my pants can attest to that.*

Right then, I hear a beep coming from Mel's phone, and she immediately pulls it out and checks her message.

I see a pained look cross her face.

"Everything okay?" I ask again.

Her mouth pulls to the side as she reads the message once more. "It's your mom. She said Gracie is having a hard time sleeping. She keeps saying she misses me."

I grab her hand and give it a squeeze. "Come on, I'll take you home."

"I'm sorry. She's not used to being away from me."

"Hey, there's no need to apologize. She comes first," I assure her.

"Thank you."

I smile, giving her one last soft kiss on the lips, and then we head out to the car. I drop her off and watch her walk up the steps to her front door since she declined my offer to walk her up. The drive over was quiet, and I could tell she was lost in thought. I don't know if she started to regret what happened, but her mind was definitely elsewhere. I just hope she's not going to pull back again.

CHAPTER 25

Melody

"Order up!"

Today's shift has been nonstop with the farmer's market laid out across Main Street. People have been in and out since I got here, and I can definitely use the tips.

I wash my hands after dropping some dirty dishes in the dish pit and tray up the hot food to take out to one of Mary's tables. They ask me for refills, and as I head back to retrieve them, I see Mary in the back filling another drink order.

"Hey, table six asked for another Pepsi and iced tea. Want me to grab them for you?" I ask.

She waves me off, already grabbing two fresh glasses. "Thanks honey, I've got it. So, when are you going to tell me who that outrageous bouquet of peonies is from?"

I stand at the computer, printing out a few tickets to have ready, and glance over at the bouquet on the shelf in the back. A large arrangement of pink and white peonies sits in a clear vase. They're from Jackson, and I'm fairly certain she knows it, but Mary loves the gossip.

Jackson has sent me flowers at work every single day for the last week and a half since our date, and they all come with a small note attached that says *For my favorite hump roper.*

"A friend," I simply reply.

"Those" —she points to the flowers— "are not flowers friends send."

I laugh at her candor.

"Maybe it's a close friend," I respond coyly.

She props a hand on her hip. "Mm-hmm. Is this the same friend that's in here a few times a week to see you?"

I shrug.

"Melody Miller, you are bad!" she says and playfully smacks my shoulder on her way out to the dining room.

I giggle. It's nice to banter with someone at work who knows my past yet doesn't pity me or look at me like I'm fragile. She's worth more than every "friend" I lost back in LA put together.

On her way out with the tray of drinks, she glances back over her shoulder. "You deserve it, honey. Enjoy yourself while you're still young."

I'm a single mom living in someone else's home, starting my life from scratch. I don't feel young at all. Although training with Summer for the last few weeks has certainly helped me feel better in my body, which is something I haven't been able to say in a long time.

As if I've summoned her, I feel my phone vibrate in my back jeans pocket and pull it out to see a text from Summer.

Summer: Are we still on for 6?

Me: Yes! Earlier if it slows down enough.

Summer: Great, I'll have the smoothies ready! ;)

A FEW HOURS, endless ramekins of ketchup, refills of iced tea, and two spilled drinks later, and I am finally clocking out and counting my tips from the day. My feet and legs are aching from running around all day, but counting the two hundred dollars in my apron is well worth it. Usually I'd find an excuse to get out of a workout, but I'm riding the high of actually making good money at work tonight, so I'm looking forward to training with Summer. Although jump rope tricks are hard, they don't feel like working out.

I walk through the doors to Jumping Jax and head to the locker room to change. I slip into my black leggings, sports bra, and oversized tee, and walk over to the mats.

Summer is already waiting with her white rope in hand, chatting with a guy I've seen frequently around the gym. I walk toward her slowly, not quite sure if I should interrupt. They look deep in conversation, and I don't want to be rude. But she spots me out of the corner of her eye before I get the chance.

"Melody!" she shouts, pats the guy on the shoulder and then walks toward me.

I watch as the guy sulks away, clearly not happy that the interaction has already concluded.

"Sorry," I tell her.

"For what?" She laughs.

"I didn't mean to interrupt."

"You didn't." Her eyebrows pull together.

"You sure? He didn't look too thrilled to watch you walk away."

She waves a hand in front of me like I'm being ridiculous. "We weren't even talking about anything. He's just friendly. He always comes to say hi."

"Yeah, because he wants you."

She rolls her eyes. "He does not."

I give her an incredulous look.

"He doesn't!"

"What's it like to be so beautiful and blissfully unaware that every man in your orbit wants to be with you?"

A laugh bursts from her chest, and she doubles over in laughter. Her ponytail flips over in her face, and she straightens up with a tear rolling down her face.

"I'm being serious," I tell her.

"Mel, the irony of that is too good."

"What the heck are you talking about?"

She cocks an eyebrow at me. "Jax."

"I'm not oblivious to him."

"Well, you were at first. And you sure are fighting it for some reason."

For lots of reasons, actually. The fact that I've got a daughter who will always need me. A child I'm not ready to introduce to a new man—a man who's not her father—until I'm absolutely certain of him. Not to mention, her father, who I haven't quite had closure with yet.

I'm not oblivious to Jackson's attraction to me. It's more like confusion as to why a man like him, who could get any woman he wants, is interested in a single mom with a good amount of baggage. A single mom who works insane hours for very little money and spends most of her time covered in sticky little kid fingers and planning her next baking day.

No. I'm well aware of our connection, but it's confusing and complicated when I'm not in the position to fully let him in.

"I'm...not," I lie.

She smirks at me, rolling her eyes. "Whatever you need to tell yourself, babe."

There's no point in arguing with someone like Summer, she's going to call you out on all of your bullshit every single time. She's the kind of friend that has your back but won't sugarcoat things and lie to make you feel better.

"How about we discuss *your* dating life," I fire back.

She purses her lips. "I don't have a dating life."

"And why is that?"

"Because the men here are freaks...aside from Jackson, of course," she adds.

I laugh. "Okay, now give me the real reason."

She smooths her hands down her ponytail. "I don't know. Maybe I'm going for the wrong kind of guy. Men our age are... still acting like they're nineteen."

My insides twist at her comment, thinking about the selfish, juvenile way Alexander behaved our entire relationship. The cheating, the lying, the gaslighting. The ironic part is that he's a few years older than I am.

I sigh. "Yeah, I know what you mean."

She gives me a knowing look. Something tells me that Summer has seen her fair share of heartbreak and betrayal, too.

"I think I need to go for someone older, independent, successful, and utterly obsessed with me. Is that so much to ask for?" she questions, throwing her hands up dramatically.

Since neither of us currently has that relationship, maybe it is.

I shake my head. "It's not a lot to ask for."

"Easy for you to say, Jackson has been obsessed with you since the moment he saw you."

I don't know why but hearing her say that makes me feel more uneasy than happy. Not that I don't think it's sweet, but all it does is remind me that I'm not being fair to him. I'm not ready to jump into things with him, so stringing him along seems unfair. I need to make a decision and either dive in head first or let him go.

"Can we jump already?" I plead.

"Okay, okay. Your mummy kicks are great. Have you been working on your side swings?"

"Yes and no."

She laughs.

"I've been working on them, but I somehow keep hitting myself with the rope when I swing the rope to the outside."

"Hmm. Show me."

I grab my pink rope in both hands and begin jumping, and then move into the side swings, but sure enough, I smack myself in the head once I try to bring the rope back to center from the outside.

Summer and I laugh when I stop and nurse my wound.

"Every single time," I tell her, half amused, half annoyed.

"I'll demonstrate again, and we'll just take it slow," Summer tells me, getting into position when Jackson strides toward us.

Our eyes meet and instantly his megawatt grin spreads across his cute face. As much as I fight our attraction, everything about him draws me in. It's like the harder I try to convince myself I should end this thing with him, the more the universe goes out of its way to give me tempting reasons to continue.

"Hey Summer. Melody."

"Jax, can't you flirt with Melody later? We're in the middle of a lesson."

My cheeks heat, and Jackson simply rolls his eyes.

"Actually, I came to let you know that I need to head out to the Denver location for a few days."

"Everything okay? Doesn't Ember have everything under control?" Summer asks.

He puts his hands in the pockets of his black Adidas pants. "Oh yeah, she's doing a great job. But with everything that happened, I told myself I was going to be more hands-on at other locations, too. I don't want anything falling through the cracks again."

Summer nods. "I understand. When are you going?"

Jackson glances at me and says, "Today."

There's instantly a pit in my stomach, knowing I won't see him for a few days. Knowing that new flowers won't be at work waiting for me. I feel stupid for being upset when I'm so unsure about where I stand with him. I do my best to ignore the unwarranted disappointment.

"Alright, what do you need from me?" Summer asks, but Jackson's attention is still on me.

His gaze bores deep into mine, and I swear he's asking me to join him. That can't be right, he wouldn't want me to go to Denver with him. Not that I could go anyway, I have a child to take care of. I can't leave her.

"Jax?" Summer asks when he doesn't respond.

He finally turns back to her. "I was hoping you'd be able to take the long shift for the next few days. I know it's a lot to ask…"

She waves him off. "Oh please, it's not like I have anything else to do."

He gives her a friendly smile. "You're a lifesaver, Sum. I owe you."

She gives him a cunning grin. "Damn right, you do. I plan on taking an extended vacation after the festival."

It's clear she's joking, but Jackson nods. "You got it. You should take some time for yourself. Especially if things go well with Wes, you'll be busy for the next few years."

"Who's Wes?" I ask.

"Jax's amazing investor friend who might be helping me make my smoothie shop dream a reality!" Summer shrieks with excitement.

My face lights up. "That's amazing, Summer."

"I'm trying not to get my hopes up, but this is a really big deal." Her face is full of hope, but I can see the trepidation. The voices in her head telling her this might not work out.

"Hey, he's going to love you and your business plan. I have no doubt," Jackson reassures her.

"Thanks Jax," Summer says.

Jackson glances back at me, lips parted like he wants to say something. But he doesn't, and unable to hold his intense gaze, I quickly look away.

"Ooookay, well, if you two are done making goo-goo eyes at each other, I'm in the middle of a training session," Summer jokes.

"I'm going," Jackson says.

I look back up to see him smiling at me.

"Have a safe trip," I tell him.

"Thanks. I guess I'll see you guys in a few days, then," he says before leaving us to our jump ropes.

I don't know why, but he seems disappointed that I didn't say more. I can't shake the feeling that he was trying to tell me something. Even when Summer and I finish our training session, and I'm on my way home, I can't get it off my mind.

Does Jackson want me to go to Denver with him?

CHAPTER 26

Jackson

Though I'm definitely more of a small-town kinda guy, there's something about the big city that makes me feel electric. Being here feels like I've made it.

When I arrived yesterday, the gym was back in great shape, thanks to Ember. She's been my rock star and has unsurprisingly transformed the train wreck into a once again flourishing establishment. Ember is similar to her sister in the way that they're both sunshine personified. They're easy to get along with, and you'd be hard-pressed to find a person who doesn't like either of them.

Ember has helped me find two new day managers to help run the day-to-day tasks, and they're proving to be great fits so far. Both women are very energetic, outgoing, and have a great sense of humor. Overall, the vibe at this location has greatly improved.

"Jackson, I have a new client sign-up. I thought you'd like to come out and introduce yourself," Ember announces, peeking into my office.

She has a hands-on style and always goes above and beyond. It was her idea for me to personally introduce myself to the new members whenever I'm in town to make them feel welcomed and seen.

I glance up from my computer. "Great job, Ember, I'll be right out."

I greet the newcomers and give them a tour of the gym, then head back to my office to get through more emails, but what I really wanna do is message Melody. I've been dying to text her all day. Her reaction when I said I was leaving was not quite what I expected. We had a great date together, and I thought we were making progress, but it feels like she's pulling back again and I don't know why.

Each day I send her flowers, and each day I receive a selfie with a sweet message thanking me. I'd be lying if I said I didn't look forward to that picture every day.

I haven't heard from her today even though the delivery receipt text alerted me that her flowers arrived a few hours ago. Today's assortment are purple peonies, with the same note I attach every day.

I decide to shoot her a text, knowing I won't see her for a few days.

> Me: I hope you like your flowers. *impatiently waiting for your beautiful selfie*

I DON'T IMMEDIATELY SEE her typing, and I shamelessly watch the screen for too long before putting it down and shifting my attention back to my work.

About half an hour later, my phone pings and I see a message from Melody. Not a text, an image. She's holding the vase of purple peonies, and her face is slightly buried in them as she inhales their scent. She's smiling, and her hair is down in loose curls. She's wearing her white Blue Bistro T-shirt, so I'd venture to say she just got off work.

> Me: You look beautiful.

FEELING BRAVE, I send another text before she replies.

> Me: I miss you.

Melody: You do?

I LAUGH, and it echoes through my office.

> Me: Of course I do.

Melody: It's been one day. 😆

> Me: I know. 🐵 How has your day been?

Melody: Good. Just got off work. About to go hump rope with Summer.

> Me: 😝

Melody: *Jump.* Every time. 🙈

> Me: Your phone has a dirty mind, Mel.

Melody: Apparently so.

Me: I'm starting to think you're doing it on purpose.

Melody: Why would I be doing that intentionally?

Me: To try and seduce me. Don't try and deny it.

I LAUGH TO MYSELF, hoping that she's picking up on my playfulness. Melody is so serious all the time that I enjoy making the effort to pull her out of her head and make her laugh.

Melody: Busted. You caught me.

Me: I knew it.

Melody: Is it working, Mr. Pierce?

Me: How formal of you.

Melody: Is it working, stud?

Melody: How's that?

Me: Not bad. Why don't you come see for yourself though?

Melody: ...

THOSE THREE DANCING dots pop up and disappear for the longest time, and I worry I've made her uncomfortable. I only intend to be playful, but when she doesn't respond at all, I can't help but worry. This woman is hard to figure out, but damn it if I don't want to keep trying.

Instead of agonizing over the conversation, and overanalyzing why she never responded, I make my rounds through the gym. I place weights back where they belong, wipe down equipment, and make sure nobody is struggling for a spot. There's nothing worse than working out alone, thinking you've got a rep and slowly letting it crush you until someone notices you fighting for your life. This is why I always make sure at least one staff member is making rounds and keeping an eye out for members' safety. It puts our clients at ease, and it makes the experience at Jumping Jax much more enjoyable for everyone.

Though the anger has died down from the now-terminated male managers, I still feel the pressure to be on top of things at all locations. The anxiety of saving face and not allowing the company I worked so hard to build crumble has caused more stress than normal. Which is exactly why I love jumping rope.

After making my rounds, sitting in a staff meeting, and having a snack I decide to get in my own workout. I have plenty of ropes at this gym but always travel with my favorite black one.

Moving my body, being physical, and pushing my body to its limits allows me to break away from the daily stressors. All my attention must go to the way my body is moving, otherwise I could end up with an injury. Physical activity doesn't allow the mind to wander very long, because you're pulled back to your moves, your screaming muscles, and the euphoric high afterward. It's one of the most rewarding things a human can do, and why I look forward to the end-of-summer festival every year. I want to introduce this lifestyle to as many kids as possible.

Not all kids have an easy childhood and can't afford the same expensive distractions other kids might be able to, but a jump rope is something most kids can obtain. And if not, that's where I come in. I happily supply the town, and those visiting each year, with a rope that I hope will be an escape for them, the way it was for me.

With my headphones blaring in my ears, and sweat dripping down my chest and back, my muscles feel warm and achy in a good way. I've worked through a routine that I have been working on to perform at the festival, and it's starting to feel fluid and polished.

I'm practicing one of the more difficult moves: double unders to mic release, as I face the entrance of the gym so I can keep an eye on the few protesters that still linger out front. They've been well-behaved, but being the last ones remaining, I know they're the most angry. Ember and the two new managers asked if I wanted to have them removed, but I decided to let them stay. I am not the man they think I am, and I'm not running the slimy establishment they're convinced it is. If they want to stay and see with their own eyes, so be it.

Just as I've finished the routine, my eyes catch on a woman sauntering up to the entrance. I watch through the glass doors as her curvy sway gets closer and more visible.

I pull my headphones out, drop the rope on the mat, and race toward her, convinced it's a mirage.

She couldn't be here, could she?

Melody's eyes lock on mine, and a smile spreads across her face. "Hi."

Her voice is soft and sweet, but excitement dances in her eyes.

My smile matches hers. "Are you really here?"

She shrugs. "I wanted to surprise you."

My eyes roam her body, like they've ached to see her. Her skintight acid-wash jeans hug her luscious curves, and what I'm assuming is a black bodysuit tucked into them accentuates her perky breasts. I glance down and see her low-top black Chucks, making her outfit sweet, yet sexy.

A bark of laughter escapes me. "I'm definitely surprised." I grab her hand and lead her into my office. "Come on."

She follows me in, watching as I close the door behind us. Suddenly, she looks nervous. "I hope this is okay."

I lean in and give her a quick kiss. "Of course it is."

"How long are you here for?" I ask, not fully understanding the reason for her visit.

Is Gracie in town with her? If not, who's watching her?

How long is she here for?

We stand facing each other, both unsure what to do. "I guess that depends on you. What you want."

Oh.

My eyebrows shoot up. She's definitely here for me.

My chest swells with excitement, but my stomach fills with unease. This woman has been hot and cold with me, and now here she is, surprising me while out of town at my work, where there's tons of prying eyes. Lots of employees that would probably be happy to start rumors that will no doubt make it to social media in no time. Protesters out front that absolutely won't miss an opportunity to dish on any news regarding me or my gym. The issue is, I don't know if it's smart for me to be seen with her yet. Not when I'm not sure where we stand or what she wants. This woman is an enigma, one who could easily break my heart. I've known it from the minute I saw her, and every time I think I'm getting through, she pulls back. So, while I'm excited she's here and I couldn't wait to see her, I'm feeling uneasy about the whole thing.

I swallow the doubts and lean in, wrapping my arms around her, and fusing our lips together. She leans into me, melting into the kiss.

"I missed you," I tell her.

"You said to come see if my seduction was working," she

says, placing her hand over my pants and quickly finding my growing erection. "Clearly, it is."

I chuckle. "Yeah, it usually does."

It's instantaneous anytime I'm around her. This woman has a choke hold on me that I've never experienced, which makes getting close to her all the more tricky. It's hard to not dive in headfirst, when I know she could change her mind at any moment and run from this. The push and pull in my own heart and mind is enough to drive a man crazy, but I can't seem to leave her be.

Her hand rubs up and down against my length. This is a more aggressive side of Melody that I've never seen, and I can't say that I hate it. But why now?

"I know you're working," she whispers. "But when you're done, do you want to do something with me?"

I nod. I want to do everything with this woman. "What did you have in mind?"

She shrugs, removing her hand. "Maybe dinner, maybe a board game."

Her coy smile earns one back. "You tease."

I nip at her lip, eliciting a squeal from her.

We're wrapped in each other's arms when there's a knock at the door, startling me. I quickly pull away from Mel and take a few steps back.

"It's open," I shout.

Ember opens the door and startles when she sees there's someone in here with me. "Oh, I'm sorry, I didn't know you had company."

Melody and I aren't together, and I don't want her to feel pressured if I try to label it, so I blurt the first thing that comes to my mind. "This is my friend. She was thinking about joining, so I was going to give her a tour."

Melody's face pinches, and her smile immediately falls.

"Oh, okay. Well, when you're done, there's a new sign-up if you'd like to come out and introduce yourself," Ember says, giving Melody a friendly, curious smile.

"Actually, I should be going," Melody announces brusquely.

"Are you sure?" I ask, feeling like a total moron.

Her eyebrows pull together as she studies my face and mumbles, "Mm-hmm."

"Can you give me a minute? I'll be right out," I ask Ember.

She nods and closes the door behind her, eager to leave the awkward tension in my office.

Melody crosses her arms over her chest. "I'm sorry, I shouldn't have come. This was a silly idea."

I grab her arms and turn her toward me. "No, I don't want you to go. I'll be off in a few hours." I pull a key card from off my desk and hand it to her. "Here's the key for my room at the Four Seasons. Let yourself in, and I'll meet you there."

She makes no effort to move or take the card.

"Please," I plead. "I really want you to stay."

She gives me a tight nod and I slip the card into her hand before kissing her cheek.

I get a thin smile before she opens my office door and hastily exits the gym without looking back.

All of my instincts want to pull her into my arms and kiss her so the entire world knows that she's mine, but she's not. And she's made that pretty clear. I don't have it in me to face another heartbreak, especially in the public eye. As much as I don't love keeping her at arm's length, maybe that's what I need to do until she proves to me that she's done running.

CHAPTER 27

Melody

Note to self: do not go out of your way to surprise a man, ever. Unless you want to suffer severe disappointment, that is.

Jackson told me how much he missed me and even hinted at me coming here in person. So I did. Initially, he looked happy to see me, but was standoffish, strange. Things only got weirder when the stunning blonde came in and interrupted us.

When she came in, Jackson practically leaped to the other side of the room so she didn't see us together. Is this someone he's fooling around with? Dating?

The Jackson I know seems to do and say all the right things, but if there's one thing I've learned, it's that anyone is capable of deceit.

Alexander, who I was with for nearly a decade, hid plenty of things from me, and we had a child together. So who's to say Jackson isn't capable of that, too?

As I make my way through the gym parking lot back to my car, I can't help but feel like I just made a huge, stupid, embarrassing mistake. I left my daughter, sacrificed valuable time with her, to come and surprise a man that clearly doesn't want me here.

Or maybe he's embarrassed of me.

Sitting in the driver's seat, I glance down at my pudgy stomach, my wide hips and thighs spread across the seat, and think about the toned and tanned blonde back at the gym. He was awfully squirrely when she came into the office, and I can't help but feel like that's his type. But what does that make me? An experiment?

I stick the key in the ignition and plan to peel out of here and not look back. Maybe I'll drive the entire way back to Blue Springs blasting A Day to Remember, venting all this pent-up rage. But I pause before I take my car out of park.

Do I make this easy for him? Let him make me feel like shit, and then let him off the hook? After everything he's said to me? After I let him into my daughter's life?

No. If this man is playing games with me, he's going to say it to my face. I have let enough men in this lifetime get away with mistreating me, and I refuse to let it happen again. I am going to get some answers.

I TAP the key card to the door of the luxury suite, because of course, that's the room Jackson Pierce is staying in. It turns green, and as I push the door open, the space before me is more apartment than it is a hotel room. I'm welcomed into a large living space with floor-to-ceiling windows that give an impressive view of the skyscrapers of Denver.

The view at nighttime must be stunning.

There's a large sectional and a table with chairs next to a separate bar area. Farther down the hall to the right is the bedroom and bathroom with an oversized tub. My quaint cottage in Blue Springs isn't half this size.

As I walk through the space, I find a large, oversized closet with Jackson's designer clothes carefully hung on hangers, and his undergarments in the drawers. I begin to get dizzy as I try to figure out which of the two versions of Jackson I know are true.

There's this big city, extravagant, wealthy side of him that terrifies me, but then there's this other side to him. The sensitive, patient, sexy, caring man that loves his mom and doesn't mind baking with Gracie. One that, aside from the car he drives and the incredibly expensive Rolex he wears, doesn't flaunt his money. It scares the living hell out of me, because which one is he, truly?

I make my way out to the main living space and over to the bar area. There's a bucket of ice, cold drinks in the mini fridge, and an array of small bottles of alcohol. While I don't drink a lot, I don't think I can handle being rejected sober.

Tequila and soda it is. There's no limes, but I don't even care. I fix my drink and sit at the large sectional, gazing out at the bustling city below.

I wonder if this is the life Jackson really craves. The busy, fast-paced day-to-day, the exciting nightlife. Blue Springs is a wonderful place to live, providing a quality of life that the city could never compete with. A way of living I've come to really love. Having come from the city, I can confidently say it doesn't hold the same appeal it used to.

I think about walking down Main Street, the smiling faces of the locals who wave and say hello. Bread Pitt, Blue Bistro, and all of the other cute businesses with rich history and familiar hello's. That's what I want. So if this is who Jackson truly is, it's better that we end things now. A rich city boy is the last type of man I'm trying to invite back into my life or Gracie's.

If I were in my twenties and childless, I wouldn't have to

worry about these things, especially so early on, but a single mom has to be ten steps ahead and always thinking of the future.

"Melody." Jackson startles me when he comes through the door.

Having been deep in thought, I didn't hear him come in.

I place my drink on the table in front of me. "I made myself a drink, I hope you don't mind."

"Not at all," he says, walking toward me with a smile. He sits next to me on the couch and faces me. "I can't believe you came here to see me."

I shrug and pick the drink back up, taking a sip.

He reaches over to place a hand on my leg, but I scoot back.

He gives me a quizzical look. "Something wrong?"

I scoff, swirling the ice in my drink. "I was going to ask you the same thing."

He leans back, giving me space. "What do you mean?"

"Are you embarrassed of me, Jackson?"

His head rears back, and his eyes widen. "Why would you think that?"

I stand, feeling the rage building. Like a blast of PTSD from all of the maddening conversations with Alexander when I'd ask him very simple questions, only to be fed nothing but lies and pulled in circles. I don't want to live that life anymore. I can't handle any more lies.

I begin pacing back and forth while Jackson watches.

"Sit and talk to me, please," he begs.

"I left my daughter with a sitter, your mother, actually, so I could come spend time with you. And for what? What was that back there? Just how many women are you fooling around with, Jackson Pierce? I know you have all the money in the world and you're used to getting what you want, primarily from women, I'd assume, but I'm not like them. I can't do this. I *won't* do this."

Jackson doesn't reply right away, and when I finally glance at him, he's grinning at me. It only confuses me further.

"Are you laughing at me?" I seethe.

The one thing I hate more than lies and deceit is not being taken seriously.

He shakes his head and rises. "No."

"Well, it looks like you think this is a joke."

He slowly approaches me, taking both of my hands in his. "You are a firecracker, you know that?"

I shrug.

I wasn't always like this. I used to be the quiet girl, the one who didn't like to rock the boat, or create tension, so I never spoke up. And it got me disrespected and walked all over. So yeah, maybe I'm a little more vocal these days, but I refuse to apologize for it.

"I like that about you, Mel."

I pull my lips to the side, refusing to talk until he gives me answers.

He squeezes my hands. "I'm not fooling around with anybody. But I am dating you. Or I'm trying to, at least."

My eyebrows pull together. "Well, what the hell was that about in your office with the perfect blonde?"

"The blonde?" he asks, grimacing.

I cross my arms and nod.

A small laugh bursts out of him.

"Okay, now you're actually laughing at me," I point out, annoyed.

He waves his hands in front of him. "No, I swear. Melody, that's Ember..."

I give him a look that says *Ooookay, and?*

"Ember...Summer's sister. She's practically my sister."

I can actually feel my face turn green. And I thought today couldn't get any more humiliating.

"Then why did you get so weird when she came in?" Even if what he's saying is true, I didn't imagine the rest.

He chews on his lip. "I did get weird, and I'm sorry. But it didn't have anything to do with her." He pauses. "I want to talk this out with you, but all I can think about is how bad I smell, do you mind if I go shower first?"

Reluctantly, a smile breaks through my angry exterior, and I nod. The small glimpses I get of his insecurities never fail to disarm me.

The other thing that scares me about this man is that even when I'm mad at him, it's hard to stay mad.

"I'll be quick. Help yourself to another drink, or there's a menu by the bed if you want to order room service."

Food does sound good. Is it rude to eat while we're in the middle of an argument or whatever this is?

Fuck it.

I pick up the phone and order two cheeseburgers, fries, and a bowl of green chili. If it comes in the middle of an argument, I guess I'll be making my point between bites of cheeseburger.

I hear the shower turn off about ten minutes later, and Jackson emerges, followed by a billowing cloud of steam that smells woodsy and manly, clean and inviting.

He's shirtless, wearing only his black shorts. His hair is still wet, in a mess of curls on his head, and small water droplets drip from the tips. It makes him look boyish and vulnerable. Nothing like the millionaire prick I was envisioning when I entered this room a few hours ago.

He pads toward me and joins me on the bed where I have been sitting since making the call for room service.

"Did you order food?" he asks.

"Yeah, I ordered us cheeseburgers."

"Thank God, I'm starving," he says, smiling.

I nervously wring my hands, still not sure how to feel about us or this situation.

"I'm sorry I upset you, Mel. You surprised me, and I guess I wasn't prepared how to handle your visit. And I reacted...unfavorably."

I give him a *No shit* tight smile.

"This was a great surprise. I want you to know that."

I rub my forehead. "I don't understand. Are you embarrassed of me? Do you not want to be seen in public with me when all those leggy blondes are around? Is that it?"

His eyebrows pull together, his tone turning absolutely serious. "No, not at all. How could you think that?"

I hold my arm out toward the door. "Did you not see yourself back there? You practically blew me off and wouldn't touch me when anyone was around. What am I supposed to think?"

He runs his hands through his hair. "Yeah, that looks bad."

I don't respond, and he reaches out and grabs my hand. "I have absolutely no reason to be embarrassed to be with you. You're a fucking prize, an absolute goddess, and I would love nothing more than to shout from the rooftops that you're mine. But..."

"But?" I ask.

"But you're not. And I'm not yours. You've made that pretty clear. And that's fine. This whole thing terrifies me, too. I don't want you to think I'm pressuring you into something you're not ready for, because I understand completely. But when Ember was looking at me, I didn't know how to introduce you. I was scared that if I slapped a label on us, you'd go running for the hills again."

"I don't run," I retort.

He raises an eyebrow at me, challenging me.

"Maybe I do a little."

"I was scared, Mel. You scare me."

The irony of that makes me laugh. I've been so terrified to let him in, get close to him, yet here he is telling me he's scared of me. What upside down, hot millionaire sixth dimension did I fall into?

"Why would you be scared of me?"

"It has to do with my ex. Shaina."

"What about her?" I ask.

Room service chooses that moment to arrive with a loud knock at the door. I'm both relieved that food is here, because I'm also starving, yet annoyed at the timing.

I'm not sure what Jackson is about to reveal, but something tells me we should probably eat beforehand because I have a feeling that afterward, neither of us is going to have an appetite.

CHAPTER 28

Jackson

The last time I was in this hotel room, I admittedly pictured Melody here with me. Just the two of us on this very bed. A small escape from our everyday lives, soaking up the company, and getting lost in each other's bodies. But not once did I envision opening up about my shitty past with Shaina and the hell she put me through.

But knowing that Melody left the gym thinking I was embarrassed of her makes me feel not only like an idiot but also an asshole.

The room service waiter wheels in a tray of food and leaves the plates on the dining table, covered. I walk him to the door, hand him a tip, and close the door.

"Oh my God, that smells delicious," Melody says.

"Should we eat first?" I ask.

"Might as well, or it'll get cold. I can't imagine those burgers were cheap."

"If it gets cold, I'll order you another one. I'm not worried about it."

She makes a face, but pads over to the table. "Let's eat."

We both tear into the burgers and take turns with the delicious green chili. That's what I love most about Colorado. Everyone has their version of green chili, yet they're all uniquely delicious. Considering the circumstances, we eat in a comfortable silence. It's always easy with Melody.

It doesn't take us long to finish, and I offer to make us both a drink.

"What were you drinking?" I ask.

"Tequila soda."

I mix the drinks up, and we head back to the couch to sit more comfortably. Melody is toying with the straw in her cup, avoiding eye contact. I know this conversation needs to happen, for the both of us, but that doesn't mean it's going to be easy.

"First off, I want to apologize if my actions made you feel like I wasn't over the moon to see you. I was surprised, and then, I guess I panicked a little."

She sighs. "I knew it."

I reach over and grab her hand. "It's not what you think." I take a deep breath, preparing myself to finally relive the worst time in my life. "Shaina is my ex. We dated for years, and I thought we were in love. It turns out, she wasn't ready to settle down."

"She broke up with you?" Mel asks softly, her eyes looking into mine, full of sympathy.

I shake my head. "Not exactly. I found out through social media that she was sleeping with my close friend. They had accidentally uploaded a picture of them kissing to her page. Though, in hindsight, maybe it was her cowardly way to end things without having to do it outright."

I put air quotes around the word *accidentally* because I never really believed it wasn't intentional. Something about the whole incident felt calculated. As if neither of them had the balls to face me and give me the truth and this was their way around having an actual conversation.

Melody raises her hand to her mouth and gasps softly.

"They had been having an affair for months. I had no idea, and I felt like such an idiot. My followers found out before I did. The onslaught of messages and tags I received, and the sheer amount of DMs with screenshots, was overwhelming. It was a humiliating way to find out. Being betrayed is bad enough, but when it becomes a public spectacle, it does something to a person. It broke me." I pause, making sure I word the next part the right way. "When I saw you today, I think I panicked about PDA with you. I think I still feel people watching and judging. It scared me because neither of us are sure what we want yet."

She gives me an understanding nod.

"Everything Shaina put me through came rushing back. It was the worst time in my life. All the whispering and staring. It was awful. The next time I go public with a woman, I want to know that we're in it together. She made me look like a fool, and as confident as I might come across, it stings. I still carry it with me."

She licks her lips. "That makes a lot of sense. I'm so sorry she did that to you."

"I wish she had gone about it in a different way, but she did me a favor."

Melody cocks an eyebrow at me. "How so?"

"We clearly weren't meant to be together, and now I get to sit here with you."

Melody's lips pull up slightly into a sad smile. "Still, nobody should have to go through that."

I watch the way her eyes are shimmering with tears, and her mouth pulls downward. She's not saying it to be polite, she's saying it because the pain is familiar to her.

"Listen, I told you because I can't have you walking around thinking there's anything wrong with you. You've been the best surprise of my life. I'm *proud* to be around you, Mel."

She sniffles and shakes her head. "I'm confused."

"About what?"

"We hang out all the time in Blue Springs. Everyone asks me about you, they know there's something going on. You visit me at work weekly. The flowers. You don't try to hide it."

My mouth pulls to the side. "Blue Springs is family. It's different there. Sure, they might love to gossip, but it's harmless. Those people have my back, and I don't worry about anything winding up on social media. The city is different. Unfortunately, I'm known by so many people here that at times it can be a bit of a circus, especially with all eyes on my gym after this recent scandal."

She mulls over my words, deciding whether to believe them or not. It sounds like an excuse, but it's not. When I'm in Denver, I become a public figure, one whose personal life has been scrutinized and used against me.

I lift my hand and cup her cheek. "Melody, I promise I'm not embarrassed of you. That's absurd, have you seen yourself?"

She rolls her eyes, as if I'm lying to make her feel better.

"Hey, don't do that. You're stunning. I can't get enough of you. You know that, don't you?"

She shrugs.

"I need to do a better job, then," I tell her.

"I get a little insecure sometimes, I guess."

"I noticed."

"We all have a past, and I can't blame you for being reactive to something that reminded you of yours. I get it more than you know." She pauses. "I don't mean to be indecisive about...us. I'm scared, too."

There's something comforting in knowing she's also scared. She has as much at stake in this as I do, and that's new for me. Shaina was well aware of how attractive she was. Men were always throwing themselves at her, and it always felt like she had a plan B if we didn't work out.

My lips curve up into a warm smile. "In the spirit of neither of us wanting to get hurt, I have a proposal."

Her eyes sparkle with intrigue. "What kind of proposal?"

"The end-of-summer festival is in about two months. How about we continue taking things slow? We can make the festival our check-in point and decide how we feel about things then. It gives us time to get to know each other more, and neither of us feels pressured to put a label on this or take it public before we're ready. What do you say?"

Without any hesitation, she smiles. "I like it."

I stick my hand out like we've just made a business deal, and she puts her hand in mine. We shake, and then she surprises me by standing and walking in front of me.

I shift on the couch so I'm facing her, staring up into her beautiful blue eyes. They're locked onto mine, and she gives me a devious grin.

"Oh he—"

I don't get to finish before she lowers herself down and straddles me. My hands instinctively find her hips and settle her in place.

"I thought you wanted to take things slow?" I ask softly.

"We can go slow. I'd just rather do it without our clothes."

Well, fuck me.

"Are you sure?" I ask.

I might have been known to sleep around a bit, but I've never pressured a woman to do anything she didn't want to, and I never would.

She nods as a wide grin spreads across her face as she pulls down the straps of her black bodysuit. "Positive."

The fabric slips down and her perfectly round, creamy

breasts are exposed. I glance up at her for approval before reaching up to caress them.

"You're perfect, Mel."

Her hands cover mine over her breasts, and she leans forward and presses her lips to mine. Her lips feel soft, and she tastes like tequila.

A quiet moan slips from her mouth into mine. My hands move from her breasts back to her hips, and I pull her harder against me. Her jean fabric, though displaying her curves beautifully, is currently pissing me off as another layer between us. All I want is to feel her skin, be as close to her as I can.

As if reading my mind, she stands, takes my hand, and leads me to the bedroom where she unzips and slowly lowers her jeans at the edge of the bed. She sits on the mattress with her pants around her ankles. She outstretches one foot, and I kneel and gently take it, happily stripping her of the layer. I do the same with the other side.

Standing, I lean over her as she scoots backward on the bed. I start to pull her body suit the rest of the way off, tossing it and her black lace panties to the floor. I stand and pull off my black shorts and underwear. My erection is already giving her its full attention, but when I glance at Melody, she suddenly looks shy.

Her arms are crossed over her stomach, and the look on her face is unreadable, but she's clearly uncomfortable.

"Melody, talk to me. What's going on in that head of yours?"

She shakes her head and forces a smile. "Just a little nervous."

I smile. "Me too."

I move back over her, spreading her legs so I can settle in between them. Leaning down, I plant a kiss on her lips, running a hand through her hair, but her arms are still awkwardly folded across her stomach. I reach down to move them to the side, but like a rubber band, they snap back into place.

I sit up. "Mel, what's going on?"

"I don't like my stomach."

One eyebrow raises. "But I do."

She looks away. "You haven't seen it yet."

"Then let me."

She doesn't respond and won't look at me. She's getting in her head again, the insecurities eclipsing the bold woman I saw a few minutes ago.

I cup her cheek, sliding my thumb under her chin and turn her toward me. "Hey, wherever you just went, come back. It's you and me here. Do you trust me?"

She chews on her cheek before nodding slightly. Slowly, her arms unfold, and she gives me access to her entire body. Before glancing down, I lean in and kiss her deeply. Our tongues swirl together like a delicious cocktail, tempting me to taste more.

"There's nothing you could show me that will change my mind," I say.

"About what?" she asks quietly, uncertain.

"That you're the most beautiful woman I've ever seen."

I sit up, and beginning at her collarbone, I lightly trace my hand downward over her soft skin. Outlining the fullness of her perfect breasts, down to her curvy stomach.

Across the front of her belly are areas of striped flesh from her pregnancy. Her tiger stripes.

This must be what she was self-conscious about.

There are four long stripes running from the middle of her stomach to a few inches below her belly button. I take a finger and softly trace down each of them.

I can feel her watching my every move with unease. I swear, I can almost feel her cringing.

"Jackson," she whispers.

I glance up at her, and her eyes are watering.

"Is this what you were worried about?"

She nods.

"Why are you ashamed of this?"

She takes a moment to answer, swallowing loudly. "Because they're ugly."

I bend down and give each one a soft kiss.

When I glance back up at her, I see tears falling down her cheeks. "These are nothing to be ashamed of. They brought your adorable girl into the world. To me, they're beautiful."

I may not know what's in Melody's past, but one thing is for sure, someone really did a number on her body image. I'll be damned if I don't spend every minute I have with her building it back up. This just became my new mission in life.

CHAPTER 29

Melody

To me, they're beautiful.

I can't stop the rush of emotion that follows. A dam breaks and lets loose everything I've been holding inside. Jackson has unleashed something in me that I can't quite explain, but it's freeing. He allows me to be myself, wholly. No filters, or scripts, or faked happiness. Just me.

I pull his lips to mine, kissing him hard as tears rush down my face. I'm aware that I probably look like an emotional maniac, but I surprisingly don't care because I know Jackson doesn't.

Alexander never missed a chance to tell me exactly what he thought of my stretch marks, which was that they're unacceptable and disgusting. To him, it was something I could "fix" in the gym. If I trained hard enough, he was convinced they'd go away. When they didn't, he decided I was eating too much. The goal post was always shifting, moving further away. It was this unattainable goal that we both knew I'd never reach, never able to accept me as I was. He wanted me to give until I had nothing left, and in the end, that's exactly what happened.

My fingers grip tighter behind Jackson's head, and I pull him closer. I don't want a breath of air between us. I spread my legs wider, and with one hand, I reach down and caress the giant erection that's been pressing into me.

His length and thickness are impressive, and all I want is to feel him moving inside of me. I stroke him a few more times, earning a quiet moan of pleasure.

"Jackson, I need to feel you."

"I want you so bad, Mel," he says, but then immediately freezes in his tracks, his movements stilling.

"What's wrong?" I ask.

"I don't have a condom," he groans, his eyes wide.

The thought comforts me, knowing he hadn't planned on coming here to sleep with anyone at all.

I chew on my lip and think it over. "I'm on birth control and I was tested recently."

"Me too. Are you sure?"

I nod. Just this once couldn't hurt. "Yes, I need you."

He grins and slides a hand between my legs. He groans with pleasure once he feels my pooling wetness. "It certainly feels like you do."

He dips two fingers inside of me while his thumb presses gently against my clit, rubbing delicious circles.

What a tease.

"Jackson, please."

He continues the slow, agonizing circles, drawing out desperate moans from my throat.

"Please what?" he taunts.

"I need you inside me," I whimper as my hips grind against his hand.

"As you wish," he says before removing his hand and thrusting into me.

I gasp loudly at the way he fills me. The delicious fullness as he presses himself deep inside of me is exquisite. Which is not a word I've ever used to describe sex. But maybe that's not what this is; somehow, this feels different with Jackson.

Maybe it's something more.

The way our bodies move, the way we fit together, the connection is deeper, more in sync. Jackson's gaze bores into mine as we shift and grind, searching for our high, and somehow, without words, he knows my body better than Alexander ever did. His hands know exactly where to go and how to move. His teeth nip at my neck and shoulders, inducing full-body tingles and goose bumps. There's nothing this man is doing that isn't sending me straight to the top of an orgasm. The way it's quickly building has me nervous in the way men are probably insecure about coming too fast. It's been a long time since I've had sex, and even longer since I've actually enjoyed it.

This? This is brand-new.

Jackson takes his time exploring my body, my skin. Savoring every kiss, every nibble.

He licks, bites, and kisses every inch of skin his mouth can reach.

With one hand, he interlocks his fingers with mine, placing them above my head while his other hand cups the side of my face, holding my gaze like he can't bear to look away. Like he can't believe this is happening.

His hard body presses into my soft flesh, but with him, the differences don't matter. We're like yin and yang. Two opposites you wouldn't expect to find together, yet somehow piece perfectly together.

Releasing my face, he reaches down and finds my swollen bud.

He's thrusting in and out at an agonizingly sinful pace while rubbing my clit, and I feel my climax climbing higher and higher until I begin to see stars.

"Jackson." I cry out his name like a prayer. Like the answer to every question I've been asking.

"Let go, baby," he instructs.

My orgasm explodes, and my entire body tenses and quakes. A glass-shattering scream rips from my throat as I ride out the wave. I feel him explode seconds after me, watching his face contort into pure pleasure. He follows my orgasm back down, and we both collapse on the bed.

I've never had an orgasm like that before, and I've definitely never screamed that way. I should be embarrassed, but maybe I feel too good to care.

Our heavy breathing is in sync as we both sink into the bed, regaining our composure.

"Wow," I say breathlessly.

Jackson lays flat on his back next to me and turns his head in my direction, giving me a lazy smile. "Yeah, wow."

"That was..." I start.

"New," he says, staring into my eyes.

Exactly.

I nod. "That was incredible."

He turns on his side. "Incredible doesn't begin to describe what that was."

I giggle. For a tough, muscular man, I've found that he has this sensitive side I wasn't sure I would like in a man. But fuck it if Jackson isn't the whole-ass package.

He presses his lips softly to mine, and when he pulls back, he whispers, "Don't hurt me, Melody Miller."

I feel a lump form in my throat, because fuck, I was thinking the same damn thing.

Jackson hops up and I hear him start the shower. Thinking he jumped in, I sit up and begin reaching for my clothes when I see him standing before me with an outstretched hand.

I glance up and self-consciously cover myself with my arms. "What?"

He nudges his head toward the bathroom. "Come on, let's get washed up and then we can order more junk food. And I already told you, no more body shaming, you're perfect."

I smile, because after the hell I went through with Alexander, he has no idea just how romantic those words really are.

After taking our time in the shower, enjoying washing each other, we settle onto the bed where we have platters of pancakes, fruit, and eggs. We were both craving a breakfast-for-dinner kind of snack.

"So you told my mother you were coming up to see me?" he asks between bites of strawberry.

I give him a sheepish grin. "Is that weird?"

"Not at all. My mother knows we're seeing each other. And she's who you feel comfortable leaving Gracie with."

Somehow, this seemingly perfect man also has the perfect mother. One that I don't feel guilty leaving Gracie with because she's become more like a grandmother to her than a sitter. She still refuses payment and always shows up with some sort of artsy craft or bakery dish for them to create together. I don't think it's a coincidence that Jackson turned out the way he did with a mother like that.

I wish I could say I was blessed with equally fantastic parents, but unfortunately, all the money in the world couldn't turn them into supportive, loving parents. We were never close, but the rift began to widen when I made the mistake of admitting that Alexander and I were having problems.

I confided in them that he was being unfaithful, and their advice was to let him "blow off steam." He was a "hard worker" in their words, and men have "different needs." When I told them I was planning on leaving, they made it very clear they disapproved and wouldn't support my decision. To them, the family connection—the money—was more important than my happiness.

I hope Jackson knows how lucky he is.

"Gracie has grown quite attached to her," I say, my voice laced with worry.

"Why do you say it like that?" Jackson asks.

"Because what if this" —I motion a hand between us— "doesn't work out?"

"Well, first off, let's try not to doom this relationship before it begins, shall we?" he replies and I nod. "Second of all, we're taking things slow, sort of, remember? We aren't going to involve Gracie or my mother. Whatever happens between us won't affect their relationship."

"What makes you say that?"

"Because my mother would never let what happens between two adults affect a child. Especially Gracie."

"Especially Gracie?" I ask.

He gives me an incredulous look. "She's crazy about her. Gracie's attachment isn't one-sided. They've really bonded. My mother texts me every time she's going to sit for her. She's always so excited and asks what sort of craft I think she might like."

My eyes sting with tears, because as evident as it was, I hadn't realized just how much thought she put into their time together. It's both sweet and painful. The way Jane freely gives her love and attention to Gracie only highlights the lack of it from her blood relatives. My parents were never that involved, and unfortunately, neither was her father.

I sniffle and giggle. "I think I might love your mom."

He laughs. "Yeah, most people do."

"Gracie's been through a lot, and as weary as I am for myself, I'm more worried for her. She likes you already. She loves your mom. I don't want her to be collateral damage in anything that happens between us."

He shakes his head and pushes the plates away. "I agree. Gracie is such a sweet, special girl. I adore her. We have two months to figure out what this is and where it's going. No pressure. If you decide to walk away, I'll understand. Gracie won't be involved until you decide to involve her. I may not be a father yet, but I know how important it is to protect her. It's your call, Mel."

It's both heartwarming and maddening that someone who hasn't fathered a child understands the need to protect her better than Gracie's own father.

"Thank you. That means...more than you know."

My eyes are misty from the entire conversation. From thinking about her not having an active father around, to knowing the people in this new town have shown her more affection than the ones who were supposed to love and protect her.

"Two months?" I ask, weary.

He nods.

"I'm on board, but as long as we're both clear that we won't be doing *this* with anybody else, too."

His eyebrows cinch together. "I would never do that to you, Mel."

"So we do this for two months, casually exclusive?"

He nods, smiling. "Casually exclusive. No pressure. Just us, getting to know each other better."

"Then we'll decide if we want to go public and possibly involve Gracie?" I ask, picturing what it would look like to walk through town holding Jackson's hand.

"Only if that's what you want."

I think it over and know it's the best case scenario. Quietly hooking up with this jump rope god in private, while still living my own life and keeping Gracie out of the drama, is the best possible situation I can think of. And if this relationship goes up in flames, the only ones who will know are me and Jackson.

"Deal." I stick my hand out to him.

He laughs, grabbing my hand and pulling me on top of him. "Buckle up, babe, you're mine for the next two months."

"You sure you don't want to back out? You've seen my not-nice side. It's not always going to be rolling around in bed."

He smirks, cupping my ass. "I'm not worried. I can handle anything you've got."

"Awful cocky, aren't we?" I joke.

His hand moves to the back of my head, his fingers twisting in my hair. "Naw, just confident."

He pulls me down, fusing our lips. The kiss is deep and passionate. His hand never leaves my hair, like he doesn't want to let me up for air. Like he doesn't want to let me go. I can't help but feel the same way.

All I can say is, if my pull to him is this strong now, lord help me for how intense this will be in two months.

CHAPTER 30

Jackson

My muscles are aching, and I'm officially out of breath. I have been going over my jump rope routine for the festival for the last hour. I asked Summer to stay late today and help me work on it, which mostly means giving me her opinion.

"It's not bad," she tells me when I drop the rope, panting for air and reaching for my water bottle.

I take a large gulp and, through heavy breathing, respond, "Not bad? What's wrong with it?"

She taps a finger on her chin. "Nothing, per se. It's missing something."

Hell. I had the same thought.

Every year I put on a routine to perform on stage at the festival to get the kids excited for jumping rope. To show them what's possible. I always try to outperform the previous year's routine, but this one is not quite ready.

"Do you have any ideas?" I ask her.

"Well, for starters, that song is not going to work." She stands up and walks over to hit pause on the music app on my phone.

"Why the hell not?"

"It's fine for the gym. But kids aren't listening to this. You need to choose something that's trending with them, one that's familiar and they'll get excited about."

"Okay, valid point."

She smirks as if to say *Yeah, I know.*

I roll my eyes. "What else, oh wise one?"

She laughs. "You definitely need to end with a mic drop, because that's always a show stopper. It looks so good, and the kids are always blown away by it. You need something in the middle, though. Something...new."

I sigh. "I'll work on it, I guess."

I join her sitting on the blue gym mats, needing to rest my legs.

"It looks great, just needs a little tweaking," she tells me reassuringly.

I purse my lips. "Thanks for staying late to help."

The corners of her lips begin to turn up. "Well, it wasn't entirely selfless."

"What do you mean?"

"A little birdie told me you had a lady visitor last week when you were in Denver."

My lips form a thin line. I don't want to say anything and incriminate myself if Melody didn't say anything to her, but who else would know? Then it dawns on me.

Summer grins. "Ember called me and said some woman came to see you, and you got all flustered and weird. Rumor has it she looked a lot like Melody."

I keep my mouth shut, and it only results in a burst of laughter from Summer.

"Can we not bring this up around Melody?" I plead.

"I thought we were past all this pretending not to like each other bullshit?"

"We are. It's not that."

"What is it then?" she asks, her eyebrows pulling down.

"We both have some...reservations, from our past. So, instead of putting pressure on us to try and figure this out or slap a label on it, we've decided to sort of be exclusive, but privately."

She lifts an eyebrow, biting the side of her bottom lip. "Hmm. That's sort of brilliant, actually."

"It is?" I ask, surprised she's not grilling me for this.

"Hell yeah. You get to fool around in secret, which, let's face it, is insanely hot to begin with. But then you also don't have the added pressure of everyone's eyes on you, debating whether you're going to last or not? That's genius."

The sneaking around has been pretty hot, I have to admit. But what I love even more is that neither of us has to face any outside pressure or embarrassment if this doesn't work out. Because as confident as I am in this, I've been sure before and been very wrong. Nobody goes into a relationship thinking it's going to end, yet most of them do.

"I'm glad you approve, but please, for Gracie's sake, keep your mouth shut."

She holds two fingers up. "Scout's honor. But you know, me, your mother, and half the town already know you two are seeing each other, right?"

I sigh heavily. "You only know because I told you, everyone else is simply speculating. Blue Springs is known for its gossipy town folk."

"Ain't that the truth. Did you hear that Trish was spotted making out with some nameless man behind Bread Pitt? I thought she was this quiet, sweet woman, and bam! Caught making out, covered in a hunky man. You think you know a person." She sighs, shaking her head in disbelief.

I laugh at her dramatic storytelling abilities. She's so animated and passionate. Trish is the owner of Bread Pitt, and overall, she has the look of a kindergarten teacher, so a rumor of her hooking up with a man is a rather juicy story for this town.

"See, I hope she learned her lesson and keeps it more private for her sake. Everyone in this town needs a hobby."

"Like sucking face with Blue Springs's newest single mom?" Summer taunts.

My cheeks redden just thinking about anyone else kissing her. "Absolutely not. That's my job."

"Right. My mistake. I guess they'll have to find something else to do, like jump rope or something."

"See, there's my favorite marketing woman. Let's get more people jumping rope, and less people discussing my love life. I've had enough of that for a lifetime."

One public relationship scandal is about all a person can take in a life span. I'm not sure I'd survive another one.

She gives me a salute. "Aye, aye, captain."

"You're such a smartass." I laugh.

"Yeah, but you love me," she announces, flipping her blonde ponytail dramatically from one side to the other.

I chuckle. "Get outta here. Thanks for your help."

"Yeah, it's so late and I have a busy night of going home to nobody." She rolls her eyes.

"Hey, you're the one who swore off dating."

She scoffs. "Because it's a freak show out there. Men are insane. What happened to the normal, fully functioning ones?"

"We are a rare breed," I say playfully, placing my hand on my chest.

She sticks a finger in her mouth and pretends to gag. "I'm serious. Even Ember has had horrible luck finding a normal guy in the city. They're either all taken, or they don't exist anymore."

"What happened with Ember?" I ask.

"Well, aside from her creepy ex-boss, the last guy she was

seeing, well, it's not my place, but let's just say she might need therapy now."

I raise an eyebrow. "Yikes."

"Exactly. You and Melody better hold onto each other."

I can't help the grin that spreads across my face when hearing Melody's name. I try to play it off by pulling off my backward cap and smoothing my hair back before putting it back on.

"You are *so* not hiding anything. Look how happy you are. It's sickening. But I'm happy for you, friend."

"Thanks, Sum."

"Do you want any help closing?" she asks.

I shake my head. "Naw, you stayed late enough as it is, go home and work on those epic smoothies you plan to make for the whole town soon."

She smiles before grabbing her bag and heading for the door. "Night, Jax."

I wave and lock the door behind her, watching to make sure she gets safely inside her Jeep.

Replaying Summer's comment in my head about going home alone, I can't help but feel even luckier to have met Melody. I may not go home to her at night, and we may not see each other every day, but she's given me something I never thought I'd get back. Hope. She's renewed my faith in relationships and in women.

Shaina did more than break my heart. She shattered my trust in relationships and women in general. I truly never thought I'd want to get into another relationship, yet here I am, pursuing a single mom. An amazing woman who, now that I know her, I can't imagine not knowing.

I want the same for Summer. She feels like giving up now, but I hope she opens her heart back up to the possibility of it someday. She has so much to offer, and anyone would be lucky to be with her.

There's no way to know where things will go with Melody. We might get to the two month mark and decide to go our separate ways. Maybe things will be too complicated to work out. But whatever happens, I know that Melody would never do to me what Shaina did. Melody would never hide something huge and betray and embarrass me. That I know for certain.

Needing to see her, I pull out my phone.

Me: Hi there. Hope I don't wake you, but I'm thinking about you.

Melody: I'm a mom, I'm almost always awake.

Me: Why? What do you do with all that awake time?

Melody: Worry, mostly.

Me: That doesn't sound fun.

Melody: Yeah, but if I don't do it, who will?

I CAN'T QUITE TELL if Melody is being sarcastic or serious. Something tells me it's a little bit of both. I've seen how serious she can be, especially when it comes to her daughter. I don't doubt at all that she spends every waking moment worrying about that little girl.

I can recall countless times when I was a young boy that I'd wake in the middle of the night and my mother was wide-awake, staring at me. When I asked her what she was doing, she'd always say, "Just looking at you." Now that I'm an adult, I wonder if that's mom code for worrying about everything that has or could happen to your child.

My heart aches knowing that my mother had to carry that by herself and knowing that Melody now carries it alone as well.

> Jackson: Want some company?

Melody: Gracie is sleeping…

> Jackson: I could sneak over. I'm a great cuddle buddy. You remember ;)

Melody: Other things seem to be clouding my memory.

> Jackson: Really? What comes to mind first?

Melody: Well, it was big and juicy…

> Jackson: Tell me more

Melody: I couldn't wait to get it in my mouth.

> Jackson: Really?

Melody: Hell yeah, the burger at that hotel was amazing.

Melody: 😂

> Jackson: Wow. That was just cruel.

Melody: Sorry. Couldn't resist.

> Jackson: You owe me now.

Melody: That so?

> Jackson: Yep, now you have to let me come over.

Melody: I don't know…

Jackson: I'll be quiet, we can hang out in the living room for a little while. Gracie will never know.

SHE DOESN'T RESPOND for several minutes. So long that I think her lack of response is a hard no. But then I see the three dots pop up and my heart starts racing.

Melody: You better be so quiet.

Jackson: Quiet as a mouse.

Melody: Even quieter than that.

Jackson: I'll be on my best behavior. See you in 10.

I FINISH CLOSING up the gym in record time, doing a very quick inspection of the weight room floor, and hoping it's presentable enough for the morning.

There's only one thing on my mind, and she's deliciously curvy and looks damn good in a pair of tight jeans. Everything else becomes second priority when it comes to her, and as exciting as it is, it also scares the hell out of me.

CHAPTER 31

Melody

If we drew straws at work to see who had to wait on bitchy Brenda, I would draw the short one every damn time.

My luck with the rotation always lands her in my section, and although she's been more bearable since Jackson's heroic tongue-lashing, she's not someone we're excited to see walk through those doors.

Truth be told, I'm surprised she had the courage to come back in here. But Blue Bistro really does have some of the best food in town, so I don't blame her.

A sheen of sweat coats my forehead from running my ass off all morning from table to table. Today is unseasonably busy for the middle of the week. Even though it's summertime, it typically doesn't get busier until later in the day, but Mary, Elana, and I have been swamped all day.

I'm in the kitchen getting soda refills for one of my tables when Mary waltzes through the kitchen door with a grin.

"Oh Melody," she singsongs.

I laugh at her. "Yes?"

"You have a hunky visitor."

She always has the same look on her face when Jackson

pops into the bistro. We have kept things between us private, but it doesn't stop the town from speculating. The only thing hotter than the hot springs is the rumor mill in town.

"I'll be right there," I say through giggles.

I saunter into the dining room and see Jackson weaving through tables in his dark shorts, black

T-shirt, black Converse, and backward cap. He spots Brenda sitting in a booth, and as he passes by, he brings his forefinger and middle finger to his eyes and then points them at her. A subtle reminder to be on her best behavior.

I stifle a laugh and drop the drinks off at a nearby table before making my way over to where he now sits two booths away from Brenda.

"Are you here making trouble?" I half-heartedly warn.

He lifts a hand to his chest, feigning innocence. "Me? Never. I'm just here for my usual. And

maybe for the scenery."

I shoot him a playful glare when he waggles his brows at me. "You're impossible."

"How's your day going, beautiful?" he asks with a sweet smile.

I pull my lips to the side. "It's okay."

His lips pull down. "Only okay?"

"It's nothing."

It's not appropriate to bash your place of employment on the clock.

"I'll put your order in," I say and turn away, but he stops me.

Jackson reaches out and gently grabs my arm. "Hey, what's going on?"

I lean in toward his table and lower my voice. "I'm fine. And I'm so grateful for this job. I owe everything to Bud and Kat. I think I'm just having a hard time justifying being away from Gracie so much for a job that feels this way."

"What way?"

Where do I even begin? It's draining, exhausting, and pays very little. But really, it's something more.

"Unfulfilling."

He nods.

"This has been an amazing way to start over. I'm so lucky they took a chance on me. I just...want more. For myself and Gracie. I guess that sounds silly. A job is a job." I swipe the back of my hand over my forehead, feeling dumb for complaining about anything that puts food on my table and a roof over our heads.

Jackson shakes his head. "That makes perfect sense. You're allowed to want anything you wish for. You deserve everything."

I give him a half smile. "Thanks."

I put his order in at the kiosk, then grab my large water bottle and take a big gulp. Guilt is clawing at me for expressing that desire out loud. It feels selfish. Though that could be the ghost of Alexander's voice in my head, shaming me for ever wanting more for myself. But the truth is, I do. I want more, and I can't shake the idea that's been knocking around my brain for the last few months.

The idea I've only said aloud to one person and feels so out of reach. But coming from two families that have more money than they know what to do with, who have used their power and influence for absolutely nothing but personal gain, I'd love to give back.

My sordid past may have influenced the idea to help women that come from toxic environments, but I've always felt like I wanted—needed—something more. Truly helping people, making a positive difference in their life, is what I want most.

But it's a silly dream. One that I'd never be able to afford without Alexander or my parents funding the idea—which neither would. So, I set my water bottle down and head back out to continue serving tables. At the end of the day, though it's not my dream job, it puts food in my daughter's mouth, and for that, I'm forever grateful.

Jackson eats his meal and leaves me a large tip, as usual, which is no surprise. The shock comes when I open the check presenter left on Brenda's table. I see that she's actually left me a decent tip for once. My service has never wavered with her. I've always maintained my friendly, attentive exterior and given her great service just like anybody else. But seeing more than a handful of coins left on the table is enough to make me think that maybe people can change.

The rest of the day flies by, thanks to a steady stream of customers, and I'm practically running out the door at the end of my shift, ready to see my little Gracie.

When I burst through the front door, Gracie and Jane are hunched over a craft, and I can hear Gracie giggling. She turns around abruptly when she hears the door close.

"Mama!" she shrieks with delight, racing over to give me a hug.

When we pull apart, I notice her face is covered in paint, and so is the majority of her hands.

"Wow, baby girl, what on earth are you two doing in here?" I ask, laughing at her rainbow-splattered face that looks more like she fell into a pail of mixed paints.

Jane stands and grimaces. "Sorry, I was going to wash her up, I swear. We got a little out of control. They're nontoxic and washable."

I laugh and raise my hand to stop her from panicking further. "It's alright. She caught me by surprise is all."

"Gracie, sweetie, let's go hop in the bath so your mother can get changed and relax a little," Jane offers.

A grateful smile spreads across my face. "That sounds like a wonderful idea. I'll get dinner started. How about we have breakfast for dinner tonight?"

Gracie's eyes light up. "With blueberry pancakes?"

I laugh and tap a finger to her nose. "Of course. Now go get cleaned up, you goofball."

She giggles and bounces away with Jane toward the bathroom.

Once she's cleaned up and dinner is ready, we sit down and ask about each other's day. I invite Jane to stay, but she kindly declines, insisting she already had other plans, leaving Gracie and me to catch up.

"I really love the painting you made for me, sweetheart," I say before stuffing a piece of fluffy pancake into my mouth.

She grins and shoves an impressive piece of pancake into her own mouth. Once she's done chewing, her next words surprise me. "I talked to Jax today."

My face scrunches in surprise. "What? When did you talk to him?"

"On the phone today. With his mommy," she says through a bite of sausage.

The mere mention of his name is enough to send a thrill through my body.

"Oh. That's nice. What did you talk about?"

She shrugs. "I told him we were painting, and that I missed him."

One side of my mouth tips up in surprise and my eyebrows shoot upward. "You miss him?"

She nods. "Yeah, he's real nice. He made cookies with us. He's funny."

I smile at her, and my heart swells at the way she is so open with her affection. Though her father might actually be from hell, she hasn't let that affect her giant heart. My biggest worry when I left Alexander was whether I was doing the right thing or not. I agonized over whether leaving her father behind would break her heart, or if keeping him in her life would.

"He should come over more," she adds.

"You think so?" I ask, not able to hide my surprise.

Her little curls bounce when she nods. "Yes, that would be okay."

I laugh. "That's good to know, baby."

Since deciding on our arrangement a month ago, Jackson has been over as often as he can. After she goes to bed, we hang out in the living room, talking quietly and making out like teenagers. It's been hard not to rip each other's clothes off, but with Gracie so close in the next room, it doesn't feel right. Especially since I'm hiding an entire relationship—or whatever this is—from her. She sleeps through the night, so I'm not worried about her noticing I'm not in the bed with her, but I'm sure it's only a matter of time before we slip.

I can't help but feel guilty for sneaking him over behind her back, but I'd rather be doing this than introducing her to a new relationship with a man who might not even be around in a few months. Life shifts quickly, and people can change their minds even faster. The end-of-summer festival is in about a month, and we have a lot to figure out between now and then.

Sure, it's fun now, but what about when real life starts seeping in, and stress begins taking swings at the relationship? The early stages are always fun, until people show you their true colors. I would be lying if I didn't say I'm still waiting to see Jackson's bad side. People can only hide who they are for so long, and this time, I refuse to ignore those signs early on. Not for my sake, but for my daughter's. It's not something we will tolerate a second time.

Once we finish eating, Gracie helps me wipe down the counters and the small table we have next to the kitchen, and we retreat to the couch since she's already had her bath. I put on a movie for her and we snuggle up together under a blanket.

It's not cold, but I love cuddling my little girl while she still lets me. Every day she looks more and more like a big kid, so I know these moments are fleeting. They say time is a thief, and I've never heard anything more true.

My phone vibrates in my back pocket, and Gracie must have felt it, too.

"Mama fart!" she shouts giddily.

I laugh and shift to pull my phone from my pocket. "It was my phone, you goofball."

She shakes her head. "No! Mama fart."

I playfully roll my eyes. "Okay, you caught me."

She covers her mouth and continues to giggle and kick her feet but quickly turns her attention back to the movie on the TV screen.

Unlocking my phone, I see a text from Jackson and can't stop the grin forming on my face. All it takes is seeing his name on my screen to make me giddy, and that alone both excites and terrifies me.

Jackson: Hey beautiful. How is your evening going?

Melody: Hi handsome. It's good. Cuddling with Gracie before bed.

Jackson: I'm jealous.

Melody: Of me or her?

Jackson: Both. I'd love to cuddle you both 😊

My heart immediately starts pounding in my chest, and although I was never a believer in "butterflies," I swear an entire swarm of them are currently fluttering around my stomach.

No, Melody, you will not fall for this man. Do not get attached.

> Jackson: Is that weird?

> Melody: No. It's sweet.

Too sweet. So sweet that I am currently having trouble breathing.

> Jackson: Okay good.

> Melody: What are you up to?

> Jackson: Finishing up at the office, missing you.

> Melody: You saw me earlier today you goof.

> Jackson: So? Can't a guy miss his girl?

What is he doing to me right now? *His girl?*

Warning bells are going off in my head right now, and I am about to be a messy puddle of stupid for this man.

> Melody: I suppose that's okay. ;)

> Jackson: Am I coming over tonight?

I DON'T REPLY RIGHT AWAY and glance at Gracie who is currently trying to force her heavy eyelids to stay open. It would be a good night, because she'll be out in about five minutes, and I am nowhere near tired yet. But with the way the conversation is going, it's making me feel like it might not be the best idea.

> Melody: I'm actually pretty tired. Today kicked my butt.

IT TAKES him a little longer to respond this time, and I worry that I've upset him. But a part of me sort of wants to see it. I've been waiting to see an ugly side of him, and maybe not getting his way will push it to the surface.

> Jackson: I understand. Get some sleep beautiful. Sweet dreams.

DAMN.

I should be relieved this is his response, and I am. But a small nagging part of me was eager to see him throw a tantrum and possibly get angry. It would make it a lot easier to walk away. Because right now, everything he's doing and saying is making me do the exact opposite. Everything he's doing is for damn sure going to make me fall in love with him. And that's not something I'm ready for.

Melody: Good night.

I SET my phone on the arm of the couch and wrap my arm around Gracie, whose eyes are now completely closed. I'll move her in a few minutes, but for now, I want to hold onto my baby girl for a little bit longer.

She's the reason I came out here, after all. To start a new life. A safe one. I did not come here to fall in love and get swept up in another man. I hardly know Jackson, and although we are becoming much closer, there's still so much we don't know about each other. There are things I still need to tell him. Things that might push him away all together once he knows.

One thing's for sure, I need to figure out how to continue seeing this man while protecting myself and my daughter, because tonight's conversation was a big warning sign that this man is nothing but trouble for me.

CHAPTER 32

Jackson

"Just a minute!" Melody shouts from inside her cabin.

She was a little short with me last night, but said she was exhausted, and I didn't want to press her. But she works so hard for herself and her daughter, I thought I'd surprise her this morning before she has to head to the bistro for her shift.

The door swings open, and she stands in front of me with her hair messily down her back, an oversized tan Colorado T-shirt, and no pants. I inhale a sharp breath and try to keep my eyes on hers, and not on her creamy bare legs.

"Jackson," she says, startled.

Her hands quickly move to the hem of her shirt, attempting to yank it down.

"Jax!" Gracie chimes in from behind her, racing toward the door and shoving past her mother.

"Gracie, hi sweetie! How are you?" I ask as she latches onto my leg in a tender embrace. I bend down and wrap an arm around her, giving her a gentle pat on the back.

She pulls back. "What are you doing here?"

Seeing them both still in their pajamas, I now feel bad arriving this early.

"I brought your mommy some coffee, and a hot chocolate for you."

I glance up at Melody's widened eyes. "You did?"

"I did." Extending my arm, I hand her the coffee and then pull the hot chocolate out of the holder and hand it to Gracie. "Be careful, it's probably still hot."

"Chocolate!" Gracie shrieks with excitement.

"Let's take the lid off and let it cool down, sweetie," Melody requests, walking back inside to place it on the table. I try my best not to stare as she bends slightly over the table, removing the top of the cup. Gracie follows, planting herself on a chair, sitting up on her knees as she dutifully begins blowing on the steaming beverage.

Melody returns to where I'm standing in the doorway, and closes the door behind us, leaving it cracked so she can hear Gracie inside.

"That was really nice of you. Thank you so much for doing this."

I rake my hand through my hair. "I'm sorry it's so early, but I knew you had the day shift."

"Are you kidding me? It's so thoughtful. Nobody has ever done this for me."

My eyebrows cinch. "Nobody's ever brought you coffee?"

She shakes her head, causing her hair to fall like a curtain around her face.

My heart pinches.

Knowing that Melody's been with men who haven't shown her the bare minimum of surprising her with a cup of coffee makes me furious. The bar is truly in hell.

"Thank you," she says softly.

I smile at her. "You're welcome."

We stand in silence, her placing one bare foot on top of the other, clearly uncomfortable in only a T-shirt.

"I like your outfit. It's my second favorite one I've seen you in."

Her shoulders finally drop and she laughs, running a hand through her long hair. "What's your favorite one?"

I lean in close and whisper in her ear, "The one where you're not wearing anything but me."

Planting a kiss on her cheek, I walk backward off her porch with a wave and mischievous grin, leaving her flushed and crossing her legs. I can't help but wonder if she's wet between them.

She lifts one arm and waves, attempting to hide the smile on her face.

"Enjoy the coffee, beautiful, I'll see you soon."

Hopping back in my car, I back out of her driveway and make my way to Jumping Jax. While last night the conversation felt off, today I can see the way she wants to be with me.

Our chemistry and connection is undeniable. But I'm trying to be smart and play it safe. Melody could easily break my heart, so some days I rack my brain wondering what I'm doing messing with a flight risk like her. But the truth is, every time I see her or talk to her, I lose the argument with myself.

This may be casual right now, but what I think we're both not saying is that we know how fucking easy it would be to fall for each other. Which is something I'm not sure either of us is ready to talk about.

"JACKSON! THEY'RE HERE!" Summer shouts.

I can hear her racing down the hall just before her blonde ponytail pops into view.

"Did you hear me, fool, they're here!" she shouts again.

"Who's here?" I ask.

"The jump ropes!" she squeals.

"Oh, thank God. I got an email saying they were going to be delayed, I was worried they wouldn't arrive in time."

"There's a million boxes out there, so come and help me move them to the back storage, will ya?"

"I mean, it is my order, so I guess I could help," I joke.

Out front, there's already a stack of large boxes waiting for us, and the truck driver is going back and forth unloading more. I sign the delivery form and thank him before we begin carrying them to the back.

Unable to help myself, I pry open one of the boxes and see bags and bags of colorful jump ropes. It feels like Christmas, and I couldn't be more excited for the festival this year. I'm excited every year, but it seems like with each new festival, it becomes a little bigger, with more and more kids excited to learn about jumping rope. It feels good to give back to people. To give kids an active outlet to escape to, no matter what their home life is like. It contributes to their health and boosts their confidence. Teaching kids a few moves and watching them practice and retain them is more fulfilling than I could have ever dreamed.

This festival may cost a small fortune, but when kids from previous years return to proudly show me their improvements since the last festival, to me, it is worth every dollar. This is for me as much as it's for the kids.

Summer walks in the storage room with a box in her arms. "Last one."

"Great, thanks, Sum."

She places the box down and places a hand on her popped hip. "You couldn't help yourself, could you?"

"What?" A goofy grin spreads across my face.

"You do this every year. As if those ropes are going to change," she says, laughing.

I chuckle. "Is it weird I love the smell of them?"

She shrugs. "No. There's worse things to be sniffing."

I lift an eyebrow. "Like what?"

"This one guy I was seeing must have had a foot fetish or something, because when we were having drinks at his place, I took my heels off because, let's face it, they feel like a torture device, and he kept trying to smell my feet."

"No, he didn't!" I bellow, unable to contain the burst of laughter that erupts out of me, nearly choking on my own saliva.

She holds her hand up. "Scout's honor. It was so creepy, after the second time, I bolted. To each their own but absolutely fucking not."

"Summer, where do you find these men?" I ask.

She gasps. "Please, *they* find *me*. I must have a freak beacon on the top of my head or something, because I cannot make this shit up. I'm like the bat signal for twisted men."

After another minute of laughing so hard, I am keeled over the boxes in front of me, I right myself to see Summer glaring at me. "It's not funny. It's a tragedy. My love life is a joke. There are no decent men left on the planet."

"Well, speaking of decent men..."

"Oh God, what? You're not trying to set me up, are you?" she says, panicking.

My eyebrows pull together. "And have you berate me if the guy has some hidden fetish? No. I was talking about Wes. Do you have your proposal ready yet? He's going to be at the festival, and he plans to be in town for a little while. If all goes well, he's wanting to help you scope out the right spot."

Her eyes light up. "Oh! Uh, sort of. I'm working on it."

"Festival is coming up," I warn.

"I know, and I'll have it ready, I promise. I want it to be perfect, so I'm tweaking some things. And perfecting some recipes."

I grin. "It's going to be perfect. He already loves the idea and is excited to work with you. Just be yourself. Don't try to be anything you're not. He'll see right through it. It's his gift."

"What is?" she asks.

"Spotting when someone's being phony, trying to impress him. It's the quickest way to get on his bad side."

She chews on her lip. "That's good to know…"

"Summer, don't worry. You couldn't be phony if you tried."

Her shoulders relax. "I just want this so badly. I don't want to screw it up."

I walk around the boxes and place my hands on her shoulders. "You won't. I already put in a good word with him. I won't let you fail."

She gives me a watery smile. "Thank you. Have I told you how much I appreciate you doing this for me?"

"Well, you could thank me by staying for the late shift tonight so I can go hang out with Melody. If you feel so inclined…"

Summer laughs and shakes her head. "Alright, whatever you need, lover boy, because soon I'll be running my very own business so you'll have to find someone else to do your bitch work."

I laugh. "You're the best!"

She flips her blonde ponytail dramatically. "Tell me something I don't know."

It hadn't occurred to me that by setting this up for her, I'd potentially be losing her at the gym. I haven't given a single thought to who I might find to replace her, because that's going to be impossible.

She's been not only my best friend, but the best manager I've had working for any of my gyms since I opened them. As hard as it's going to be to replace her, I'm still elated for her, because Summer works damn hard and not only does she deserve it, but she's also earned it.

CHAPTER 33

Melody

I'm not sure there's any better feeling in the world than coming home after a long shift and taking off your bra and shoes. Second only to seeing my daughter's beautiful face.

Once we're settled at the small table in the kitchen, eating dinner, I ask about her day. "You've been having fun with Jane?"

"Yeah, Mommy, she's so much fun. More fun than Grandma," she innocently responds.

Since we've been in Blue Springs, I haven't heard from my family, nor has Gracie really asked about them, so I haven't had much reason to bring them up. It makes me wonder if Gracie has been more aware of our living situation than I even knew. Kids sense things, picking up on more than we think they do, so it pains me to think of her knowing just how awful her father and my family can be.

She's asked about her father a few times, but the curiosity always seems to come more from worry than yearning. But this is the first time she's mentioned my mother, who was a seldom-seen grandmother.

"I'm glad, baby." I keep my response short. If she wants to

talk about them, I'll never stop her, but I'm not entirely eager to keep the conversation going, either.

Gracie takes a spoonful of the green chicken chili soup I made, not bothering to swallow before she speaks. "She said there's a big festival with lots of kids. Can we go, Mom? Can we? I want a jump rope. She said I can have one."

The way her blue eyes sparkle and light up from the notion of going to the festival is enough to make me crack a smile, thoughts of my past life long forgotten, if only for the time being. "Of course, baby. I think that's a great idea."

She pumps her small fist into the air in a show of victory. "Yay! You're the best."

I laugh.

"You jump rope with Summer. I want to try, too," she tells me.

I place my elbow on the table and cradle my chin, giving her all my attention. "Yeah, I do. I think you'll be really good at it. Better than me." I lean in close and whisper in her ear. "Maybe even better than Summer."

When I pull away, I can see her eyes widen with excitement and a huge grin spreads across her face. Even if I wasn't planning on going to the festival, the look on her face now would have absolutely sealed the deal.

Truth is, going to the festival both excites and terrifies me. It'll be a turning point for Jackson and me, and I have no idea what that'll look like.

Will we both be all-in?

Or will one of us be left standing alone and exposed?

I can already tell how easy it's going to be to fall for Jackson Pierce. Not *if*, but *when* I do. Though it's not something I am anywhere near ready to admit aloud. And after hearing about his past, I know he has similar trepidations. Who could blame him after what he's been through?

I shake my head, trying to erase any thoughts of falling in love with Jackson. This is fun for him, and it needs to be that for me, too. Otherwise, I fear I'll be the one holding a one-sided love letter with a return to sender stamp on the front of it.

It wouldn't be the first time.

Gracie's slurping pulls me from my thoughts. I glance at her and she looks up at me from under her lashes. "Ooops."

She giggles and I can't help but join in. Every day, I watch her small face grow a little bit older, and these silly moments happen less and less. One day I'll be looking into the face of a grown woman, so I stare just a little bit longer, wanting to memorize all of her tiny features while they're still present.

AFTER I'VE GOTTEN Gracie tucked into bed and snoring like the tiny train that she is, I sneak out to the living room for a bit of "mom time." I pour myself a glass of white wine from the fridge. The first sip is crisp and refreshing. Even though the sun is no longer out, the nights tend to hold onto the day's warmth longer than I expected for a town in Colorado.

With my glass of wine in hand, I retreat to the couch and flip on a show for background noise, turning it on low so as not to wake Gracie.

I've quickly gone through my first glass and am returning to the couch with my refill when I see my phone light up on the coffee table. When I swipe it open, there's a text from Jackson.

Jackson: Hi beautiful.

A smile instantly spreads across my face, and I quickly take a sip of wine, willing myself to play it cool, even though he can't see me.

Melody: Hey handsome.

Jackson: I was thinking...

Melody: Oh yeah? What about?

Jackson: You mostly.

I bite down on my bottom lip, the smile too strong to be held back this time.

Jackson: Is Gracie sleeping?

Melody: Yes...

Jackson: Come out front.

My heartbeat accelerates at the thought of him being right outside.

I set my phone down and peer through the front window to see Jackson casually leaning against his car in the driveway in gray sweats, a black shirt, and his backward cap. I slowly open the front door and snick it closed behind me. I don't make it down the few small steps before Jackson has made his way to me, wrapping his arms around my middle.

I hear him inhale deeply as he presses himself tightly against me. "I missed you."

I giggle. "What are you doing here right now? Are you crazy? Gracie could have been up."

When we separate, his eyes are full of mischief. "Maybe. That's why I asked."

He slowly pushes me backward until my back meets the front of the house and he has me pinned. One of his hands rests on my hip, and the other is cradling the side of my face as I crane my neck to look up at him.

"Jackson..." I whisper before his mouth crashes into mine.

His tongue slips into my mouth and sweeps across mine, forcing an involuntary moan to slip out before I knew it was coming. My hands fly to his back as I attempt to press us even closer together, arching my lower half into him more deeply.

When we finally come up for air, I'm breathing heavily.

He caresses my hair. "Hi."

A dopey smile lingers on my lips. "Hi."

"You taste like wine," he whispers seductively.

I chuckle. "I may have had a glass when you texted. How long have you been out here?"

He shrugs. "Not long. I took a shot that Gracie might already be sleeping and hoped that you wouldn't be."

"You got lucky," I say, knowing that I very easily could have fallen asleep tucked in next to Gracie.

He presses his lips to mine softly. "Yes, I did."

My stomach flips.

Don't read into things.

Don't read into things.

I should tell him goodnight and go back inside. I should tell him we need to stop sneaking around like this.

I *should* tell him all of that. But instead, I offer him a drink.

He eagerly nods and we quietly step into the living room. I

carry over the two glasses of white wine, and we settle into the couch. The TV is still on low, so we sip our wine in silence while he caresses my bare legs that are now thrown across his lap. I typically sleep in an oversized shirt and panties, so there's not much between us.

I try not to focus on how good his hands feel on me. The way I swear I can feel electricity flowing from his skin to mine. And I really try to ignore the way he looks painfully *right* sitting next to me.

As we finish off the first glass, his hands have seamlessly made their way higher, now caressing the flesh of my inner thigh. It takes all of my energy to focus on the TV, but I couldn't tell you what's on the screen, because I'm too preoccupied squeezing my legs together.

"You should stop doing that," Jackson whispers.

I glance over and the lust in his eyes could set my flesh on fire.

"Doing what?"

"Biting that bottom lip."

Not realizing I was, I pull it back into my mouth, and pop it back out again. "Why?"

"Because I'm having a hard enough time keeping my hands to myself when all I want to do is pull that pouty lip into my mouth and bite down on it."

His hand squeezes my thigh when he says it, and like a release button, I relax my legs.

He raises an eyebrow. "Melody…"

I nod, and we both set our wine down. As soon as the glasses hit the table, he pulls me onto his lap so I'm straddling him on the couch. I wiggle until I'm flush against him, practically grinding my pussy against him as his length grows beneath me.

I still get a flash of anxiety, my self-consciousness making me want to hover over him, but after so many times of him forcing all of my weight down, I've become more comfortable with him, and myself.

"You're bad," he whispers.

A sly grin spreads across my face. "Only sometimes. But I can be good, too."

A look akin to shock plays over his face, never having seen this side of me. I could blame the wine, but the way I want him is all me. The playful and carefree way I want to be with him is a lot easier to indulge in when the wine is silencing the fears and the doubts that hold me back.

I continue grinding against him, extracting a low groan from his throat. His hands firmly grip each side of my ass as he follows my movements. Leaning down, I bite his bottom lip, causing him to smirk. His hands move from my ass to the skin under my shirt.

Moving from my back toward my front, I tense up. He must feel it, because he pulls his hands from me.

I'm looking into Jackson's eyes, but all I can hear is Alexander in my ear whenever he caught a glimpse of my stomach.

"Are you still on a diet?"

"Have you been working out this week?"

"Gracie isn't a baby anymore, you should have lost this weight by now."

I know he was being an asshole then, and I know it now. But it doesn't take away the sting. The way it feels when someone you love with your whole heart looks at you with disgust. When they look at you like you're worthless because you've gained weight.

Does that sort of shame ever go away?

"I thought we talked about this," Jackson says in reference to my negative self-talk.

"It's hard, I can't help it sometimes."

His eyes fall to where his hands were a moment ago.

"I have an idea," he says before lifting me off him with ease and flipping me onto my back on the couch in one swift movement.

"Whoa," I say, giggling before slamming a hand over my mouth to stifle it. My head instinctively jerks back to the bedroom where I hope Gracie is still sound asleep.

Jackson places himself over me, slowly lifting my shirt with his eyes on me the entire time. He lifts it a few inches before stopping and waiting for me to give him permission to keep going.

I nod and he glances down, continuing to lift the hem of my shirt. He exposes my pink lace panties but pays them no attention as he keeps lifting. He stops just before reaching my breasts. Then he does something that surprises me.

He bends down and places soft kisses on my stomach. Just like the first time.

From top to bottom, he presses his lips to my flesh over and over. Each kiss causes full-blown goose bumps to erupt from the top of my head to my toes. My skin is tingling and hot from his kisses, but also from the emotion it evokes.

I find myself batting my lashes to fight the tears. A few sneak by and slide down my cheeks. When Jackson glances up at me, he takes a thumb and softly brushes them away.

"I'm sorry," I say, feeling foolish.

I cover my face in embarrassment.

"I'm sorry," he says back.

I remove my hands and lift my head to look at him. "What? Why?"

"I'm sorry you were ever with someone that stripped away the confidence a woman like you should have."

I scoff. "A woman like me?"

He nods. "Yes. The most beautiful, perfect woman I've ever known."

Beautiful? Perfect? How can he say that when he's got a hard stomach of chiseled abs, and he's leaning over a woman with a mom belly and stretch marks that I've spent years wishing away?

My eyebrows pull together, trying to figure out how he can see me this way. If he truly feels this way, or if he's just really good with women.

His thumb presses between my eyebrows, smoothing out the crease I formed. "You can choose not to believe me all you want, Mel, but it won't stop being true. I take one look at you, and I can't quit thinking about everything I'd like to do with you. To you." He presses himself into me. "Can you tell?"

Fuck yeah, I can tell.

"Don't let one idiot take your identity because he was too blind to see your worth." He puts his thumb under my chin, lifting my eyes to his when I try to look away. "Look at me. I see you."

With that, he completely disarms me. I decide right then and there that I'm no longer going to let Alexander come between me and the life I'm trying to create here. He's taken enough from me and I won't allow him to take one more thing.

Jackson has had to talk me off the ledge so many times that I should know him better at this point. He is all good, and tonight, he is all mine.

I place my forefinger to my lips, and pull Jackson up with my hand in his, leading him through the house to the back door. Bringing a blanket with me, I lead us outside. I slowly close the door behind us, and gesture over to the flat round swing that hangs from the roof of the porch.

Jackson sits on the edge of the swing, waiting for my next move. There's a slight breeze in the air, but it's still mostly warm out. The sky is dark, but there are a million stars lighting up the sky. The only sound comes from crickets and frogs at a nearby stream.

I don't know what makes me so bold, other than the fact that he's right. Jackson sees me. He sees me the way nobody ever has. His praise gives me the confidence to lift my shirt over my head, letting it drop to the porch.

I wrap the blanket around my shoulders and place one leg on each side of Jackson, straddling him on the swing. He places his hands on my hips to steady me as the swing starts to sway with our movement.

I bend down, but before I press my lips to his, I tell him, "I see you, too."

His misty eyes surprise me, but not as much as him flipping me until I'm under him again. He strips down, and then slowly slides my panties off, like he's savoring every inch they travel. I may have my insecurities, but the way Jackson Pierce looks at me makes me feel like I've been chiseled to perfection out of clay. Like I was made just for him.

He lingers over me longer than I like, making me ache, making me needy. "Jackson, please."

"As you wish," he says, spreading my legs apart and placing himself between them.

Though I'm not a prude, I've never been one who needs sex the way I seem to whenever Jackson is around. And I've definitely never had sex outside, underneath the stars. But I can say with certainty this will not be the last time.

It's safe to say that this man is changing me, and I really like this new version of myself. But my hesitation remains. He may say all the right things now, but I have no idea where his heart will be at the end of summer. And I'm realizing that terrifies me most of all.

CHAPTER 34
Jackson

"**A**re you serious?" Melody shrieks with excitement.

I nod, unable to hide my equally excited smile. "Wes was really inspired by the idea and can't wait to meet up with you and talk more about it."

At first, I wasn't sure if it would be overstepping to talk to Wes, but as soon as I saw the eagerness in his face at the idea, I knew I had to try.

When I came over this morning to drop off coffee and hot chocolate for her and Gracie, I couldn't resist giving her the news.

I'm smiling, but internally, I'm bracing for impact. Melody isn't a woman who accepts anything that even remotely looks like a handout, so I'm worried this could backfire on me.

Melody places her hands on the side of her head, shaking it in disbelief. "I don't know what to say. I never thought...I never thought my idea could be real."

"You're okay with this?" I ask with relief.

A wide grin spreads across her face and she nods her head. "Of course. This is unbelievable."

The Melody I knew from a couple of months ago might have

told me to fuck off and scolded me for meddling. But this Melody, *my* Melody, knows that everything I do is with the intent to see her flourish.

I pull her in for a hug, giving her a gentle squeeze. "I'm glad because you deserve all of your ideas to become reality, Mel."

I feel her squeeze back before we release, and she leans up to give me a kiss. Not a deep, passionate one. A quick one. Like a married couple seeing each other off for the day. Like we've done it a thousand times. Like we'd do it a thousand more.

As heated and delicious as the other kisses are, these might be my favorite. They're comfortable, out of habit. They tell me that I'm not the only one quickly falling deeper by the day.

"Thank you," she tells me sweetly.

"Happy to do it. But the credit is all yours, it's your idea."

The last few weeks I have been in a Melody bubble. From the first night we had sex on her back patio under the stars, something shifted.

At first, it was nighttime sneaky sessions, but after Gracie caught us cuddling on the couch one night when she woke up to pee, it quickly morphed into dinner invitations. I worried that Melody would pull back after Gracie caught us, but she surprised me by leaning into it. We are still trying to be casual, and we don't show affection around Gracie, other than a quick hand squeeze, but things have become more serious. We've fallen into a comfortable pattern.

I have always thought Gracie was an adorable, sweet girl, but getting to spend more time with both her and Melody lately has made me absolutely melt for her. I'm not entirely sure what the story is with her father, but I know he's out there somewhere. After getting to know her, I couldn't imagine walking away from her for any reason. Gracie has this ability to make you fall in love with her, and I think it's safe to say that it runs in the family.

Melody runs her hands through her hair. "I better get started, I only have a few weeks to prepare!"

We're coming up on the end of July, which means the summer festival is only about two weeks away. Not only is my schedule about to get insanely busy, but I'm also only a few weeks away from having to figure out where I want things to go with Melody. And Gracie, for that matter.

While there's no doubt that I'm falling for her, it's a lot to consider. She's been opening herself up to me more and more. And letting me into her daughter's life is not to be taken lightly. But there's still a whole other side of her, her past, that she's kept hidden from me. I know it's hard for her to talk about, which is why I don't force it. But I can't say that it doesn't worry me.

Before either of us decides to jump into this relationship with both feet, I don't think it's unfair to know what I'm getting into. Melody has her insecurities, and though she may not believe it, I have plenty of my own.

I'd like to know what happened with Gracie's father. Why he's not around, and how their relationship ended. The way she's so tight-lipped about it worries me that she may not be entirely over him.

What if I open up at the festival and tell her I want us to be together only for her to tell me she still has feelings for her ex? I couldn't possibly compete with Gracie's father, nor is it a dynamic I desire to come between. Melody has every right to keep her family together if that's what she wants. But I deserve to know what I'm up against.

With Shaina, it was always a losing battle. I thought I was what she wanted, but I was only ever a placeholder for her. Someone to serve as a safety net and boost her confidence while she did whatever the hell she wanted. I would've rather known up front that she was never serious about me. If I know what I'm up against, I can protect myself.

"You've got this, Mel, you're going to be great," I try to reassure her, despite the grimace she's currently displaying.

"I hope so."

With Gracie preoccupied with licking the whipped cream off her hot chocolate, I sneak a kiss to the top of Mel's head. "I should be going, but I can't wait to see what you come up with."

"Thank you for the coffee. You don't have to keep doing that, you know."

I smile. "It makes me happy."

"Why?" She giggles.

I shrug. "Because it makes you happy."

Melody bites her bottom lip in that irresistible way that she knows I love. I narrow my eyes at her in warning and shoot a look over to where Gracie sits before glancing back at Mel. She's playing with fire and she knows it.

I'll deal with her later when I've got her all to myself.

Though we don't do sleepovers, neither of us can resist our nighttime get-togethers. If I'm the adrenaline-seeking junkie, she's the endorphins I actively seek out.

"See you later, Gracie girl," I shout across the room.

"Wait!" Gracie shouts as she shoots off her chair and races over to give me a hug.

I give her a squeeze, soaking up the affection she so freely gives.

It may not be the best idea to bring me around Gracie so much before Melody and I have made our decision, but after she caught us cuddling together, it was even harder to hide things. Not only that, but it feels right. Other men might be intimidated to step into this family where another man once stood, but not me. I consider it an honor.

Though, the only problem now is, if I lose Melody, I lose Gracie, too.

SWEAT IS DRIPPING down my face and back as I reach for my towel and ringing phone.

"That looked really good!" Summer shouts at me from across the mat over the music.

I flip over my phone and see an incoming call from Wes. I shake my phone at her and point toward my office. Summer gives me thumbs-up and nods as I take the call where it's quieter.

"Hey Wes," I say through labored breathing.

"Jackson Pierce, how the hell are ya?" he asks brightly.

Wes is generally a chipper man. He's not Mr. Sunshine, but he's always upbeat. He's a very direct, and sometimes, impatient man, so he's earned the reputation of being kind of an asshole. But he's one of the best, most generous people I know.

"Not bad, man, how are you?"

"I can barely understand you with all that heavy breathing. Did I catch you with your pants down or something?" he asks jokingly, although, possibly serious.

I sink down into my office chair, wiping myself with a towel. "Hilarious. I just finished a jump routine. Practicing for the festival."

"Ah, Mr. Pierce the perfectionist."

I huff out a laugh. "I guess so. So what can I do for you? I'm usually the one to call you."

"That's true, you can be a pest," he jokes.

Wes is a busy man. He has his hands in a multitude of different businesses, which always has him traveling or in some meeting or another. Which typically means, yes, I'm the one calling him, not the other way around. So this call has definitely piqued my interest.

"Yeah, yeah, yeah. Just tell me what you want." He enjoys giving me a hard time, so I can't resist giving him one back.

"Nothing, really, I had a few minutes so I thought I'd check in on things and see how your girl's proposal was coming along."

My mind instantly goes to Melody when he says "your girl," until I realize he's referring to Summer.

"Oh, Summer, yeah, it's going good," I stutter.

The line is silent for a moment too long and I realize he caught the delay.

"She'll have it ready; she's excited." Maybe if I keep talking, we can blow past my awkward moment.

"Who is she?" he asks.

No such luck.

"What do you mean?" I ask coyly.

"Don't try and bullshit me. The woman you thought I was referring to just a moment ago. Because you sure as hell didn't have Summer on your mind."

He calls me out and he's not wrong. I don't know why I even tried to lie. What I told Summer about him is true, this man can spot bullshit two miles away. And apparently over the phone.

"It's Melody."

"Melody? As in, the woman we just spoke about who is also currently preparing a proposal for me? That Melody?"

"Maybe," I respond slowly.

A deep chuckle erupts on the other side of the phone, and I can picture his head thrown back.

"What?" I ask.

"I never thought I'd see the day."

"See what?" I ask.

"You in love again."

Warning bells go off in my head. I have had those thoughts a few times myself, but I haven't said them aloud. Nor do I plan to.

"Whoa, slow down. We're just hanging out," I defend.

"Don't get your panties in a bunch, Pierce. It's okay, you can tell little ol' Wes. It'll be our secret," he taunts as another burst of laughter escapes his lips.

"You know what, you can really be an asshole," I deadpan.

"So I've heard," he says through his fit of laughter.

"Well, maybe you should consider working on that."

"Naw. I have too many friends as it is, imagine if word got out that I was nice and mushy like you, I'd never get a second to myself. Sounds like a nightmare."

He's full of shit. We both know he's not an asshole, and we both know he only keeps his walls up to protect himself. Much the same way I do.

"I'm not mushy," I protest.

"Sure, you're not. That's why you're getting protective and defensive over this new broad."

"Watch it," I warn.

Another burst of laughter. "See."

Though nobody is in the room to see me, I cringe from the way my cheeks heat.

So what if he's right? Big deal. It's no secret I like Melody. We've been seeing each other for a few months now. It doesn't mean I love her. I'd know when I'm in love, right?

I shake my head. "Whatever, man. Laugh all you want, but one day, a woman is going to burst into your life and completely change the trajectory of every plan you made for yourself. Wait and see."

"The day that happens will be the day hell freezes over, my friend. I very much enjoy my life the way it is. No commitments, no confusion, no drama. Just a beautiful woman whenever I want. Easy peasy."

I'm not sure if he's trying to convince me or himself.

Wes is a notorious playboy, but he is always upfront about his intentions. He never lies or leads women on, which is still a step above most relationships from the men I know. He's just a man who likes to have a good time.

Though, I'm certain it's still an act, a cover, to protect himself. I know because I was the same way before Melody entered my town and my life.

But he was right about one thing. When it comes to Melody, I am most definitely protective, and as that thought enters my mind, I can't help but wonder: have I been in love with her this entire time?

CHAPTER 35

Melody

"Melody! It's five thirty, what are you still doing here?" Kat scolds from across the kitchen as she exits her and Bud's office.

"Elana never showed for the night shift so I stayed late to help the night crew."

Kat props one hand on her hip in the motherly way that prompts me to give her a sheepish smile. She's been nothing but kind to me since I arrived in Blue Springs and more of a mother than my own ever was to me. But that's just how Kat is. She's caring and comforting in a way that makes you want to seek her out when you're having a bad day because her warmth is like a hot cup of cocoa on a snowy day. She instantly makes things better. It makes perfect sense that she and Jane are such close friends since they both embody so many of the same qualities.

She wags a finger in my direction. "You work much too hard and you've been here since 8 am. You get home to that beautiful little girl of yours and enjoy the night with her."

I don't mind staying to help, but I do have dinner plans with Jackson and Gracie tonight, and it's all she could talk about as we dozed off to bed last night. Lately she's been almost as eager to see him as I am, which makes me feel less bad for sneaking around with him behind her back.

My rationality is that it's safer for her this way. Right now he's a family friend, so there are no expectations. If it turns into more, then we step into dangerous territory.

I finish wiping down the counter and grab some glasses to restock the shelf. "Okay, I'm going, I swear."

I untie my apron and roll it up as I walk to Bud and Kat's office for my purse.

"Have a good night, you two, I'll see you in the morning," I say, giving them a wave.

"'Night, young lady," Bud drawls out as Kat says, "Good night, sweetheart."

As much as I love working for Bud and Kat, and how wonderful they've been to me, I can't help but daydream about new possibilities. A dream that, with Jackson's help, I could open my very own safe house for women. After hearing that he spoke to his friend Wes about making this a reality, it has made coming to Blue Bistro even less fulfilling.

Don't get me wrong, I'm incredibly grateful for the blind chance Bud and Kat took on me, but there's only so much enjoyment one can get out of serving burgers to impatient tourists and regulars of Blue Springs week after week.

Though I'd be lying if I said I wasn't nervous to quit. What do I know about running a safe house? Why would anyone trust me to keep them safe? And, to top it off, I'm scared to let Bud and Kat down. I don't want to seem ungrateful, like the work here isn't good enough.

Is it awful to want more?

I exit the doors of Blue Bistro into the warm summer air, heading for my car. The sidewalks are littered with townsfolk and tourists alike. Though Blue Springs isn't a huge tourist destination, it still draws a crowd from nearby Colorado towns.

It's a friendly, quiet place, and snuggled up against beautiful mountains, with hidden hot springs, the views don't get much better than this.

When I first came to Blue Springs a few months ago, I had zero expectations about it. I didn't know if I would spend a month here or a year. But now, with August upon us, I can't help but picture Gracie growing up here. Creating a life here wouldn't be so bad. Putting down roots and finding a place of our own here sounds more appealing the longer we're here.

I wish I could say it's primarily due to my newfound freedom, but I know there's another large factor contributing to my happiness. A six-one, chiseled, jump-roping man with curly brown hair that brings me and my daughter hot beverages in the morning simply because he wants to, and knows how to do things to my body that I didn't know were possible.

Jackson Pierce has quickly gone from a delicious accessory in my life to a daily staple I'm beginning to depend on.

I've also gained an incredible friend in Summer. She's been warm and welcoming from the minute we met, and it's not something I've been accustomed to. My circle back in LA was full of drama and backstabbing, so you never really knew who you could trust. Actually, that's a lie, I knew I couldn't trust any of them.

As hard as it was to leave LA, it would be even harder to leave Blue Springs, for very different reasons.

As if I've summoned her with my mind, my phone rings at the same time my engine roars to life.

"Hey Summer."

"Hey girl, what are you doing?"

"Just got off work, heading home."

"Want to get in a jump workout with me?" she asks eagerly.

"I wish I could. I'm actually racing home because I have dinner plans with Jackson and Gracie."

"Both of them?" she asks incredulously.

I laugh awkwardly, because it does sound pretty official when I say it aloud. "Yeah, but it's no big deal. It's dinner...as friends."

There's silence on the line and I can practically feel her smug smile and eye roll from the other side.

"Well damn," she responds, sounding disappointed.

"What's going on?"

"I may have ulterior motives for asking you to work out with me," she confesses.

"Should I be scared?" I joke.

"No, but I am."

"What are you talking about?"

Silence, and then she word vomits so fast I can't catch every word.

"You need help with your proposal for Wes?" I ask, dumbfounded.

"Of course! Unless you don't want to."

I laugh. "Oh my gosh, no. I am happy to help, it's just...I was going to ask you to help with mine. I'm freaking out. I have never done anything like this before, and I'm going to screw it up."

I voice the doubts that have been bouncing around in my head for the last week since Jackson gave me the news. There are only two weeks until the festival and I have no idea where to begin. I have done my fair share of googling, but it would be nice to talk to someone who knows what they're doing.

When he first told me the news, I was shocked. I had a minor fit of panic that I quickly stomped out once I saw the excitement on his face. Jackson isn't a man who does things for others to benefit himself. Over the last few months, he's proven to be a man who goes out of his way to make others happy simply because it makes him happy.

Allowing myself to enjoy the news without wondering what

was in it for him might have been the moment I realized things have changed; I've changed.

It may have been the exact moment I realized that I'm in love with Jackson Pierce.

"Why don't you ask Jackson?" she asks.

Because I don't want to look like an idiot.

"Why don't *you* ask Jackson for help?" I echo back.

"Touché."

I'm surprised Summer isn't going to Jackson for help, having known each other for most of their lives. I can't imagine she has too many self-conscious moments that arise between the two of them.

"Summer, I'm happy to help, but I really have no idea what I'm doing, either. I think Jackson would be more helpful to you."

I can practically see her blonde ponytail swish back and forth when she says, "No way. He can proofread them when we're done. Now, when are you free so we can work on these?"

I laugh at her stubbornness. "I could meet up with you tomorrow after work, if Jackson doesn't need you."

A boisterous laugh bursts out of her. "I could say the same thing to you."

"He only needs me at night," I say before I can think better of it. "Wait, I didn't mean...oh God, that came out wrong."

All I hear is laughter on the other end of the phone as Summer relishes in my accidental slipup that isn't entirely false, but not entirely true, either.

"I just meant he needs you more during the day for work purposes," I correct.

"Melody, babe, no need to clarify. I know *exactly* what you meant," she says through another fit of laughter.

"Good luck figuring out the proposal by yourself," I bluff, because let's face it, I need help even more than she does. And I'd rather not go running to the man I'm sleeping with and tell him that I'm, in fact, not capable of doing this. I'm sure that'll really boost his confidence in me and make him glad he put himself out on a limb for me. Just a single mom who has no clue what she's doing. Fantastic.

"No, wait!" she shouts. "I'll be good, I promise."

I can still hear her laughing, though she's doing a much better job at stifling it.

I can't help but giggle along with her.

"So, tomorrow? Where do you want to meet?" I ask.

"Rocky's?" she suggests.

"You want to write our business proposals at a bar?" I laugh.

"Why not? I'm so stressed about this, and I'm definitely going to need a drink."

She has a point.

"Okay, I'll text you when I'm off tomorrow."

"Sounds good. Thanks, Mel."

"No problem."

"Have fun with your 'friends' dinner. Just one question."

"Shoot."

"If it's just a casual, friendly dinner, why wasn't I invited?" she taunts and then bursts into laughter again.

"I'm hanging up now," I say before actually hanging up. But not before hearing her cackling even louder on the other end.

The truth is, these dinners aren't so friendly anymore. They started out that way. A way to get to know each other better, and it's been good for Gracie to have a positive, happy male figure around. But now they've become so frequent that the lines have blurred. In the matter of a few weeks, it's like we've turned into a little family. It feels comfortable and safe. Two things we've never been accustomed to.

From living at home with my parents, to living with Alexander, I've always felt on edge. My existence always felt transactional. As if my presence, and my love, were never enough. I always had to provide something for someone else.

For my parents, I had to be the perfect daughter to keep up the flawless family image they wanted. Then they molded me into someone a man like Alexander, and his family, would want to marry into.

With Alexander, he had the same upbringing, so he held the same expectations of me. I had to portray the quintessential woman at his side, never questioning him. In his eyes, he provided for us, so that was reason enough for him to do as he pleased, no matter how much it hurt me or his daughter.

Safe and comfortable are two words I'd never used to describe my homelife either with my parents or Alexander. Maybe that's why it's been so easy to fall for Jackson.

Am I ready to admit aloud that I'm in love with him?

He has no expectations of me and does things for Gracie and me simply because it makes us happy. He's gentle, funny, and kind in all of the ways I always dreamed a man could be. He stands up for me and has protected us in a way that allows me to let my guard down with him. I've seen myself grow into a new version of myself, and while I may not be completely at ease, I've surprised myself with how easily I've let him into my and Gracie's life.

I pull into my driveway a few minutes later, eager to see the man I love. Excited to make dinner with him and my beautiful daughter, because we deserve to be this happy. After all we've been through, it's time that Gracie and I finally get our happy ending.

CHAPTER 36

Jackson

A splash of red wine colors the counter as I attempt to fill Melody's glass.

"Oh no, messy!" Gracie shrieks dramatically in the way little kids do.

Melody laughs while tearing a paper towel and wiping away the spot. "See, all better."

Gracie palms her forehead theatrically. "Oh my."

Both Melody and I laugh as Gracie shakes her head, cracking a smile. She's clearly trying to entertain us, and it's working.

I've been looking forward to this dinner with my two favorite girls all day. It took all of my effort to focus during the two conference calls I had earlier today, which is absolutely not like me. I always put business first, never letting women be a distraction the way Melody has become for me. I can't say I hate it, especially now that our middle-of-the-night trysts have evolved into something more. Much more.

I watch as Melody sips the red wine, a little spilling past her plump lips, and I can't help but stare. At her lips, and the way her red dress hugs every curve.

"Jackson," Melody warns.

I take a step closer to her. "Yes?"

"Stop looking at me like that."

I cock an eyebrow. "How am I looking at you?"

"Like I'm going to be dinner instead of the pasta on the stove," she playfully scolds me, but I know she thrives off my undivided attention. The way I can't seem to tear my gaze from her. Her smile tells me as much. The way her body gravitates toward me solidifies the assumption.

A smirk dances on my lips. "Oh, I can arrange that if you'd like."

Her eyes drift downward to where Gracie is sitting at the table just a few feet away, smushing Play-Doh with her small hands. She may not be paying attention, but her ears don't miss much. She's so smart.

Her eyes shift back to mine and she shakes her head. "You're playing a dangerous game."

"Maybe, but I'm a great opponent. I don't mind losing."

She sucks in a breath and bites her lower lip in that sexy way I can't resist. We're caught in a stare down, both of us scared to move. The air is static with electricity, daring one of us to inch closer and make the connection. But our lust bubble pops when Gracie shouts from the table.

"Mommmm."

Melody rapidly blinks and steps away from me. "What, baby?"

"It's stinky," she says, pointing to the stove where, sure enough, the sauce is burning and bubbling over the pan, making a mess.

"Shit," Melody curses under her breath.

"How's it looking?" I ask as I watch Melody frantically stir the sauce, turning off the flame.

"Well, it's definitely done, if that's what you're asking."

We both laugh.

I walk behind her to grab the plates, letting my fingertips graze across her back as I whisper into her ear. "Good, because I'm starving."

Her body shudders as I hand her the plates.

"Jax, sit with me!" Gracie shrieks from the table.

"Of course I'm going to sit next to you, sweet girl," I respond.

As much fun as I'm having, I've really been enjoying spending time with Gracie, too. It's a dynamic I never saw for my life, nor was it something I thought I'd like as much as I have been. Not that I dislike kids. But after my relationship with Shaina exploded, the fairytale family ideal became collateral damage.

Somewhere in the last few weeks, though, these two have opened me back up to the possibility of more. As tantalizing as it is, "more" terrifies me. Scares me to my core because the more you have, the more can be taken away from you.

The vodka sauce penne pasta is creamy and so indulgent that hardly a word is spoken while we work on clearing our plates. Even Gracie, who's always chatting away or making some sort of sound effect, is silent while she eats.

It's a comfortable silence. The kind that only comes when you're in the company of people you can unapologetically be yourself with. The kind I could get used to. The kind I think I've already gotten used to.

Melody clears the table and begins cleaning up the kitchen, forcing me into the living room with Gracie, despite my offer to clean. I've never been the kind of man that requires or needs a woman to clean up after him. I enjoy doing things for the woman I'm with. My happiness comes from making my partner happy.

I sip my wine on the couch while Gracie sits on the floor in front of it, coloring a picture on the coffee table. She's humming a tune quietly, and when I turn my head, I can hear Melody humming a tune of her own as she wipes down the countertop. I find myself smiling from ear to ear at the comfort I find myself in around these two. I could blame the wine for the way my heart is pounding in my chest and the butterflies flipping around in my stomach, but it's not the wine. It's them. They make me undeniably happy in a way I haven't been in a very long time.

Not the kind of happiness that comes from the high of accomplishing a goal, but the happiness that comes from the mundane moments in life.

Melody grabs her wine glass and makes her way over to me on the couch, sitting closer to me than she typically does when Gracie is around. While we may tiptoe very closely on the line, we are careful to never cross it in front of Gracie.

"Thank you for a delicious dinner," she tells me.

I made the sauce, but she put as much effort into dinner as I did. "You're welcome. Thank you for the wonderful company."

Her entire face lights up, but I see hesitancy in her smile.

"What?" I ask.

She chews on her lip. "I wasn't sure how this" —she motions between us and Gracie— "would look. Or how it would feel."

I rub her hand with my thumb, nodding. I wasn't sure myself.

"I thought it might be weird, or that it may be awkward for both of you. But..." she trails off, so I finish.

"It's not."

She shakes her head. "Not at all."

A bright smile stretches across her face, and I can't help but return one as my chest swells with love.

Am I in love? Is that why this word so easily keeps crossing my mind, threatening to slip past my lips?

I clear my throat and take another sip of wine to break the

tension. I'm not saying it tonight. Not here, not in front of her daughter, putting them both on the spot.

Shake it off, man.

Melody, clearly sensing the shift, changes the conversation. "I'm meeting Summer for drinks tomorrow."

"Oh yeah? That sounds fun."

She takes a sip of her wine, popping one shoulder up.

I give her a quizzical expression. "Is it not going to be fun?"

She laughs awkwardly. "No! I mean, yes, it will be. I just mean that it's not a casual girls night. We're meeting up to work on our proposals."

"That's great, I was wondering how they were coming along."

She grimaces.

"That good, huh?" I laugh.

"Ooooh yeah," she responds sarcastically.

"You know it's going to be great, right?"

"I...I've never done this before," she reluctantly admits.

I give her a warm smile. "I thought that might be the case."

"You knew?" she asks with surprise.

I chuckle and nod.

"Why would you risk your reputation on me, knowing I have no idea what the heck I'm doing?"

"My *reputation*? First of all, Wes is a close friend of mine. Second of all, we all start somewhere. You can't get anywhere unless you start with your first one. And last," I say softer now, intertwining our fingers, "I believe in you. So even if my reputation were at risk, I wouldn't be worried at all."

Her eyes mist over, and she gives me a warm, watery smile, so I give her hand a squeeze.

"Hey, I mean it," I reiterate.

She nods, and then pulls her hand back, quickly wiping away the stray tear that slipped down her cheek.

Thank you, she mouths.

We spend the next hour watching whatever movie is playing for Gracie while she colors. I don't pay it much attention, because I'm focused on the slight buzz I'm getting from the wine, and the way our bodies feel together. The way her skin feels warm and soft beneath my hand as I caress her leg. The way her hair smells like coconut every time she turns her head and I get a whiff of it. The way she's been melting deeper into me as the evening progresses.

It's not until my phone dings on the arm of the couch that I realize how late it's getting. I have an early day tomorrow, and more meetings that I need to be present for, so I really should be going.

"Oh shoot," Melody whispers as she checks her own phone. "Gracie, sweetie, it's time for your bath."

Gracie whips her head around and gives her best pouty face. She's a hell of an actress with her entire bottom lip pushed out, widened doe eyes, and hands pressed together in prayer. "Please, Mama, five more minutes."

"Gracie. It's already really late, sweetheart. You've had way more than five extra minutes."

"Two more minutes?" she counters.

A half laugh, half gasp bursts from Melody. "You little rascal. Nice try, but it's time for your bath. You were playing around in the dirt and you stink like sweat."

Gracie groans dramatically, though I can tell she's not really angry, this is just the way they banter. Mother and daughter, testing each other's limits.

"I should probably get going, too," I say.

"No!" Gracie pops up, standing in front of me.

"Sweetie, he has things he needs to get done, too," Melody explains.

"Please, can't he stay and help me get ready for bed?" she begs.

I glance over at Melody, who raises both hands in surrender, then turn back to Gracie's pleading eyes. "I can stay a bit longer as long as it's okay with your mom."

"Mom, can he? Pleeeese?"

Melody releases a heavy sigh of defeat. "A little bit longer. Don't think this is getting you out of bedtime, because it's not."

Her words are firm, but her tone is soft.

"Yay! Thanks Mom, thanks Dad!" she shrieks, giving us both quick hugs before hopping off to the bathroom.

Dad?

Did she just call me "Dad"?

Did she mean to?

I glance over at Melody to see she's equally stunned. Her eyes are wide and misty as she stares after Gracie, and she's placed a hand over her mouth. Either suppressing a happy or saddened sob. But for a few moments, neither of us speaks or moves, processing the moment.

Like trying a new move for the first time, I let the word slowly stretch across my mind to see how it feels. I never expected to hear those words out of Gracie, or anyone, for that matter, so I never needed to think about how it would feel to hear it. She thinks of me as a father figure, and as scary as that could seem, it doesn't feel scary at all.

It feels right.

If I thought loving Melody made my heart swell, after hearing Gracie call me Dad, I fear the organ may no longer fit inside of my chest.

After Shaina, I turned everything off. I went from feeling every negative emotion known to man, to feeling absolutely nothing.

Like a switchboard, Melody has managed to turn it all back on, rebooting my entire system. In one evening, I can go from feeling turned-on, to proud, to loved, and now, accepted and wanted. Needed. With Melody and Gracie, I feel every damn thing.

This changes everything and I know one thing for sure, I no longer fear where Melody stands, because I know where my heart is.

I am in love with Melody Miller and when this festival arrives, I plan on showing her exactly how much.

CHAPTER 37

Melody

"**A**re you trying to get me drunk, Summer?"

"Maybe. Is it working?" She winks at me.

My shoulders shake with laughter. "Yes, actually."

Summer sips her cocktail, raising her chin with a prideful grin.

"These are really good, but I don't think we need another round. We haven't even started to work on our proposals," I remind her.

Summer's long blonde hair lies in loose curls over her shoulders, framing her face. The light blue baby doll dress she's wearing under her jean jacket makes her eyes pop even more than they already do.

She flips her hair over one shoulder and places her elbows on the table. "We will work on them, I promise. I just needed a few drinks first."

"Are you okay? I've never seen you like this."

She sighs, resting her chin in her hands. "Ugh. I know."

I laugh.

"Are you laughing at me?" She tries her best to sound offended.

"I'm relieved. I'm so nervous about this damn thing."

Now it's Summer who's laughing. "Oh God, what did we get ourselves into?"

I shrug, taking a sip from my own beverage. The server comes back with two fresh drinks for us, and we hand off our empty ones. We clink our glasses together, immediately taking a sip.

"Jackson actually made me feel a lot better about it last night. So even though I still have anxiety about the whole thing, I don't think he's going to let either of us fail," I say, trying to comfort not only her, but myself.

"What did he say?"

"How much he believes in me." Summer doesn't reply, waiting for more. "I know it doesn't sound like much, but it meant a lot to me. Nobody's ever told me that before. I could feel that he really meant it."

Summer gives me a warm smile and reaches across to squeeze my hand lying on the table. "He does mean it, Mel. I'm glad you two found each other."

The smile that appears any time I think about Jackson surfaces, and I've now dubbed it my "Jackson smile," because I've never been so giddy over anyone or anything in my life the way I am with this man.

Especially after last night.

"I have to tell you something," I confess.

Summer's eyes bulge, a million thoughts probably going through her head right now. She grabs my hand and flips it over, eyeing it suspiciously.

"What are you doing?" I ask, giggling.

"Just making sure you two didn't go and elope without me," she jokes.

I pull my hand back. "Definitely not."

"I know how you two are with each other, it's not that far-fetched."

I playfully roll my eyes.

Summer takes another sip and then sits back. "Okay, okay. Tell me, what's juicier than you two getting married?"

"Well, for the record, we did not get married," I reiterate and Summer rolls her wrist, urging me to continue. "But Gracie did call him 'Dad' last night."

"What?!" Summer, who had been taking a sip of her drink, apparently swallows wrong and nearly chokes to death on her drink. She coughs loudly with her hand to her chest for so long that I round the table and give her a few smacks on the back in case she's really choking. Once she's finally cleared her throat of the liquid, she takes a deep breath and then her jaw drops.

"I know," I tell her, still in shock about it myself.

"Yeah, this is...huge. What did Jackson say or do? What did you do?" she asks eagerly.

"I didn't say anything!" I say, laughing. "I wasn't sure how to respond. I had no idea how Jackson was going to feel or respond, so I just sat there until he reacted first."

"How did he react?"

"He was silent for a minute, and then he leaned in to kiss me, like, really kiss me. Hand on the back of my head and everything. Then got up and helped Gracie get ready for her bath. It was sweet."

"Neither of you two said anything about it?" Summer asks in disbelief.

I shake my head.

"Oh my gosh. He didn't say anything about it at work today. I'm dying to know what he's thinking right now."

I chuckle. "You and me both."

Summer swirls the straw around in her drink. "So, how do you feel about it?"

Good question.

When that word left Gracie's mouth, it shocked me to my core. I haven't heard her utter that word since we left, aside from the very few times she's asked about her father. So it's not something I'm used to hearing anymore. It never occurred to me that anyone might take that place or step into that role for her. Especially so soon.

Jackson and I have yet to decide where things are going. Are they going well? Yes. But have we had a conversation to discuss our intentions going further and where that leaves us and Gracie? No.

Our plan was to wait until the festival, which felt like it was racing toward us, but after last night, I wish it was tomorrow so I knew exactly what he was thinking and feeling.

I lay awake all night, replaying Gracie's words. How they so casually flew from her mouth. As if she's said it a million times.

When I uprooted our lives and drove us to Colorado, I spent countless nights wondering if I had done the right thing by her. People always say, "A girl needs her father." But is it still true if said father is only causing her and her mother pain?

I spent years waiting and hoping for Alexander to change. Once Gracie was born, I really thought things would turn around for us. I thought once he saw her beautiful face, he would realize how important his family was, and he would prioritize his family. But if anything, Gracie's existence only pushed him further away. He used her as an excuse to "work more"—which really only meant him staying late at the office to fuck his secretary—and he was home even less than before.

Carrying the entire load of parenthood has been no easy feat. But it's not the responsibility or the work that bothers me.

It's the burden of questioning every decision I make. Not knowing if it's going to benefit or hurt her in the long run. Wondering if I'm going to wind up screwing her up despite my best efforts. Fearing that one day Alexander will come back and fill her head with lies that I've taken her away from him, when we both know the truth. He never really wanted us to begin with.

Hearing Gracie call Jackson "Dad" opened up old wounds, but it also opened my eyes. Gracie does need a father, but it doesn't mean that person needs to be Alexander.

Summer is looking at me expectantly while my mind runs wild.

I take a deep breath and tell her the truth. "I don't know."

She gives me a knowing look. "Hey, that's okay. I'm sure it caught you both by surprise, and it's a lot to take in."

"It's not that it was bad or I disliked it."

"Then what is it?" she wonders aloud.

"It scared me."

She doesn't speak, but gives me a sad, understanding smile.

"Everything about Jackson scares me, to be honest."

"Because you love him," she states matter-of-factly.

I can't hide it anymore. I've stopped lying to myself about it, and I can no longer lie to anyone else, either.

I nod.

"I know, Mel."

"I have to think about Gracie. If Jackson doesn't feel the same way. If he decides this has been fun, but he's not ready to be a dad, it's not just me that loses him, it's Gracie, too. I can handle being hurt, that's nothing new. But I cannot watch her heart break. Not again."

Summer sighs. "I can't speak for Jackson, but I do know that he's absolutely crazy about you. I've seen the way he lights up when your name comes up in conversation. I've seen you two together. What you two have is special. It's real. That much is true."

"But it doesn't mean he's ready to be a dad. Hell, I don't think he's even ready for a relationship. I don't know if I'm ready for all of that," I confess.

"Now *that*, I completely understand. I have put myself out there for so many men, and here I am still single. It's the Wild West out there. But," she says when she sees the look of panic on my face, "no man has ever looked at me the way Jackson looks at you."

Can it really be that simple? Can the way Jackson looks at me tell me everything I need to know? Because I've seen it. I know the look she's talking about. Sometimes I feel like I could ignite from his gaze. But that's just lust, isn't it? It's no secret that we have intense chemistry, but has that transformed into more for him, like it has for me? Is it possible he's fallen in love with me? Not only me, but my daughter, too, in this short amount of time?

"Talk to him. I know you two have this whole agreement to wait until the festival. But I think things are beyond that now. Have dinner together and talk. Figure things out."

I sigh. "Look, if you're going to give me reasonable solutions and be rational about this, I'm not sure this friendship is going to work out."

She laughs. "I know, I can be so wise at times."

"What do I tell him?" I ask, hoping she really does have all the answers.

"The truth. Lay it all out there, Mel. I know you're scared, but whether he's in the same place as you are right now or not, he's not going to hurt you or Gracie. That much I know for sure."

Summer's conviction is so strong, I have no choice but to believe her. She's his best friend and has been their whole lives. She knows him best, so if she's saying I can trust him, I can.

He seemed surprised, though not confused or upset last night, so I keep telling myself I'm likely overreacting. I'm worrying for nothing. Still, I can't quiet the voice in my head that tells me it's asking too much. That he only wanted the fun, secret relationship, and didn't sign up for a whole-ass family.

But what if I'm wrong? Are there men who actually want a family instead of just the image of having one? I couldn't convince Gracie's actual father to participate and show up in our lives even though he was bound to her by genetics. And I think that's what worries me the most: the man that should have loved her unconditionally couldn't, so how could anyone else?

Summer, being the great friend that she is, sensing my downward spiral in the silence stretching between us, orders another round. "One more round, and then we order food, because we have boss-girl things to do. Dreams to chase and goals to crush. No matter what happens, we have this and we are going to kill it. You with me?"

I smile and lift my drink to her already lifted one and clink. "Let's do it."

I can't control what happens with Jackson. All I can do is be honest and let the cards fall where they may. If he decides to walk away, I still have my beautiful daughter and this amazing opportunity to hold onto.

After years of being with the wrong man, it's been hard to let a new one come into my life. Hard to believe they're not all bad. But now that I have and I see how good things can be, how they *should* be, it scares me to think it's all about to slip through my fingers. It seems too good to be true, because after all, look at us. I'm sure people look at Jackson and me together and wonder what the hell he's doing with a woman like me.

I've had to work hard to convince myself that I deserve a man like him, despite not looking like Summer or any of the other painfully beautiful women at his gym that I'm sure drool all over him on a daily basis.

But one thing I absolutely will not do is try to convince Jackson or any man to be with me. Or that Gracie and I are a good thing, because that, I know for a fact. So if Jackson Pierce isn't ready for my daughter, then it's his damn loss.

CHAPTER 38

Jackson

"Jackson Pierce!" Summer's high-pitched shriek barrels down the hallway and into my office before she does.

Her blonde hair floats around the corner as she practically sprints into my office and drops into the chair across from me.

"Something I can do for you?" I ask nonchalantly.

She shoots me a silent, accusatory stare.

"What did I do?"

She lifts a manicured eyebrow. "Anything you'd like to tell me?"

I tap a finger to my temple. "Hmm, no, not really."

She purses her lips and rolls her eyes at me.

"Well, since I know you had drinks with Melody yesterday, I'm going to assume that a conversation about me was had," I reply.

Summer clutches her chest dramatically and lowers her voice. "Gracie called you 'Dad.'"

I let out a breath and lean back in my chair.

"Jackson Pierce. What is going on in that mind? So help me, if you hurt them..." she warns.

I lift a hand for her to stop.

"I'm not going to hurt them."

"Well, what on earth was that response about?" she asks, frowning.

"It's been a lot to absorb."

She nods.

"Did I upset her?" I ask, worried that my lack of acknowledgment may have given Melody the wrong idea.

The truth is, it made me feel damn good when Gracie said that. My concern was for Melody. I didn't want to put her on the spot and react without knowing how it made *her* feel.

Summer shakes her head. "Anxious and worried, maybe."

I release a long puff of air, raking a hand through my hair. "That makes two of us."

Summer laughs.

"Something funny?"

She nods. "Yeah. The two of you."

"Why's that?"

"Since you two started seeing each other, you've both had this crushing fear of getting hurt or in your case, humiliated again," she says pointing at me. "But the whole time, you've both been all-in, whether you realized it or not."

"What are you saying?"

"That you two need to get over your shit and realize you both love each other. The only way either of you is getting hurt is by letting those fears come between you."

"How can you be so sure?" I ask, looking down at a fingernail I'm picking at.

She gives me a warm smile. "Look at you, Jackson. Look at her. You two are in so deep you can't see what's right in front of you."

That's not entirely true. I see her. Oh, I definitely see Melody.

But simply "getting over" the fear of rejection and humiliation isn't as simple as she makes it sound.

"Says the woman who's sworn off dating because of a few bad dates," I challenge with a huff.

If it's so easy to get over your shit, let's see her do it.

I shoot her a glare, and she rolls her eyes at me again. "Hey, it's way more," she says, sweeping her arm across the front of her, "than a few bad dates, first of all. Second of all, that's completely different. I don't have someone showing up for me day after day, looking at me the way you two look at each other."

Even without Summer's lecture, I wasn't planning on going anywhere. I know I'm in love with Melody. I'm not sure where she stands, but I'm ready to put it all out there, and let Melody make her choice. Maybe she's unable to fully show me where she's at because I haven't been able to. Perhaps Summer is right, and we are both too terrified to show our cards first.

"I'm going to tell her I'm in love with her," I confess.

"Well, duh."

I stand, grabbing my wallet off the desk.

"Wait, you mean right now?" Summer shrieks, popping up from her own chair with excitement, bouncing from foot to foot.

I laugh. "No. Well, maybe. I don't know. I just need to see her."

I hear Summer squeal as I bolt out of my office with no real plan in mind. My only focus is getting into my car and driving to Melody's place. Our agreement was to wait until the festival to make any decisions, but I can't wait a few more weeks. Melody and Gracie are my future, and I want them to know it, so they can make the best decision for themselves.

As I exit the gym, the flower shop across the street catches my eye and I decide that something this epic needs something extra. I don't want to show up empty-handed. I slip into the small shop and grab two bouquets of peonies. Red for Melody and pink for Gracie. Next, I head over to Bread Pitt and order their favorite drinks to take as well.

Driving up the road toward Melody's, I find my nerves growing. As hard as I'm trying to "get over" my shit right now and admit to my dream girl that I love her, it's not that easy. My palms are sweating, and my heart is racing.

I anxiously tap at the steering wheel, forcing myself to stay within the speed limit.

There's a chance Melody doesn't want the same things I do. It's possible that a serious relationship is the last thing she wants. Hell, I've had to practically drag her into hanging out with me to begin with.

Doubt begins to creep in, but I keep my foot on the gas pedal.

Don't be a coward.

I see her cabin come into view and I place my car in park. I check and recheck my appearance in the rearview mirror.

This is the point of no return. Time to show my cards.

I knock loudly on the door with both bouquets in one hand, anticipating seeing her beautiful face appear when the door opens. But when it does, it's not Melody or Gracie that I see.

"Mom?" I laugh. "I didn't realize you were here."

She gives me a quizzical expression. "You didn't see my car out front?"

Nope, sure didn't.

My tunnel vision for seeing Melody clouded the fact that I parked next to my mother's car, and Melody's isn't even here.

I hear Gracie's little feet racing for the door, and when she appears in the doorway, her eyes go wide. "Wow! Those are beautiful!"

I extend the pink bouquet. "These are for you."

"For me?" she practically whispers, her eyes wide as saucers.

"For you, sweet girl."

She carefully grabs the bouquet and retreats into the house.

"Come on in. Melody is at work right now. She has the night shift. Do you want me to place these in some water?" my mother offers as we walk into the living room.

I shut the door behind me. "No, I think I'll take them to work. I was looking forward to seeing her."

My mother tries to hide a grin.

"What?" I ask.

She smirks and leans in to kiss my cheek. "I'm happy for you. For you both."

I've never been able to keep much from my mother. We've always been close, so it's not a surprise that she knows exactly why I'm here.

"Oh, I almost forgot. I got Gracie a hot chocolate."

I leave the red peonies on the leather car seat and remove Gracie's drink from the holder to bring it inside. She grabs it excitedly and pops the lid off to lick the nearly melted whipped cream. It's her favorite part.

"I would have brought you a coffee, but I didn't realize you were here," I tell my mother apologetically.

She waves me off. "Oh please, at my age, I can't drink caffeine in the afternoon, I'll be up all night."

I stand there awkwardly for a moment, not really knowing what to do now.

"Go get your girl. I'm fine with Gracie. But call me with the details."

I laugh. "You're incorrigible, Mother."

She squeezes my arm. "Yeah, but you love me."

"You're right. And thank you."

"For what?" she asks as her eyebrows pull together.

"For being an incredible mother. An amazing single parent. Just for everything you've done for me. It can't have been easy."

I have only seen my mother cry a handful of times in my life. She's one of the strongest women I know, and while she doesn't hide her emotions, she's not prone to tears. But as I stand before her, I can see her eyes watering up.

It's a moment before she responds, and I can't help but notice the way her voice is cracking and thick with emotion. "Thank you for making it all worth it."

I hug her and Gracie goodbye, and as much as I hate the quick visit with my mother, I have another woman I'm dying to see. A woman I hope to one day call mine.

THE DRIVE back over to the main street in town takes longer than it did to drive to her house. But it's not the nerves this time. Seeing my mother and Gracie calmed me and made me realize just how sure I am about all of this. A small flicker in my chest tells me that Melody feels the same way. That she wants the same things I do.

I park behind the gym in my usual spot and take a deep breath before I head over to Blue Bistro. There's no way I can blurt out "I love you" while she's at work, but I still need to see her. To bring her a small surprise, so she knows I'm not going anywhere.

Based on the conversation I had with Summer, it seems that I left Melody with some unanswered questions. So, at the very least, I can show up today and let her know that she has nothing to worry about. The confession can wait, because I want it to be special for her. She deserves for it to be perfect.

With the red peonies and coffee in hand, I make my way over to the bistro through a throng of people idling outside the front. They are giving hugs and appear to have just finished dining. I squeeze around the crowd and slip inside, eagerly anticipating Melody's sweet face. That perfect smile.

I stand at the front and scan the restaurant, but don't see her. Maybelle stands at the hostess stand, smiling at me.

"Hi Jackson, table for one today?" she asks.

"I'm looking for Melody."

"Oh, she's around here somewhere. I can go look in the back and let her know you're here, if you'd like."

"Great, thanks."

She slips away and disappears through the kitchen doors for a few moments and then saunters back out alone.

"She's in the back preparing a few things, she'll be out in a couple minutes."

I give her a gracious smile. "Thank you."

"Hi, can I help you?" the hostess asks someone behind me.

I step to the side so new patrons can filter in.

"Pardon me," I say, stepping out of the way of a tall man behind me.

Even though it's not quite dinnertime yet, the restaurant seems to be filling up quickly. As I wait for Melody, I glance around and see that the dining room is nearly full. I internally frown because I had hoped Melody could sneak out for a few minutes with me, but it doesn't look likely.

I'm daydreaming about what I'm going to say to her when I hear the man at the hostess stand say her name, and as if the volume was just turned up, my attention is immediately drawn to his conversation.

"You're looking for Melody?" Maybelle asks the man.

He nods.

"Who should I say is looking for her?" she asks.

"Tell her it's an old friend," the man responds slowly, smoothly, in a tone that makes my skin crawl.

I immediately dislike him.

Blue Springs has its fair share of tourists, but in our small community, we all mostly know one another and their families. So it's always a bit alarming when a stranger comes around asking for one of our own.

"Okay..." Maybelle responds somewhat reluctantly and then retreats from her post, making her way back toward the kitchen again.

Unable to bite my tongue, I turn to the man. "You're a friend of Melody's?"

He turns to face me, and his expression is cold. Hard. He's wearing tan slacks that are rolled at the ankles, his white loafers on display. His collared shirt under a blue knit sweater is strange for the summer weather, and his short hair is slicked back in a way that tells me this man is all about control.

"Who's asking?" the man retorts.

I puff my chest, unable to stop the laugh that bubbles out of me. "Her boyfriend. Who the hell are you?"

The man takes one hand out of his pocket and extends it toward me in a professional, yet unfriendly, dominating manner. "Nice to meet you. I'm her husband."

Husband.

My ears instantly begin to ring as I slowly back away.

He couldn't be her husband. Melody isn't married. She's never mentioned that she ever was or is currently married.

I don't have much time to react before I see Melody's body swaying in our direction. Her eyes are on me, and she's wearing the widest smile. A few moments earlier, and I'd have returned it.

I'm frozen in place, unable to shake myself out of it.

"Melody," the man next to me calls brightly, turning toward her.

And as her gaze drifts from me to the man next to me, I watch the recognition hit. Her smile falls and all I see is confusion and panic. She looks guilty.

Yeah, I'd have the same look on my face if I were her.

CHAPTER 39

Melody

Drinks with Summer last night were fun and productive. Aside from the cocktails being addictively delicious, the company was exactly what I needed.

We had girl talk, and I was able to voice my concerns and sort out some of my thoughts about Jackson. And still managed to get quite a bit of actual work done. Though the proposals aren't finished, we did make a huge dent in the process, and I'm feeling cautiously optimistic about it all.

I really enjoy my time with Summer. At first, I wasn't sure what to expect from someone like her. I'm used to women who look like her backstabbing and gossiping about me, but that's far from the person Summer is. She's warm and loyal and cracks me the hell up. Her confidence radiates in a way that's motivating, instead of cocky.

It's not that she thinks she's better than anyone else, she's just sure of herself. I find myself wanting to be around her because she's the kind of woman I strive to be more like. The kind of woman I hope Gracie turns into one day. One who doesn't let anyone else's opinions derail her plans or view of herself.

Coming into work today, I found myself in a much better mood, despite the slight hangover I woke up with. We didn't go crazy, but man, I just can't drink the way I used to in my twenties. Three drinks now take three to five business days to recover.

I'm preparing all the condiments for the night shift, cleaning them off, and preparing all the fruits and side work needed before the rush begins. The bistro is already buzzing with customers, but if these things don't get finished, we'll be running around like crazy when the actual rush hits.

"Melody," Maybelle singsongs as she enters the kitchen.

I glance up to see her smiling face. "Hi, do I have a table?"

"You have a visitor," she says with a coy expression.

"Who is it?"

"It may or may not be the handsome man who finds himself in your section almost every day of the week."

I laugh. I could be jealous that she called him handsome, but it's no secret Jackson Pierce is a hot commodity around here. His good looks are hardly a secret.

"I'm just finishing up, I'll be right out."

"You got it, girl," she tells me, and then pushes her way back out to the dining room.

Though I'm still anxious about where things stand between Jackson and me, I find myself giddy that he's here to see me. That must be a good sign, right?

I finish slicing the limes, placing them in the dish over ice, covering it with the lid. I slide the gloves off my hands and discard them in the trash bin at the end of the counter and make my way out front.

Jackson is standing at the front with a bouquet of the most beautiful peonies in his hand. I can only see his profile, but even that makes me break out in a wide grin. He slowly turns toward me, but his expression doesn't match mine. He looks horrified.

And then I see why. Or hear, rather.

"Melody."

That voice, that familiar deep timbre that instantly gives me chills. I'd know it anywhere.

My eyes reluctantly drift away from Jackson.

Alexander.

My skin turns cold, and before I can respond—to either man —Jackson drops the bundle he was holding and angrily storms out of the restaurant, leaving me standing face-to-face with the man I ran away from only months ago.

I'm PACING the small area of flooring that runs from my bedroom to the front door. Bud and Kat, seeing me hyperventilating in the walk-in cooler, sent me home, despite the busy day. I tried to protest, but could barely form a thought, let alone a sentence.

Seeing Alexander face-to-face in Blue Springs felt like cold water pouring down my back. No, it felt like seeing a ghost. One who haunted me for years. One I thought I had left behind.

Once I arrived home, Jane, seeing me distraught, offered to take Gracie for ice cream. I managed an emotionless nod. Gracie was excited for a sweet treat and luckily none the wiser. So I've been pacing the cottage, wondering what the hell he's doing here.

I'm turning back toward the front of the house for another lap when a knock at the door stops me in my tracks.

"Melly, it's me. I want to talk." Alexander's nickname for me sends a shudder down my spine.

"About what?" I shout through the door.

"Us," he responds, his voice dripping with an unfamiliar sweetness.

I don't miss the way he doesn't mention Gracie.

Chewing on a fingernail, I struggle with what to do. Alexander isn't a man that's used to hearing no. He's a man who gets his way. What will happen if I don't let him in? What will happen if I do?

"Come on, babe, I only want to talk. Please," he pleads.

What if time away is what he's needed? What if all these months gave him the space to realize what he lost?

I slowly open the door. His arms are propped high on the door frame, and his downward gaze lifts to mine. "Melly."

I give him a quick smile.

As always, his hair is perfectly styled, and he's dressed to impress. To men like him, image is everything. I used to find the effort endearing, but now I see it for what it really is—control.

He straightens and places his hands in his pockets, planting a sheepish grin on his face. "Can I come in?"

I chew my lip nervously. "Just for a minute."

Considering he's Gracie's father, don't I owe it to him to see why he's traveled all the way to Colorado?

Stepping back, I push the door wider to give him access. He takes a few steps inside, looking around. The intoxicating cologne he wears instantly clouds my senses. It used to render me helpless to his desires, but now it makes my stomach roil. A stark reminder that I was never the queen in his twisted game, I was merely a pawn to create the perfect image his family required of him.

He lets out a small laugh, rubbing the back of his neck. "Wow, it's, uh, smaller than what you're used to, huh?"

I ignore the snide comment, not only because it's not worth the fight, but because he's not wrong. It's tiny compared to the near palace I lived in with him. The cold dwelling that I tried to make a home for many years, but spent more time crying alone in, instead.

Crossing my arms, I stay by the door, guarded and wary. "What are you doing here?"

He turns to look at me, his eyes raking from head to toe. "You look good, Melly."

I'm still in my work uniform, and the Alexander I knew would never allow me to leave the house looking this way. To get my hands dirty would be below his standards.

"What do you want?" I ask.

"To talk."

"Why?" I ask defensively.

I'm doing my best not to sound too curt, but this entire situation has thrown my world off its axis. I feel cornered.

"I want you to come home."

I snicker. "I am home."

He takes a few steps toward me, but I back away until I'm flush against the door.

My apprehension doesn't deter him, and he closes the distance between us. Lifting a hand to my cheek, he responds. "No, home with me."

For a moment, a split second, I close my eyes at the softness of his touch, the tenderness of his voice. It takes me back to the man I fell in love with. Before the mask came off.

His voice becomes a whisper. "Things are different now. I miss you."

It could be so easy to believe things will be different. That we could be a family again. Life would be so much simpler, going home with my daughter's father. Piecing our family back together, instead of acknowledging my failed marriage, is everything I ever wanted. But the words I've been needing to hear from him for so long don't feel the way I thought they would.

I open my eyes and see his slimy grin. The one that says he knows he's getting his way. Slapping his hand away, I move around him, taking large strides until I'm out of his space.

"You gave me your written consent to take Gracie away months ago. You didn't try to stop me. You didn't even say goodbye to her."

He glares at me, not appreciating being challenged. "I wasn't thinking."

"You haven't reached out in all that time, either. You've had plenty of time to think."

His eyes harden, but I can see the effort he's making not to lose his cool. Yet.

"No," I mutter.

"No?"

"We've been gone for months. I begged you for a year. An entire year to help me fix things. I cried to you, pleaded, and told you how unhappy I was. You didn't want to listen, so we left. You let us leave. Not once have you tried to contact us. What the hell have you been doing?"

His face transforms from the smug grin to disdain. The look that challenges me to keep questioning him. In the past, I would have backed down. I wouldn't have pushed him. Not after seeing how far he takes things. But I'm not the same broken girl I was in LA.

"Can you tell me Gracie's shoe size? Any of her favorite foods? Do you know what songs she needs to fall asleep? Do you?" We both know he can't answer a single one of these questions.

He's had years to get to know her, spend time with her, and he's neglected to do either because he's been more concerned with his bank account and whatever skirt he's chasing.

All the feigned kindness I saw from him is long gone. He works his jaw, and his eyes fill with fire. "We are a family, and you are my wife. Enough playtime. You're done making me look foolish, you're coming home with me."

His image. It's always about his image.

"It's time for you to leave, Alexander."

He scoffs like he can't believe I have the audacity to tell him what to do. "I'm not going anywhere without you."

Warning bells erupt in my head. I've seen this look from him before.

He takes slow, deliberate steps toward me, and I match each one, moving away. He grabs a vase with pink peonies in it from the table and violently throws it against the wall behind me.

I scream, covering my head with my arms as glass shards explode around me.

"Alexander, stop. You need to go or else," I warn weakly.

"Or what, Melody? You'll have your boyfriend come and take care of me? Try it. My lawyers will have him in handcuffs so quickly. You forget how much money, how much power I have."

I've never forgotten. He's wielded it over me our entire relationship. The retort is always stored as ammo, ready to detonate whenever he decides I'm behaving out of line.

"You never reached out. We weren't hiding. Please, just go," I beg, trying to hold the tears at bay.

My mind reels back to my last night with him, when very similar circumstances played out. When the glass came within inches of hitting Gracie. It was the last and final straw. Alexander has yelled and belittled, manhandled and threatened me, but that was the first time he put Gracie in any real danger.

One time too many.

I was okay with that being my life. I made peace with it because it's what I chose. But I couldn't live with myself knowing that was also going to be Gracie's story.

Alexander takes quick steps, and before I can move out of reach, he shoves me to the ground, placing his body over mine. Strong arms pin me down, and long legs hold mine in place. His face is reddened, and his typically slicked back hair is becoming disheveled. His eyes bulge from their sockets as they bore into mine. The mask he wore to lure me back with him is long gone. He looks like a stranger, but I suppose he always was.

"Please. Let me up and we can talk," I plead.

"Oh, now you want to talk? How about we do something else instead..." His suggestive comment causes bile to rise in my throat.

Using every muscle in my leg, I attempt to raise it and kick him, but he's much stronger than me, and by the smirk on his face, he knows it.

I begin to scream. "Heeeelp! Somebody, please!"

He releases one hand from my arms to cover my mouth.

My eyes water as I violently shake my head from side to side, attempting to free myself of his sweaty, salty hand. But it's to no avail. His anger only seems to make his hold that much more secure.

Thank God my Gracie isn't here.

"What the fuck is going on here?" A female voice shouts from the front door.

As quickly as he had me pinned, Alexander releases me and is on his feet. I gasp for air and scramble to my feet.

"Summer," I croak out.

If I thought Alexander's face was angry, the look on Summer's face is absolute fury.

"If you put one more hand on her, I will gut you like a fish. Do you hear me, you sick fuck?" Summer threatens in a tone I've never heard from her. Her typical bubbly exterior has been replaced with pure venomous rage.

Alexander smooths his hair back, trying to collect himself. "I think you have the wrong idea. I'm Melody's husband, and we were just, uh, role playing."

"And what game is that? Rapist and victim?" Summer barks back, calling it exactly as she sees it.

He doesn't respond, but glares in her direction.

"I've already called the police, and it's a small town, so they'll be here before you can start that overpriced, piece of shit car in the driveway."

"You bitch," he snarls.

Summer laughs. "Yeah, throw a tantrum, that'll show me."

Summer's eyes briefly flick to where I'm pressed against the wall. "Are you okay?"

I nod.

Sirens begin to wail loudly, and within seconds, there are police bursting through the door. Summer explains that she's the one who called, and points to Alexander, describing what she walked in on. The police waste no time throwing cuffs on him, while another officer comforts me and asks if I'd like an ambulance to go to the hospital. I decline. All I want is my baby girl.

We stand in the kitchen while the officers take a statement from both Summer and me while Alexander sits in cuffs out front screaming, "You lying bitch!" over and over.

They inform me that under the circumstances, and with an eye witness, they will be issuing a TPO—temporary protection order—but that I will need to file with the judge if I want to make it permanent, as this will only last three days.

Summer thanks them, but before they take him out to their cruiser, I make my way over to him, standing tall and projecting my voice. "Alexander, I want a divorce."

He spits in my direction, and the officers yank him toward the cruiser.. I don't take a breath of relief until I see him secured inside the vehicle.

I turn back, and Summer wraps herself around me in a tight hug, apologizing that she didn't get here sooner. I don't know why or how she's here to begin with. I'm only glad she didn't arrive a few minutes later.

A part of me always knew Alexander was bad news, but

there's another part of me, a louder part, that insisted on seeing the good. So no matter how many times it happened, I was always surprised to see the ugly side of him surface.

If Gracie wasn't involved, I may have spent forever with the man. In a weird, full circle kind of way, Alexander may have been the one to break me, but he gave me the one thing I cherish most in the world, and that little girl became the very thing to finally free me from him.

CHAPTER 40

Jackson

My phone rings for the fourth time in the last hour. I glance at the screen, groaning when I see it's Summer again.

I decline the call and flip it over on the bed. I'm not ready to face my best friend's positivity when I've been duped again. Jackson Pierce, forever the laughing stock. Nope, I'm not ready to hear how things are going to work out. Her glass-half-full speech will have to wait.

It's been two days since I ran out of Blue Bistro after meeting Melody's husband. A husband whom I was never informed she had.

What was I? The summer fling before she went home to her real family? Fuck that. I have nothing to say to her, and I have nothing to say to Summer, who has adopted Melody as her new best friend.

I should be at work right now, but I'm not ready to face anybody. My social media is currently disabled, and I'm sure I'll have a heap of humiliating messages waiting for me. I was prepared to put everything on the line for her. Against my better judgment, I shoved all my worst fears down and was ready to take the leap with her, and for what? To land in the exact same situation I was in with Shaina.

Well, not exactly the same. At least her husband isn't one of my friends. Though it stings all the same.

The kicker is that Melody hasn't even reached out. Not a single call or text message. Though, if I was caught red-handed, I might not have much to say, either. Any future we may have had got obliterated, but her lack of effort to make amends shows me how little I must have meant. Clearly, our relationship was entirely one-sided.

Do I sound a little pissed off? Yeah, maybe I do. But I refuse to apologize for my anger, because I gave all of my effort to a woman, yet again, only to be blindsided and betrayed. Maybe this is my lot in life, to forever be betrayed by the women I love.

My phone pings on my bed, alerting me of a text message.

Summer: Call me. I need to talk to you.

I SCOFF. She's not checking on me, which means she's clearly taken Melody's side.

Jackson: Busy.

Summer: Stop being a stubborn ass, and CALL ME

ME? I'm stubborn? What in the hell have I done wrong that I owe a conversation to anyone at this point? Last time I checked,

Melody is the one that hid a marriage while she was in a relationship with me.

I spent so much time opening up to her about my history with Shaina, my fears going into a new relationship. And she was hiding this the entire time? She had ample opportunity to tell me the truth but waited until the two men she was involved with crossed paths.

Until she was *caught*.

I'm not the one who lied, and as far as I'm concerned, she's no better than Shaina.

The last few nights haven't granted me more than a few hours of sleep, so rather than get into a text message argument with my friend, I resolve not to reply. Whatever happens with Melody and me shouldn't come between me and Summer, so there's no need for a conversation about it. I told her I was taking a few days off work and she said she has it handled, so unless that's changed, I don't have anything else to say.

I didn't tell Summer about what happened, so I haven't talked to her about any of it. But it's been a few days and now Summer is blowing up my phone, so I'm assuming Melody has filled her in.

Somehow, even though I've slept a maximum of six hours in the last few days, my body feels like it's buzzing with energy, so I decide to get in a run and work on the jump rope routine for the festival.

Thoughts of the festival usually fill me with joy and anticipation, but right now, it's filling me with nauseousness. The sinking feeling that the festival is when we had planned to, hopefully, take our relationship to the next level. But now, it will forever be a reminder that the woman I saw forever with betrayed me before we could even get there. I find myself cursing her for ruining this for me. The festival was mine and I let her in, and now it's tainted.

I do my best to shake off any thoughts of Melody as I hop on my treadmill. After a two-mile run and a thirty-minute run-through of the routine, I take a quick shower to clean the layer of sweat and grime off my skin. I towel dry and dress, contemplating what to do next.

I should eat, but nothing sounds good. I should sleep, but I can't shut my mind off. I'm supposed to be going back to work tomorrow, but the thought of facing Summer, or anyone, for that matter, makes me want to crawl into a hole.

I've never been spineless or one who's easily intimidated, but I'm having a hard time wondering what the world could be saying about me right now. Having the confrontation happen in public, in a gossipy small town, doesn't instill much confidence that the news hasn't made its rounds yet. It's been two days, which means it's likely circled every gym location already.

As much as I'd love to continue playing hermit and hide at home, I can't let Summer continue to hold things down at work. I'm the boss and I need to man up and take care of things. I can be irritated with Summer all I want, but she's still doing me a massive favor by letting me sort through my shit in private while she takes on the extra workload for me.

It's still early, but I give in and decide to try and get some shut-eye anyway. Though, as soon as my head hits the pillow, my phone goes off again. Another call, but this time it's from my mother.

I feel like an asshole when I decline.

Within a minute, a text from her comes through.

Mom: Call me ASAP.

MY MOTHER ISN'T much of a texter, nor would she send a cryptic message like this unless it was an emergency, so I call her back immediately.

She answers on the first ring. "Jackson, where the hell are you?"

Her voice is more accusatory than anything.

"I'm at home, why?"

"You need to come over," she demands.

I sigh. "I'm not really up for socializing, is everything okay?"

"Hold on," she says before I hear a muffled conversation and some scuffled noises before she returns. This time, her voice is much lower. "Melody is here."

I blow out a huff of air. "Mother, look, I appreciate you trying to play devil's advocate here, but—"

She cuts me off before I finish. "Jackson Pierce, this is not what you think. Stop being a stubborn ass and get over here like the man I raised you to be. She needs you. They both do."

What the hell is that supposed to mean?

"What's going on?"

"Not over the phone. Come over and I'll explain everything," she tells me with a tone of finality.

She's not going to let me argue this further. As much as I'm dreading seeing Melody right now, I can't ignore the urgency in my mother's voice. Something serious is happening, and I have no clue how it involves Melody and me, but I guess I'm about to find out.

I PULL on a pair of gray sweatpants, a white tee, and my baseball cap. My mind is racing with what I could be walking into.

Why is Melody at my mother's home?

Summer and my mother have been known to meddle, but I'm not sure they would go to these lengths to get us talking. Something's up.

My mother's home comes into view, causing my pulse to race. I know Melody is here, but why do I also see Summer's vehicle outside?

I feel more confused than ever.

I park and take a deep breath, attempting to steel my nerves before going inside. Before I've even left my car, I see Summer marching down the pathway.

She throws herself into me, wrapping her arms around me. I hear her sniffle.

"Summer, what's going on?" I ask as she presses her face into my shoulder.

I feel her head shake.

When she pulls back, she quickly wipes her bloodshot eyes and gives me a sad smile.

I place my hands on her shoulders, holding her steady as I take in her appearance. "You guys are scaring me. Are you okay?"

She nods. "I'm glad you came."

Feeling like an asshole for not responding back to her, I apologize.

Summer takes a calming breath. "I don't blame you for not responding. There's no way you could have known."

"Known what, Summer?" I ask, noting the edge to my voice.

She grabs my hand, pulling me toward the house. "You should hear it from her."

I don't know whether the *her* she's referring to is Melody or my mother.

Inside the house, it smells like fresh baked goods, cookies, maybe. There's a TV on quietly in the living room, and I can hear Gracie laughing at whatever show is playing. The sweet sound is almost enough to disarm me. But when we round the corner, I see Gracie on the oversized couch with Melody and my mother flanked on both sides of her.

Both women turn back to look at me, though Melody quickly turns back to the TV, but not before I notice her red-rimmed eyes.

My mother stands and approaches me, folding her arms around me in a warm embrace before turning back to Gracie. "Gracie, I think those cookies have had enough time to cool. What do you say we try a few and then break out the modeling clay?"

Gracie's attention pulls from her show and she shrieks with excitement before she realizes I'm standing in the entryway. "Jax! I missed you!"

She races toward me, and I instinctively bend and lift her tiny frame. She wraps her arms around my neck and lays her head on my shoulder like it's the most comfortable place in the world.

"Hi, sweet Gracie. I missed you, too. I'm going to talk with your mommy for a bit, and then I'll come do the clay with you."

"O-kaaay," she drags the word out in a pouty tone, though she makes no complaint as I set her back on the ground and she prances off with my mother to the kitchen.

Summer follows after them, leaving Melody and me alone. I'm not sure what conversation we're supposed to be having or why, so I continue to stand awkwardly in the entryway.

Melody has yet to turn back around to look at me, and something tells me this is just as awkward for her, if not more.

A part of me wants to be stubborn and force her to make the first move, but Summer's words are ringing in my head, so I let my guard down and take a seat next to Melody on the couch.

Her head swivels in my direction, but she doesn't make any eye contact. She's wearing what looks to be pajama bottoms and a loose-fitting T-shirt. Her hair is in a messy knot on the top of her head, and she's not wearing a drop of makeup. It's clear she's been crying, and the dark circles under her eyes are telling of long, sleepless nights, and yet I can't ignore how beautiful I find her. The pull that she still has over me.

It takes everything in me not to reach over and grab her hand like I usually do. Not to kiss her face like I've gotten used to doing. Not to comfort her when I know she's hurting, because I'm hurting, too. All the anger in the world can't override the love I have for her.

Her palms press into the cushion as she shifts her body to fully face me. I watch as her mouth opens and closes, about to speak, but thinks better of it.

We're both working up the nerve to say something, anything. The three women here clearly know something I don't, and aside from not wanting to deal with this yet, I don't have the slightest clue why I'm even here.

Why Summer is here.

Why Melody is here.

Every instinct I have is to get up and leave, because I'm sure I'm only going to hear more lies. More deceit that'll make me look like a fool. But I can't make my feet move. I'm planted on this couch with her, finding myself eager to hear what she has to say. Unable to turn away from her, even now. Especially now.

I take a deep breath and force the words out. "So you've been married this whole time?"

She nods her head slowly, as if it hurts to move. My stomach turns sour, and it's not until Melody raises her arm to tuck a piece of stray hair behind her ear that I see it.

Deep purple bruising marks her wrist, and I can't help but notice they resemble the shape of fingers.

Who the fuck had their hands on her?

CHAPTER 41

Melody

"Pack a bag, you're coming with me," Summer demands.

The police car backs out of the driveway with Alexander in the back, and now that the adrenaline is wearing off, my hands and legs have begun to shake for the last several minutes. I'm trying to process what just happened, now sitting on the couch with Summer by my side.

"How were you here?" I ask.

"Jane called me, said you looked shook up and to come check on you."

Thank God for Jane. Because I know exactly what would have happened if Summer didn't show up when she did.

"Do you have a suitcase or a duffle?" she asks, rising from the couch.

I nod, pointing to my room. "Where are we going?"

"Jane's place. She told me to bring you there. Gracie is already there, we can bring some things for her, too. Let's get you out of here for a few days."

I nod, not having the energy to tell her that all I want to do is climb into bed and hide from the nightmare that is my life.

For the next several minutes, I hear Summer rummaging around in my drawers and going back and forth to my bathroom, tossing any essential things I might need into the purple suitcase. She doesn't seem to mind that I'm not helping.

Summer lugs the large suitcase out of the room and rolls it down the hallway, placing it at the front door and taking a seat next to me. She pats my leg with one hand. "Are you ready?"

"I'm gonna use the bathroom, give me a minute," I tell her in a fragile voice I hardly recognize.

I suddenly feel exhausted, and it's hard to keep my eyes open. But I make my way to the bathroom to splash some cold water on my face. After I have my daughter in my arms, I'll be able to relax and sleep. Gracie and my bed are all I want right now.

We make the short drive to Jane's place, and I all but burst through the front door and into my baby girl's arms.

They say that when kids get hurt, they can hold it together, and it's not until they see their mom that their emotions flood out. The same is true for mothers when they see their children.

Everything pours out of me as I hold her tightly. Tears and snot slide down my face as I cradle my baby girl into my body as tightly as I can. Every emotion is flooding out, right there on the floor of the entryway. Jane and Summer watch on, not saying a word. Summer holds a hand to her mouth, likely stifling a sob, and Jane's eyes are downcast, as are the corners of her mouth.

Gracie holds on to me and rubs my back. "It's okay, Mommy. Don't cry."

Her words only make my sobs harder and louder, and I manage to choke out a muffled, "I'm sorry."

An apology that my child has to console her crying mother.

An apology that I had to protect my baby from her father.

Two things that should never happen.

Yet, here we are, in a life that I never thought I'd be living, making decisions I never thought I'd have to make.

The tears finally stop, and I smooth a hand down Gracie's hair. "I'm okay, baby. Mommy's sorry."

Her small hand cups my face. "Mommy sad?"

I nod.

"Aw," she says with a sad face, and then plants a kiss on my cheek. "I love you, Mommy. We can make you cookies! Cookies will make you feel better!"

I find myself chuckling. My sweet girl, who couldn't possibly know what just occurred, thinks cookies are the answer to my tears, and my God, I love her for it. Thank God she's small and oblivious to the pain her father has caused. One day, he'll have to answer to her and explain why he chose himself over her. I will never make excuses or cover up what he's done. I will freely answer any questions she has one day, and she will have the freedom to make her own choices. But for now, I'm grateful that all she's concerned with is cookies.

"Gracie, what a wonderful idea, dear," Jane chimes in.

We rise from the floor and make our way to a spare bedroom Jane has set up for me. The queen-size bed has fresh sheets on it and a floral duvet. A bouquet of flowers sits on the side table, and the entire place smells warm and inviting. Like clean laundry and fresh flowers.

I toss my luggage in the closet and shut the door. Jane takes Gracie by the hand and tells me they're going to bake some treats so I should rest. Summer has filled her in on the situation, or at least the gist of what happened at the cottage. Now that I've drained my body of every drop of water, I'm grateful I don't have to retell the story. Relive the details.

My head hits the pillow, and the last thought I have before I quickly doze off is how sweet Gracie's giggle sounds in the other room.

WHEN MY EYES FLUTTER OPEN, the room is dark and the house is quiet. I roll over to glance at the clock on the side table. One in the morning.

Gracie.

I practically jump from the bed and out into the hallway, where I see Summer walking toward my room with a glass of water. She jolts when she sees me, slapping a hand to her chest.

"Shit, Mel, you scared the hell out of me."

I rub my eyes. "Where's Gracie?"

She extends the water toward me, and I down half of the glass in one gulp, becoming very aware of the pounding in my head.

"She's in bed. She's fed and bathed, cuddled up with Jane on a make-shift bed in the living room. We didn't want to wake you."

I pant a few heavy breaths after chugging the water.

Summer giggles softly. "Thirsty?"

I smile and nod. "Guess so."

"Hungry?" she asks.

My stomach growls in response, so I nod.

She nudges her head to follow and leads me down the hall toward the kitchen. Jane slips from the bed with Gracie and quietly pads over to where I'm seated at a dining table, downing a plate of pasta, eating like there's no tomorrow.

When my frantic gaze meets hers, she pats my hand. "She's still sound asleep. We had a fun-filled evening. Don't feel guilty for a moment that you were sleeping. It's what I was hoping you'd do."

My nose stings, and a lump at the back of my throat threatens more waterworks.

Her kind words and comforting tone feel like a warm cup of tea with honey, soothing away any soreness. I've always had to carry the weight of the world on my own. That "village" everyone talks about was never something I was awarded when I had Gracie, so while this is everything I've always wanted, it's foreign to me.

"What can we do?" Summer asks after I've finally placed my fork down on the ceramic dish.

I shrug. "I don't know. I never thought he'd show up like this."

"He's behind bars. You're safe now," Summer says, attempting to comfort me.

I scoff, wiping my once-again sniffling nose. "For how long? He'll post bail by tomorrow."

"Honey, I know this has been a lot. I can't even begin to imagine where your head is at. In the interest of keeping both you and Gracie safe, I'd like to offer my home to you both for as long as you'd like." I open my mouth to tell Jane we couldn't impose, but she raises a hand to stop me. "None of that. Now, I'd also like to add some unsolicited advice, if you don't mind, and suggest you file a permanent restraining order against that man."

I sigh. It's not a thought I haven't already had myself, but actually going through with it is something else. Something a woman never dreams she'll have to do. The man you shared marriage vows with, the one you made love to and had a child with. No woman ever thinks it'll be her in a situation like this. Until she is.

My gaze lingers on Gracie who's sound asleep, sprawled out on the mattress without a care in the world. "I will. I also need to serve him divorce papers."

Jane squeezes my hand. "We'll help you take care of all of that, honey."

Summer gives me a warm smile and a wink, but I can see the way her eyes are red and puffy with circles underneath. They haven't slept because they've been worried about me.

"I'm sorry about all of this...chaos. And to impose on your lives this way."

"Melody, listen, honey, I am a patient woman, but I will not stand for you continuing to speak about yourself as if you're a burden. I love you and your daughter very much, so you, my dear, are going to have to learn to accept it." Jane's firm but kind voice causes my shoulders to shake slightly and a soft laugh bubbles out of me. Something I didn't think was possible at a time like this.

I nod, offering her a genuine smile.

"Come on, Mel, let's get some rest," Summer suggests.

"I'm going to lie with Gracie in the living room. Summer, you can take the bedroom, if you'd like."

She nods. "If you're sure."

I nod and then rise to clear my dishes. Padding over to the living room, I see Gracie sprawled out on a mattress from a pull-out couch that looks as big as the one in the bedroom. Her little foot is sticking out from the covers, and I can't help myself as I walk by and give her cute toes a little squeeze.

Something tells me there are a lot of hard days ahead but seeing her safe and content gives me all the strength I need to surge forward. Whatever happens between Alexander and me, no matter how he plans to slander me when the divorce papers arrive—which he will—I will be ready. No matter what happens with Jackson and me, it doesn't matter. As long as I have my baby girl, I know we can get through anything.

"Oh God. I might throw up," I tell Summer when she informs me that Jackson is on his way over to the house.

After explaining what happened at the bistro, and lifting Summer's jaw off the floor, she insisted we call him over. But to be honest, I wasn't ready before today. I needed time to sort through everything that had happened.

A few days have passed and I'm in a better headspace to see him, so Summer had Jane call him over. He was too angry to respond to Summer's calls or texts, but Summer knew he wouldn't deny his mother.

"Deep breaths, it's going to be fine. He's only upset because he's thinking of Shaina right now. This is probably giving him flashbacks of what happened with her, but he doesn't know the truth. When he does, you'll see that nothing has changed. You two will be fine," she assures me.

I release a heavy exhale, doing my best to believe her, but as I hear car tires crunching gravel outside, I can't ignore the jackhammer in my chest.

Summer's eyes go wide. "He's here, I'll be right back."

Before she takes off, she gives my hand a tender squeeze.

Summer is outside for several minutes, and Gracie plops down next to me on the couch and asks for one of her favorite cartoons. I flip the channels until I find something she'll like.

While she's zoned out on her show, I'm chewing on a fingernail, self-consciously wondering if I should have changed into some decent clothing before he arrived. A part of me didn't think he'd actually show up. The look on his face at the bistro was volatile. I've never seen him look so angry or hurt. I'm the one that hurt him, and I feel sick about it.

Footsteps sound against the wood floors as Summer and Jackson make their way inside. I quickly glance over to see them in the entryway but can't make myself hold the gaze. I feel ashamed, embarrassed, and scared to hear what he thinks of me.

Jane comes and snags Gracie away for more baking after my girl gives a warm welcome to Jackson, which comes as no surprise since she's been asking about him all morning. The girl loves him and I can't blame her. I only hope I didn't permanently screw everything up for her—and me.

After a few awkward minutes of him standing a few feet away and me not having the courage to start the conversation, he finally decides to sit next to me. I'm racking my brain trying to figure out how to start this damn conversation.

Hi, how are you?

I had an eventful few days, how have yours been?

I know we're not a couple, but I'm going to be staying at your mother's house for a while.

All of it sounds stupid when I think of saying it aloud, but Jackson surprises me by speaking first.

"So, you've been married this whole time?"

His face turns red as soon as I nod, and I think he's going to get up and leave, but then his eyes zero in on my wrists. The skin that's covered in bruising from Alexander's hands. Suddenly, the fire in his eyes looks different from the hurt I saw seconds ago. He looks positively pissed.

CHAPTER 42

Jackson

My heart is in my throat as Melody begins speaking. I don't know what I was expecting, but it wasn't this.

"Gracie's father was abusive. Mostly emotional, but toward the end, it became more physical." Her voice is low, likely so it doesn't reach Gracie's ears. "He spent most of our marriage having an affair with his secretary, as well as other women in his office. I tried to confront him, but he always made me feel like somehow it was my fault. I felt so lost at one point that I finally spoke with my parents about what I should do, and they told me that because he works hard and provides for me, I needed to overlook it. Wealth became his free pass for every infidelity. I should have left years ago, but I was scared. Scared to have a failed marriage, scared to disappoint my family. Scared of him."

A lump forms in my throat as I try to retain the emotions raging inside. My fists are curled tightly on my lap, but I don't speak. I can't help but think how her aversion to wealth makes a lot more sense now.

"He was...*is*, very controlling. But when I saw those two pink lines, I really thought things would be different. I thought it would be the change he needed to be better. But he wasn't prepared for the amount of work and dedication children require. He became even more withdrawn. Alexander was home less frequently, and when he did show, he was usually angry. None of it was okay, but it was bearable. Then one night..." Her voice trails off and she turns her head away from me as the tears begin cascading down her cheek.

She quickly wipes them away, and clears her throat, steadying her voice to continue. "We were arguing, a run-of-the-mill evening for us. I was expressing how unhappy I was and begging him to listen to what I was saying. But he got defensive and started screaming about all the things he provided me. He grabbed something nearby, shouting about how much it cost. I can't recall what it was, but I do remember that Gracie had walked into the bedroom just as he threw it in my direction. He nearly hit her and couldn't even apologize or check to see if we were hurt. He grabbed his keys and stormed out, leaving both Gracie and me crying in the bedroom, surrounded by glass. It was the night I packed our bags. The next morning he returned, smelling like stale alcohol, and I asked him to give me written permission to take Gracie, which he did, and we left."

My head is dizzy with information. Overloaded with emotion. Her story has sucked all the air out of the room. I can hear Gracie giggling in the kitchen with my mother, their voices distant but clear. But in the living room with Melody, it's silent. Tears spill down her face, and I fight whether I should comfort her or give her space.

"I—" I begin, but she cuts me off.

"I should have told you I was married. It's been my intention to divorce him but haven't had the time or the money to get it done. Keeping it from you was never meant to embarrass or hurt you. I've been ashamed of my past, scared of what it might say about me."

For a man who usually stands tall, I now feel about two inches high. My stubbornness made me think the worst of her the last few days. Thinking she would ever hurt me. Any and all anger I felt before coming over has dissolved into something heavier to bear.

I scoot closer and gently grab her hand. "Please don't apologize. You don't owe me any explanation. I'm sorry I didn't give you the chance to explain. I was being stupid."

Her story is horrific but doesn't quite explain why he was at the bistro asking for her. The way he came in and asked for her as if she would be expecting him. Or where he currently is. "Is he still here?"

She shakes her head. "He was arrested a few days ago."

My blood heats, and my pulse quickens. "What happened?"

She shrugs, and rubs her wrists, drawing my eyes back to the bruising. "He showed up at the cottage wanting to talk. The details don't really matter, but it didn't go well. Luckily, Gracie was with your mother and asked Summer to come check on me." She pauses to sniffle. "She's my angel. You've got one hell of a friend."

"She's your best friend now, too," I tell her. Lately I've seen how close they've become, and it fills me with pride that two women I think so highly of have forged such a close relationship.

"I'm lucky she showed up when she did," Melody says grimly.

I don't even want to know what she means by that and can only imagine what happened at the cottage that the cops needed to be called. The last two days, I have been pouting and stewing in my own misery, while she's been dealing with this hell.

"I'm so sorry I wasn't there," I say sheepishly.

She gives me a sad smile, shrugging. She doesn't seem angry, but she should be angry with me. I wasn't there for her. Didn't give her the benefit of the doubt. I let my insecurities cloud what I know about her. Melody isn't a stranger. I know who she is, and yet, I so easily pushed her away. She didn't deserve that.

"Thank you for telling me. I can't imagine how difficult all that has been. But I want you to know that you have nothing to be ashamed or embarrassed about. What happened to you and Gracie is wrong. Nobody deserves that."

She nods. "I know that. Now."

"So, what happens next?" I ask.

"I'm not sure. I need to file for divorce. He's probably posted bail and is on his way home to his lawyers. He'll find a way to make me pay for this."

I caress her hand with my thumb. "I won't let that happen."

"I wasn't sure you'd come," she confesses morosely, eyes glued to our hands.

"I never should have reacted that way. It won't happen again," I say firmly.

The embarrassment and anger from the last few days hasn't diminished but has shifted from her to myself. I'm embarrassed at my reaction, and angry that Melody had to face that monster alone.

I will never let her down again.

She lets out a long yawn, and her shoulders slump, as if telling me her story has literally lifted a weight from her but drained her all the same. "I guess I'm staying with your mother for a while. So I need to run home and grab a few things. Summer packed me a bag but seems to have forgotten that I need more than one pair of underwear."

"Can I go with you?" I'm unable to resist asking, because now more than ever, I don't want her out of my sight.

She nods, the corners of her mouth lifting just slightly. "I'd like that."

Melody tells Gracie that we're going back to the house, and

she insists on riding along. My mother and Summer look hesitant, but I assure them I'm going, too, and they will be safe. Melody tells my mother we will be quick, and while Alexander is a monster, he's not stupid enough to come back and start trouble with a TPO against him.

The ride back to her cottage is quiet. The radio is low, and Gracie is humming to herself in the back seat. Melody stares out the window, lost in thought. I take a risk and reach over to grab her hand. She surprises me by intertwining our fingers and squeezing my hand. The small gesture fills me with hope.

We pull up to the cottage, and with only Melody's car out front, we sigh in relief that there are no unwanted visitors. I kill the ignition and reach for my door handle, but Melody places her hand on my arm.

Our eyes meet, and she glances at Gracie before turning back to me. "Do you mind if we go in alone? I'll be quick. I just need a minute."

I give her a reassuring smile. "Of course, I'll wait outside for you. Shout if you need help carrying anything out."

She mouths *thank you*, exits the car, and opens the back to unbuckle Gracie from her car seat. I watch as she carries her up the few steps and into the house. The way she's holding onto Gracie tells me it's more for herself than her daughter.

I turn the car back on, letting the music play softly, roll the window down, and prop my elbow up on the ledge. While the last few days have felt dark and uncertain, today feels lighter. The sun is shining, and for the first time in a long time, I've never been more clear about what my future looks like.

The leaves are rustling in the tall trees that surround the cottage as a soft breeze blows through. The air smells of pine and freshness. Perhaps a sign of things to come: a fresh start.

Melody has been inside for almost ten minutes, and as much

as I want to check on her, I don't want to intrude when she's asked for some privacy.

My stomach begins to growl, and suddenly all I can think about is a big juicy burger from the bistro, so I decide that I'll pick up some dinner on the way back to the house so nobody needs to fuss over cooking or cleaning. Just a delicious, hearty meal and all my favorite girls.

Another five minutes tick by, and I'm beginning to get antsy. I drum my fingers on the window ledge as my patience wears out. I reach to turn the car off and see Gracie burst through the front door. I smile when I see her little mess of brown hair flopping around, but my smile quickly vanishes when I see the tears streaming down her face.

I turn the radio volume down, the music immediately replaced by Gracie's crying and screaming.

Hopping out of the car, I quickly scoop her up. "Are you okay? Where's your mom?"

Through snotty cries, she chokes out a sentence, one word at a time, that turns my blood cold. "He...has...her."

Before I've had time to think about what I'm going to do, I place Gracie in the back seat and instruct her to stay there. I hand her my phone with 9-1-1 on the screen and tell her to press the green button and tell the operator what's going on before racing into the house.

I nearly trip up the steps and fall through the door to see Melody pinned against the wall by Alexander's arm pressed across her throat. His back is to me, but I can see the fear on Melody's face. Her eyes are wild and full of tears. She lets out a raspy croak that he stifles with his other hand.

"Shut up. You and your bitch friend are going to pay for calling the cops on me. Did you really think that would keep me away? Did you forget who I am?" he shouts, spittle flying across her face, evident by the way she's squeezing her eyes shut.

I close the distance and grab him by the shoulders, ripping him off her. Catching him by surprise knocks him off-balance and he flies to the floor.

"Jackson," Melody cries, throwing herself behind me.

I wrap one arm behind me to hold her, quickly trying to plan my next move.

"You must be the man that's been screwing my wife," Alexander boldly accuses.

I scoff.

"Surprised you'd notice when you've been screwing every woman in LA."

His eyes narrow to slits, and his mouth puckers as if he's tasting something sour.

He rises, puffing his chest out and taking slow steps toward me. "Who the fuck do you think you are?"

"The man that's going to permanently rearrange your face unless you get the fuck out of here."

He lunges for me at the same time I push Melody as gently as I can out of harm's way. His body crashes into mine. The impact sends me scrambling backward, and I try to find my footing. His hands fly around me like a spazzed-out madman. Each swing is a miss; I successfully dodge each one. Every time he's unable to make contact with my face, his own becomes redder with fury.

I finally manage to shove him backward, giving me a moment to breathe with a few feet now between us.

I'm strong, but I'm not a fighter by nature. I don't enjoy hurting others, unlike this sadistic fuck. But if he keeps rushing me, refusing to back down, I may not have a choice.

I glance to my right and realize Melody is no longer in the cottage.

Good.

But it's all the time Alexander needs to force himself on top of me. He throws his arm across my throat, the same way he had done with Melody, and is winding up for a swing at me.

He's baring his teeth like a wild animal, and saliva is dripping down his mouth. "This is my family and I'm not going anywhere, do you hear me?"

When it comes to anger, he might have me beat, but he hasn't accounted for one important factor. I'm a hell of a lot stronger than he is.

I flip us around until he's on his back on the floor with me on top of him. Pulling my arm back, I release it with a precise punch, knocking this city slicker out cold. "That's where you're wrong pal, this is *my* family."

THE COPS once again take Alexander away in handcuffs, assuring us that this time there will be no bail set under the new circumstances. Violating the TPO means serious jail time for him.

Melody and Gracie sat huddled and sobbing in the back seat of my car when I came outside, and it nearly broke me to see them that way. To know this is the kind of lifestyle they'd been enduring.

I held them both until the cops left, and I helped Melody with the rest of her things so we could return to my mother's. I called in an order to the Bistro, so all I had to do was run inside and pick it up.

We all ate together in the living room as a family. After we cleaned up and the girls showered, we made the bed in the living room where the three of us crashed together, and I held them both tightly in my arms, silently promising to never let them go.

CHAPTER 43
Melody

I roll over and smack right into a hard, muscular chest. Jackson groans in his sleep, so I throw my arm over him, rubbing his shoulder and back. Gracie has long ago hopped out of the bed, so I scoot closer and pepper his chest with soft kisses.

He responds by slipping his arm over my waist, giving me a light squeeze.

"Good morning, handsome," I whisper.

He moans softly, his eyes slowly prying open. "Good morning, beautiful."

We have graduated from the living room to the spare bedroom, and Gracie, Jackson, and I have been sleeping in there every night.

Gracie has adapted to the new, temporary arrangements seamlessly, and not one night has gone by that she didn't drift off by telling both Mommy and "Daddy" good night. Each time she calls Jackson "Daddy," I can see the affection radiating off him. My heart swells, and I can feel it ache in my chest. Gracie finally gets to experience what having an active dad around is like, and there's nothing that could ever compare to that.

If the encounter with her father left any residual effects, I haven't been able to tell. Maybe Gracie never had to let go of Alexander because he never gave enough of himself for her to latch onto.

The last week has been stressful, yet hopeful. With the help of Jackson and his mother, I immediately filed for divorce, and a judge issued a permanent restraining order against Alexander. Before, it was my word against his, but now I have three witnesses who've seen what he's capable of. He's as good as screwed. We were able to get my restraining order rushed, and the judge granted immediate protection after the TPO had expired.

Not only did Jackson help me with all of the necessary paperwork, but he also paid every fee to the courts to ensure it was all taken care of as quickly as possible. Though the divorce won't be official for many months, it's a start in the right direction. With everything in motion, I finally feel like I can breathe again.

Gracie has been keeping busy with her new and improved lemonade stand that Jackson and Jane helped her create. She will be attending the festival next week with her very own kiosk. We've decided to call it *(No) BS Lemonade*, after both Blue Springs and Blue Bistro for their donation of all the blueberries we'll be using in the lemonade. Needless to say, she's over the moon about it.

"Where's Gracie?" Jackson asks, his head jerking up.

Through everything, Jackson has been attentive and protective in a way I haven't seen before. He hardly lets us out of his sight, and when he does, he's constantly checking in. While we've been staying at his mother's house, he's had state-of-the-art cameras installed along the perimeter of the cottage.

I cup the side of his face, caressing him softly, directing his head back down. "She's with your mother. She's fine."

He lays his head back down, his shoulders sagging from the release of tension.

I can't count the number of times Jackson has apologized for the way he reacted that day in the Bistro. Nobody could have known what was really going on. Hell, I might have had the same reaction if our roles were reversed. Lord knows I had my own meltdown when I thought he was messing around with Ember.

We're all human, and we do the best we can to protect ourselves. Once you've been hurt, it's hard to put yourself back out there. I understand more than anyone why he would assume I betrayed him.

Jackson's back at work, and we've all been doing our best to let things go back to normal, or as normal as they can be. Though, when I have the mornings off, he makes the effort of going in late to work also, so we have more time together.

After everything we've been through, all of the extra attention could feel suffocating for some people, but not to me. This is the first time in my life that I have someone who actively puts in the effort and wants to be around Gracie and me. Jackson chooses us day after day, putting us above all else, and I can confidently say that while we haven't allowed ourselves to say it, I've never felt more loved.

The intensity of the situation had the words on the tip of my tongue many times. To let him know that I am in this. But we don't need words. We say it with every touch. Every kiss. Every lingering goodbye before work. Every intense gaze before we part ways.

I don't want it to seem impulsive. When I say it, I want Jackson to know it has nothing to do with what happened.

We lie together a few more minutes before he needs to get up for work. I make the three of us and Jane a large breakfast before he slips into his shoes and heads to the door.

"I'll see you later, sweet girl," he tells Gracie, planting a kiss on the top of her head.

This always makes her giggle and blush, her face radiating with affection.

He turns to me and presses a deep and passionate one to my lips.

Things have quickly turned serious between us, and I'm loving every moment of it. For the first time, it feels like I belong, instead of feeling like I'm trying to convince the man I'm with that I'm worthy of him. No, now I've got a man who proves to me and Gracie day after day just how lucky he is to have us in his life, and that's something worth fighting for, no matter how scary it might feel.

"GIRL! You and me. Tonight. Rocky's," Summer shouts as she enters Jane's home, strutting toward me.

I thought it might be weird staying at Jane's house this long, but the truth is, I've never felt at home anywhere else the way I feel here. Not only is Jane accommodating, but she's sweet in a way that goes beyond playing host. She truly treats Gracie and me as family. Always has.

Clearly, Summer feels just as comfortable here.

"What?" I ask, laughing.

The great thing about Summer is, she always manages to put me in a good mood. She's sarcastic, witty, and funny in a way that makes me temporarily forget we've just been through a week of hell. She doesn't make me talk about it or relive it. Summer has been treating us like nothing is out of the ordinary, and I am truly grateful for that.

She hands me a clear bottle filled with her latest smoothie

recipe and slaps down a folder of papers on the kitchen table where I'm coloring with Gracie. "Our proposals! We have less than a week. We need to polish these things up!"

I unscrew the cap to the bottle and take a large gulp of the orange-colored concoction. "Oh my God, Summer, this is incredible."

She pops one shoulder up, smirking. "I know, right? This one might be my new favorite. I just love peaches, don't you?"

I laugh. "You say that about all of your recipes."

She purses her lips. "Hey, I can't help it if they're all fantastic. I could be opening a store, like, an actual store! So they better be."

"They're all amazing. People are going to be lined up around the corner for them," I assure her.

"Not if I don't finish this damn thing first!" she shrieks, pointing to the file.

The urgency in her voice makes me giggle. While I should be equally stressed about it, after everything that just happened, I can't find it in me to spin out over something like this.

I'm taking it seriously, don't get me wrong, but I'm also not going to make myself crazy with perfection about it. All we can do is our best, and Wes is either going to love what we have to offer or he's not.

"I'm off tonight, but I was going to hang out with Gracie. She wanted to put the final touches on her lemonade stand."

"Grandma can help me. Go play with Summer," Gracie chimes in.

Is my daughter sending me off on a playdate?

She's started calling Jane "Grandma" and I don't think there's one of us that isn't elated by it.

Summer and I exchange curious grins, and I glance down at Gracie who hasn't even glanced up. "Sweetie, I need to ask Jane.

I can't just assume she's free to watch you. She might have plans."

"She doesn't!" Jane shouts, coming down the hallway.

I laugh, shaking my head.

Summer holds out a hand as if to say *See*.

Jane rounds the corner with a hairbrush in hand, pointing it directly at me. "Melody Miller, haven't you learned yet that I live for time with my Gracie? Go," she demands, flicking her hand at me. "You and Summer have fun, we'll have a little girls night of our own."

I chew on the inside of my cheek. "Are you sure?"

She challenges me with a raised eyebrow.

I hold my hands up in surrender. "Sorry, sorry. I got it. I guess you've got yourself a date, Sum."

Summer squeals at her victory.

Jane disappears down the hall and Summer takes a seat at the table with Gracie and me. "How are you two doing? Really?"

Summer isn't one for prying, but I know she's been itching to check in on us. She's the best friend I've ever had. Actually, she might be the only real friend I've ever had. By now, everyone back in LA would have heard about what happened with Alexander, and not one "friend" in our inner circle has reached out to me. Even with him behind bars for the next few months, nobody can swallow their pride to check in on us.

My own parents have yet to call or send a text, though I did receive a bouquet of flowers with a generic "Get well soon" card attached to it, which I immediately tossed in the trash.

The lack of effort is hardly shocking, but it stings all the same. There are few people in this world that should be hard-wired to love you no matter what, so it's a bitter reality when you've fought your whole life to be noticed by them, only to be treated like a burden.

I grew up in a home where I never wanted for anything,

except the things my family couldn't provide. Love. Affection. So, as I glance down at Gracie, smiling and humming a tune to herself as she colors, I can't help but feel like I'm doing something right. The way she's openly affectionate with others, always eager to show and receive love. It's a concept that's still somewhat foreign for me when it comes to anyone other than Gracie. But I'm slowly letting go of those old behaviors, because we deserve more.

"We're..." I start slowly. "Okay. There have been some hard nights, and some hard questions to answer." I roll my head in Gracie's direction. "But we're good. Jane and Jackson, and you, have made what could have been a really dark time bearable."

The time I spent feeling guilty about a divorce and feeling ashamed of "failing" has long since passed. I no longer carry the shame or guilt about my decision to leave. I may not be to blame for our relationship ending, but my crime was refusing to believe him when he showed me who he truly was.

When Alexander showed up here, I finally saw with clear vision what any future with him would have looked like. He's angry and needs professional help, but we can't be a part of that.

One day, for Gracie's sake, I hope he makes the right changes to become the man and father Gracie deserves, but that's on him. I no longer carry the burden of his actions. Alexander will do what Alexander wants, as he always has, and letting go of that has been the biggest gift I've given myself.

Summer sips on her own smoothie, smiling warmly at me. Her hand slips over mine and gives it a squeeze.

"I don't know if I ever really thanked you for—" I start, but Summer stops me, so I don't need to finish.

"Well, first of all, you did. Second of all, you don't ever need to thank me for that. You two are family now. We protect our family. I will always be in your corner, Mel."

Her words make my eyes misty. They're simple and should

be so obvious. But it's the first time I've understood what it actually feels like to be cared for, to be protected.

When we first came to Blue Springs, Colorado, I was scared to open up and let others in, but now that we have and felt how good life can be, the only thing I'm scared of is letting them go.

So holding on is exactly what I plan to do.

CHAPTER 44

Jackson

The air is filled with the scent of sweet fried dough, fresh fruit, and pine.

It's a sunny August day, with not a cloud in the sky, and the festival couldn't have landed on a more perfect date.

Half of the town is busy running around trying to finish setting up before the festival begins, and a sea of people flood the grounds. There's excitement buzzing in the air, and I am more than ready to kick things off.

Colorful tents stand tall and balloons reach for the sky, swaying overhead. Everyone has a smile on their face, and the energy is high. This day has always meant a lot to me, but now it's become a local tradition that I get to share with the entire town of Blue Springs.

Soon there will be kids running in every direction, high on sugar and adrenaline. It's the highlight of my year, and I cannot wait to hype up a new generation of kids about fitness and jumping rope.

"Jackson, you want these over here?" Summer calls out, walking up with two of my employees who each cradle a box of ropes.

I direct her over to the front of the stage where we have tables set up for the assorted ropes. "Let's pull them out and spread them on these tables."

They immediately get to work setting out each rope and heading back to the truck for more boxes.

"Summer, is your tent already all set up?" I ask, knowing she has been stressed, not only about the festival, but about the proposal, which she and Mel finally completed.

She shrugs. "I think so."

"You think so?" I laugh.

"I know you still have a lot of things to finish…"

"Put those ropes down and go take care of your smoothie stand. I can manage," I playfully demand.

"It's fine, I—"

I don't let her finish. "Go, or when Wes arrives, I'll be sure to tell him every embarrassing story I know about you."

She narrows her eyes, placing her hands on her hips in a wide stance. "You wouldn't dare."

I raise one eyebrow and give her a sly smile. "Wanna bet? Post-competition diarrhea?"

Her lips purse like she just sucked on a lemon. "You're a monster, Jackson Pierce."

I laugh. "Go. I have this, I promise. This is a big day for you. Make sure you're all squared away."

She thanks me, gives me a quick hug, and skips off to her tent halfway down the lot.

As much as I'd love the extra help, I know that today marks a new beginning for her. Once Wes meets her and reads her proposal, there's not a chance he won't want to invest, so I better get used to not depending on her anymore. Summer has always been destined for greatness. She's smart, savvy, and everybody loves her. There's no doubt that by this time next year, she'll be one of the most successful businesses in Blue Springs.

I help the guys unload more boxes of jump ropes as we track back and forth and can't help but steal a glance at my girls setting up their very own spot for the festival. Gracie's lemonade stand shines with its old-fashioned appeal, in contrast to all of the tents. The oversized lemon and straw decals she added to the front are playful and sweet, just like Gracie.

Melody glances up and catches me staring at her with the same goofy grin I always seem to be sporting around her. Her expression mirrors my own and she blows me a kiss. There's a million things to do, so I'm trying to stay focused. But all I can concentrate on is the other reason I'm elated that today has finally arrived. But first I need to get through the jump rope routine I've been practicing for weeks, because after all, creating excitement around exercise for kids is what today is all about.

Noon arrives much quicker than it usually does, and somehow, everyone manages to get set up on time. The space is already filling with families from both near and far. Most of the locals are vendors, but everyone else seems to be in attendance as well.

There's music playing from the stage, bubbles and laughter begin spilling out in every direction, and it all adds to the magic of this fun-filled day.

I'm making my rounds, checking if anybody needs any last-minute help, when I hear my name called. I turn around to see a tall, tanned, dark-haired man in a suit strutting in my direction.

"Wesley Griffin, how the hell are ya?" I greet, walking toward him.

He grips my hand in a firm shake, leaning in to pat my back. "What are you, my mother?"

"Sorry, *Wes*," I correct.

My eyes trail over his attire, noticing he stands out like a sore thumb. "What's with the suit? You look like you're here to shut us down for not having the right permits, not to enjoy a festival."

He places his hands in his pockets and glances down at himself. "This is how I always dress. What's the problem?"

I shake my head, laughing. I'm in basketball shorts, a black tee, black Converse, and a backward cap. Everyone else in attendance is taking advantage of the warm day, wearing sundresses and shorts. But not Wes. He stands before me looking like he's about to attend a board meeting.

"Well, you're going to make one hell of an impression, I'll give you that." I clap him on the back and guide him through the festival. "Come on man, let's go meet my girls."

I introduce him to Melody, who is ecstatic and eagerly hands over her proposal. The two seem to hit it off immediately, and even Gracie seems taken with him. He can be a hard-ass when he needs to be, but right now I'm seeing my friend Wes, not businessman Wes.

He assures her that he'll look over the proposal this evening and she will be hearing from him soon, and if everything is as I have told him, she should be expecting good news. The sparkle in Melody's face hearing that her dream is about to come true is all-consuming, and I can see her trying not to explode with excitement. She wants to burst with joy, as evidenced by her wringing hands, but she's trying her best to come across calm and collected, which I find irresistibly adorable.

"So that's the woman you're in love with, huh?" Wes asks when Melody's out of earshot as we stroll down the line of tents.

Half of my mouth turns up in a grin. "Yeah, that's her."

"She's a sweet woman, her daughter, too. What a cute kid. I'm happy for you, man."

"What about you?" I ask.

"What about me?" he echoes.

"Any women you're crazy about?"

He throws his head back with an abrupt chuckle. "Lots of them. Just last week there was Theresa, and then Ashley."

I roll my eyes. "Come on man, I'm serious."

"The only thing I'm serious about is my business. That life is great for you, but it doesn't interest me."

I laugh. "Fair enough."

"Remind me who we're about to meet," he says as we make our way down the line of tents, through the thickening crowd.

"Summer Hart. My best friend."

"Ah, the smoothie queen," he deadpans.

"Wait until you taste them," I tease.

Summer already has a long line of people eagerly wanting her smoothies, which is great timing when I arrive with Wes.

I wave both arms in the air to get her attention as we make our way to the front and around the side of the tent.

"Hi!" she shouts over the music and noise from the crowd. "Give me just a minute, I'll have Ember cover me!"

She turns back to the tent, having a quick conversation with her younger sister Ember who is in town for the festival. She's blonde like Summer, but a little shorter, and a lot quieter. Though she's the more reserved sister, she's an equally loyal and dependable friend to have around. She has been doing a fantastic job at my Denver West location and took a few days off to join us for the festival.

A few minutes later, Summer steps aside with her proposal, offering it and an open hand to Wes.

He shakes it firmly, though doesn't return the bright, eager smile she's giving him.

Wes opens the proposal, flipping the first page, grunting, and then closing it again. "So, smoothies?"

I almost chuckle at the way he abruptly switches from laid-back Wes, returning to business mode.

Summer seems confused, too, her eyes darting between us. She clears her throat. "Uh, well, yeah. Would you like to try one?"

His mouth pulls to the side, and he raises an eyebrow before nodding. "Sure. Give me your best one."

Before Summer turns back to her blenders, I swear I see a sheen of sweat break out across her forehead.

While she's making his drink, we stand in silence, and he never takes his eyes off her.

She returns, quickly handing over the orange drink, and I don't miss the way her hand slightly trembles.

He takes a few long sips, grunting to himself, but offers no feedback.

Summer's the first to speak. "This is my newest recipe. It's a peach protein. I call it Peach Punch."

He makes another grunting sound before responding dryly, "We'll be in touch."

"Alright, sounds good. T-thank you," she stammers awkwardly.

The entire interaction is bizarre so I can't blame her for her reaction. I stand next to him, feeling the awkwardness stretch between the three of us.

Is he having an aneurysm or something?

Summer waves before quickly returning to her growing line, and we make our way around the crowd and head toward the stage.

"Bro, what the fuck was that?" I ask when we've made our way to the side of the stage.

"That might be the most beautiful woman I've ever seen."

His blunt confession nearly makes my jaw drop. It's not what I expected him to say.

"Listen, that's my best friend, so you keep your filthy hands off her. You hurt her and I'll kill you."

He chuckles. "Noted."

Though he seems to hear my warning, his attention is glued to the blonde a few tents away who's back to slinging smoothies with a toothy smile spread across her face.

"I'm gonna go make my rounds, see what this little town has to offer," he tells me before heading off into the sea of tents.

Not long after, I spot Summer jogging toward me in her pink leggings and matching sports bra.

"Man, you've had a steady line all afternoon. I know that bodes well with Wes."

She scoffs, leaning to one side with her hand on her hip and her other one flipping around theatrically as she speaks. "What the hell is that guy's problem?"

"Wes?" I ask.

She gives me a look that says *Duh*.

"He's just all business."

"Gee, I couldn't tell by the suit ensemble he wore to a freaking festival. Who does that?"

I laugh because, well, she's right. It's a bit strange, but we all have our quirks, and Wes just likes to dress nicely.

"He's not all bad," I try to reassure her.

"He was kind of a dick, Jackson."

"It was kind of weird, I'll give you that. It's just the first meeting, I'm sure he was nervous like you were."

She rolls her eyes and purses her lips like she can't fathom the idea.

"Let's hope his business skills are a hell of a lot better than his people skills," she warns, poking her finger in my chest before storming off.

Speaking of people skills, her own are lacking a bit right now.

I laugh as she jogs back to her tent.

Wes meeting the girls today was a big deal, but I had no idea it was going to take this strange turn.

All I can say is, the next few months are going to be very interesting.

CHAPTER 45

Melody

"Gracie, this is the best lemonade we've ever had, isn't it, Bud?" Kat dramatically slurps her lemonade, making loud approving noises.

Gracie's hands are clasped in front of her and her cheeks are pink from the praise.

"Thank you for supporting her small business," I tell them.

Kat waves me off. "Are you kidding me? We're going to find some snacks to stuff our faces with and then we'll definitely be back for more. Save us a cup."

I wasn't sure what to expect from today, considering we're not a legitimate business in town. This was more for Gracie to feel included, and word must have gotten out because we've had a line all afternoon. Though, the warm weather helps.

Pulling Gracie into a side hug, I lean down and whisper into her ear, "I'm proud of you, sweetheart."

She hugs my leg, smiling up at me. "Thanks, Mommy."

All afternoon we've been greeted with warm smiles and friendly townsfolk. August has been kind to us, but these warm, breezy days are going to quickly disappear. Today, everyone is in a great mood, excited to be out and enjoying the good vibes.

I finally met Wes, who was as professional as they come in his suit and tie, but also quite the charmer. Gracie couldn't help staring at him, and who could blame her? He is undeniably handsome, and if I wasn't stupid in love with Jackson Pierce, I might have had a hard time looking away.

He seemed enthused to work with me, and the way he interacted with Gracie made me feel like he's a good guy to have around. If Jackson trusts him, so do I.

I saw him chatting briefly with Summer, and I'm dying to hear how it went with her, but it'll have to wait, because Jackson is about to take the stage.

The music cuts off, and spectators begin to flood around the front of the stage where Jackson now stands, holding a mic. "Blue Springs, wow! You really showed up today. Thank you, everyone, for being here. This event is so special to me. Fitness, and jumping rope, specifically, has been my passion for most of my life. It's gone from a fun hobby to how I make a living, and for that, I'm forever grateful. Thank you to everyone who supports Jumping Jax and those who have consistently showed up to these festivals to show support.

"Fitness has given me so much to be thankful for, but I don't want this to be about me. Today is about the kids. So if you haven't already, kids and adults alike, come to the front and grab a jump rope. I've prepared a small performance, so sit back and enjoy. And as always, if anyone is interested in learning a few of the moves you see today, stay behind. I'll be holding a mini class here in a bit."

He tosses the mic to a man standing nearby, and the crowd erupts into applause, quieting when new music begins.

He starts slow with a one leg heel touch, one leg opposite side, and repeats for a few beats until the music turns into a faster rhythm, when his feet begin moving double time as he performs straddle doubles into backward shuffles. The moves are quick but precise, and the crowd is captivated by the chore-ography.

I try to make my way closer, but the crowd is dense with everyone attempting to do the same thing. Every child in the crowd looks astonished as their eyes stay glued to Jackson's impressive movements. If I hadn't already known what he's capable of, my own jaw would be on the floor.

Jackson has always had an inviting aura about him. From his genuine smile, to his generous heart, he's the most addicting man I've ever met. I'm equally transfixed by him.

His music mix switches from fast songs to slower ones, which displays his wide array of talent. The performance goes on for several minutes and his forehead begins to glisten with a slight sheen of sweat. It's a warm day, and he is giving his all. He ends the routine with my second favorite move, the mic drop.

Jackson saves my favorite move just for me. Which I'm already picturing him doing later.

Did it just get hotter?

The entire crowd erupts into applause as the music fades out and he gives a courtesy bow toward the audience before hopping down and shaking the hands of parents and kids, who are eagerly awaiting to chat with him.

I feel a tap on my shoulder and turn to see Summer at my side. "Take a look at your man."

I laugh, unable to hide my smile. "He did so good. That routine came together so well."

She nods. "I knew it would. He lives for this yearly routine."

I glance back up, beaming with pride for the wonderful man who's now taking pictures with kids up on stage, looking like summertime Santa.

"So," Summer starts. "Did you meet the investor?"

My face twists into confusion at her phrasing. "Wes? Yeah, I did. I saw you two talking. Isn't he great?"

She grimaces, shrugging one shoulder.

"What's that about?" I ask.

"I don't know. He was kind of an ass."

The lemonade I was just sipping nearly shoots from my mouth. "What the heck happened?"

"He was sort of rude, don't you think? And what's the deal with the suit on one of the hottest days of the year?" she rambles on, clearly annoyed by the man.

My forehead wrinkles in surprise. "I thought he was great. Gracie loved him. It may not be a good idea to call the man making your dreams come true an ass."

She flips her blonde ponytail behind her shoulder. "Well, obviously, I won't tell him that. But he needs to work on that attitude. Just because he's hot doesn't mean he can treat people however he wants."

Guess I'm not the only one who noticed.

Already, my mind is spinning with what's to come in the next few months. In just one meeting, Summer is flustered by a man she thinks is hot. I've never seen her get so easily worked up over a guy. And there's not a man on earth, aside from Jackson, who wouldn't give his left leg for a date with her, so something tells me there's a good chance Wes is attracted to her as well.

I don't get to respond before she continues to grumble about him. "Jackson told me he was probably nervous or something, but clearly, he was a perfect gentleman to you. So what the hell?"

I playfully smack her arm. "Summer! You're already complaining to Jackson about him?"

She gives me a look that says *So what?*.

Placing my palm on my forehead, I sigh dramatically. "Oh Summer."

"Listen, he may be out here doing us both a favor. But if he thinks his money and influence is going to be a get-out-of-jail-free card to treat me like crap? Oh honey, no. He has another thing coming," she asserts, looking at me for confirmation.

She's right, I know better than anyone that's a dangerous road to go down. Though I had a great encounter with him, she's correct. Under no circumstance does any man get the right to treat a woman poorly because he thinks his money gives him the upper hand.

I nod my head in agreement. "You're right. But let's give him the benefit of the doubt. If he decides to go into business with us, it's a good idea to start off on good terms. Maybe hold off on jumping down his throat for now."

"Alright, but only because you asked so nicely. However, if he makes one snarky remark, I can't be held responsible for what I say. I won't hold my tongue."

I laugh and pull her into my side with one arm. "I know, and that's why we love you, Summer. You're spicy and fiery."

She throws her arm around me. "Oh, I'll bring the heat. And don't you forget it."

ABOUT THIRTY MINUTES LATER, after the crowd has finally dispersed from the stage and everyone is perusing the tents again, Jackson manages to find his way back to me. I lift my head to see him practically running in my direction. He rounds the side of the lemonade stand, looking like a man on a mission, and pulls me in for a kiss.

Gracie stands to the side, organizing her cups, straws, and lids. We don't typically show much affection around Gracie, so when we pull apart, I look behind me to see her gazing up at us with hearts in her eyes and a smile on her lips.

I turn back to Jackson. "Wow, that was—"

"I love you, Melody Miller."

I feel my face heat and my heart race. "What?"

His hand caresses the side of my face. "I'm in love with you, and I couldn't wait another minute to tell you. I've been dying to say it all day."

Tears well in my eyes. I pull his face to mine, kissing him deeply. The man I've been falling for since I moved to Blue Springs, a man who, not only on paper, is perfect, but has shown me he also lives up to his credentials, just admitted he's in love with me.

When we pull apart, I see slight panic in his eyes and I realize I haven't responded. I hold his face between my hands. "I am so in love with you, Jackson Pierce."

"You are?" he asks.

I eagerly nod my head.

Gracie latches onto us with one arm wrapped around each of our legs. "I love you guys, too!"

Jackson scoops her up, wrapping around us both. "I love you too, Gracie. Thank you for making me a dad."

My emotions take on a mind of their own, and tears stream steadily down my face. For a moment, I forget we're in public, because all I can see is the bubble I'm in. My family bubble. As Gracie lays her head on Jackson's shoulder, I can see exactly what the next ten years will look like. What they'll feel like. And it's pretty damn good.

When I came to Blue Springs, I was running away from my problems with no plan for the future. But it turns out, this whole time I was actually running toward our future. One I didn't foresee for us, and one that's turned out better than I ever dreamed it could be.

From the moment Jackson began pursuing me, I was scared, terrified to open myself up to another man. I was intimidated by his looks. But looking as good as he does is just a byproduct of doing what he's passionate about. It's never been about looks for him. It was about doing what he loves, every day.

It's easy to be intimidated by his abs and rippling muscles, but he's much more than that. Underneath, he's the sweetest, most genuine and generous man I've ever known. Someone I don't need to explain my feelings to, because he always knows.

Jackson Pierce isn't all muscle, he's all heart.

He was equally scared to open up to me, but his bravery and vulnerability made me believe that I, too, could be brave.

He showed me that you won't always be ready for the life you want. Sometimes you just have to jump for it.

Epilogue - Jackson

TWO MONTHS LATER

"Mommy, my room is *huge*," Gracie shrieks, racing down the hallway.

I finally convinced Melody to ditch the cottage, so we packed them up and moved them into my house. She was hesitant at first—which is very on-brand for my sweet Mel—but I was patient and made it clear I wasn't going anywhere, and after the three of us sharing the bed night after night, she finally decided that a little more space wouldn't be so bad.

Truthfully, the timing couldn't have been better with the weather getting cooler. The cabin is warm, but Melody has yet to experience one of our brutal Colorado winters, and that small fireplace in her living room wasn't going to cut it.

We have spent most of the weekend decorating Gracie's new room, which has been the perfect blank canvas for her to pour her creativity into.

The afternoon was spent going from store to store in search of a big girl bed, curtains, paint, pictures for her to hang, and decorative hooks for her coats and sweaters.

Gracie had a field day picking out all of the new decor, and I got pure joy out of watching her mother nearly croak when I swiped my card before she had the chance.

She complained that she didn't want me spoiling her, and that she could pay for it, but I assured her it made me happy to do it. At the risk of sounding crude, I have more money than I could ever spend, and two new beautiful reasons to spend it. So, she can complain all she wants, but she's going to have to get used to me spoiling her.

"Let's put those new sheets and blankets in the wash so they're clean for bedtime, sweetie," Melody suggests, and she and Gracie set off for the laundry room.

Melody took the weekend off to move, and Bud and Kat were more than willing to accommodate. They've adopted her as much as the rest of us.

I never expected to become a father this way, or at all, really, but in many ways, this is so much better. I may not be her biological father, but I get to choose her. Every day, I wake up knowing that while I wasn't there from the beginning, I get to be there for everything else. Choosing to love and protect Gracie is the easiest thing I've ever done.

They blew into town one spring day, and Blue Springs has never been the same. Melody and Gracie fit seamlessly into our small town, and in many ways, it feels like they've always been here.

Wes has met with Melody several times over the last few months, and most recently, they've closed on a nearby property that will be the ground floor for her project "Lemonade Stand." Gracie came up with the name, and I saw a light bulb go off in

Melody's head. When I asked her why she decided on that one, her response surprised me.

"Lemonade Stand will be a symbol for hope. To remind the women who come here that just because you only have lemons, it doesn't mean you can't make lemonade, and one day, even a lemonade stand. I want them to know that life has so much possibility, and it can be so sweet if they give it the chance. Lemonade Stand will be our symbol for not letting the sour parts of our lives overtake the sweet ones."

Her passion for this project has been inspiring to watch unfold. Each time she returns from a meeting with Wes, I can see the excitement and joy radiating off her. It's only a matter of time now before she's going to be needed full time and will be able to put her days of waiting tables behind her. I've tried to get her to quit for weeks, but she's stubborn and insisted she never wanted to be reliant on me. Though the provider in me wishes she would, I have to respect it. She's a hell of a woman.

I grab a bottle of water from the fridge and watch Melody and Gracie comfortably move around the house, organizing their things and making themselves at home. When Melody passes by, I reach out and catch her by the waist.

"Well, hello there." She giggles, moving into my body.

"Have I told you that I love having you two here?"

She taps a finger against her bottom lip. "Oh, only about ten or twenty times."

"Maybe I'll tell you ten or twenty more."

I squeeze my fingers into her sides and she lets out a squeal. "Jackson Pierce, are you getting frisky with me?"

"Maybe. Would that be okay?" I ask, smirking at her. My eyes drop to her lips, where she's currently biting that plump bottom lip that I'm dying to taste.

"I think it's about time we christen that big bed you have in your bedroom," she teases, slowly pressing her body into mine.

"Our bedroom," I correct.

I pull her face to mine, sealing my lips over hers. My tongue sweeps across her mouth, lapping up all her sweetness. I grip the back of her legs and lift her onto the granite countertop, stepping between her legs, our faces never separating.

My hands are frantic, itching to explore, but Melody quickly pushes me off and hops off the counter when we hear Gracie's little feet skipping down the hall.

"Tease," I joke.

"Just wait to see what I have in store for you later," she taunts, leaning forward and nipping my lip.

I laugh, loving this lighter, friskier side of Melody. In the last few weeks, I've seen a drastic change in both her and Gracie. Any reservations they had previously have almost disappeared. It's like the last wall she was holding up has finally crumbled down and I'm able to see all of her. The biggest compliment has been watching both Melody and Gracie unleash their goofy side. If they can be comfortable enough around me to let those guards down, then I know I must be doing something right.

Epilogue - Melody

"I'm going to get a sprinkle one. Ooh, and a maple one. Oh, and a chocolate one!" Gracie rambles on as we make our way over to Bread Pitt for breakfast.

I officially handed in my notice at the Bistro this morning, and I have to admit, it was bittersweet. But with the grand opening of Lemonade Stand in just over a month, it was crunch time.

As glad as I'll be to no longer be waiting tables, this job gave me a new start. Bud and Kat helped me get back on my feet, and Blue Bistro will always have a special place in my heart.

Gracie and I spent last night baking them a cake and had Jane write "thank you" in icing on the top, because I am nowhere near the baker that she is. I handed them my notice along with the cake and a bouquet of flowers. We shared a tearful embrace, and I assured them that they'd still be seeing a lot of me. Blue Bistro is still the home of Jackson's favorite blue cheese burger, after all.

Mary, though sad to see me leave, gave me a motherly hug and told me how proud she is of me. Two things I never received from my own mother. I'm not ashamed to say that I held on to her for longer than standard hug etiquette probably dictates.

Now I'm hand in hand with Jackson on one side and Gracie on the other as we walk over to Bread Pitt. I'm looking forward to a warm coffee and pastries.

"Sweetie, let's start with one, and go from there. I'm not sure we need all of that sugar," I tell her, earning a pouty bottom lip.

We push through the front door, and the sweet scent of pastries fill my senses, as does the strong, fresh aroma of coffee beans.

"Gracie!" Trish calls out when she sees us walk in.

"Hi! We want all the donuts!" Gracie proclaims.

I hold up a hand. "Uh, we will have one donut, as discussed."

Jackson laughs next to me, and I squeeze his hand.

"What?" he asks innocently.

"Don't encourage her," I say, but I know it's a waste because Jackson would absolutely buy Gracie every pastry in this shop right now if I wasn't opposing it.

Trish hands us each one donut, steaming coffees for Jackson and me, and a hot chocolate for Gracie. We thank her and take a seat next to the window and stuff our faces with the fresh pastries.

My phone pings, and I see a text from Summer.

Summer: Urghhh.

Melody: Uh oh, is that the war cry for all things Wes related?

Summer: When is it not? 💀

I GIGGLE, covering my mouth with a napkin and trying not to spit out my chewed-up donut.

"What?" Jackson asks with a grin.

"Summer," I say, shaking my phone. "Another crisis with Wes."

My phone pings again.

> Summer: How am I going to survive starting an entire business with the man when we can't even get past finding a building for it?

> Melody: Maybe you guys should make out and get rid of all that sexual tension. 😒

> Summer: This isn't a sexual tension issue, it's an arrogance issue. The man is a menace.

> Melody: Hang in there. This is your dream, remember? Surely you're not going to let one man stand in your way.

> Summer: You're right. Fuck him.

> Melody: Not a bad idea.

> Summer: Stop.

> Melody: Sorry, couldn't help it.

I PUT my phone back in my pocket as we finish our treats and sip our coffee. Jackson and I laugh over the situation with Summer and Wes. They've been at each other's throats since the day they met. Although he's made no move to pull out of the deal, they fight more like a married couple than business partners.

Jackson leans in, plants a kiss on my mouth, and whispers in my ear. "Let's finish these and drop her off at my mother's. There's another set of lips I'm dying to taste."

I blush, biting my bottom lip.

Jackson runs his thumb across my lip, his eyes full of fire.

He has this incredible way of making me feel sexy and loved even when I'm stuffing my face with a donut. Something that never would have happened with Alexander. As I sit here, being utterly myself, not wearing a stitch of makeup, carefree about how many calories I'm consuming, Jackson sits next to me, undressing me with his eyes and whispering dirty things into my ear.

How could life possibly get any better than this?

The End

Stay tuned for Summer's book, *Summer Heat*, coming soon.

Acknowledgments

Thank you to everyone who has followed me from my spicy romantasy era, into my small-town era. This has been such a fun series to create, and I hope you all love it as much as I have.

To my loving man Leo, thank you for being the kind of man that I pull inspiration from to create these swoon-worthy book boyfriends. I never would have had the courage to publish any book without your love and encouragement. Thank you for always believing in me.

To my loyal alpha reader and best friend Hannah Sulewski, thank you for always being the first set of eyes on my manuscripts. I'm grateful for every comment, and suggestion you give. This book was so special to me, and I hope it will always be a reminder of how strong you are, and how worthy of good things you are. I love you.

Hannah Bird, thank you for always being available for advice, and for being a thorough set of eyes on my books. Luckily you didn't have to remind me to dress my characters this time, but there were plenty of other things that would have slipped by without your keen eye. This will always be such a special reminder of what I accomplished during a very difficult pregnancy. Thank you for being my pregnancy twin and going through the daily woes right along with me. We did the damn thing! I love you!

Ali Salvino, what would I have done without you? Your excitement for this book has been the best thing to see. Between creating edits for promos, designing the entire cover, and overall keeping me hyped about it, you have been my absolute angel. Thank you for being an incredible friend, and hype woman. I am so grateful for you! I love you!

To the rest of my amazing gals, Jennalee, Sam, Jen Davis, Ally Griffith, and all my other hype women, thank you for sharing my content, being my beta/arc readers, and overall being incredible hype women! I have such a loving community behind me, and I don't know what I've done to deserve you all. Thank you from the bottom of my heart for following along on this journey with me.

Also by Jackie Egan

Standalone:

One Last Message

Weapon of Mass Seduction Series

Soul Snatcher

Curse Breaker

About the Author

Jackie lives in SoCal with her two beagles. She enjoys spending time with her fiancé and two daughters, staying active, and visiting the local wineries. She has turned her lifelong love of reading into creating stories for others to enjoy. When she's not in mom mode, you can catch her writing, or enjoying a new book.